To my muse,
for sticking with me all these years.

ACKNOWLEDGMENTS

To my daughter, Chloe, for listening patiently to me talk on and on about my dream of becoming an author

To my sister and BFF, Lori, my steadfast cheerleader, manager, sounding board, and therapist. Without her unwavering support, this book never would've seen the light of day.

To my brother, Matthew, who's been asking me for years: "So, when are you going to publish a novel?"

To my parents, Herb and Barbara, for always being there for me and believing in me

To Sheila Trask: Thank you for the constructive, encouraging and insightful editorial feedback.

To my beta readers: Lori, Dominique, Ashley, Angela, Amy, Cassie, Jenny, and Becca, for your feedback, insights, and encouragement.

To book reviewers Catherine Bibby of Rochelle's Reviews and Alice Laybourne of Lunalandbooks: Thank you for your kind and generous support.

Vulnerable

McIntyre Security Bodyguard Series — Book 1

april wilson

This novel is a work of fiction. All places and locations mentioned in it are used fictitiously. The names of characters and places are figments of the author's imagination. Any resemblance to real people or real places is purely a coincidence.

Visit www.aprilwilsonwrites.com to sign up for the author's e-mail newsletter to be notified about upcoming releases.

ISBN-13: 978-1517390822
ISBN-10: 1517390826

Published in the United States of America
First Printing October 2015

1

*B*eth found herself wandering aimlessly through the library, wondering what she was doing there so late. It was well past closing, and all the lights were off. Moonlight streamed through the windows, casting long, sinister shadows on every surface.

She shivered, then looked down at herself and realized she was naked. *"It's just a dream. Don't panic."*

But that was easier said than done when she heard the heavy footsteps.

No! Not again!

She searched frantically for a place to hide, running through the tall stacks of books, her heart thundering painfully. When she came to the double doors that led to the stairwell, she pushed through them. The doors closed behind her with a resounding clang, leaving her in pitch black darkness.

The footsteps grew louder, heavy, dull thuds on the polished floors that drew ominously closer.

She wrapped her arms around her naked torso, as much for comfort as for warmth. Too late, she realized the footsteps were coming up the stairs. *Oh, God, he's in the stairwell!*

As she backed into the corner, she walked right into a pair of bruising hands that gripped her arms hard.

"There you are, you little bitch," he said, in that gravel voice she'd never been able to forget. *"You can't hide from me. Haven't you learned that by now?"* He pushed her down to the cold cement floor.

"No!"

She screamed.

"Beth, wake up!"

Her first instinct was to fight the slender hands that pinned her down. Beth yanked her hands free and began to batter the dark shape hovering over her.

"Ow!" cried an outraged female voice when Beth's fist connected with something soft. "Beth, stop! It's me!"

Her eyes shot open, and she was practically blinded by the ceiling light. She tried to sit up, but a pair of determined hands pinned her to the bed.

Beth looked up into a pale, freckled face framed with sleep-mussed red hair. "Gabrielle!" she gasped, struggling to catch her breath. Her heart was pounding so hard it hurt, and her lungs felt tight. Too tight, as if they were being squeezed in a vise. "Can't breathe!" she wheezed, groping blindly for the top drawer of her nightstand.

Gabrielle leaned over and opened the drawer, grabbing Beth's rescue inhaler. "I've got it. Relax."

Gabrielle shook the inhaler, then angled it at Beth's mouth. Beth pulled the inhaler into her mouth and administered the medication. Then she lay back and closed her eyes while the medication did its job. And just like that, all the fight left her.

"Are you okay?" Gabrielle said, returning the inhaler to the drawer.

"Yes," Beth rasped, taking a hesitant breath. She pulled the quilt up to her chest.

Gabrielle turned off the light, crawled into bed and slipped beneath the covers. She rolled Beth to her side and spooned behind her. "It's okay," she said, stroking Beth's hair back from her hot, damp face. "You're safe."

"He found me in the library." Beth tried to suppress the echo of the terror she'd felt. "I was in the stairwell and it was dark. He grabbed me."

Gabrielle wrapped her arm around Beth's waist and snuggled up against her. "It's okay. It was just a dream."

Beth began to shake, a delayed reaction to the surge of adrenalin. She felt chilled to the bone, despite having a sheet and a quilt covering her. Even Gabrielle's body heat wasn't enough to warm her. Those god-awful nightmares always left her feeling so vulnerable. The shaking intensified.

"Go back to sleep, Beth," Gabrielle said as she tightened her arm around Beth's waist. "I'll stay with you tonight."

Faint light spilled into Beth's bedroom from the hallway, but Gabrielle didn't bother to get up and turn it off. Beth always slept better with a light on.

"Shane?"

Shane McIntyre turned away from the surveillance report he'd been reading on his computer and looked up at his executive assistant.

"Detective Jamison's here to see you. Shall I send him in?"

Shane nodded. "Thanks, Diane. Send him in."

Chicago Homicide Detective Tyler Jamison walked into Shane's office and paused just over the threshold. The man was dressed in his trademark black suit and tie, crisp white dress shirt, and polished black loafers. He was tall, with a trim, muscular build. His dark hair was cut short, tidy and conservative like the rest of him.

Tyler scowled as he glanced around the spacious, high-rise corner office, his sharp gaze taking in the modern furnishings and the million-dollar view of N. Michigan Avenue. He eyed Shane accusingly. "Apparently I'm in the wrong business."

"The choices we make, Detective." Unfazed by the man's disapproving tone, Shane rose from his chair and met Tyler halfway, extending his hand in greeting. "Hello, Tyler."

Tyler nodded brusquely as they shook hands. "Shane."

While the two men had crossed paths professionally many times, they weren't exactly friends. Their respective careers brought them together with some regularity, but their personalities were too much at odds to allow for an easy friendship. Tyler Jamison was a stickler for doing things by-the-book, while Shane's motto was more along the lines of *do whatever it takes.* The two men usually ended up butting heads, but they'd always managed to keep things professional between them.

"Have a seat, Tyler," Shane said, returning to his desk chair. "What can I do for you?"

Tyler sat in one of two chairs parked in front of Shane's desk. "I'm here on a personal matter."

Shane leaned back in his chair, not bothering to hide his surprise. He'd never known Tyler Jamison to mix the professional with the personal. "All right. What do you need?"

"I want to hire your firm." Tyler laid a black leather portfolio on Shane's desk and opened it, withdrawing two manila folders. "I have two subjects here. One requires around-the-clock protection. The other — well, I'm hoping you can help me send him back to prison."

Shane picked up the first folder and opened it. An 8x10 color photograph of a young woman's face was clipped inside the front cover. It was a candid shot, and the subject looked pensive. The girl, who looked to be in her early twenties, had long, pale blond hair and large blue-green eyes — a stunning mix of innocence and sensuality.

Shane glanced up sharply at Tyler. "Who is she?" But as soon as the words were out of his mouth, he knew. It was in the eyes. Tyler and this girl had the same ethereal blue-green eyes.

"She's my sister," Tyler said. "Beth."

"I'm guessing she's the one who needs protection," Shane said, frowning as he studied her photograph.

Tyler nodded, his expression tight. "Unfortunately, yes."

Shane took one last look at the young woman's photograph. She had an oval face, a smooth pale complexion, and lush, full lips that would undoubtedly bring some lucky bastard to his knees. But it was her eyes that grabbed his attention. He could get lost in those eyes. "How old is she?"

"Twenty-four."

Shane knew Tyler had to be in his early forties, which made him old enough to be this girl's father. "And she's your *sister*?"

"Yes," Tyler said, interpreting the skeptical look on Shane's face. "She was a late surprise for our parents."

Shane laid down the girl's folder and picked up the other one. It contained a booking mugshot of an overweight man in his mid-40s with pale splotchy skin, heavy jowls, and a greasy brown comb-over. The man's dark eyes were bloodshot and watery.

Shane peered up at Tyler, a sick feeling in his gut. He knew where this was going; otherwise Tyler wouldn't be here. "And this guy?"

"Howard Kline," Tyler said. "He's the bastard who abducted Beth from her front yard when she was six years old. A neighbor remembered seeing a plumbing van parked outside our house at the time of the abduction. We were able to track the kidnapper — and Beth — through the van. That's him eighteen years ago."

Shane scanned the attached report on Howard Kline. Kline had been living on a farm with his widowed mother at the time. He was convicted on multiple counts and sentenced to 30 years in prison. Just looking at the smug expression on the bastard's face made Shane see red.

"We located her about twelve hours later," Tyler said. "I was a uniformed officer then, fresh out of the academy. I was the one who broke down that cellar door and found her bound and gagged, lying naked on a dirt floor. She suffered from severe hypothermia and dehydration, but she was otherwise uninjured. Thank God."

Tyler swallowed hard, his eyes radiating pain. "Some nights I can't sleep for thinking about what might've happened to her if we hadn't found her so quickly."

Shane nodded, saying nothing. On the outside he appeared calm, but on the inside he was roiling. The thought of anyone hurting a child was more than he could tolerate. The idea of someone hurting this girl — it made him want to break something.

"Kline's going to be released early on parole next week," Tyler said. "I have no idea if he's still a threat to Beth or not, but I can't take any chances. I need you to protect my sister and help me put Kline back in prison. Will you do it?"

Shane nodded as he closed the folder on Kline. "I'll put together a plan, and we can meet tomorrow to go over it."

Tyler took a deep breath and visibly relaxed for the first time since entering Shane's office. "Thank you, Shane." His eyes looked bleak. "The thought of Kline hurting Beth again is more than I can bear."

Shane looked at Tyler, his expression hard. "I won't let this guy get within a mile of your sister." He had three sisters of his own, and he knew damn well how he'd feel if one of them was in danger.

Tyler shifted uncomfortably in his chair. "About the cost — "

Shane shook his head. He had a pretty good idea how much money Tyler earned as a detective. "Don't worry about the cost, Tyler. We'll work it out."

"I'm going to pay — "

"Tyler, it's not an issue," Shane said. "Now, how's Beth handling the news of Kline's impending release?"

Tyler tucked the empty portfolio under his arm and stood. "She doesn't know," he said. "And she's not going to."

Shane held his tongue as Tyler left his office. Of course Beth needed to be told about Kline's release, but that could wait. There'd be plenty of time to argue with Tyler about it later. Right now, he had work to do.

He texted the operatives he wanted in his conference room at 8 a.m. sharp the next morning. Then he picked up the dossier on Beth Jamison and flipped it open to gaze at her photo once more.

The next morning, Shane sat at one end of the conference table, Tyler at the other. It was a good thing they were at opposite ends of the table because, if Shane could have reached Tyler, he would have throttled him.

"You have to tell her, Tyler," Shane said for the umpteenth time, glaring at the man. "We can't adequately protect someone who doesn't know she needs protecting." Shane felt for the guy, he really did. But to keep Beth in the dark about Kline's release was foolish, not to mention outright dangerous.

"No," Tyler said, a muscle twitching in his tightly clenched jaw.

"Tyler — "

"No, Shane! Beth suffers from severe anxiety because of what this monster did to her. I don't want her to know he's about to become a free man. End of discussion."

Shane sighed as he made a concerted effort to rein in his temper. Keeping Beth Jamison in the dark went against his professional instincts, but he didn't want to waste time sitting here arguing. He wanted to get the teams out in the field to do their initial reconnaissance.

Shane diverted his attention to the striking redhead sitting next to Tyler. "What's your opinion, Ms. Hunter? You know Beth better than anyone."

Tyler had introduced Gabrielle Hunter as Beth's housemate and best friend. The two girls had met in college, and they'd been best friends ever since. So far, Gabrielle had been silent on the topic.

"Leave Gabrielle out of this, Shane," Tyler said. "She's here because I want her in the loop. She's my extra set of eyes on Beth. That's all."

Shane glanced at Tyler, then back at Gabrielle. "Ms. Hunter, how do you think Beth would take the news about Kline's impending release?"

Gabrielle peered hesitantly at Tyler, then looked at Shane. "She wouldn't take it well. She's absolutely terrified of Howard Kline."

Shane sat back in his chair and considered his options. Arguing with Tyler wasn't going to accomplish anything — the man would only dig his heels in deeper. And Shane wanted to get his people out in the field now. "We'll take the issue up again later," he said, looking directly at Tyler. "For now, I'll abide by your request."

"It's not a request, Shane," Tyler said, his voice hard. "She's my responsibility, and I make the decisions where Beth is concerned. If you can't accept that, I'll find someone else who can."

Shane shook his head. "That won't be necessary."

He glanced around the table at the operatives in attendance, who were watching the Shane/Tyler throw-down with great interest. "Miguel will head up Beth's covert protection team. AJ will supervise the electronic surveillance on Howard Kline." Shane looked at his brother Jake, who was seated to his right. "Jake will head up the team keeping visual surveillance on Kline."

Shane consulted the report in his hands. "Beth and Gabrielle share a townhouse in Hyde Park?"

"Yes," Tyler said. "I own the building. I installed a top-of-the-line security system, so it should be pretty secure."

Shane looked at Tyler. "You won't mind if Jake checks out the security system?"

Tyler looked like he did mind, and he took his time contemplating the request. Finally, he relented. "Fine. Gabrielle can let him in to look at it when Beth's at work."

"That won't be necessary," Shane said, glancing at his brother.

"What, he's just going to break into the house?" Tyler said, not bothering to hide his irritation.

Jake McIntyre ran a hand through his dark hair. "It's not much of an evaluation, Detective, if I don't see how easy it is to beat."

Shane nodded at Jake. "Do it."

Then Shane looked down the table at Tyler. "One last thing," he said. "I have a connection to the administration at Kingston Medical School. I can get someone placed inside the library so we can keep a visual on Beth while she's at work. Since it's a public building, I'd feel better if we had someone on the inside."

"No," Tyler said. "I don't want anyone in the library. Beth works in a secured room, and no one can get in there without being buzzed in. She's safe enough at work. Besides, it would be too conspicuous to have someone in there with her."

"I was thinking of Lia," Shane said, nominating his youngest sister. "They're about the same age. Lia would be the perfect shadow, and Beth would never know."

"Hell no!" Tyler said, slamming his fist on the tabletop. "I've met your sister, Shane. I don't want that psychotic delinquent within a hundred yards of Beth! The goal is to *protect* my sister, not corrupt her."

Shane didn't take offense at Tyler's characterization of Lia. Lia was indeed a wild child — there was no point in denying that — although she was neither psychotic nor delinquent. Lia was one of Shane's best undercover operatives. And she was exactly what Beth needed.

"All right," Shane said. "We'll play it your way."

For now.

2

two weeks later...

The moment Beth walked into Clancy's Bookshop on Friday evening, a week's worth of stress simply melted away. This was her happy place. Being surrounded by books was like a balm to her frazzled soul. While most of her friends were out clubbing, she was happiest alone with a good book.

After work, she'd gone home and grabbed a quick dinner. Gabrielle had left her a plate of lasagna to warm up, a salad, and — best of all — a dish of chocolate mousse. Then she'd hopped a cab downtown to spend the evening in her favorite place.

As usual for a Friday evening, the store was packed. Beth worked her way over to the New Releases table to check out the hardbacks. She scanned the shiny new covers and even picked up a couple of them to read the inside jacket copy. Then she moved on to the racks of newly released paperbacks.

After making a circuit of the first floor, meandering through the magazines and newspapers, Beth reached her favorite part of the store — the Romance section. She'd always been a die-hard romance fan, ever since reading her first romance novel as a teen. She loved the intense passion, but more importantly, she loved the happily-ever-afters. They made up for her own abysmal track record in the romance department.

When it came to intimacy, she was a complete disaster. Guys didn't take kindly to their girlfriends crying in bed — or even worse, screaming at them to stop. It was a mood killer every time. She was destined to end up alone because she had more issues than any one man could handle.

At least she had her book boyfriends and her vibrator. They never let her down. But more importantly, she never let them down.

After browsing the display of new romances, she picked up a couple of paranormals that looked promising. She was always in the mood for some hot alpha heroes. Then she drifted over to her guilty pleasure — the erotica aisle. She skimmed the new releases, and an anthology of spanking stories caught her eye. She pulled that one off the shelf and tucked it with the others in the crook of her arm.

Shane knew he was in trouble the minute he laid eyes on Beth Jamison. Her photograph had rocked him, but seeing her in the flesh had sealed the deal. She was just as stunning in person as he'd feared.

As he watched her from across the room, he had to admit he'd never wanted a woman more. Just looking at her now made his body feel hot and his skin too tight. His dick twitched in his trousers, and he had to shift his stance to accommodate his growing erection. *Fuck!*

He wasn't even supposed to be here in the first place. He'd been working late at the office when Miguel had called to tell him Miles Bennett — who was scheduled to watch Beth that night — had been taken to the ER with a severe case of food poisoning. Shane had jumped at the chance to take Miles's shift just so he could get a look at this girl with his own eyes.

He had absolutely no business sniffing around Tyler's little sister, and he damn well knew it, but he couldn't get the image of her out of his head. Every time he looked at her photograph, his pulse kicked into overtime. That had never happened to him before, and now he needed to see her in person, if just to get her out of his head once and for all. Innocent little blonds simply weren't his type.

Just a half-hour earlier, he'd been sitting in his office with Jake going over the latest surveillance report on Howard Kline. Jake's team had been tailing Kline for the past five days and had next to nothing on the guy. After being released from prison, Kline had moved in with his elderly, disabled mother in a low-income neighborhood on the south side. Since then, he almost never left the house, other than to meet with his parole officer and his court-appointed therapist. Other than that, he'd been living in complete seclusion with his mother. That alone was a red flag.

You'd expect a guy just getting out of prison after 18 years to go out and live a little — grab a beer, go to a movie, get laid. But not this guy. He was living the life of a recluse. In some ways, that was a good thing. If he was holed up at home, he wasn't out on the streets looking for Beth Jamison. The downside was Jake and his team hadn't been able to get a good feel for him. And that was a problem, because they needed to know what this guy was thinking.

When the call had come in that Miles was out of commission for the night, Shane had jumped at the chance to take his place.

"I'll be there in fifteen minutes," Shane had told Miguel.

"Why you?" Jake had said as soon as Shane ended the call.

Shane had stood, grabbing his phone and keys. "Why not me?"

"Because you're the CEO of this outfit, and you don't do field work," Jake had said.

"Well, I'm doing field work tonight."

Jake had shaken his head in disgust. "You're an idiot. This has bad news written all over it."

And now here he was on a Friday night in a bookstore of all places, feigning interest in a shelf of architectural books two aisles away from where Beth Jamison stood perusing romance novels.

He shifted his position to get a better view. He'd seen her photo, but that was just a head shot. Now he saw the whole package. *Damn.* She was just as exquisite in person as he'd feared.

He already knew her stats. She was five-eight, 125 pounds. She was taller than average and rather on the slender side. This evening, she was wearing a peach dress and a lacey white sweater. Her long legs were bare, and she wore a pair of flat brown sandals. She didn't have much in the way of curves, but her long blond hair, parted in the middle, framed a lovely face. She looked so... delicate. No wonder this girl needed protection. She didn't look like she could fight her way out of a wet paper bag. The thought that someone might want to hurt this girl made his chest tighten.

Shane watched her, mesmerized. On the outside, she looked very serene — calm and cool — but he knew appearances could be deceiving. According to her emotional profile, she was anything but serene. Tyler had described her as excruciatingly shy and timid. She was uncomfortable around strangers, and she suffered from severe anxiety and asthma.

And she had nightmares, apparently a lot of them. Gabrielle Hunter had described those in great detail, including the ear-splitting screams in the dead of night, along with the panic attacks that often followed.

Kline had really done a number on this poor kid.

Beth was on the move now, and Shane changed positions again to keep her in his sights. His job suddenly got a whole lot more interesting when she turned a corner and moved into the erotica section. *Holy shit.* He hadn't seen that coming.

He watched as she scanned the erotica shelves and selected a book, adding it to the small pile in her arms. When she headed toward the back of the store, he followed, more intrigued by the second.

When Beth took a seat in one of four oversized armchairs positioned around a low table covered with discarded books and magazines, he moved into position. She set her stack of paperbacks on the table in front of her and tucked her purse beside her in the chair. When she picked up one of her books and started reading, Shane tried to catch the title — his curiosity thoroughly aroused — but he couldn't see it from his current vantage point.

When the young couple seated around the table got up and walked away, leaving Beth alone, Shane did the unthinkable. He took the seat directly across from her.

She was so engrossed in her book, she didn't even seem to notice that someone had sat down at the table. *Damn it!* Someone needed to teach this girl to be more aware of her surroundings.

Sitting so close to her now, he had no trouble reading the title of her book. An anthology of spanking stories? *Really?* His dick shot hard as a pole, and he had to shift in his chair to ease the pressure in his trousers. Never in a million years would he have guessed that little Miss Jamison liked a bit of kink. It was almost enough to make him rethink his stance on innocent little blonds.

As Shane watched her, he noted her flushed cheeks and quick breaths. She was getting aroused! He almost had a heart attack when her tongue slipped out to wet her bottom lip. *Fuck!*

She shifted restlessly in her seat, and he couldn't take his eyes off her. Watching her body's response to that damned book was causing him serious physical pain. He had to cross one ankle over his knee to hide the obvious erection tenting his trousers. Honestly, he wasn't a stalker, but right now he sure as hell felt like one.

The girl was lost in her own world, completely oblivious to the fact that his gaze was locked on her like a heat-seeking missile locked onto a bonfire. It was a good thing Tyler had hired protection for her, because she was doing a lousy job of taking care of herself. He could be anyone sitting here ogling her. Hell, he could be Howard Kline, and she probably wouldn't have noticed.

Suddenly, Shane wanted to get her attention. He wanted to see those exquisite eyes on him. He wanted to see those lush lips turn up in a shy smile. But more than anything, he wanted to hear her voice.

And that was when he made his second mistake of the evening.

"Is that a good book?"

Beth flinched at the unfamiliar male voice, low and tinged with amusement. A rush of liquid heat surged through her, pooling low in her belly. She was already aroused from reading stories about bare-bottom, over-the-knee spankings, and that provocative male voice had just tipped her right over the edge. As her hands started shaking, she kept her gaze fixed on the book in her lap.

Please don't be talking to me.

She could see in her peripheral vision that the chairs on either side of her were vacant. So she peeked up under her lashes and cringed when she saw the tip of a man's black loafer and a bit of charcoal trouser leg across the table from her. It was just the two of them seated at the table, so of course he was talking to her! He had to be.

Oh, my God. Kill me now.

Her pulse started racing, and her chest tightened. She pulled in a deep, shaky breath in an attempt to stem her sudden rush of anxiety.

Closing the book, she laid it face down on her lap and covered it with both hands, feeling just like a kid who'd been caught with her hand in the cookie jar. *Busted!*

She kept her eyes glued to her lap because she couldn't bear to look a complete stranger in the face — let alone one who knew she was reading erotica.

Of course, it had to be spanking stories she'd been caught reading. That was her deep, dark secret. There had to be something seriously wrong with her. She was an intelligent, educated woman with a bachelor's degree in literature and a master's degree in library science, and yet she secretly got off reading about girls having their bottoms spanked.

This was beyond mortifying, and she didn't know what to do. Maybe if she simply ignored him, he'd get the hint and go away.

No such luck.

"I'm sorry if I embarrassed you."

The sound of his voice made her tremble, and her heart was beating so hard now she could feel her pulse pounding in her throat. Why couldn't the floor just open up and swallow her whole? *Right now. Please.* And why did he have to have a voice like a sex god? It was low and just a little bit rough. Just the sound of it made her belly quiver.

"Hello? Miss?"

In the end, it was his gentle persistence that was her undoing. She glanced up and found herself ensnared by the sight of him: short, thick hair the color of fine chocolate — slightly tousled as if he'd run his hands through it — a sexy five-o'clock shadow on a handsome face with a strong jawline and a perfect blade of a nose. Leaning back in his chair, dressed in a charcoal suit and white dress shirt, sans tie, he looked like a disreputable heart-throb on the cover of GQ. A pair of striking, electric blue eyes held her gaze as he waited for her reply.

God, no man should have such beautiful eyes.

She knew she was staring, but she couldn't help herself.

And then he offered her the most disarming smile she'd ever seen on a man... a perfect, slightly crooked smile that set butter-flies loose in her belly.

"Hello," he said. He rose from his chair and reached across the table to offer her his hand. "Shane McIntyre."

The top button of his shirt was undone, and Beth could see a hint of brown chest hair peeking through the opening. Given the suit and shirt, he looked like he'd just come from the office. If so, he must have had a really long day as it was nearly ten o'clock in the evening. He looked at her expectantly, his hand hanging patiently in the air as he waited for her to take it.

She felt like an idiot as she sat there staring at him, still trying to get over the fact that this guy was even talking to her. What did he say his name was? She racked her brain and came up blank. She'd be lucky to remember her own name, let alone his.

Eventually, her engrained good manners prompted her to reach out and clasp his hand, which was warm and dry in hers. His grip was firm, yet gentle, and when he gave her hand a little squeeze, a tingle shot up her arm. She released his hand abruptly, as if she'd been burned by the contact, but he held on to her hand. When he smiled again, the corners of his blue eyes crinkled with tiny laugh lines.

She swallowed, her throat dry. What was he waiting for? *Oh, right. Her name.* "I'm Beth." Her voice was little more than a husky whisper.

When she attempted to pull her hand free from his, he released it and sat back down. "It's a pleasure to meet you, Beth."

Just hearing him say her name did something wickedly wonderful to her insides. Her heart beat frantically, though. God, why did she have to be like this? For the millionth time, she wished she was more like Gabrielle. Gabrielle would smile and flirt with him and not think twice about it. Instead, Beth sat there trapped in her own insecurities, poised to run.

She felt the tell-tale signs of rising panic as her chest constricted painfully and her heart pounded. The adrenalin rush had started, and it was fight-or-flight time. And, for her, that meant flight. She carefully laid the spanking book face down on the table with the rest of the books she'd picked up and shot to her feet, clutching her purse. "Excuse me. I have to go."

As she walked past him, Shane reached out and gently caught her hand. "Beth, wait. Please."

She froze, staring at the long fingers that enveloped her hand. He wasn't hurting her; in fact, he wasn't exerting much pressure at all, and yet she felt utterly trapped.

"Don't go," he said, rising to his feet.

Now that he was standing, she realized how tall he was. He had to be at least six feet tall, maybe taller. His shoulders filled his suit jacket well. For that matter, his entire body filled his suit well. Just looking at him made her flush with heat from head to toe.

"Stay a while," he said. "Why don't you join me in the café? Can I buy you a cup of coffee? Or a bite to eat, if you're hungry. Whatever you'd like."

He gave her an encouraging smile, and she just stood there staring at him.

She looked down at their joined hands, and when she tried to pull her hand free, he released it.

"Sorry," he said, giving her that damnably charming smile once more.

She looked away as her chest constricted painfully. The last thing she needed was to have a full-blown panic attack in public. She wanted so desperately to stay, just for a little while, but she didn't dare. She already knew how it would end.

"It's getting late," she said, looking away. "I really should go."

"Please don't," he said. "I didn't mean to chase you off. I'm sorry."

She felt a delicious fluttering low in her belly, and she was so tempted to try. But she knew it would be a waste of time. She shook her head. "No. I'm sorry, I can't."

"It's okay, Beth."

She looked up at him, astonished by the compassion she heard in his voice. It was almost as if he *knew*. But how could he know? He didn't even know her! It wasn't okay! *She* wasn't okay! She would never be okay.

"I haven't eaten since lunch," he said. "Keep me company in the café while I wolf down a sandwich. You don't even have to talk to me, if you don't want to."

Was that his idea of a pick-up line? Surprisingly, she laughed. In addition to being drop-dead gorgeous, he was funny, too. Self-deprecating. And kind.

"Take pity on me and say 'yes,'" he said.

Shane reached for her hand again, and this time she let him hold it, simply because it felt so good. It was such a simple thing, to hold hands with someone, but she honestly couldn't remember the last time she'd done it.

Her gaze was drawn to the heavy silver watch on his wrist —

a Rolex, she noted, with one of those complicated watch faces with the tiny dials that men seemed to love so much. There was a dusting of brown hair on the back of his hand, and his fingers were long and tan, his nails clean and trimmed bluntly at the tips. When she wondered what those long fingers would feel like on her body, her belly clenched tightly.

"Just one sandwich," he said. "I'll eat fast, I promise."

She grinned, unable to help herself. To her surprise, her panic began to subside. His fingers felt so good against hers, so warm and solid. She studied their joined hands, his much larger one engulfing hers.

His thumb slowly stroked the back of her hand, and her erratic heartbeat slowed. Her body was responding to him, to his voice, to his touch. She was shocked when she realized he made her feel... *safe*.

Feeling safe was the one thing she craved more than anything. It was such an elusive goal, always just out of her reach. Right now, she was so desperate to hold on to it that she was willing to take a risk.

"Okay, I'll stay," she said. "But just for a little while."

$\mathcal{e} \mathcal{O}$ 3

Shane strove for nonchalance, but inside he was reeling. It wasn't just her looks that had knocked him for a loop, although she was probably the most alluring natural beauty he'd ever met. No, it was her presence — the way she'd looked at him, the sound of her voice, her gentle poise. Despite her anxieties, she'd conducted herself with grace, remaining calm on the outside when she was probably anything but calm on the inside. She may be saddled with a lot of anxiety, but she wasn't a coward.

Her physical response to him had floored him. He'd felt the instant attraction between them, clear as day. And on some level, she must have felt it, too. Her cheeks had flushed when he took her hand, and her pupils had dilated. He doubted she was even aware of her response to him, but he sure as hell was.

"Shall we?" he said, endeavoring to dial down his own body's response. His heart was hammering in his chest, and he needed to redirect his thoughts to something more mundane so his dick would settle down. The last thing he wanted to do was scare her off.

He led her by the hand through the aisles of books toward the café at the front of the store. Her hand felt so small in his, and that stirred up all kinds of protective feelings in him. When she tried to gently extricate her hand from his, he gave hers a reassuring squeeze, but he didn't release her hand this time. He smiled at her, gauging her reaction. She smiled hesitantly back.

He knew this had to be difficult for her, given her history and her fear of strangers, and he was trying hard not to come on too strong. He should just let her go and walk away, but the impulse to take care of her hit him hard. She reminded him of a wild rabbit, skittish and fearful, ready to flee at the first hint of danger. Damn it, she needed someone to take care of her.

He was naturally a dominant personality. As the eldest of seven children, he'd always been the leader. He'd always looked out for his three younger brothers, defending them from schoolyard bullies, teaching them how to hold their own, when to fight and when to walk away. He'd taught them how to take care of themselves. He'd watched over his three younger sisters, too, keeping a watchful eye on them, threatening their boyfriends with dire consequences if they stepped out of line.

He was a protector at heart, and he liked playing that role. That's why he started McIntyre Security — to protect people. So he wasn't surprised to find himself wanting to play that role with Beth.

As they walked through the store, Beth found herself furtively studying Shane. She couldn't help noticing every little thing about him, like the way he walked with a smooth, confident stride, or how tall he was — at least half a head taller than she was. She found herself drawn to him, mesmerized. And she wasn't the only one. Several of the women they passed followed Shane with their eyes. They'd catch a glimpse of him and do a quick double-take, their eyes widening in appreciation and lingering on him. Honestly, she couldn't blame them. She was finding it difficult not to stare at him.

When a curvy blond in a skin-tight, cobalt blue dress and matching stilettos stepped directly into Shane's path, he brought them to an abrupt halt, catching Beth when she stumbled.

In her towering heels, the woman was nearly as tall as Shane.

She looked him directly in the eye, her ice blue eyes cold and hard as diamonds. When the woman glanced at Beth, she scowled, her kohl-lined eyes narrowing as she assessed Beth from head to toe.

The woman's full, round breasts looked like they were about to spill out of the low neckline of her dress. Those couldn't be real, Beth thought. Instantly, she felt self-conscious. The woman had a perfect hourglass shape, with eye-popping breasts, a trim waist, and curvy hips. Her professionally sun-streaked blond hair was swept up in a graceful chignon, and her lips were painted a deep red. She was a walking advertisement for elegance and sex.

Beth was painfully aware of how she fared in comparison. She had no curves to speak of, no hips, and hardly any breasts. She typically didn't wear make-up other than occasionally some lip gloss, her clothes were bohemian thrift shop, and her sandals were flat and well worn.

"Hello, Shane," the blond said, her voice low and sultry. She ran a glossy red fingernail down the front of his white shirt.

"Deborah." Shane's voice was cool as he subtly shifted out of the woman's reach.

The blond smirked at Beth, not even bothering to hide her disdain. "Who's your little friend?"

"None of your business." Shane sidestepped the woman and led Beth right past her.

Beth was taken aback, by the woman's acerbic tone and by Shane's blunt dismissal of her. Obviously, these two had some kind of history, and it didn't appear to be a good one. She glanced back and was surprised by the woman's blatantly hostile glare.

Shane squeezed Beth's hand. "Sorry about that."

She hurried to match his longer strides. "Who was that?"

"No one. Forget about her." Shane looked at Beth and stopped, his expression softening. His free hand came up to touch her face, his thumb brushing lightly across her bottom lip. He frowned.

"What?" she said, feeling defensive, as she was sure he was

comparing her to the other woman.

"You are so damn beautiful," he said, shaking his head.

As they reached the café, Beth wondered if she'd lost her mind. She wasn't the type to just hook up with a stranger in public.

Shane led her to a cozy table for two by the window overlooking the sidewalk out front, where there was still plenty of weekend foot traffic. He grabbed two menus tucked inside the condiment rack and handed one to her.

She perused the menu even though she already knew it by heart, mostly to give herself something to do so she wouldn't sit there mooning over him. She honestly didn't feel like eating. Her stomach was in chaos, and she was still a little shaken from the run-in with that woman.

Shane closed his menu and looked at Beth. "What would you like? I'll go place our order."

Our order. As in the two of them, together. Was this a date? She honestly wasn't sure. Had he just picked her up? And she'd let him? Good grief, what was she thinking?

"I'll have a small Pomegranate Blueberry Smoothie, please," she said, slipping her menu back into the condiment rack.

"Just a smoothie? That's all? You sure you don't want something to eat?"

"That's all, thank you. I'm not hungry."

"I'll be right back," he said, standing.

She watched him walk to the counter to place their order. He was speaking to the cashier when Beth's phone buzzed with an incoming text. She pulled her phone out of her purse, already knowing who the message was from.

Hey sis. What's up?

It was Tyler's nightly text, just touching base to make sure she was all right. Her brother was very protective, very paternal and, yes, very bossy, but she honestly didn't mind. Sometimes she found it a little smothering, but she would never complain.

She owed him so much. She texted him back.

Having a smoothie at Clancy's. You?

Tyler worried about her, partly because of his personality, but mostly because of her past. He'd been just barely out of the Chicago Police Academy when she was abducted, and he'd never gotten over it. To be honest, she hadn't either. She didn't think she ever would. Beth's phone buzzed again.

Watching the game w/guys @ Rowdies. How about lunch tomorrow? Pick u up @ 1130?

She sent a quick reply.

Sounds great. See you then.

Beth was tucking her phone back into her purse when Shane placed a smoothie on the table in front of her and his sandwich, chips, and coffee at his spot.

"That was my brother," she said. "If I don't reply, he'll send out a search party."

Shane laughed. "Not a problem."

Actually, she wasn't kidding. Tyler would send out a search party if he couldn't reach her; he'd done it once before when she'd let her phone battery die. When she didn't reply to his message, he'd tracked her down himself.

Beth took a sip of the deep purple smoothie, savoring its sweet and tart flavor. The cold cup felt good in her hand.

Shane watched her take another sip. "Is it good?"

She nodded. "It's delicious. Thank you."

"You're welcome." He picked up his coffee and took a sip. "Are you and your brother close?"

She nodded. "Yes."

"Do you have any other siblings?"

"No, just my brother."

"I'm the oldest of seven."

Her eyes widened in genuine surprise. "I can't even imagine what that's like."

"Just imagine a lot of noise and chaos, and you'll have it," he said, smiling.

She smiled back. "When I was little, I used to beg my mom for a little brother or sister, but it never happened. My dad died when I was a baby, and my mom never remarried. I don't think she ever got over losing him."

They sat in comfortable silence while Shane polished off his sandwich and chips in record time.

He hadn't been kidding, Beth thought. The man must have been starving. When he was finished eating, he leaned back in his chair, observing Beth as he leisurely sipped his coffee. She kept her eyes on her own cup, fiddling with her straw and taking slow sips of her smoothie.

"Would you like anything else, Beth?"

"No. This is perfect," she said. She could feel his gaze on her, and it made her nervous. His attentiveness was both flattering and nerve racking.

"So, do you come here often?" he said, and then he winced. "That sounded really lame, didn't it? But it was an honest question."

She smiled. "I come here almost every Friday evening. It's my way of unwinding at the end of the work week, which is rather ironic considering I work in a library."

He took another sip of his coffee. "Sounds as if you like books."

"I do. What about you? Do you read?"

"I read a lot, mostly nonfiction," he said. "One of my brothers writes military thrillers, and I read his books. He's actually quite good. His last three hardcovers hit the number one spot on *The New York Times'* bestseller list."

"That's impressive," she said. "What's his name?"

"Jamie McIntyre."

"I'll have to watch for his books."

"I'd be happy to loan you my copies." He laughed again. "That sounded like a pick-up line, I know, but I meant it."

Shane set down his coffee cup, his expression turning serious. His mind had been racing since she'd agreed to come to the café with him. But now what? Now that he'd met her, he couldn't just walk away and never see her again. That was unacceptable. So where did that leave him? "I'd like to see you again, Beth. Will you have dinner with me one night this week?"

Her heart stopped in her chest, and she stared at him. He really was trying to pick her up; it wasn't just wishful thinking on her part.

"Beth?"

There was something in the tone of his voice that resonated with her. It was part patience and part command.

"Beth, you can talk to me."

Talk to him? He made it sound so easy. She shook her head.

"What's wrong?" he said.

"It's just that...." She couldn't even finish her sentence. How could she possibly explain to him how difficult it was for her to open up to someone? She'd made it her life's goal to avoid conflict and stress, and that meant avoiding people, especially men. This man, with his beautiful eyes and strong hands, made her feel vulnerable in a way she'd never felt before. He made her want things she'd resigned herself to living without.

"It's just what, sweetheart?" he said.

Hearing him call her that — *sweetheart* — pushed her over the edge. She was going to burst out of her own skin any second. Her heart began to race, and her chest tightened.

Beth grabbed her purse. "Thanks for the smoothie. I'm sorry, but I have to go."

She was halfway to the exit when she heard him call her name, but she kept running. When she reached the glass doors, she pushed through them and stepped out onto the sidewalk, the warm, humid summer air making it hard to breathe. The street was crowded with cars and pedestrians, but she caught sight of an available taxi just a few yards away. She made a beeline for the cab, but before she could open the door and escape, Shane was at her side.

"Beth, wait." He grabbed her shoulders and turned her to face him.

The concern in his expression made her knees go weak, and

she felt lightheaded.

"I'm sorry if I came on too strong," he said. "I didn't mean to scare you."

Sweetheart. When he called her that back in the café, it made her realize just how much she wanted that in her life. How much she wanted to be someone's sweetheart.

Shane released her to retrieve a business card from his wallet and handed it to her. He leaned forward and put his lips to the side of her head, his warm breath caressing the shell of her ear as he whispered to her. "You're overwhelmed, Beth. I get that. It's all right."

The sound of his voice, low and sensual, made her shiver.

He straightened and pointed at the card in her hand. "That's my card. My name, work number, and private number."

Beth looked down at the card, too stunned to take in any of the details.

"Call me, Beth. Day or night, it doesn't matter. Just call me, please. I want to see you again."

Beth closed her trembling fingers around the card and drew it to her chest.

Shane reached out and brushed the edge of her cheek with his thumb. He leaned toward her, and her heart nearly stopped when she thought he was going to kiss her. But, at the last moment, he pulled back and smiled ruefully. She stood frozen in place, her heart thundering painfully in her chest.

"Call me, Beth," he said as he opened the cab door.

Beth slid into the backseat of the cab. And as she sat there shaking, Shane leaned into the cab and secured her into the seatbelt.

The cab driver, a rotund man with a thick head of white hair, glanced back impatiently. "Come on, folks. I don't have all night."

Shane glared at the driver, then pulled out his wallet again to withdraw several bills, which he shoved into the driver's outstretched hand. "Make sure she gets home safely."

"Shit, man!" the driver said, eyeing the bills. He shoved them into his shirt pocket. "Thanks!"

Shane looked down at Beth one last time, his expression tight. "I'll be waiting for your call." Then he shut her door.

"Close the windows and lock the doors," he said to the cab driver through the open front passenger window.

"You got it, buddy!" the driver said, immediately engaging the locks and putting up the windows.

As the cabbie put the car in drive, Beth looked down at the card in her hand. It was printed on white linen paper and embossed with charcoal gray text.

Shane McIntyre
Founder and CEO, McIntyre Security, Inc.

Beth recognized the prestigious address of his office building. It wasn't far from the high-rise building that housed the restaurant where Gabrielle worked.

She slipped Shane's card into her purse, and then leaned back in the seat and allowed herself to relive the feel of his lips against her ear as he'd whispered to her. She lost herself in the memory of his voice, so close and intimate, and the feel of his warm breath against her ear.

As the cab pulled smoothly into the flow of traffic, she turned to glance out the rear window for one last look. Shane stood on the sidewalk exactly where she'd left him, his gaze locked onto her cab as it drove away.

He was still watching when the cab turned a corner.

As soon as Beth's cab disappeared from sight, Shane headed for the parking garage where he'd left his car. He couldn't help wondering what the fuck had just happened back there. He must have lost his mind, because he'd broken nearly every rule in the company handbook. He'd violated protocol and compromised the entire operation. If he weren't the owner of the company, he'd fire himself on the spot.

But it wasn't his unprofessionalism that surprised him the

most. It was the fact that he'd been poleaxed by a submissive little blond. And she was submissive — there was no doubt in his mind about that. Submissives really weren't his type. He tended to date Federal court judges and surgeons, bank vice-presidents and attorneys. He dated women who knew what they wanted and weren't afraid to take it. And Beth — she was none of those things. She wasn't his type, and she was ten years younger than he was. So why the hell was he reeling like he'd just been blindsided?

He'd never met a more sensuous, more enticing woman in his life, and he wanted her — desperately. Knowing her background, he'd tried not to come on too strong. He'd tried to rein himself in. But he wasn't used to treating women with kid gloves. Still, he hadn't imagined that instant connection between them, the heat, the attraction. Her body had given off all kinds of signals that she was interested, but still she'd run.

Damn. She was going to be a hell of a lot of work. And, shit! Tyler was going to kill him. There was no doubt about that, because now that he'd met Beth, everything had changed. This case had become personal for him. No matter what it took, he was going to become her lover. And then, her safety would be his responsibility.

4

Shane was still officially on bodyguard duty for the next six hours, which meant he'd be parked outside Beth's townhouse until someone relieved him at the end of his shift. On the way to her house, he stopped at a fast food drive-thru to grab two large black coffees and a couple of sandwiches to hold him over. As he pulled away from the drive-thru, a call came in. He synced his phone to the car speakers. He'd been expecting this, and he figured he might as well get it over with.

He sighed. "What is it, Jake?"

"What the fuck do you think you're doing?"

"My job."

"Since when is field work your job?"

"Since tonight. You knew I was filling in for Miles."

"Shane, let someone else do it. You can't work all day and then do surveillance all night."

"Yes, I can," Shane said. "Go bother someone else."

Jake made an exasperated sound. "I'll do it. I can be at her house in twenty minutes."

"I said I've got this, Jake. Give it a rest. How's Miles?"

"He'll live, but he's been admitted to the hospital overnight for observation."

"Is anyone with him?"

"Yeah. Liam is."

"Good," Shane said. "Keep me updated." And then he ended the call.

On the drive home, Beth kept replaying Shane's parting words: *Just call me, please. I want to see you again.*

Had the sexiest man she'd ever met tried to pick her up in Clancy's? And did he really expect her to call him? He couldn't have been serious.

She was shaken out of her reverie when the cab pulled up in front of her house.

The cabbie hunched down to look out the front passenger window at her address. "Nice place," he said.

"Thanks."

The cab driver glanced back at Beth with a satisfied grin on his face. "Tell your boyfriend thanks for the tip. He made my entire quota for the night."

"Sure," Beth said, even though she had absolutely no intention of seeing Shane McIntyre again. "Thanks for the ride."

Feeling a little dazed, she walked up the stone steps to the front door and let herself in. Once inside, she reset the security system — one of Tyler's demands.

The interior was dark, except for the light coming from a stained-glass lamp on the hall table. The lamp cast a warm glow throughout the narrow foyer, making the dark mahogany floors gleam with a beautiful luster. A handsome grandfather clock that her paternal grandfather had given to her grandmother for their first wedding anniversary stood in the foyer, its large, gold pendulum swinging gracefully as it marked the passing seconds. A burgundy floral runner ran the length of the foyer, leading to the kitchen in the rear of the house.

She loved this old house. Every time she stepped through the front door, she felt a sense of peace, a sense of homecoming. Knowing that her grandparents had lived nearly a half-century in this house gave her a sense of continuity that she cherished.

Like the other brownstones in her modest neighborhood, the

building wasn't very wide. The front staircase hugged the left wall of the foyer, leading up to a landing and a hallway that led to three small bedrooms and a bathroom.

The house was quiet, as Gabrielle wasn't home from work yet. As one of the top ranked sous chefs at Renaldo's, Gabrielle worked the very desirable evening shifts and didn't get home until a little after midnight. But as much as Beth loved Gabrielle's company, she was relieved that her best friend wasn't home. Right now, she just wanted to be alone.

She left the light on in the front hall for Gabrielle and headed up the narrow staircase to the second floor, walking past the landing and the bathroom to her bedroom at the end of the hall.

Beth switched on the light in her bedroom, a vintage crystal chandelier that hung in the center of the room. It was an old-fashioned light fixture for an old-fashioned house.

Much of this house still bore her grandmother's loving touches from the '40s. The walls in Beth's bedroom were a pale blue. White lace curtains hung in the two tall windows that overlooked the back courtyard. The bedroom furniture was mahogany, too, and had once belonged to her grandmother.

After tossing her purse onto the bed, she walked into the tiny adjoining closet and kicked off her sandals, then stripped out of her clothes and hung them up. She grabbed a nightgown off a hook on the back of the closet door and headed down the hall to the bathroom to wash up for bed.

She frowned when she caught sight of her reflection in the bathroom mirror. Her eyes seemed a little bruised, thanks to the faint purple shadows beneath her lower lids. Her complexion, which was usually pale thanks to her Swedish mother, was still flushed from her encounter with Shane.

Comparing herself to the blond bombshell in all her striking, curvy glory, Beth thought her own reflection was quite unremarkable.

Shane made good time. Luckily, he arrived on Beth's street just as someone was pulling out of a street-side parking space just four doors down from her townhouse. From his vantage point, he had an unimpeded view of her front door.

It was a quaint street of brownstones in very nice condition, decorated uniformly with window boxes filled with colorful flowers and decorative wrought-iron fences. The faux gaslight streetlights made for good visibility.

At the rear of the house, he knew, was a small yard enclosed by brick walls and a one-car garage that housed Beth's Mini Cooper. An alley provided access to the garage and backyard. Jake had installed an extensive system of covert surveillance cameras at the rear of the property covering the alley, the garage, the backyard, and the back of the house. Those cameras were monitored 24/7 back at the office, and Shane could access those cameras at any time from an app on his phone — like he was doing now.

He shut off the engine and prepared to settle in for a long night. If he'd known he was going to be sitting in his car all night, he would've arranged to trade the Jaguar for the Escalade. He certainly wasn't going to be able to stretch out his six-foot-two frame in the tight confines of the vintage car. After a couple hours of sitting here, his right leg would be giving him hell thanks to the two metal rods in his right femur.

As he took a sip of coffee, he wondered what the hell he'd said that had sent Beth running like that. He laid his phone on the front passenger seat and glanced at it. She wasn't going to call him, damn it. He'd wanted to ask for her number, so he could do the calling, but that would've been too much, too soon. He'd just have to be patient. He'd give her a few days to call him, and if she didn't, then he'd improvise another chance meeting.

He'd already broken a whole slew of rules. Why not break a few more?

Beth switched her bedside lamp to the nightlight setting and slipped between the cool white sheets. She tried to relax, but she was too wound up to sleep. Her thoughts kept drifting to Shane's business card, which she'd tucked into her purse.

She lay quietly as the minutes ticked by, waiting for her heart rate to slow. Call him? No way. That was so not happening. Half an hour later, she was still awake, edgy and restless. She grabbed her purse and pulled out his card. The URL for his company's website was listed on his business card, so she pulled out her Kindle and fired it up so she could check out his website.

His company's website was impressive, with a sleek, modern design. According to the *About Us* page, they offered personal protection and state-of-the-art security systems in over a dozen countries. Personal protection... as in bodyguards. They also had a division that designed and installed state-of-the-art security systems for museums, universities, hospitals, and government installations. They had a list of patents longer than her arm, and their client list read like a *Who's Who* of Fortune 500 companies.

She clicked on a link that took her to the bios of the company executives and her eyes went right to Shane's photo at the top of the page. She read his bio, surprised to learn he'd spent 10 years in the military. After he left the military on a medical discharge, he'd gotten his MBA at the University of Chicago and started his business. Still, she knew next to nothing about him, other than the fact that he was keeping her up tonight.

Frustrated, she put both her Kindle and Shane's business card back into her purse. What might have happened tonight if she hadn't run off? What if she'd stayed and talked to him? What would he have done? For a moment, standing outside the cab, she'd been sure he was about to kiss her. He'd leaned right into her, his eyes glued to her mouth, but at the last moment he'd pulled back. If he had kissed her, she probably would have run away screaming, and he probably would have considered himself lucky to have avoided that nightmare.

"You're such a fucking headcase!" That's what Kevin — her first and only serious boyfriend — said when he walked out on her. He was right, of course. And she hadn't dated anyone in the three years since. The one time she'd taken a chance had back-

fired on her in a big way.

"Ooh!" Frustration was eating at her. She turned on her side and wrapped her arms around the spare pillow, wishing she had someone to snuggle with. She closed her eyes and remembered the feel of Shane's lips against her ear as he'd murmured to her. His voice had been low and just a little rough, enough to make her insides quiver. His warm breath ruffling her hair had made her shiver. Just thinking about him — thinking about what might have happened — stirred up inconvenient feelings she'd rather not have to deal with right then.

She felt herself growing increasingly restless, until sleep became the last thing her body wanted. She could feel the blood pooling in her sex, making her flushed and achy. Her sex began to throb as if it had a mind of its own and knew what it wanted.

Pressing her face into the cool pillowcase, she remembered the feel of his hand holding hers. God, she wanted more of that. She wanted those big hands on her again. She wanted those long fingers trailing over every inch of her body. Unfortunately, her body and her mind were at odds with each other.

Knowing one surefire way to shut down her thoughts, she rolled to her back and reached up underneath her nightgown and into her panties. She was already so wet, her sex flushed with heat and unrelenting need. She discarded her panties, kicking them off somewhere under the sheets, then spread her legs and slipped her finger between the slick folds of her sex, sinking it into her core. She was so wet from just thinking about Shane — she couldn't imagine what it would be like if he were actually here. The wetness spilled out, and she spread some of it to her already-sensitive clitoris.

It had taken barely any stroking at all before her belly began to quiver, before her muscles tightened in anticipation of her release. She stroked herself relentlessly as she reached for the oblivion she so desperately needed. She pictured Shane, imagining running her fingers through his hair. She wanted to tug on those beautiful strands and pull him close. She wanted to... damn it, she wanted him.

Desperate now, Beth opened her legs wider and surrendered to the inevitable tumult. Her muscles locked as her finger rocked her clit. She closed her eyes and imagined it was Shane's finger stroking her, that it was his touch driving her crazy. His face was there in her mind when her body exploded into a mind-numbing orgasm. Waves of blinding pleasure radiated from her core, coursing through her body and stealing her breath. She was alone in the house, so she allowed herself the rare luxury of crying out her pleasure.

All too soon, the waves receded, her limbs like jelly now, boneless and limp. She didn't have the energy to find her panties, so she straightened her nightgown and rolled to her side, wrapping her arms around the spare pillow and wishing it were a warm male body. Tiny, residual tremors from her orgasm coursed through her body, and now she could finally relax.

As she drifted off to sleep, she heard Shane's voice in her head. *Just call me, please. I want to see you again.*

Her throat tightened with longing and regret as she pressed her hot face into the pillow. She couldn't call him. She just couldn't trust someone that much.

5

Nearing the end of his overnight shift, Shane desperately needed to stretch his legs, but there just wasn't enough room in the Jaguar. He was stiff, exhausted, and hungry. If he stood in for Miles again, he'd sure as hell do it in the Escalade with a giant thermos of black coffee and a stash of food.

Sitting in that plush corner office was making him soft.

To make things worse, Beth hadn't called. He hadn't actually expected her to call, but still, there'd been that tiny hope she might. So he'd had six hours to sit here and think about her, reliving their encounter and trying to figure out exactly what had made her run. And thinking about her all night — remembering the delicate scent of her skin... how soft her hand had felt... how good her hair had smelled — had left him with a raging case of blue balls. He hadn't felt this sexually frustrated since... well, since never.

Miguel Rodriguez showed up at 0545 hours, fifteen minutes before Shane's shift was up. Miguel had texted him a heads-up of his impending arrival, and Shane vacated his parking spot just as he saw Miguel's black Mustang come around the corner.

After leaving Beth's street pre-dawn, Shane debated whether to head to the penthouse apartment on Lake Shore Drive in the Gold Coast or to the house in Kenilworth. He typically spent his weekends on his estate in Kenilworth, right on Lake Michigan.

But the penthouse won out because the idea of leaving the city just now didn't sit well with him. And, yeah, it was just an excuse to stick close to *her*. In case she did call.

Now that he'd met Beth, he realized why Tyler worried so much about her. The thought of someone trying to hurt her made him go a little nuts. The girl had absolutely no defenses.

Shane parked in his reserved slot in the underground parking garage of his apartment building and took the express elevator up to the penthouse floor. He stepped out into the private foyer and then walked into the apartment, which was silent at the moment, thank goodness. He really didn't feel like explaining himself to anyone right now.

He'd half expected to find Cooper waiting to ambush him. While he loved the man like a brother, he wasn't in the mood to be grilled. And Cooper would grill him. The man missed nothing.

He headed down the hall to the master suite, which was his private domain. Once in his own space, he stripped off his clothes, dropping them to the floor, as he headed for the bathroom. Right now, the only thing he wanted to do was alleviate a very persistent erection.

He stepped into the granite and glass walk-in shower and flipped a couple of switches. Hot water shot out instantly from six different shower heads, and he groaned as he walked into the spray. His dick bobbed in the air, ruthlessly defying gravity like it had a mind of its own. The damn thing had been tormenting him all night, so he finally took hold of it and grabbed some body wash and began stroking.

A cold, clinical hand job held no appeal for him right then, so he closed his eyes and indulged himself in the remembered scent of Beth's warm skin. He needed her scent in his nose again. Hell, he needed it all over his body; he wanted to be covered in it. He'd barely touched her, and yet he couldn't get her out of his head.

He pictured Beth as she'd looked sitting in that damn cab,

gazing up at him with those big, soulful eyes, looking so damned lost. It had killed him to send her off alone in a cab. He'd wanted to take her home himself, but he could hardly have done that when she was in full flight mode. She wasn't ready for that yet.

He'd had just enough presence of mind at the time to let her go — to give her some space. But his retreat was only temporary. One way or another, they'd be seeing each other again, soon. The only question was, how long did he have to wait?

Shane braced himself on the granite wall with one hand and pumped his erection with the other. He conjured up a pair of Caribbean ocean eyes, wide with anticipation. *God, he wanted her.* He wanted to feed his cock into her sweet body, one inch at a time, and watch her face as he filled her. He wanted to take her slowly, prolonging her pleasure and his, but he also wanted to drive his cock into her so hard and so deep that he banished thoughts of any previous lovers from her head.

His shout was loud and hoarse when he finally lost control and unloaded against the shower wall with a violence that surprised even him. *Fuck!* Cooper probably heard that.

Shane pulled on a pair of gray sweats and one of his old Marine Corps t-shirts and padded barefoot to the kitchen. If he couldn't satisfy his sexual appetite, at least he could fill his belly. He was grateful to find a pot of fresh coffee in the maker, and he knew he had Cooper to thank for it.

He threw together a deli sandwich — that was about the extent of his food preparation skills — and parked himself on a stool at the kitchen counter to eat, suck down some coffee, and peruse yesterday's newspaper.

Cooper walked into the kitchen dressed for business in jeans and a black t-shirt, his empty gun holster strapped to his muscular chest.

Shane nodded in greeting. "Thanks for the coffee. You heading out?"

"Thought I'd go to the shooting range," Cooper said. "What

about you? It's Saturday. I thought you'd be in Kenilworth already."

Shane swallowed a mouthful of hot coffee and shrugged, aware of Cooper's scrutiny. Apparently word got around fast. "I thought I'd stay in town this weekend."

Cooper leaned against the counter, crossing his arms over his chest. "And why is that?"

And here came the interrogation. "Do I need a reason to sleep in my own apartment?"

"No," Cooper said. "I'm just wondering if this has anything to do with your moonlighting last night as a covert bodyguard after putting in a full day at the office. Do you plan to sleep any time soon?"

"I already have a mother, Cooper. But thanks."

"Yeah? Well, your folks aren't here right now, so guess what? I get to do the honors. I promised Peggy I'd keep an eye on all you kids."

Shane threw Cooper a quelling glance, then picked up his plate and coffee. "I'll be in the office. I'm going to finish eating, read the case reports from last night, and check e-mail. Then I'll grab some shuteye. Satisfied?"

Cooper nodded. "Just doing my job, boss," he said, grinning.

Shane dropped into his desk chair and booted up his PC. He was exhausted and needed sleep, but of course he'd never admit that to Cooper. Cooper was old enough to be his father, but he had the energy of ten men. As far as Shane knew, the man never slept or took a break. The hypocrite.

As he ate, Shane read the new case reports that had come in from the field overnight. He would have to write one himself on his overnight surveillance of Beth, but he'd leave out the fact that he'd hit on her. He'd also leave out the part about his raging all-night hard-on.

His company had about two dozen surveillance jobs under-way in the city right then, but the only one he was interested in at that moment was Howard Kline. The Kline surveillance team had reported a quiet night. While Shane had been camped outside of Beth's house, Kline had been at home with his mother watching reruns of 1980's sitcoms until the wee hours of the morning. Kline's inactivity worried Shane. The man hardly ever left the house, and that just wasn't right. It was a huge fucking red flag. He made a mental note to go out on one of the surveillance runs himself, so he could get a firsthand glimpse of Kline. He could tell a lot about a man from watching him.

He took a few minutes to write up his own report from the night before, leaving out the many ways he'd screwed up. He refrained from mentioning that he'd held her hand and whispered in her ear as he'd inhaled her tantalizing scent. Damn.

He read the report his brother Liam had filed on Miles' trip to the ER and subsequent hospitalization. It must've been one hell of a case of food poisoning, the poor guy.

Shane picked up the desk phone and dialed Liam's cell.

"Jesus, Shane," his youngest brother said with a voice that sounded like crushed gravel. "It's six-thirty on a Saturday morning! Something had better be on fire."

"How's Miles?"

"You woke me up to ask me that?" Liam made a disgusted noise. "Miles is fine. He'll be sprung from the hospital sometime today, and he should be able to return to work this evening."

"Tell him that won't be necessary," Shane said. "I'm taking over his shift with Beth Jamison until further notice. Give Miles a couple days off to recuperate, and then assign him to another case."

"Why the change?" Liam said.

"Just do it."

Beth woke Saturday morning to the warm, yeasty aroma of homemade pancakes. She cracked open her eyes and blinked at Gabrielle, who sat on the side of her bed holding a wooden tray. Gabrielle was dressed in black yoga pants and a purple sports bra, and she looked gorgeous, as always.

According to the digital clock on her nightstand, it was eight-thirty. "You've already been out for a run and made breakfast?"

"Yep. Four miles," Gabrielle said, grinning at Beth. "Now rise and shine, sleepy head."

Beth glared at her best friend. Gabrielle's cheeks, which were flecked with a light dusting of cinnamon freckles, were flushed, and her green eyes sparkled. She looked far too amazing for this early on a weekend morning. She was gorgeous, with a body to die for, and she cooked like a boss. She was going to make some guy very lucky one day.

Beth groaned as she rolled over to hide her face in her pillow. "I hate you."

"Come on! I made pancakes," Gabrielle said. "You love pancakes."

Beth rolled back and eyed the tray in Gabrielle's lap. There was a stack of three enormous pancakes on a plate, a small pitcher of maple syrup, two forks, napkins, and a glass of what Beth knew was fresh-squeezed orange juice. Gabrielle never took short-cuts in the kitchen.

"Thanks, Gabrielle," Beth said as she scooted up in bed to lean against the headboard. "I really don't deserve this."

Gabrielle set the tray on Beth's lap. "Of course you do. You're my best friend."

"Then I guess I don't deserve *you*." Beth picked up the knife and cut the stack of pancakes in half. "I hope you're planning to share this with me. I couldn't possibly eat this much. Besides, Tyler's picking me up for lunch in a few hours."

Gabrielle grinned as she picked up the extra fork. "Why do you think I brought two forks?"

Beth took a bite of the pancakes and moaned. "Oh my God, this is so good," she said. "Thank you."

"You're welcome. So, did you have a good evening last night?"

Beth's face heated. "I did, actually. I sort of met someone last night at Clancy's."

Gabrielle looked at her in surprise. "You 'sort of' met some-one? Who?"

Beth shrugged. "His name's Shane McIntyre. He gave me his number and asked me to call him."

Gabrielle's eyes narrowed. "Really."

Beth took another bite. "He bought me a smoothie in the café. He was really nice, but I kind of freaked out on him and bolted."

Gabrielle laid down her fork. "Are you going to call him?"

Beth shook her head. "No. He's way too far out of my league. Besides... well, you know."

"Yeah, that's probably for the best," Gabrielle said.

Tyler arrived at half past eleven and let himself in. Beth ran down the stairs to meet him.

Her brother stood in the foyer dressed in his typical week-end attire — black jeans, a white collared shirt, and a pair of black running shoes. She had to admit, from a purely objective perspective, her brother was all kinds of hot, if you liked your guys tall, dark, and controlling. No wonder he couldn't keep a girlfriend.

Tyler ruffled the hair on the top of Beth's head. "Ready, kiddo?"

She ducked out from beneath his hand and smiled. "Yes."

Tyler had been calling her "kiddo" for as long as she could remember. She'd always been a kid to him, and probably always would be.

Beth grabbed her purse from off the hall table. "Bye, Gabri-elle! I'm leaving!"

"Bye!" Gabrielle called from the kitchen. "Have fun!"

Tyler steered Beth out the front door and locked the door be-hind him.

She walked down to the curb and found the front passenger

door of Tyler's black pick-up truck locked. Glancing back, she spotted Tyler back at her front stoop reading something on his phone. His brow was heavily furrowed, and he was frowning. After he keyed a quick response, he slipped his phone into the holder at his waist.

"Sorry about that," he said, jogging down the front steps.

Tyler unlocked her door with his key fob, and she slid into the truck cab.

They drove a couple of miles in silence, which was unusual for them. Tyler usually grilled Beth on how her week went. But today, he seemed preoccupied.

"Was that work?" she said. "On your phone?" Her brother never stopped working.

"Yeah," Tyler said. "Just something about a case I'm working on."

When they entered the restaurant, they were seated promptly in their favorite back corner booth. A petite brunette with short, curly hair and dimples arrived to take their order: a large, deep dish pizza with everything. Tyler ordered a Coke for Beth, and a bottle of the local Goose Island summer ale for himself. When their server returned with their drinks, her eyes lingered on Tyler.

"Our server is crushing on you," Beth said, once the girl had gone.

Tyler scowled. "No, she isn't. So, how was work?"

"It was fine."

She told him all about her week, and he entertained her with a story about an extracurricular departmental game of basketball that had gone bad that week — ending with both of them laughing so hard they had tears in their eyes. They were still laughing when their pizza arrived.

"Thanks," Tyler told the girl, as she set the pizza on their table.

"Can I get you anything else?" she said.

"No, thank you," Tyler said. "This should do it."

"Okay." She smiled at him, showing off those dimples. "Let me know if you change your mind."

"I will, thanks," Tyler said.

Their server stood there smiling at Tyler for a few more seconds, and then she blushed and walked away.

"See? I told you she was crushing on you," Beth said, grinning at her brother as he placed a slice of pizza on her plate.

Before he could reply, his phone buzzed with an incoming call. When he gazed at the screen to check the caller ID, a flicker of surprise crossed his face.

"Excuse me," he said as he accepted the call. "What is it?" He listened intently for half a minute. "Understood. But now's not a good time. I'll call you later." And then he abruptly ended the call.

"Work again?" Beth said.

"Yeah. Nothing to worry about." Tyler smiled at her. "How's your pizza?"

After they finished their meal, Tyler paid the bill, and they left. When they got back to her house, he double parked and walked her up to her door.

"Beth, do you need anything?" he said, as he unlocked her front door with his key.

"No, thanks," she said. "I'm good."

"How about money?"

Beth smiled at her brother. She loved him dearly, but sometimes he drove her nuts. "Nope. All good."

He nodded. "Let me know if you need anything, okay?"

"I will. Thank you, Tyler."

Tyler leaned down and kissed her on the cheek. "Call me if you need anything, kiddo."

"I will."

He started to walk away, but then he turned back and wrapped his arms around her. "Be careful, Beth," he murmured.

"Be vigilant. And always let Gabrielle know where you are and when you'll be home."

"I will."

Tyler seemed a little shaken. He was always protective of her, but this was different. He was worried.

"I love you, kiddo," Tyler said, reaching out to muss her hair again.

This time she let him do it.

Beth walked through the kitchen and out the French doors to the backyard where she found Gabrielle working in her herb garden. With its neat little rows of carefully marked plantings, the herb garden was Gabrielle's pride and joy.

Beth crouched down beside Gabrielle and began pulling weeds from between the flourishing oregano plants.

"How was your lunch?" Gabrielle asked.

"Good. Tyler seemed a little distracted, though."

"Oh?" Gabrielle said, moving over to weed around the dill plants.

"Yeah. Something's bothering him. And then he got weird right before he left, reminding me to 'be vigilant.'"

"Well, you know how protective he is of you."

"I know," Beth said. "But this was different. He told me to always tell you where I am."

"We do that anyway, Beth. That's nothing new."

"I guess," Beth said.

6

After finishing up paperwork and returning e-mails, Shane headed to his suite and crashed. He needed a few good hours of sleep if he planned to camp outside Beth's house again that night. During his time in the Marines, he'd learned to fall asleep anywhere at any time. That skill came in handy in his civilian life, too.

He woke at noon, hungry. He grabbed his socks and running shoes and headed to the kitchen. Cooper had left him a note telling him to help himself to the leftover Chinese food in the fridge, which he did. He guzzled a bottle of water, then headed down to the gym on the 14th floor.

The gym was crowded, which was good. Maybe he could find someone to spar with. Kicking the shit out of someone sounded like a really good idea. If he couldn't find someone in the gym, maybe he could talk one of his brothers into going a few rounds with him.

After a quick warm-up, he grabbed an employee to spot him and hit the bench press. The physical strain of lifting 280 pounds helped him rein in his thoughts. After he finished with the bench press, he ran three miles on the indoor track, setting a grueling pace that helped him stay focused. Otherwise, he was liable to do something stupid like check in on Beth. If there was a problem, his people would let him know.

About the time he was done running, a text came in. He stepped off the track and checked the message. It was from the surveillance team assigned to monitor Kline. Finally, something:

K's on the move. On foot.

Shane texted back:

Watch and report.

He wanted to know Kline's every move. If the guy sneezed, Shane wanted to know. If Kline was on the move, he wanted to be sure it wasn't in Beth's direction.

He texted Miguel, who was on duty watching Beth.

Report Bookworm location. K on the move.

Bookworm. Shane grinned at Beth's nickname. It was definitely growing on him. When Miguel had first come up with the nickname, Shane hadn't liked it much.

"The Bookworm's home from work, safe and sound," Miguel had reported once via a phone call to Shane.

"Don't call her that," Shane had said.

"Why not? She's a librarian, for God's sake, and she hangs out in bookstores. Ergo, the girl's a bookworm."

Since Shane couldn't argue with Miguel's reasoning, the name had stuck.

Miguel texted back:

Bookworm still at lunch w/T-Rex @ Mario's.

Another text came in from the team shadowing Kline:

K walked to public library. Using PC.

All right! Now they would finally get somewhere. Kline surely wasn't surfing the Internet for cookie recipes.

Shane replied to the Kline team:

Alerting IT. Stand by for forensics team.

Shane called AJ Byer, head of the IT department. "I want a computer forensics team mobilized and ready. Howard Kline is using a PC at a public library. I'll have the surveillance team send you the exact location. As soon as Kline leaves the library,

I want a team on that computer. I want to know everything he did. Every search, every keystroke."

"No problem, Shane," AJ said.

Shane headed upstairs to the apartment. After a quick shower, he parked himself on one of the kitchen counter barstools and booted up his laptop. Another text came in from Kline's surveillance team:

K left the library on foot, heading home.

Shane replied:

Secure the PC. Forensics en route.

The Kline surveillance team confirmed the order:

Roger that.

Shane called AJ. "Kline just left the library. Someone from the surveillance team will hang back at the library to guard the PC until your folks get there."

"Got it," AJ said. "We have the location, and the forensics team has already left. Their ETA is 30 minutes."

An app on Shane's phone chimed, alerting him to the fact that he was about to have company. Someone had entered the passcode to the private elevator. He checked the bank of CCTV monitors in the kitchen and saw Jake and Liam in the elevator. They were undoubtedly here to give him a hard time about his whereabouts last night, but at least they had the decency to bring food. A moment later, Shane heard a ping as the elevator doors opened in the foyer.

"We heard there are some developments," Liam said as he came through the foyer doors. He was carrying two large pizza boxes, which he laid on the counter.

Jake walked in reading an incoming message on his phone. He headed for the fridge and grabbed bottles of beer, handing one to Shane and one to Liam.

Shane opened a pizza box and pulled out a slice. "Thanks for the food. I'm starved."

"No problem," Liam said. "Anything concrete yet from IT?"

"Not yet," Shane said. "The forensics team is en route to the library. We should be able to get some good intel from his browser history."

Liam opened his beer.

The three brothers sat on barstools at the counter, eating pizza and drinking beer.

Forty-five minutes later, Shane's phone chimed with an incoming call. "AJ, I'm putting you on speaker." Shane synced his phone with the speakers in the kitchen. "Liam and Jake are here too."

"We've got problems, Shane," AJ said. "Our perp was a busy boy at the library. He searched for second-hand computer shops and cheap Internet plans."

"Figures," Shane said. It was only a matter of time until Kline got himself an Internet connection at home.

"He also searched for local employers who hire ex-cons," AJ said.

"He needs an income," Liam said, grabbing another slice of pizza. "To pay for the second-hand PC and Internet service."

"He tried to download some porn, but the library filters caught him," AJ said. "But here's the kicker, Shane. He ran a search on Beth Jamison. He accessed her home address and phone number. He searched for her on social media websites, but he didn't find much there. She has a Facebook page, but it's restricted to friends only. He also went to the Kingston Medical School website and viewed a map of the campus."

"Fuck," Shane said. "Thanks, AJ. Send me the full report when forensics is done."

Shane called Tyler Jamison, whom the guys had aptly nicknamed T-Rex. He knew Tyler was with Beth, but this couldn't wait. Tyler answered on the third ring, and it was noisy where he was — they must still be at the restaurant.

"What is it?" Tyler said, his voice coming through loud and clear over the speaker.

"Kline just searched the Internet for Beth's address and telephone number on a PC at the public library," Shane said. "Threat confirmed."

"Understood," Tyler said. "But now's not a good time. I'll call you later."

Shane texted Miguel, who was parked outside the restaurant where Beth and Tyler were, and gave him the update. *Threat confirmed.*

"I guess it's official now," Liam said, pulling another beer out of the fridge. "You want one?" he asked Shane.

"Yeah." Shane caught the bottle Liam tossed his way.

Jake grabbed another slice of pizza. "Defcon 4. Now we wait for him to make a move toward Beth, and we nail him."

Shane realized he'd been hoping that Kline had moved on by now, but no such luck. Kline was still fixated on Beth. Covert surveillance on Beth was no longer enough; he wanted close personal protection on her 24/7. He'd be having a talk with Tyler as soon as he could arrange it.

"Anyone up for a few rounds in the ring?" Shane said, finishing off his second beer. Right now he needed an intense work-out. When he and his brothers hit the mat, it was no holds barred.

"I am," Liam said, hopping off his barstool. "I'm always happy to kick your ass. What do you feel like? Jiu Jitsu? Krav Maga? Kickboxing?"

Jake laughed. "Be careful, Liam. The boss is in a shitty mood. You know how he gets when he's like that. He fights mean."

Shane stowed the leftover pizza in the fridge, and the three of them headed down the hall to the martial arts studio. Liam and Shane hit the locker room and stripped down to shorts and muscle shirts.

A few hard rounds in the ring with Liam would feel good, if his brother didn't manage to pummel the shit out of him first. He and his brothers were pretty evenly matched — they were about the same size, with similar builds and musculature. But

Liam clearly had an advantage; he was a martial arts instructor who'd played professional circuits for several years during his rebellious phase. And Liam hit hard.

Shane handed his phone over to Jake to monitor the incoming chatter from the field while Shane and Liam climbed into the ring.

The martial arts studio was part fight club and part hang-out. A boxing ring stood on one side of the large industrial-looking space. The other side featured a full-service bar with a small kitchen and plenty of seating. There was even a kick-ass sound system and a small dance floor. The floors were wood, the interior walls were weathered red brick, and the lighting fixtures were steel and glass. It was called "industrial chic," according to his sister Sophie. Having an interior designer in the family came in handy.

Jake made himself comfortable on a black leather sofa across the room. "This had better be good," he said, leaning back and crossing his leg.

The brothers had their own method of fighting, their own version of kickboxing meets back-street brawling with a little fast-and-hard thrown in Krav Maga-style.

Liam threw the first punch. Shane dodged the half-hearted move and followed up with a sharp jab to Liam's right side.

"Hey!" Liam groused when Shane's fist connected with the side of his torso.

Shane shrugged. "Too bad. You were slow."

Now Liam was pissed. Good. So was he. And Shane wanted to play hard.

"I told you he's in a shitty mood," Jake said.

"Oh, it's on, asshole," Liam growled, coming at Shane with a roundhouse kick that sent Shane halfway across the ring.

Shane regained his feet and shook it off. "You'll have to do better than that, Liam."

Liam came at him again, getting in several good hits, but Shane was okay with that. If Liam was going to play hard, then so was Shane. They went at it, pummeling the hell out of each other. It was fast and furious, fists and feet flying, along with a whole lot of sweat and a few splatters of blood, especially when the edge of Shane's bare foot connected with Liam's mouth. They took turns knocking each other to the mat.

"Are you two *trying* to kill each other?" Jake asked as he stepped up to the edge of the ring.

Both brothers were panting from the exertion, drenched with sweat and a little bloodied. Liam looked like he'd have a black eye, and Shane was definitely favoring his right leg.

"Nah, we're just having fun," Liam gasped as he drove his foot into Shane's right kidney.

Shane hit the mat, using his inertia to roll right back up onto his feet. He drove his foot into Liam's side, knocking Liam down and following up with a headlock.

"Want to join us?" Shane said, breathing hard. He released his hold on Liam and jumped back to avoid retaliation.

"No, thanks," Jake said. "I'd rather not piss blood for a week."

After a solid hour of merciless pounding, Shane and Liam called it a draw and headed to the locker room for showers.

As the two men were getting dressed, Shane looked at Liam. "At some point, I want you to give Beth Jamison some basic self-defense lessons."

Liam's brow arched. "Seriously?"

"Yeah. She's completely defenseless. She needs to learn situational awareness and some basic defensive moves, at least enough to stall an attacker."

Liam shrugged. "Sure, no problem. Let me know when."

Jake poked his head through the locker room doorway. "We've got company. Tyler's downstairs, asking to come up."

"Oh, there's a surprise," Liam said, pulling on his jeans.

"Send the elevator down for him," Shane said. "I'll be right out."

Shane was surprised it had taken Tyler this long to come to the apartment. He knew Tyler's curt response on the phone wasn't the end of it. Tyler certainly couldn't have spoken to him in front of Beth. Now the arguing would begin.

He pulled on sweats and a t-shirt and headed to the foyer to meet Tyler.

As soon as the elevator doors opened, Tyler stepped out and glared at Shane. "I want that fucker behind bars!"

"So do I," Shane said.

Tyler followed Shane through the foyer doors into the apartment.

"I can't believe they let him out!" Tyler shouted. "What the hell were they thinking? He's no longer a threat to society, my ass!"

Shane shook his head. "Believe me, Detective, when we find something we can use to take him down, we'll let you know."

Shane walked into the kitchen and opened the fridge. "Want something?"

"Yes," Tyler said. "Beer."

Shane tossed a bottle of beer to Tyler and grabbed a sports drink for himself.

Jake and Liam walked into the kitchen.

"The IT report on the library PC just came through," Jake said, handing a sheet of paper to Shane.

Shane skimmed the report quickly, his expression grim.

"Let me see that," Tyler said, grabbing it from Shane. Tyler scanned the report and blanched. "God damn it," he said, looking a little pale. "He's really looking for her."

Tyler handed the report back to Shane. "I was hoping he'd forgotten about Beth. He's a pedophile, and she's not a kid any longer."

"Yeah, but she's the one that got away," Shane said, hating the words as soon as they came out of his mouth. "He probably blames her for the past 18 years he spent locked away."

"What can we do?" Tyler said, dropping onto one of the barstools. He took a long pull on his beer. As the reality of the situation hit him, he seemed a little lost.

"I have covert surveillance on her 24/7," Shane said. "But I want to escalate that to close personal protection."

Tyler shook his head. "No close bodyguards, Shane," he said. "I don't want to scare her."

"She should be scared, Tyler!" Shane said, slamming his fist on the counter. He took a deep breath. Fighting with Tyler right now wouldn't help Beth. "Kline is a free man, and he's looking for Beth. She needs to know that."

"No," Tyler said, coming off the barstool. He began to pace. "Shane, you don't realize what this would do to her!"

Shane really wanted to take Tyler Jamison into the boxing ring for a few rounds. Tyler was lean and muscular, probably pretty damn tough, but Shane didn't think he was used to the kind of intense hand-to-hand combat that he and his brothers preferred.

"What about the roommate?" Shane said, thinking of the redhead. "Are you going to brief her?"

Tyler nodded. "Yes. I'll update Gabrielle. She needs to be fully aware of the situation. It'll make her more vigilant."

"Aren't you afraid the roommate will spill the beans to Beth?" Jake said.

"No," Tyler said. "Gabrielle won't tell her. She won't want to scare Beth."

"That's an awful lot of pressure on the roommate," Liam said. "If your sister finds out what's been going on behind the scenes, she's going to be pissed at both you and Gabrielle."

"I'll deal with that if and when the time comes. Right now, I just want Beth to live a normal life. I don't want her to feel like she's under a microscope."

"At least let me get someone inside the library," Shane said. "Miguel can get into the library, but he doesn't have any visibility into the Special Collections room where Beth works. I want someone in there with her, Tyler."

The detective mulled it over, then shook his head. "She's perfectly safe in there," he said. "She works in a secured area, and she has a co-worker in there with her. The threat's not inside the library, Shane. It's outside where she's vulnerable."

"She spends eight hours a day in there," Shane said, struggling to keep his temper in check. Tyler was letting his emotions cloud his judgment and possibly putting Beth in danger in the process. "That's eight hours when we have absolutely no visibility on her. I don't like it."

"No," Tyler said. "I don't want to risk it."

Shane watched Tyler pace. The guy obviously loved his sister, and he just wanted to keep her safe. Hell, they all wanted her safe. But Tyler was wrong to hide this from Beth. And now Shane was caught in the middle. He'd gone against Tyler's wishes by making contact with Beth in the first place. When Tyler found out what Shane had done, he'd want Shane's head.

And he will find out, Shane thought. The sooner, the better.

7

Monday morning brought pouring rain, so Beth drove her electric blue Mini Cooper to work. The Mini was her treat to herself after finishing graduate school and getting her first professional job. It was a bare-bones model, but she loved it nonetheless.

She arrived just as another employee was leaving, and she happily scored a spot close to the library's main entrance. Huddled beneath her black-and-white polka dot umbrella, she raced into the building dodging water puddles.

Devany Roth waved eagerly from the reception desk as soon as Beth walked through the doors. "Hi, Beth!"

"Hi, Devany," Beth said, trying to catch her breath. She shook the raindrops off her umbrella and folded it up. "How're you?"

"Not bad for a rainy Monday," Devany said. "But I guess that's not saying much, is it?"

"No, it isn't," Beth said, chuckling.

"Do you want to grab lunch today?"

"Sure. That'd be great," Beth said. "I'll come get you at noon."

Beth sat at her desk staring blindly at her computer screen. She'd been trying to make sense of the same e-mail for the past ten minutes, but hadn't made any progress. Her encounter over the weekend with Shane McIntyre kept replaying in her mind like an animated GIF, looping endlessly, over and over. She didn't know what to make of him. But after the way she'd run out on him, he probably hadn't given her a second thought. She'd missed her chance.

"Beth? Honey, are you okay?"

She glanced up to at her co-worker, Mary Reynolds, who had walked up to her desk. Mary was petite, with short, silver hair cut in a pixie style that seemed very appropriate for her elfin face and large hazel eyes.

"I'm fine," Beth said, trying for a convincing smile.

"You seem preoccupied this morning," Mary said, regarding her with a perceptive gaze.

Beth shrugged. "I had a busy weekend. I guess I'm just tired."

The phone on Beth's desk rang, and Mary wandered back to her own desk as Beth answered it. It was Devany.

"Beth, there's a student asking to come into the Special Collections room. He doesn't have an appointment — do you have time to fit him in? He asked for you specifically."

"Sure, I can fit him in," Beth said. Her next student appointment wasn't for another hour yet. "Send him up."

Beth stayed at her desk until she heard the knock on the Special Collections door. When she opened the door, she found herself looking at a familiar face. First-year student Andrew Morton stood sheepishly at the door.

"Hi, Beth," Andrew said, grinning at her.

"Hi, Andrew," she said, surprised to see him. She stepped out of the way as he came through the door. Andrew was starting to become a regular.

"Thanks for seeing me on short notice." Andrew laid his backpack on one of the study tables in the room and pulled out a sheet of paper, which he handed to Beth. "I need these books," he said, tossing his blond bangs.

She quickly scanned the list. "Have a seat, and I'll get your books," she said, heading for the stacks.

"How was your weekend?"

Beth jumped when she heard Andrew's voice directly behind her, causing the tiny hairs on the nape of her neck to stand up.

"It was fine," she said, taking a steadying breath. It was an innocent enough question; there was no need to overreact. Still, he made her nervous. She stopped when she came to the shelf she was looking for, and he careened into her.

"Sorry," he said, grabbing her shoulders as if to steady her. His hands clasped her far longer than necessary, and she had to shrug out of his hold. His cologne was overpowering, and she was finding it difficult to breathe. Much more of this and she'd need her inhaler.

Beth pulled away from Andrew and took a book off the shelf. When she turned, Andrew was standing so close she had to step back to avoid bumping into him. Apparently, he was not well versed on the concept of personal space.

"I'll put this on your study table," she told him, sidestepping him and heading back to the middle of the room. "You can get started on your research while I locate the rest of the books on your list."

Andrew followed Beth back to the study table.

"Have a seat, Andrew," Beth said, pointing to a chair. She glanced across the room and noticed Mary watching them intently through the glass walls of their office.

Andrew sat reluctantly, and Beth went to retrieve the other books on his list. When she returned a few minutes later, she laid them on his table and told him to call for her if he needed anything else. When she returned to her desk, Mary was waiting there for her.

"That boy has a crush on you, Beth," Mary said, her eyes on Andrew as he cracked open one of the books. "This is probably the fourth time he's been in here this month. I thought I was going to have to peel him off you. Are you okay?"

"I'm fine. Just having a little trouble breathing. He went a little overboard on the cologne."

Beth could feel the signs of an impending asthma attack. Her chest had tightened and it was becoming harder to catch her breath. Her anxiety levels began to spike, and she felt flushed. When she started coughing, she retrieved her inhaler from her purse, shook it, and administered the medication.

Mary gently rubbed Beth's back. "Are you okay?"

Beth nodded, not yet able to speak.

"In the future, if Andrew needs anything, I'll deal with him," Mary said.

Beth took a tentative breath. "Thanks," she said. "He gives me the creeps."

The week progressed as usual for Beth. Every day that passed was a day she didn't call Shane. She'd programmed his cell number into her phone, but she had yet to push the send button. She just couldn't do it. Every time she'd tried to get with someone in the past, she'd ended up having an ugly, all-out panic attack, and she just didn't want Shane to see her like that.

Andrew Morton showed up at the Special Collections room on Wednesday afternoon, again without an appointment. This time, Mary offered to help him while Beth hid out in the packing room.

"Beth, I'm afraid you have an unwelcome admirer," Mary said a few minutes later, as she walked into the back room. "He made his excuses and left as soon as he realized I would be the one helping him today."

Beth looked up from the box of periodicals she was unpacking.

"He was very unhappy," Mary said, looking concerned. "He seemed... agitated."

"Maybe if I avoid him for a while, he'll get tired of stopping by."

"Maybe," Mary said. But she didn't seem convinced.

That night, Beth dreamt she was in the Special Collections room long after the library had closed. The lights were dimmed, and she was in the stacks, wandering aimlessly. Suddenly someone was there with her, right behind her. She could feel hot breath on the back of her neck.

"Mary?" she said, turning. But deep in her heart she knew it wasn't Mary.

"Hi, Beth."

Andrew.

"Do you have an appointment, Andrew?"

He shook his head, his tousled blond hair sweeping across his forehead. "No." He smiled at her.

"You shouldn't be here."

"I don't need an appointment to see you."

Andrew reached out to touch her face, but she backed away. He pressed forward, and she kept backing away, until her back hit the wall. He advanced on her, an arrogant grin on his handsome face. The lights went out suddenly, and it was pitch black in the room. Strong, rough hands grabbed her wrists, squeezing them as he pinned her to the wall.

"Andrew, stop it!" she cried. "You're hurting me!"

The temperature dropped precipitously, and she began shivering. No matter how hard she struggled, she couldn't get free. Then he began to tear the clothes from her body as if they were made of wet tissue paper. He pushed her down to the floor and crouched over her. She could feel his foul, hot breath on her face.

"You can't hide from me, little bitch. Haven't you figured that out yet?"

That gravelly voice was unmistakable. That wasn't Andrew!

She took a deep breath and screamed as loud as she could.

"Beth! Wake up!"

Beth's eyes shot open, and she was blinded by the light hanging over her bed. Gabrielle stood beside the bed in her PJs.

"Gabrielle!" Beth gasped, sitting up. She struggled to catch her breath, her heart pounding wildly.

"Are you okay?" Gabrielle said.

"It was Andrew! He... it was like the other time, but it was *An-*

drew. And then it wasn't Andrew; it was Kline."

Beth lay back in her bed, gasping as she willed her heart and respiration rates to slow.

Gabrielle switched off the ceiling light and climbed into Beth's bed. "Go back to sleep, Beth. It's okay."

"You can't keep this up, Shane," Liam said, walking into Shane's office Thursday morning.

Shane glared at his youngest brother. "Don't you ever knock?"

Shane had been operating on about four hours of sleep each day all week, and it was starting to take its toll. Diane had managed to avoid him completely for the past two days, resorting to e-mails and voice messages to communicate with him. He'd started to notice people going out of their way to avoid him in the hallways and gym. Even his own brothers had made themselves scarce the past couple of days.

But it wasn't the lack of sleep that was making him so damned irritable. It was Thursday, and Beth hadn't called. He'd finally accepted the fact that she wasn't going to. If he wanted to see her again — and he sure as hell did — then he'd have to arrange it himself. She wasn't going to make it easy for him.

The problem was, he didn't know *why* she wasn't calling. Was she simply not interested? If that was the case, he'd leave her the hell alone. He wasn't a stalker. But if she was just too shy to call — or worse yet, too afraid — then he wasn't giving up on her. He'd do whatever it took to get past her fears.

Liam dropped into one of the chairs in front of his desk. "We all know what kind of hours you've been keeping this week, bro," he said, crossing one leg over the other.

"Liam, go away." Shane looked up from the report he'd been reading and glared at his brother's smug face. "Isn't there something you should be doing? If not, I can fix that."

"What the hell's gotten into you? Jake told me you made contact with the Jamison girl last week. Is that true?"

Shane looked at his brother. "I did." *And yes, it was a mistake.*

"And her name's Beth, not 'the Jamison girl.'"

"You fucked with a covert surveillance, Shane."

"And?"

"And now you're watching the girl yourself?" Liam studied him.

Of his three brothers, Liam was the quiet one, the intuitive one. Shane glared at Liam, willing him to leave.

"Okay," Liam said, throwing up his hands. "You've gone over the deep end. Fine. But you can't keep working around the clock. You have to have some downtime, and you need sleep or you're going to screw up even worse."

He couldn't very well argue with Liam, because his brother was right.

"Here's the deal," Liam said. "Tonight, I'll take your shift while you get a solid eight hours."

"Liam — "

"It wasn't a suggestion, Shane."

Liam was right, and Shane knew it. If one of the others were acting like he was, Shane would have already pounded some sense into him. Or her.

"All right," Shane said, knowing this was an argument he wouldn't win.

"Good," Liam said, smiling smugly at him. "That wasn't so hard now, was it?"

Jake walked into Shane's office, a scowl on his face. "What wasn't so hard?"

"Trying to talk some sense into this idiot, that's what," Liam said.

Jake took the chair beside Liam. "Gentlemen, we have a problem."

Liam scoffed. "You mean besides Shane's unprofessional conduct?"

"What is it?" Shane said, glaring at Liam to shut him up.

"IT hacked into Kline's PC so they could monitor his Internet activities 24/7."

"What'd they find?" Shane said, dreading the answer.

Jake frowned. "For one thing, Kline's downloading a ton of really violent porn. He's also accessing of ton of child pornography — we can report him to the feds on that; that should be good for more jail time. But — here's the kicker: he's stalking Beth online. Just an hour ago, he used an online mapping site to get directions to her townhouse and to the Kingston University campus. He's also been searching online classifieds for handguns."

"Shit," Liam said.

Jake nodded. "Yeah. Defcon 3."

Shane ran his fingers through his hair. "He's going to make a move on her," he said. "It's only a matter of time. We'll have to be ready."

"Should we bring Chicago PD in on this?" Jake said. "They can arrest him for possession of child pornography. That'll put him back behind bars for a while at least."

"No," Shane said. "We'll handle this. I don't want a temporary solution. Kline needs to be neutralized permanently."

8

You aren't going to call me, are you?"

Oh, my god. Shane. Beth recognized his voice instantly, but she kept her gaze fixed on the shelf of books in front of her, stunned into silence when she realized he was standing right behind her.

"I figured you might be here tonight," he said.

Shane laid his warm hands on her bare shoulders, and they felt so incredibly good she couldn't help leaning back against him.

His mouth moved in close to her ear, and he whispered to her, his warm breath ruffling her hair. "If you tell me to take a hike, I will," he said. "I'll walk away, and I won't bother you again, I promise. But I'm going to go out on a limb here because I think you *are* interested."

When his arms came around her waist, she melted into him. She was so tired of fighting this, fighting herself. How many nights had she lain awake in her bed that week, fantasizing about him, wishing she had the courage to try one more time? Well, damn it, she was going to try.

"Well, what's the verdict? Do I take a hike, or can I stay?"

She shivered when she felt his lips in her hair. Why did his touch make her go weak in the knees when every other man's touch made her cringe? "Stay."

He sighed, and she felt the tension leave his body.

He must have been peering over her shoulder at the shelf of books in front of her, because he said, "*Fifty Shades*, huh? My sisters read those books. I'll bet he spanked her, didn't he?"

A very unladylike snort burst out of her before she could contain it. "Yes." She couldn't help chuckling. "A few times."

He turned her so that she was facing him, and she lost herself in his heated gaze. She hadn't imagined how beautiful his eyes were. His irises were such a bright and clear blue, with tiny flecks of gold. They seemed to penetrate right through her, missing nothing. He looked devastatingly handsome in a pair of well-worn jeans and a tucked-in, blue button-up shirt. She wasn't sure which was sexier — this casual look or the CEO dark suit and white dress shirt persona. Right now the top button of his shirt was undone, exposing his tanned throat, and he looked rakishly sexy. Unable to resist the urge to touch him, she reached out and laid a tentative hand in the center of his chest.

He covered her hand with one of his own, and his gaze darkened. "Do you recommend them?" he said, his voice rough.

For a moment, she couldn't remember what they were talking about. *Oh, right, the books.* "I highly recommend them," she said, taking the bait and feeling a tad bold. After all, he'd admitted that he'd come here specifically to see her even though she'd left him in limbo all week. There were probably a thousand other things he could be doing tonight, and no shortage of women he could be doing them with, but he'd chosen to come here instead. To find *her*. She felt a warm fluttering low in her belly.

"There should have been more spanking and less Red Room of Pain," she said. "Ana liked the spanking; it was the other stuff she wasn't so keen on. Not that I blame her." She didn't know what on Earth had possessed her to say that, but his gentle sense of humor put her at ease. She felt she could say anything to him, and he wouldn't judge her.

"Red Room of Pain?" He grinned. "I think I can guess what that's about. But it's his loss. I'm not one to miss opportunities."

Shane tugged gently on a tendril of hair that had escaped her ponytail, and she felt a corresponding tug between her legs. For crying out loud, he was just playing with her hair!

He tucked that strand of hair behind her ear, and then he brushed her cheek with the edge of his thumb. She closed her eyes, savoring his touch.

"How about we go somewhere a bit more private where we can talk," he said. "Anywhere you'd like."

She swallowed past the lump in her throat and nodded. If she was going to try one more time, she'd have to go outside her comfort zone. "Okay."

"Good." He grinned at her, clearly pleased with himself. "Step one accomplished."

"Step one?"

"Getting you to say 'yes' to me. That was step one."

"What's step two?"

"Step two is getting you to tell me why you're so fearful."

Her smile fell, and she tried to pull away.

"Whoa, relax," he said, holding onto her. "There's no hurry. I won't pressure you." He brushed her bottom lip with the pad of his thumb. "Now, where do you want to go? How about a quiet place where we can have a drink and talk?"

"That sounds good." She was shocked that she'd even agreed to this.

"Where would you like to go?" he said.

It had to be somewhere public and somewhere close by, so they could walk. She wasn't about to get in a car with him. If she was going to do this, at least she wasn't going to be stupid about it. "How about Café del Sol? It's usually quiet this time of night, and it's just a few blocks from here. We can walk."

"That sounds like a plan," he said, offering her his arm. "Shall we?"

She took his arm, feeling as if she'd just thrown all caution to the wind.

They stepped out onto a bustling sidewalk teeming with pedestrians, as it was still early for this part of downtown on a Friday night. Shane's professional instincts kicked in, and he found himself scanning the crowd, watching for threats. He knew Kline was at home watching television, but old habits were hard to break.

"The restaurant's this way," Beth said, pointing to the right.

He took hold of her hand, lacing their fingers together, and they started walking.

"I read your company's website," she said. "Are you a bodyguard?"

He smiled. "Generally, no. I usually do management type stuff — the boring stuff no one else wants to do. Occasionally I work out in the field, but it's rare." *Like this past week.*

"Who are your clients?"

"All sorts really, but mostly people in high profile positions — celebrities, politicians, corporate big-shots — the type of people who tend to attract unwanted attention. We also design high-end security systems for corporations and governments."

"My brother works in law enforcement, here in Chicago." She might as well get that out there, because if anything came of this, he'd have to deal with Tyler sooner or later.

"Is he a cop?" he said, hating the need for subterfuge. Still, he was thrilled that she was finally starting to open up to him. The sooner she did that, the sooner he could tell her who he was. "I hope he's not going to arrest me for corrupting his sister."

Beth laughed at that, but not because she thought it was funny. Her brother could actually become a serious problem where Shane was concerned. Tyler wouldn't like the fact that she was dating an older man. And the difference in their ages would be just the beginning of Tyler's objections.

"He's not a patrol officer," she said. "He's a homicide detective. And he's very protective of me, so yes, he might arrest you. Consider yourself forewarned." She smiled at him when she said it, but she really meant it.

Shane smiled. "Don't worry. I promise not to give your brother any reason to arrest me." He lifted her hand and kissed it. He'd do whatever was necessary to keep Beth from getting caught in the middle.

"Here we are," she said, coming to a stop.

Shane opened the door for Beth, and they walked inside. The restaurant was small and quiet, furnished with mismatched tables and chairs. They were greeted by a smiling teenage boy with dark hair and piercing dark eyes — Luis, according to his name tag.

"Two?" the boy said in a heavy Spanish accent, as he grabbed two menus.

"Si, por favor," Shane said.

"Can we sit outside, on the patio?" Beth asked.

Luis nodded at her. "Si, seniorita."

They followed their young host through the restaurant and out the back door to a patio enclosed within four brick walls. The patio was quite small, having room for only four tables. Fortunately, it was empty at the moment. It was a cozy space, with lit candles on each of the wrought-iron tables, hanging flower baskets and several potted trees.

Luis laid their menus on a table in the far corner. "I'll be right back with chips and salsa."

Shane pulled a couple of bills out of his wallet and handed them to the boy as he whispered to him in Spanish.

"Si, Senior!" Luis said, staring in awe at the bills in his hand. "Muchos gracias!" And then the boy raced back into the restaurant.

Beth took the seat Shane had pulled out for her. "Thank you. What was that all about?"

"I rented the patio for the evening."

Beth chuckled. "What's the going rate for a patio these days?"

"A couple hundred bucks." It was a small price to pay for privacy. He didn't want any prying ears making her feel self-conscious.

"Oh, my god!" she cried. "You didn't have to do that!"

"Yes, I did," he said, smiling as he handed her a menu. "I'll never get you to open up to me if they seat other customers out here with us."

And there was that disarming smile of his again, stirring up the butterflies in her belly. She couldn't help returning his smile, losing herself in his gaze. When the door to the restaurant opened, she jumped and looked away, grateful for the distraction.

Luis stepped outside carrying a tray laden with two glasses of ice water, salsa, and a bowl of tortilla chips. "Ready to order?" he said, as he set the glasses and bowls on the table.

Shane looked at Beth. "Would you like something to eat?"

"No, thank you. I'm not hungry. The chips will be fine."

"It looks like we're just having drinks, then," Shane said to the boy. "I'll have a Corona. Beth, what would you like?"

"I'm not much of a drinker," she confessed, dipping a chip into the salsa. "Maybe a Strawberry Daiquiri?"

"The lady will have a Strawberry Daiquiri," Shane told Luis.

After Luis disappeared back into the building, Shane reached out for Beth's hand and brushed his thumb across the back of it. "There are a hundred questions I want to ask you, but I'm afraid most of them will send you running."

Beth took a long sip of her water, and he suspected it was just a distraction to hide her nervousness. So he changed tactics.

"Why don't you ask me something instead?" he said.

Her eyes widened, and she smiled. "Okay." But then she hesitated.

"It's okay. You can ask me anything."

"Well, there is one thing I should ask," she said, a little sheepishly. "You're single, right?"

He looked at her pointedly. "Beth, if I weren't single, I wouldn't be sitting here with you."

She blushed. "I'm sorry. I guess that was a stupid question."

He shook his head. "No, it wasn't stupid. Women can't be too careful, can they? To answer your question, yes, I'm single. I'm not seeing anyone right now." He grabbed a tortilla chip and scooped up some salsa. "What else would you like to know? Ask away."

"Why did you leave the military?"

He grinned, realizing she must have read his bio page on the company website. That meant she'd been curious about him. Good. "I received an honorable discharge on medical grounds."

"What happened?"

"I was in a building that blew up," he said. "I sustained a lot of injuries to my arms and chest, but the worst damage was to my right leg. My right femur was pretty much pulverized." He slapped the top of his leg. "After four surgeries and two steel rods, I'm almost good as new, although I set off metal detectors everywhere I go."

She laughed at that, just as he'd intended.

"I went state-side for rehabilitation, but it was pretty obvious I'd have to start thinking about a new career. So when the Marine Corps discharged me, I came home to Chicago and started my business."

"That's awful. How did the building blow up?"

"I blew it up."

"You did?" She looked shocked. "Why did you do that if you were still inside?"

He shrugged. "It was necessary. You do what you have to do in a war situation."

Beth leaned back in her seat, shaking her head. "I can't even imagine doing something like that."

"Now it's my turn," Shane said. "I get to ask you a question. And it's an easy one, I promise."

"Okay." But she looked less than eager.

"You're... how old? Early twenties?"

She nodded. "Twenty-four."

He picked up another chip. "I'm thirty-four. Do you have anything against dating older men?"

Her grin faded, and for a moment he regretted bringing up the difference in their ages. It didn't matter one bit to him, but maybe it did matter to her.

"I don't have a problem with it," she said. "But my brother will. Our father died when I was a baby, and my brother — Tyler — sort of assumed his role. He won't approve of me seeing you.

I might as well warn you now."

Shane sighed. He hated putting her in that kind of position. "Beth, you're an adult," he said gently.

"I know, but... there are extenuating circumstances." She looked down at the table top, her finger absently tracing the patterns in the wrought iron swirls. "I have... issues... that affect my life. He worries about me."

Shane squeezed her hand. "You do seem a little shy. Very shy, in fact," he said. "It's all right. I don't mind."

Luis returned to their table to deliver their drinks. Beth took a wary sip of her slushy red concoction and smiled.

"Do you like it?" Shane asked, watching her reaction.

She took another sip and nodded. When she licked the sugar crystals on the rim of the glass, Shane's jaw clenched.

"Are you dating anyone?" he asked, because she'd expect him to ask. He already knew damn well she wasn't.

She shook her head as she sipped her drink, trying not to laugh. If he only knew how ridiculous his question was. "No."

Shane put down his Corona, and his gaze turned hot and direct. "I want to see you again, Beth."

She took a big swallow of her daiquiri to mask her reaction to his blunt question. Was he talking about dating, or just hooking up? She forced herself to ask the question. "Are you asking me out on a date?"

"Yes."

She stared down at her glass, surprised to find it was nearly empty. She desperately wanted to say yes to him, but it was hard for her to trust people. She knew so little about him, and more importantly he knew so little about her. He probably thought she was like any other girl her age, carefree, adventurous, sometimes a little reckless. She was anything but.

The alcohol she'd drunk had hit her system now, and it made her feel a little brave — but not nearly brave enough to get through this conversation.

He frowned, and she thought for sure he was reading her mind. If he could read her mind, he'd most likely change his.

"Beth, I realize we just met — "

"Yes!" Oh, my God, she said it.

His brows lifted in surprise, as if he'd been expecting her to say no. "Yes?"

"Yes." She held up her empty glass. "I think I'll have a refill."

Shane chuckled and shook his head. "I think one's enough for tonight, don't you? Especially if you're not going to eat anything. I don't want you to lose your head and blame it on the alcohol tomorrow."

Lose her head? Over what? What was he expecting to happen tonight? When he brought her hand to his mouth and kissed her knuckles, she felt a jolt of electricity shoot up her arm.

"This place will be closing up soon," he said, checking his watch. "Would you like to come back to my apartment for a little while? It's not far from here. We could talk, get to know more about each other. And when you're ready to go, I'll drive you home."

The idea of going to his apartment set off all sorts of alarm bells in her head, and her heart started racing. Could she really do that? Go to his place? Go home with a practical stranger? She knew so little about him.

"Beth?"

She looked at him. "Hmm?"

"Would you like to come over for a while?"

Was she actually considering doing this, or was it the daiquiri talking? Was she really ready for this? Her friends did this sort of thing all the time. Gabrielle would do it. And technically, wasn't this their second date? Did that make it all right?

Shane squeezed her hand. "You can say no, sweetheart. If it's too soon, you can say no."

She swallowed hard, her pulse beating wildly.

He smiled ruefully. "How about if I just drive you home instead?"

Part of her was relieved by the reprieve he was offering. But at the same time, she was tired of being alone. She really did want to try. The thought of going home alone and lying in bed wishing things were different was depressing. And as for Shane? He'd always been a gentleman. He'd never done or said anything inappropriate. And, my God, she wanted him.

She frowned. "Why did you change your mind?"

"Because I saw the panic on your face," he said. "The last thing I want to do is scare you off, Beth."

"Well, maybe I want to go to your apartment tonight."

He looked rather skeptical. "You do?"

Beth shrugged. "Sure. For a little while." She could do this.

Shane stood and held out his hand. "All right, then. Let's go."

9

After Shane paid the bill, they left the restaurant and headed for the parking garage two blocks away. It was half-past eleven now, and the pedestrian traffic had thinned out considerably.

Shane opened the front passenger door of his silver Jaguar for Beth, and she slipped inside. He leaned in to latch her seatbelt.

"I can do that myself, you know," she said, grinning at him as he adjusted the fit of her seatbelt.

He grinned back at her. "I know." And then he gave her a quick kiss on the lips before shutting her door.

Beth sat in stunned silence as Shane walked around to the driver's side. She could still feel his soft, warm lips on hers. Even though it had been nothing more than a peck, so light and quick it had ended almost as soon as it had begun, her lips tingled. She touched her fingertips to her mouth and smiled.

"I thought I'd get that out of the way," he said, as he latched his own seat belt. His gaze was hot. "Now you don't have to worry about when it's coming. We've already done it. The next time we kiss, we'll be old pros at it."

The city was lit with millions of sparkling lights that flashed by in a colorful blur as they headed north on Lake Shore Drive. The city was on their left, and Lake Michigan was on the right — a massive body of water that stretched as far as the eye could see. The lake was a beautiful sight at night, moonlight shimmering on the glassy black surface of the water.

"Where's your apartment?" Beth said.

"In the Gold Coast, right on Lake Shore Drive."

She'd never spent much time in the Gold Coast before — it was way too rich for her blood. Studying Shane's profile, she reminded herself that she was probably just one in a long line of women he'd taken back to his apartment. *Don't read too much into this.* It was probably just a hook-up. People did this sort of thing all the time. It was no big deal.

"You okay?" Shane said, glancing at her.

She smiled at him. "Sure. Fine." But with each passing minute, she felt less fine.

Beth pulled out her phone. "I'd better let my roommate know where I'm going. If I'm out later than usual, she'll worry." She composed a quick message to Gabrielle:

Met up w/Shane McIntyre downtown. Going to his apt in Gold Coast. Don't worry.

She hit Send before she could change her mind. If she was going to do something this crazy, she should at least let someone know where she was going.

Her phone chimed almost immediately with a reply:

How the hell did u run into him AGAIN?!?

She winced when she read the message. Gabrielle could be as bad as Tyler sometimes.

Shane glanced at her from the driver's seat. "Was that from your roommate?"

"Yes."

She keyed in a quick reply to Gabrielle:

He was at Clancy's.

And then she stowed her phone in her purse.

She snuck a quick peek at Shane. He seemed quite relaxed behind the wheel, his left hand on the steering wheel, his right hand resting on the gear shift, just inches away from hers. She studied those long, tanned fingers gripping the gearshift, imagining what they would feel like on her body, touching her, stroking her. It had been so long since anyone had touched her that she'd forgotten what it was like. She sighed.

Shane grabbed his phone and handed it to her. "You have my number. Do you mind giving me yours?"

With each exchange of personal information, she felt like she was sinking deeper and deeper into whatever it was they were doing. And she wasn't even sure what that was. What did he want from her, besides the obvious? Was it just sex? She didn't think he could possibly be interested in anything more serious.

They had the same brand of phone, so she quickly keyed in her number and added it to his contact list before she could change her mind. Then she handed his phone back.

Shane reached for her hand and laced their fingers together. She'd never realized how sexy a man's hand could be. His hands were no stranger to hard work, she realized, noticing numerous nicks and scars on the back of the one she was holding, especially along the knuckles. He'd clearly been involved in more than one brawl.

With her index finger, she traced a scar that started on the back of his hand and extended past his wrist and up his forearm. "How did you get this?"

"That's a souvenir from Afghanistan," he said.

"Does it still hurt?" she asked, skimming her finger along the pale, jagged scar.

His hand squeezed hers tightly in response to her soft touch. "No, it doesn't hurt," he said. "Mostly, it's numb because of nerve damage."

As Shane turned into a circular drive, Beth looked up at the modern glass and steel apartment building that towered above Lake Shore Drive. Judging by its impressive exterior and prime location, she figured it had to be one of the most prestigious properties in the Gold Coast — probably in all of Chicago.

Shane pulled into an underground garage, stopping at an electronic gate to enter an access code to gain entrance. He parked near the bank of elevators in a slot marked PRIVATE.

As he reached over to release her seatbelt, a curious feeling came over her, as if a gentle wave of well-being flowed through her. She hardly knew this man, and yet he made her feel *safe*.

Shane reached over to touch the tendrils of her hair that had escaped her ponytail, letting the strands slide through his fingers. "Everything okay?"

She nodded. "Fine."

"I'll get your door," he said.

They walked hand-in-hand through the cool, well-lit garage to a bank of elevators. Shane led Beth to the last elevator, which was marked PRIVATE, and punched a code into an electronic keypad. The elevator doors opened, and they stepped inside the car. He punched another code into yet another keypad inside the car.

"Why is this elevator private?"

"Because it's reserved for the penthouse apartment," he said as they began ascending.

He owns the penthouse. She couldn't even begin to imagine how much that cost. She'd heard stories about the price tags on apartments like this — they were astronomical, to say the least, certainly in the millions of dollars. Apparently the security business paid pretty well.

Her eyes scanned the interior of the elevator — it was one of the nicest elevators she'd ever been in. Three of the walls were brushed steel, and the fourth was a floor-to-ceiling mirror set in a gold frame. Gold light fixtures adorned the walls, and there were two security cameras positioned overhead.

She glanced at the mirrored wall and was startled by their reflections. Shane turned heads wherever he went. When she caught sight of her own reflection, she inwardly cringed. She was hardly the kind of woman one would expect to see standing next to Shane.

While Shane might look at home on the cover of *GQ*, she certainly didn't look like she belonged on any magazine cover. Her hair was probably her best feature, but it looked a little worse for wear at the moment, strands of it having come loose from her ponytail. She looked like the farmer's daughter gone wild. Her sundress was wrinkled after a long day at work, and her sandals had certainly seen better days. With no make-up on, she looked pale and rumpled next to Shane, and she couldn't help wondering why she was even here.

Her heart rate kicked instantly into overdrive, and alarm bells started to peal loudly in her head. Her chest tightened painfully, and the air seemed too thin in the confines of the elevator. Without much warning, she was well on her way to a full-blown panic attack, and being inside a small, enclosed space wasn't helping.

The elevator came to a gliding stop, and the doors opened to an elegantly appointed foyer. Shane took Beth's hand and started forward, but she didn't budge.

He stopped and looked back. "What's wrong, sweetheart?"

The expression on her face must have told him plenty, because he stepped back into the elevator car and pressed a button on the control panel. The elevator doors remained open.

Shane's hands settled on her shoulders, and he peered down into her face. "What is it, Beth?"

She was in way over her head, and she started shaking, her breaths coming fast and shallow. She couldn't breathe. She needed her inhaler. She needed to leave, now! It had been foolish to even think she could do this.

"I need to go home!"

Shane studied her for a moment, his expression mostly one of concern, but she thought she also detected a hint of disappointment.

His hands slipped down her arms to clasp her hands. "I'll take you home. No problem." He squeezed her hands gently. "But can we talk for a few minutes first?"

She nodded, feeling all kinds of guilty for bailing on him. He'd done nothing wrong. In fact, he'd been an absolute gentleman all evening. He wasn't to blame for her emotional damage.

"Can we talk out here?" he said, and he led her out of the elevator into the private foyer. "What happened?" he said. "I recognize a panic attack when I see one. That's fine, honey — I just need to understand what caused it. Was it something I did?"

She'd expected him to be angry, but he wasn't. Now that she was out of the elevator, her alarm bells began to quiet. The foyer was quiet and spacious, well lit by an elaborate crystal chandelier hanging high overhead. She could finally breathe again.

"It's not anything you did," she said. "I just... changed my mind." She was embarrassed now, and she looked down at the polished hardwood floor, wishing a hole would open up and swallow her.

"You changed your mind about coming over tonight? Or about seeing me?"

She glanced back up at him, surprised by his question. He hadn't done anything wrong. "About coming over tonight. Not about you."

Shane smiled. "Thank God." When she tried to look away again, he tipped her face back up to his. "It's okay, Beth. You're allowed to change your mind. But can you tell me why?"

She shook her head. "I'm not ready for this. I do want this ... you ... but I'm not ready."

He nodded. "All right, we'll slow it down. I'll take you home. Come here, sweetheart."

Shane pulled her into his arms, and she laid her cheek against his shirt, the top of her head hitting just underneath his chin. The rhythm of his chest rising and falling with each breath was comforting. Her arms slipped around his waist, and they simply stood there holding each other. Her pulse gradually slowed as the anxiety faded.

"Lights, twenty-five percent," Shane said, and the lighting in the foyer dimmed to a faint glow.

Beth tensed instantly.

Shane looked at her. "What's wrong?"

God, he would think she was a complete idiot if she told him she was afraid of the dark. What 24-year-old was afraid of the dark? "It's dark."

Shane's arms tightened around her. "Lights, fifty percent."

The lighting level increased, and Beth relaxed as she looked up at the multi-tiered chandelier above their heads. The dangling crystals twinkled, casting flickering prisms of light on the foyer walls.

"Better?" he said, rubbing her back.

"Yes."

Shane's hands came up to her face, his thumbs brushing her cheeks. "Beth, don't be afraid to tell me what you need. Whatever it is, I want you to tell me."

"I'm sorry for messing up our evening," she said. She chuckled, trying to make light of the situation. "Why do you even bother with me?"

"Because you have me under your spell, and I'll do anything to get you to kiss me."

She laughed then, relieved that he wasn't planning to ditch her at the first opportunity.

"I hope someday you'll tell me why you have such anxiety and let me help you with it."

"You could Google it," she said, a little too flippantly. Now he was pushing, getting a little too close for comfort. Just the thought of telling someone about what happened made her a little crazy. "It was all over the news."

He shook his head. "I don't want to Google it, Beth. I want you to trust me enough to tell me yourself."

She pressed her face against his chest, and then his lips were in her hair. "I promised I'd take you home, and I will," he murmured. "But before we go, can I kiss you? I'd really like to kiss you. I've wanted to since I first saw you."

"You already kissed me," she reminded him. "Remember? When we first got into the car?" She certainly remembered.

He chuckled. "I mean a real kiss."

The thought of his lips on hers brought back the butterflies with a vengeance. They were rioting now, and she felt anxious and queasy, but in a good way this time. It had been a long time since she'd been on a date, and an even longer time since she'd been kissed.

"If you don't want to, that's — "

"No, I do," she said, her hands grasping his waist. As she held onto him, the heat from his body warmed her, and she melted into him. He smelled so good, a tantalizing mixture of warm male skin, soap, and a hint of cologne. She wanted to wrap herself up in him.

She gasped when his lips touched hers, warm and gentle. She sucked in a shaky breath and shivered. His touch was electrifying, setting off an aching hunger deep in her bones. He slowly increased the pressure of his mouth on hers, and his lips coaxed hers open.

The kiss started off slow and languorous, and he lulled her into a sweet, sensuous haze. She was hypnotized by him, forgetting everything except for the exquisite pressure of his lips on hers. His lips, firm and soft at the same time, nudged hers apart. When she opened her mouth to him, his tongue slid in and found hers, teasing it with light strokes. This was certainly not her first kiss, but it was definitely the best. She swayed, and his arms tightened around her to provide support. She made a soft, inarticulate sound of need, and he groaned in response, increasing the pressure of his mouth on hers.

"My God, you are so sweet," he murmured against her mouth. His hands came up to cradle her face, and their breaths mingled as his mouth continued its gentle assault on hers.

Shane's mouth dipped lower as he planted kisses along the graceful line of her jaw, and then down to her throat where he felt the wild fluttering of her pulse beneath his lips. "Shh, it's okay," he breathed against her pulse point, alternating kissing and suckling gently.

His mouth returned to hers with a hunger that seemed just a bit out of control. She knew she should stop him, but when he started sucking at her mouth, taking small, painless bites of her lower lip, she felt her own body go up in flames. His lips coaxed hers open, and his tongue swept inside, stroking hers, making sweet love to her mouth.

Liquid heat pooled low in her belly, and her muscles started quivering. Her legs felt like jelly, and she didn't think she could stay upright much longer. She was shocked by how much she wanted him. Really wanted him, then and there, more than she'd ever wanted anything in her life.

Beth gasped when she felt his broad palm settle over her left breast. His hand burned through her dress and bra as he cupped her flesh and molded it to his hand.

"Your heart is racing," Shane said. "I hope in a good way."

"Mmm." She laid her hand over his and pressed it hard against her flesh. She wished she could feel his hand on her bare skin right now, feel the heat and the roughness of his palm. Her nipple puckered beneath his touch, and he brushed the taut little peak through her clothing with the edge of this thumb. Even through her clothes, his touch was electrifying.

She whimpered into his mouth.

"Jesus, Beth," he groaned, pulling her tight against him.

She felt his erection prodding her belly, hard and insistent. Wetness flooded her sex, and she felt hot and achy. Suddenly, his fingers were there, pressing right through the fabric of her dress against the needy place between her legs. She cried out at his touch, her body shuddering as his fingers closed in on the apex of her sex.

Before she even realized they'd moved, she felt the wall at her back. Shane's hands cradled her face, holding her head still as his mouth ate at hers. She gasped and slipped her arms around his waist, and she held on for dear life as he kissed her like she'd only ever dreamed of being kissed. She was making desperate noises now, sounds she'd never heard herself make before.

Her body went up in flames as she pressed herself against his hand, shamelessly rocking herself against the pressure in an attempt to assuage the terrible ache he'd created.

He pulled up her dress and slipped his hand inside her panties, his finger sinking between the plump folds of her sex. He groaned loudly when he encountered her slick, wet heat.

"My God, baby," he groaned, his finger slipping inside her tight, wet channel. "Let me make you come," he said, looking at her with a fiercely burning gaze. "Let me. Say yes."

She nodded, torn between an insane arousal and utter mortification that she was letting him touch her like this.

"Say it!" he demanded in a hoarse voice. "Say yes!"

"Yes!"

ಉ 10

H old up your dress," Shane said, his voice rough and urgent.

Partly in shock, she obeyed, her legs shaking so badly she didn't know if she could stay on her feet.

She gasped when he touched her core, collecting some of the wetness he found there and bringing it to her clitoris, spreading it on the tiny nub of flesh. He pressed the slick pad of his finger firmly on her clit and began a concerted effort to drive her out of her mind.

She shuddered as Shane alternated the pressure on her clitoris, teasing her as he stroked her with firm, relentless movements. The onslaught of sensation drove her higher and higher, sending her on an upward spiral she'd never experience before. The pleasure was nearly unbearable, and she could barely breathe. Her whole world narrowed down to that one little spot. She stood on wobbly legs, one hand holding up her dress while the other clutched at his waist for support. His hot mouth covered hers, and he drank in her cries.

Shane released Beth's mouth and gazed into her flushed face. Her pupils were dilated, her cheeks suffused with pink. Her nostrils flared with excitement as he continued his gentle assault on her. He was desperate to make her come, to feel her fall apart in his arms and hear her cry out. Her tantalizing scent was in his nose, and all he could think about was pleasuring her. If he had to send her home, he wanted to give her something to remember him by.

He felt her body tense and knew she was close. Beth dropped her dress and clutched the front of his shirt with both hands, holding onto him for dear life. When she swayed, he wrapped one arm around her waist and pulled her against him. When her climax hit, she pressed her face against his chest, muffling the soft keening sounds she made in his shirt.

Shane felt dangerously close to losing control then and there, and he had to struggle not to come in his jeans. "That's it, baby," he groaned, his lips in her hair as he stroked her back as the residual tremors rocked her body. "Let it happen."

Shane had barely done more than touch her, and it was the most thrilling sexual experience Beth had ever had. She knew how to take care of herself, but she'd never experienced an orgasm with someone else before.

She lifted her hot face from his shirt and looked up, ready to take the biggest risk she'd ever taken. "I want you."

Shane kissed her tenderly, his lips clinging to hers. He pulled back to look at her, and his gaze locked onto her bottom lip, which was swollen from his kisses. He couldn't remember wanting a woman this badly.

His expression was rueful as he shook his head. "I touched you because I had to, not because I wanted to seduce you. I told you I'd take you home, Beth, and I'm going to keep my promise."

She took in a shaky breath and shored up her courage. "But I want this."

"So do I, honey," he said, brushing her hair back. "Believe me, so do I. But we're going to wait until you're ready. *Really ready.* I don't want to mess this up."

She was torn. Part of her wanted to take the "out" he'd given her, but part of her wanted him now. And she was afraid that if she didn't act on it now, she might never get another chance.

He kissed her once more, so sweetly she felt like crying. By the time she realized what he was doing, he'd straightened her panties and dress and was leading her back into the elevator, while she walked in a climax-induced fog.

She was still in a daze as the elevator began its descent. Shane smiled as he slipped his finger into his mouth and sucked on it.

Her face burned with mortification when she detected the faint scent of her arousal in the air and realized he was sucking her juices off his finger. Oh, my God.

"There's no reason to be embarrassed," Shane said, watching the pink color her cheeks. He reached out to cradle her face in both hands. "Will you have dinner with me tomorrow night, here at my place?"

Her beatific smile made him catch his breath.

"I would love that," she said.

"It's a date. I'll pick you up at six. If you like, we can come back here to my place and have a quiet dinner. Then we can talk and work on that 'getting to know you' stuff."

"You cook?" she said, surprised.

He grinned. "No, I dial. I have plenty of friends in the restaurant business. We can order in anything you like. What will it be? Italian? Chinese? French? Thai?"

"I like it all, but Italian sounds good."

"Italian it is," he said. "I'll call my friend Peter Capelli and ask him to send something over."

"Peter Capelli? Isn't he the owner of Renaldo's? My roommate works there."

"He is, and he owes me some favors, so I'm going to call one in."

When the elevator came to a stop, they stepped out into the garage.

"Let's get you home," Shane said, steering Beth to his Jaguar.

As Shane buckled her into her seat, Beth found herself distracted by the sight of his long fingers. She watched the tendons flex and contract and thought about where those fingers had been just minutes before. At the memory of how those fingers brought her such blinding pleasure, her belly did a little somersault. She couldn't imagine what those hands would feel like stroking her all over. The thought made her dizzy.

He tugged on her seatbelt to tighten it, then leaned forward and kissed her gently, sucking her bottom lip into his mouth. "I like taking care of you. Does it bother you?"

She shook her head, smiling. "I don't mind."

It was true; she didn't mind. She knew a lot of women would be offended. Gabrielle would have considered it patronizing, and she would have swatted his hands away and asked him if he was insane. To Beth, it was comforting.

Shane leaned forward and kissed her again, although this time his kiss had some heat behind it. She shivered when his tongue traced the seam of her lips.

He stroked her cheek with the pad of his thumb. "You take my breath away, you know that?"

She blushed. *Same to you, mister.*

He smiled. "It's late. Let's get you home."

Traffic was light at this late hour, so it was an easy drive south to Hyde Park. Beth sent a quick text to Gabrielle to let her know that she was on her way home.

As they sat in comfortable silence, Shane stroked the back of her left hand, which he'd laid on his thigh. Beth rested her head back in her seat and closed her eyes, enjoying his touch.

She must have drifted off, because suddenly they were parked in front of her house.

"Somebody's up past her bedtime," Shane said, smiling at Beth as she blinked under the bright light of a street lamp. Shane unbuckled his seat belt and then hers. "I'll get your door."

Beth watched him cross in front of the car, admiring his physique and the powerful way he moved.

When they reached the top of her front steps, Beth unlocked the door and they stepped inside. The front hall table light was on. The upstairs was dark, as was the front parlor to the right, but there was a light on in the kitchen at the back of the house. "Gabrielle?" Beth called.

"In the kitchen!"

Beth took Shane's hand. "Come and meet my roommate."

Shane knew he was taking a hell of a risk as he followed Beth down the hall to the kitchen. He just hoped Gabrielle Hunter would keep her cool and not blow his cover. He had no idea what to expect from Gabrielle.

Gabrielle looked up as they entered the kitchen, and her eyes widened in instant recognition when she spotted Shane.

Shane gave her a direct look, willing her to play it cool.

Gabrielle stood at the island counter making a sandwich, and there was a bottle of red wine and a half-filled glass on the counter. "I've had a really long day, I'm starving, and it's late," she said, glancing pointedly at Shane as if these things were his fault. Then she looked at Beth, a too-bright smile on her face. "Aren't you going to introduce me to your new *friend*, Beth?"

"You didn't have to wait up, Gabrielle," Beth said as they came into the room. "I texted you that I was on my way home."

"Pardon me for worrying about you, Beth," Gabrielle said, cutting her sandwich in half with a little more force than necessary. Gabrielle's voice was tight as she glared at Shane. "It's not like you to go home with strange men."

Ouch. She was mad as hell at him, but at least she hadn't given him away. Yet.

"This is Shane McIntyre," Beth said to her roommate. Then she glanced at Shane, and he couldn't help noticing that her smile had slipped a little. She'd definitely picked up on Gabrielle's hostility. "Shane, this is my roommate and best friend, Gabrielle Hunter. Gabrielle's a sous chef at Renaldo's."

"Nice to meet you, Gabrielle," Shane said, eyeing Gabrielle directly. To his utter relief, Gabrielle held her tongue. "Renaldo's is one of the best restaurants in Chicago," he said, sending her an olive branch. There was no reason they had to be enemies. After all, they were on the same team. "Congratulations. I know those sous chef positions are difficult to come by."

Beth was watching her friend closely, but Gabrielle was avoiding her gaze.

Gabrielle picked up her plate, wine glass, and bottle. "I'm heading upstairs, Beth, now that I know you're home safely," Gabrielle said pointedly as she walked away. "I'll wait for you upstairs."

In other words, *He's not staying long, is he?*

"Okay, Gabrielle," Beth said, a small frown marring her brow. "I'll be up in a few minutes."

Shane tamped down his irritation at Gabrielle's manner, but he certainly couldn't complain. She'd held her tongue, even though it hadn't looked easy for her. For that, he was grateful.

"It was a pleasure meeting you, Gabrielle," he said, as she walked away.

"Likewise," was Gabrielle's parting comment.

Beth watched at a complete loss as Gabrielle disappeared up the back staircase. Her hostile behavior didn't make any sense. Gabrielle didn't even know Shane.

"I'm sorry," Beth said to Shane. "She's usually very friendly."

"It's all right. She's probably just tired from a long day. It's late, and I'd better let you get to bed." He drew her to him and kissed her.

"Maybe she had a rough night at the restaurant," Beth said.

"Or," he said, playing with a loose tendril of her hair, "maybe she's just a tad protective of you. I can appreciate that."

Shane removed the band holding Beth's ponytail, and the strands fell forward, framing her face. He kissed her again, his fingers threading through the silken strands. Obeying the gentle coaxing of his lips, she opened her mouth for him, and his tongue slid inside. She could feel his erection prodding her belly.

He broke away from the kiss with a guilty grin on his face. "Sorry. I couldn't help it. When I'm around you, I want you."

She smiled at him. "Thank you."

"For what?"

"For not getting mad when I freaked out at your apartment. I appreciate that. A lot of guys would have gotten angry."

"Beth." He shook his head. "I hope I never get angry at you for expressing your honest feelings. It was just too soon. I understand that." His hands cupped her face. "I'm in no hurry here, sweetheart. Well, actually I am in a hurry because I want you. But you know what I mean. I told you — I want to take care of you. That means meeting your needs. All of them. And if cutting the night short was one of your needs tonight, so be it. We'll get there."

He kissed her again, and Beth felt the heat of his palm through her blouse as his hand covered her breast. She looked down at his big hand molding her flesh, gently kneading it. Feeling a sudden pang of inadequacy, she tried to pull back, but his other arm slipped around her waist, holding her to him.

"What is it?" he said, looking into her eyes. "What just happened?"

"Nothing."

"Beth." His voice was even, but firm. "Talk to me."

Well, wasn't he master of the universe. He was patient, but she also knew he could be very persistent. She had a feeling they'd be there all night if she didn't answer him.

"It's just... I'm not..." She couldn't say it. "Never mind. It's not important." She tried again to pull away, but he held her.

"Sweetheart, I told you before, there's nothing you can't say to me. I saw that flash of panic in your eyes, and I'm not leaving until you tell me what put it there."

"My breasts aren't very big," she said, nearly choking on the words.

Shane struggled to suppress a smile, and Beth wanted to hit

him.

He brushed the edge of his thumb over her nipple, sending a shockwave of pleasure through her body. Then he unbuttoned the top few buttons of her dress. Before she could even protest, his fingers slipped inside her clothing and pushed aside the material to reveal her left bra cup. Then his hand slipped into her bra, nudging the white cotton fabric down.

Shane looked down at her bare breast; they both did. The nipple was puckered from the attention and exposure to the cool night air, a tight little dusky pink bud atop a small mound of pale, creamy flesh. He leaned down and licked her nipple before he took it fully into his mouth. He sucked on the little bud, and then his teeth tugged oh-so-gently on her nipple. When she felt a corresponding rush of warmth low in her belly, she arched into him, crying out. His mouth moved quickly to cover hers and catch the sound.

He kissed her long and deeply, his tongue stroking hers, teasing it, dominating it. When he pulled back, he gazed down at her. "Your breasts are absolutely perfect," he said. "Are we clear on that?"

She nodded.

"Good. Now, are we still on for dinner at my place tomorrow evening?"

"Yes."

"Great. I'll pick you up at six."

"Okay," she said, still reeling from the memory of his hot mouth on her breast.

He chuckled as he released her. "Good night," he said, and he kissed her one last time, a sweet, languorous kiss. "Sleep well, Beth. I'll see you tomorrow."

"Goodnight," she said, smiling.

She walked him to the door, and then locked up and headed upstairs.

Gabrielle was sitting in an armchair in the upstairs landing, waiting for her. A third of the bottle was gone.

"Did you drink all that by yourself?" Beth asked.

Gabrielle looked up and sighed. "No. It was already open. It's late, Beth. I'm going to bed. I just wanted to make sure you got home okay."

After the way Gabrielle had acted downstairs, Beth had been sure Gabrielle was planning to read her the riot act. But now Gabrielle just seemed tired. "Gabrielle, what's wrong?"

Gabrielle shook her head. "Nothing's wrong. I just had a really long day, and I'm tired. I need sleep."

Beth didn't believe her for a second. "Are you sure?"

"Everything's fine. I just need to hit the sack," Gabrielle said. "So do you. It's late."

"Yes, Mom," Beth said, rolling her eyes, which made Gabrielle smile. Sometimes Gabrielle was so much like Tyler. They were both overprotective, and they both thought they knew what was best for her.

Beth appreciated the concern, but sometimes it got to be too much. "Goodnight, Gabrielle. Thanks for waiting up for me."

"Wait!" Gabrielle grabbed her arm. "Beth, what do you know about this guy?"

"I told you. I met him last weekend at Clancy's, and we started chatting. I ran into him again tonight."

"You just *happened* to run into him again?"

"Yes. Well, he'd asked me to call him, but I didn't, so he came looking for me tonight at the bookstore — I told him I go there on Friday evenings. We talked, and then we walked to Café del Sol for drinks."

"Don't you think that's kind of weird? That you just happened to run into him again?"

"Gabrielle, don't go reading anything into this. He's very nice. He was a real gentleman tonight. Don't be so suspicious."

"He seems a little old for you."

"He's thirty-four," Beth said, shrugging. "It's not a big deal."

"Wait until Tyler finds out," Gabrielle said. "Your brother will throw a fit."

Gabrielle was certainly right about that.

"We're consenting adults. That's all that matters," Beth said. "I'm having dinner with him at his apartment tomorrow night. Well, I guess it's tonight now. He's picking me up at six. He's going to have Renaldo's send dinner over. Can you believe that?"

"Beth, Renaldo's doesn't deliver."

"Shane said he knows Peter Capelli, and that Peter will send dinner over."

"I'll believe that when I see it," Gabrielle said.

Beth said goodnight to Gabrielle and headed to her room to get ready for bed. After a quick trip to the bathroom to wash up, she crawled between the sheets and stretched out, groaning with pleasure.

It was probably just her imagination, but she thought she could still feel the gentle tug of Shane's mouth on her breast. She'd thought she was going to burst into flames right there in the kitchen. And then there was the orgasm he'd given her in the foyer of his apartment; her insides still felt like liquid. She hadn't even had sex with him yet, and he was already the best lover she'd ever had. She smiled a stupid giddy smile. Maybe she could do this.

Moonlight filtered through the sheer lace curtains, casting a soothing glow in her room. As she lay there in her bed, her eyelids growing heavy, a fleeting thought occurred to her. The thought grew into a stark realization, and she suddenly felt sick.

Shane had driven her home tonight, but she'd never once told him where she lived.

~ 11

Beth was wide awake now, her heart racing. How could Shane have driven her home from his apartment when she'd never told him where she lived? She'd dozed off in the car on the drive home, and somehow they'd ended up at her front door. She hadn't thought about it at the time, but now the alarm bells were pealing loudly in her head, accompanied by flashing red lights.

How had he known where she lived? She lay there fretting, and it wasn't long before the anxiety bus rolled right over her. It was full-blown panic attack time, and she started to hyperventilate. She tried using the imagery and breathing exercises her therapist had taught her to control her heart rate and breathing, but they weren't helping. No happy place was going to pull her out of this downward spiral. She'd gone too far, too fast.

She replayed all of their conversations in her head, and she was sure she'd never given him her address. And he had never asked.

Beth grabbed her phone from the top of the nightstand and called Shane's number, not caring that it was now one-thirty in the morning. She needed an explanation.

Shane answered on the second ring. "Beth? Is everything all right?"

"How did you know where I live?" Her voice was little more

than a choked whisper. "You drove me home tonight, but I never told you where I live, and you never asked." There was silence on the other end. "How did you know, Shane?"

She heard a muffled curse, then his voice, low and calm.

"Beth, I can explain."

"How!" she cried. Her adrenaline levels were through the roof. "How did you know?"

And then, to her utter mortification, her emotions crashed from exhaustion and adrenal overload, and she started crying. Abruptly, she ended the call.

Her phone rang half a minute later. "What?" she said.

"I'm coming back," he said, sounding a little winded, as if he were running. "Meet me at the front door."

She jumped out of bed and raced down the stairs. It wasn't until she got downstairs that she wondered how he could possibly get back to her house so soon. He'd left at least a half-hour ago. He had to be almost back to his apartment by now.

Beth ran to the front parlor window and peered outside. There he was on the sidewalk in front of her house. He jogged up her front walk, and she met him at the door.

"How did you get here so fast?" she asked as he stepped inside.

Shane closed the front door behind him and locked it. What to tell her? He sure as hell couldn't tell her he'd been parked outside, on duty. "I was parked down the street," he said, sticking to the truth as much as he could. God, he hated lying to her.

"What? Why? You should have been home by now."

"I pulled over about a block from here to check my phone messages and answer some e-mails."

"At one-thirty in the morning?" She couldn't help the incredulity in her voice. She was seeing red flags everywhere now.

"Yes, Beth," he said, with a calculated hint of exasperation in his voice. He had to deflect her attention. Guilt for deceiving her was riding him hard, but he had no choice. "I have a business to run. My employees work shifts around the clock in this city. I was just trying to catch up on work."

"And just what are they doing at one-thirty in the morning?"

"The same thing they do all hours of the day or night. Surveillance and personal protection. That's what we do, and we do it around the clock. I don't keep nine-to-five hours, Beth. I'm always working. I took time off this evening to be with you, and now I have to make up for it."

"Oh." And just like that, she lost a good deal of her steam.

"Now, can we get to the reason why you called me?"

She frowned. "How did you know where I live?" She thought back to the evening they'd shared, replaying everything they'd done, how he'd kissed her, how intimately he'd touched her. Now she simply felt violated, and the thought made her sick.

"Beth, honey, your address is public information." At least that much was true. Shane tried to pull her into his arms, but she stepped back as his words sank in.

Public information. She felt like an idiot. Of course. Fifteen seconds on the Internet would pull up her address, her phone number, and more information than she would care to share with the entire world. Privacy was a thing of the past now, courtesy of the Internet, whether she liked it or not. She was a very private person, and she never posted personal information on the Internet. But public information was easy to obtain.

That quickly, her adrenaline levels crashed and exhaustion overcame her. Shane caught her as she swayed, then picked her up and carried her to the sofa in the front parlor. He eased down beside her on the sofa and reached for her hand.

"I'm sorry I scared you," he said.

When she tried to pull her hand away, he held on to it.

"Beth, I'm in the security business. Finding information is a big part of what we do. Getting your address was nothing — a moment's work. I didn't even think about it. I'm sorry I didn't think to mention that to you tonight, but it honestly never crossed my mind. I never meant to scare you."

Shane held her hands, warming them and trying to still their trembling. She watched him with wary eyes.

"Please say something, sweetheart," he said.

His explanation seemed perfectly reasonable, and she had no

reason to doubt him. But it wasn't easy for her to trust someone.

"I have trust issues." Her voice was little more than a whisper. "The panic kicked in, and I reacted. I didn't stop to think. I'm sorry." Even now, her heart was racing.

He nodded. "Why do you have trust issues? Who abused your trust?"

When she didn't answer, he scowled. And then he asked her point blank. "Beth, did someone hurt you?"

She nodded. But she was so not going there tonight. She'd had enough trauma for one night.

"Physically?" he said. "Or emotionally?"

"Both, I guess. But mostly emotionally."

"Jesus." It was hard to hear her say it. He released her hands and ran his fingers through his hair and took a deep breath. "Will you tell me about it?"

Beth shook her head. "I'm tired, and I don't want to talk about it."

Shane nodded. "Fair enough." He stood and lifted her into his arms. "I'll carry you up to your bed."

"I can walk," she protested.

When he set her on her feet, she stumbled. She would have fallen if he hadn't caught her.

Shane swept her back up into his arms. "I'm carrying you. No argument."

"But I'm too heavy."

He chuckled. "Sweetheart, I bench press more than twice your weight every day. I won't even break a sweat."

No one had carried her to bed since she was a small child, and the experience now was a little unnerving. True to his word, though, he didn't break a sweat as he carried her up the stairs. But a memory burned into her mind resurfaced, and she remembered the night Tyler carried her out of that cellar. She shoved the memory away.

"Which bedroom is yours?" he asked.

She pointed down the hall. "The last one."

Shane carried her into the room and gently deposited her on

the bed, covering her with the sheet and quilt.

"Can I stay tonight?" he said, brushing her hair back from her face. He couldn't stand the thought of leaving her right now; if she panicked again, he wanted to be here. "I don't want to leave you alone right now."

Her first instinct was to say no. He'd seen too much of her already, and she was feeling very emotionally exposed at the moment. But she couldn't bring herself to do it. The truth was she wanted him to stay. It gave her a thrill to have him here in her bedroom. "Okay."

Shane closed the bedroom door, and Beth watched him with wide eyes as he quickly stripped down to his boxers and walked around to the other side of the bed.

He slid in beside her and pulled her close. "You're exhausted, sweetheart. Try to sleep."

She closed her eyes and tried to calm her racing mind, but the proximity of his warm body made it hard to relax. The heat radiating from him and his masculine scent stirred her senses, tantalizing her. Her hand ended up on his chest, measuring the rise and fall of his breaths. She could feel his strong, steady heart beat beneath her fingers.

Shane laid his big hand over hers and began to stroke the back of her hand. Hypnotized by his touch, she began to relax. She crashed hard and fast as sleep pulled her under.

The last thing she remembered was feeling his lips in her hair as he murmured something she didn't quite catch.

12

Shane woke instantly in the wee hours of the morning to the sound of screaming. He sat up and took immediate stock of his surroundings.

Beth's bedroom.

He looked at her in the dim light, barely able to make out her restless form. *She's having a nightmare.*

Her frightened whimpers pierced his heart. "Jesus, Beth!" He grabbed her by the shoulders and shook her gently. "Wake up, sweetheart!"

Startled, she opened her eyes and looked around frantically as if trying to orient herself. She blinked up at him in the darkness. "Tyler?" She was still half asleep, her voice hoarse and her chest heaving as she reached for him.

"No, honey," he said. "Not Tyler. Shane." He brushed the hair back from her hot face.

Her wits must have returned in a rush, because she sat up, gasping. "Shane!"

He steadied her. "You're okay, sweetheart. I've got you."

She rubbed frantically at her chest.

"It's okay," he said, his hand on her back. "You had a nightmare."

"Can't... breathe!" she gasped, reaching for the top drawer of the nightstand. She fumbled blindly inside the drawer, until

Shane leaned across her and located her inhaler.

"Here, Beth," he said, handing it to her.

She shook it briskly, then pushed the inhaler into her mouth. After she administered the medicine, drawing it deeply into her starved lungs, she lay back down and closed her eyes. In seconds, she started to relax and soon began breathing easily again.

He studied her. "Are you all right?"

She nodded shakily. "Yes."

But she didn't look all right to him.

Beth looked at the digital clock on the nightstand, which read 4:30. They'd had only three hours of sleep. She groaned. "I'm sorry I woke you."

"It's okay, sweetheart," he said, just as her bedroom door burst open and Gabrielle rushed in.

Gabrielle stopped abruptly at the sight of Shane sitting shirtless beside Beth in the bed. A bright light from the hallway spilled into the room, blinding them.

"She's okay," Shane hastened to say. "It was just a bad dream."

"I know what it was," Gabrielle said, breathless and still half asleep herself. She gave Shane a sharp look. "What the hell are you doing here? You left!"

"I came back," he said.

"Obviously," Gabrielle said, glaring at him.

If looks could kill, Shane figured he'd be a dead man right now. Gabrielle looked like she wanted to carve him up with one of her fileting knives.

"I was upset last night, and I called him," Beth said, hoping to defuse Gabrielle's hostility toward Shane. "He came back."

Gabrielle transferred her glare to Beth. "If you were upset, you could have come to me."

Shane knew Gabrielle wasn't angry as much as she was hurt. "It was me she was upset with, Gabrielle," Shane said, attempting to placate her.

"Oh, for fuck's sake!" Gabrielle threw her hands up in disgust and glared at them both. "Whatever! I'm going back to bed."

"Sorry for waking you, Gabrielle!" Beth called as Gabrielle

stalked out of the room, slamming the door shut on her way out. The hallway light switched off, and a moment later Gabrielle's bedroom door slammed shut.

Beth flinched.

"She'll be all right," Shane said. "Don't worry."

Shane lay back in bed and pulled Beth close, tucking her into his side. She was still trembling from the aftermath of her nightmare. He wrapped his arms around her in an effort to comfort her.

Beth turned toward him, laying her head on his shoulder and stretching her arm across his chest. He waited a few minutes until the shaking stopped and she began to relax. It was time to get her to start opening up to him, and her nightmare was the perfect opening. They had a lot of ground to cover between the two of them before he could tell her everything.

"Do you want to talk about it?" he asked, stroking her arm as it lay across his chest.

Her finger began drawing patterns in the hair on his chest, and she sighed. "No."

His cock stirred instantly at her light touch, and it was a struggle to keep his mind on his train of thought. But he didn't want to be distracted at the moment. Getting her to talk to him was too important.

"Are you sure? I'm a good listener," he said. "I've been known to vanquish a few nightmares in my day. It's what I do for a living, you know."

"It's not that easy," Beth said.

"I didn't say it would be easy, honey." His hand found hers, and he laced their fingers together, mostly to still her nimble fingers, which were driving him crazy. He brought her hand to his mouth and kissed the back of it, amazed at how silky soft her skin was. "Were you dreaming about the person who hurt you?"

"Yes," she said, reluctantly.

Beth pulled her hand from his and ran the tip of her index finger over his nipple, causing it to pucker instantly. His dick started twitching in his boxers.

He made a rough sound in his throat and recaptured her hand, stilling it. "Beth."

She tugged on her hand, and he released it. Then she resumed her slow exploration of his chest, her fingertips following the contours of his torso, outlining his muscles and following the shapes of his bones. She traced his collarbone down to his breastbone, her fingernails gently scraping his chest hair. When her fingers followed the trail of hair that led down his abdomen, his hardening cock rose up beneath the covers.

"Sweetheart, now's not the right time," he said, trying to do the right thing though it was getting more difficult.

Beth's face burned. Why was this so hard? She'd read enough romances to know perfectly well how to seduce a man, but she wasn't sure she could pull it off.

She was desperate for something to take her mind off her nightmare, to dispel the lingering traces of *that monster* from the edges of her memories. So she took a huge leap of faith. She slipped her fingers beneath the bedding and quickly found what she was looking for. His erection was tenting his boxers now, and she took hold of him through the fabric. He was as hard as a steel rod in her hand, and she was shocked by the girth of him. She tried to imagine him fitting inside her. *Good God.*

Shane groaned, his entire body responding helplessly to her touch. "Baby –"

Beth tightened her grip on his erection, giving him a tentative squeeze, and his body bowed off the bed.

"Fuck!" His hand came down over hers, but this time he didn't try to still her fingers. His chest heaved with his rough breath. "Beth!"

She took courage from the ragged tone of his voice. She wanted to forget the nightmare lingering in her mind like an oily black cloud. She wanted to forget everything except for the man in her bed. And she knew of only one thing that would accomplish that. Oblivion.

"I want you, Shane."

She wasn't used to initiating sex, but right now it felt right. It felt *necessary*. He was hard as stone in her hand, and the sound of his harsh breath soughing in his chest gave her some sorely needed confidence. She slipped her hand inside his boxers and wrapped her fingers around his bare flesh, shocked at how hot he was. Her fingers traced the line of a thick, pulsing vein that throbbed just beneath the velvety skin covering his rigid penis.

His voice was strained. "Beth, honey, I don't think — "

She stroked his cock from the root upward, caressing his velvety soft skin. Her fingers crested up and over the crown of his penis, and she felt a trace of wetness there, which she caught with her palm and spread over the fat head of his cock. It was like putting a lighted match to dry tinder.

Shane groaned loudly as he shoved his erection into her tight fist. He grabbed her face and pulled her to him for a blistering kiss.

"Beth," he groaned against her mouth. "God!"

Shane's mouth was fierce on hers, eating at her, sucking and biting as if he wanted to devour her. His tongue pushed into her mouth, twining and twisting with hers. Before, he'd always been such a polished kisser, but right now it was just primal.

"Christ, you make me lose my mind," he groaned into her mouth. "I am so fucking desperate to be inside you."

"I'm not stopping you," she said as her heart hammered in her chest. She reveled in his violent reaction.

Shane tore his mouth from hers, scowling as he looked at her. His hand covered hers, slowing her strokes. The knowledge that it was Beth's hand on him had him so damn close, and he sure as hell didn't want to come in his boxers. "Do you have any condoms?"

"What?" She had never in her life bought condoms.

"Condoms. Do you have any?"

Beth shook her head. "No. Don't you? I thought guys always

carried condoms."

He barked out a short, harsh laugh. "I'm sorry to disappoint you, but I don't have any on me right now." He groaned. "No condom, no sex, sweetheart. Unless you think your roommate keeps a stash of them?"

"Oh, God no!" she hissed. "I am not asking Gabrielle for a condom!"

Shane chuckled. "I don't blame you. Earlier, I thought she was going to castrate me. I don't want to antagonize her any more than I already have."

Beth groaned when his words finally sunk in. *No condoms, no sex.*

Shane levered up and turned them so that she was lying down, and he loomed over her.

Beth looked up at his grinning face. The bastard! How could he be so flippant when she was burning up here?

"I know what you need," he said. His mouth descended on hers, tasting and teasing hers with slow, languorous kisses.

He was right. She needed this. She needed *him.*

Shane threw back the bedding and slipped his hand underneath her nightgown. His fingers traveled up her torso, skimming past her underwear as he pushed her nightgown up to her waist. Her belly quivered beneath his fingers as he rimmed her belly button with the tip of his index finger, making her squirm in response. Then he reached higher and cupped her left breast, kneading the small mound gently and marveling at the softness of her skin. He squeezed her nipple lightly with his thumb and index finger. When she stiffened, he released her nipple and stroked it gently.

Shane's hand plumped her left breast, molding her soft flesh into a little mound. He gently pinched her nipple again, then rolled it between his index finger and thumb. She cried out as his touch streaked along her neurons to a spot between her legs that just seemed to grow hotter and wetter with every touch.

"You are so fucking beautiful," Shane said, gazing down at her. "I would give anything to be inside you right now." There was a wistful frown on his face. "But I'll just have to improvise."

"Improvise how?"

He kissed her again, a sweet mingling of their mouths. Then he dipped his head down to her breast and drew her nipple into his mouth, teasing the peak with quick lashes of his tongue. When he sucked her languidly, drawing on her nipple with his tongue and lips, her body bowed.

Shane released her nipple and scooted down the bed, kissing and nibbling his way down her belly.

"Where are you going?" Beth reached for him in a futile attempt to draw him back up. Her heart rate kicked into overdrive as a sinking suspicion formed.

"Not very far, I assure you." He pressed his face against her white cotton panties, right over her mound, and inhaled deeply through the fabric. Before she could react, he had her panties down her long legs and had tossed them over his shoulder and onto the floor. His eyes were locked on her sex as he petted her curls.

Beth pressed her legs together tightly. "Shane, no! What are you doing?" It had been almost 24 hours since she'd showered, and the last thing she wanted was Shane sticking his face between her legs.

"I'm improvising," he said. "We don't have any condoms, so I'm going with Plan B." His hands were on her knees now, and he tried to open them, but she resisted. "Open your legs, sweetheart," he said, patting her knee.

"No."

"Why not?"

"You can't do that."

"Why not?" he said, not even trying to suppress the grin on his face.

"Because!"

"Beth, open your legs." He was using that tone again — that *you-will-do-what-I-say-even-if-it-takes-all-night* tone.

Why did that turn her on so much? She should yell and scream and call him a bully, but, instead, she felt herself growing even wetter. Still, he had no business sticking his face down there right now. "No!"

"Sweetheart."

"Maybe some other time," she said. "After I've showered."

"Showered? Honey, you don't need to shower. I want to taste you, not some floral body wash. If you don't open your legs right now and let me in there, I'll lay you over my knees and spank you."

An undignified snort escaped her before she could rein it in. She didn't know which would be more horrifying: his mouth on her down there or a spanking. She gazed down the length of her torso at him, surprised by the earnest smile she saw on his handsome face.

"Pretty please," he said.

Reluctantly, she relaxed her legs and let him pry them apart, and the air felt cool on her hot, damp flesh. He settled himself between her thighs, his face just inches from her crotch. She groaned, covering her eyes with one hand.

She shuddered when she felt his warm breath between her legs. Honestly, she didn't know if she could do this. "Shane — "

"Relax, sweetheart," he said.

"But I haven't — "

"Beth, honey, there is no reason on Earth why I wouldn't want to put my mouth on you *right this minute*. If you'll let me put my mouth on you, I promise to make you come until you can't see straight."

When she felt his fingers gently open her folds, she raised her head and watched in horrified fascination as he touched the tip of his tongue to her clitoris. His tongue lapped at it, and her entire body jerked as if she'd been shocked by a live wire. She cried out a garbled and inarticulate sound.

"It's okay, honey." He flicked his tongue against her clitoris, and she jumped. His broad shoulders filled the space between her thighs, pinning them wide open, and he pressed forward. "Just relax."

She dropped her head back on her pillow and growled in

frustration. "Relax? Are you crazy?" How the hell could she relax with his face between her legs?

No guy had ever done this to her before. Sure, she'd read about it a million times and always found it thrilling, but she wasn't prepared for the reality of it — the intensity of it, the thrill. It was just too much — his hot mouth, his breath, his tongue, teasing and invading. Her body shuddered as pleasure ripped through her, from her heated core straight up her torso. Her body bowed off the mattress as high-pitched and desperate sounds came out of her.

Shane's hot tongue took two big swipes of her slit, and then suddenly his mouth was voracious and demanding. His tongue zeroed in on her clitoris, lashing it relentlessly, battering that tiny, sensitive piece of her until she was rocking her hips against his mouth, crazed with an exquisite pleasure that left her breathless.

Shane worked at her, stroking, nibbling, sucking. At one point, his teeth gently latched onto her clit, and the sensation was enough to make her want to scream. She had to cover her mouth with her hands.

Her belly clenched when a wave of intense pleasure radiated out from the little bud that was the focus of his attention. When she felt his finger swipe down her slit and tease the opening to her core, she began to thrash. He held her steady with one hand on her quivering belly, while he slipped his index finger slowly inside her opening, gently pushing through swollen, wet tissue. His finger curled inside her, searching as he stroked her. He lingered in one spot, stroking slowly and methodically, and she trembled as an unfamiliar anticipation built deep inside her.

He glanced up at her. "You okay?" he said, sounding a little breathless.

Beth nodded, too mortified to speak as she watched him.

Shane continued stroking inside her, bent on a slow, methodical campaign to drive her insane. She felt the sensation grow, swelling and peaking like a tidal wave as it picked up energy, just waiting to be unleashed. He was relentless in his goal, stroking her mercilessly. She recognized the impending explosion, so she grabbed the pillow beside her and covered her face with it in a desperate attempt to muffle her cries.

Finally, when the most tumultuous orgasm she'd ever experienced ended, Beth removed the pillow from her damp face, sucking in lungfuls of air. "Oh, my God," she gasped, her voice little more than a throaty whisper.

Shane wiped his face on the sheet, then came up over her on all fours, smiling down as he kissed her soundly. "Has anyone ever done that to you before?"

She was shocked to smell and taste herself on him, earthy and salty. "No."

"I didn't think so," he said, looking very pleased with himself.

"So that was Plan B," Beth muttered, once she'd caught her breath.

"What did you think?" he said as he collapsed beside her on the bed, a little breathless after his exertions.

"If that was Plan B, I don't think I'd survive Plan A," she said. "Maybe it's a good thing we didn't have any condoms."

Shane chuckled. "Did it pass muster?"

Beth laughed. How in the world could he be so sexy and reassuring at the same time? He'd pushed her past her comfort zone on a couple of occasions, but he'd never pushed her this far.

As her racing heart began to slow and breathing became easier, Beth closed her eyes and savored the residual tremors of the best orgasm she'd ever had. She remembered him threatening to spank her earlier, and she imagined herself lying across his lap, his broad hand on the curve of her butt. After what he'd just done to her, the idea of baring her bottom to him didn't seem quite as shocking as it once would have. Maybe it would be fun to try.

"Are you okay?" Shane said as he pulled her close.

"More than okay," she said, her limbs like jelly.

He tugged her nightgown down over her thighs and then

covered her to the waist with the sheet and quilt. As her eyelids started drooping, she felt his lips in her hair.

"Can you sleep now?" he said in a low voice.

She felt his erection pressing insistently against her hip. "But you haven't—"

"Next time," he said. "Tonight was about you. Go to sleep."

But he'd just given her a mind-blowing orgasm. Surely she should return the favor.

"Sleep," he said, almost as if he'd read her mind. He rolled Beth to her side, wrapping his arm around her waist, and spooned with her.

Beth sighed. She liked this. She liked *him*. She liked how she felt when she was with him. For the first time, she could see herself letting go with someone, not just with sex, but with a lot more — with herself. She could see herself telling him everything, about the darkness and about her nightmares. She wanted that so desperately.

When she shifted her legs, she realized she was bare beneath her nightgown. "My panties are on the floor."

"I know." He seemed unconcerned.

She laughed. "I was just wondering if I have the energy to find them."

"You don't. Now go to sleep." His hand slipped beneath the bedding and found its way between her thighs.

"Okay," she whispered.

13

"How long is she going to sleep?"

Beth woke to Gabrielle's plaintive voice.

"As long as she needs, Gabrielle," Shane said, his voice quiet. "She had a rough night. Let her sleep."

"She never sleeps this late."

"Well, today she's sleeping in. Go away before you wake her."

Beth cracked open her eyes, surprised to find the room so bright. She looked at the clock beside her bed. It was after ten! Gabrielle was right; she never slept this late. "I'm awake," Beth said.

Gabrielle stood in the bedroom doorway dressed in her running clothes. Her face was flushed, and her red hair was damp. "Do you want breakfast?" she asked Beth.

Beth rolled onto her back and looked at Shane propped up in bed beside her. He was dressed in faded jeans and a t-shirt, and there was an open laptop computer on his lap. His hair was damp, and Beth realized he'd already showered.

"Good morning," Shane said. He leaned over and kissed her gently on the mouth. "Did you sleep well?"

"Yes."

Plan B had certainly done the trick. After that mind-blowing orgasm, she'd fallen into a deep, undisturbed sleep. In fact, it was the most restful sleep she'd had in a long time.

"Where did the laptop come from?" she said. He hadn't had it with him when he came back last night.

"A friend brought it to me this morning along with a change of clothes. I thought I would work here a while and let you sleep. You'll need your rest for tonight."

"What's tonight, Shane?" Gabrielle said.

Beth had already told Gabrielle she was having dinner with Shane. Why was she playing dumb?

"We have a date tonight," Shane said. "Dinner at my place."

Beth felt a curious fluttering in her belly when Shane referred to their plans as a date. Were they really dating? And what, exactly, did that mean to Shane?

Gabrielle eyed Shane suspiciously, and then she looked at Beth. "Does Tyler know about this *date?*"

When Beth didn't answer, Gabrielle smirked at Shane. "Tyler is her brother, her very *protective* older brother," Gabrielle clarified.

"Beth's an adult, Gabrielle," Shane said. "She doesn't need her brother's — or anyone else's — permission to date."

"Obviously, you haven't met Tyler," Gabrielle countered. "Or have you?" she said, cocking an eyebrow at him.

"He hasn't," Beth said, sitting up. This couldn't go on. She really needed to find out why Gabrielle was so hostile toward Shane. Beth had dated before, and Gabrielle had never acted like this.

Shane went back to typing on his laptop.

"I need a shower and tea, in that order," Beth said, swinging her legs over the side of the bed. She smoothed her nightgown down over her thighs, trying to hide the fact that she was bare ass naked underneath.

"Missing something?" Gabrielle said, as she bent over and picked Beth's panties up off the floor.

"So that's where those went," Shane said, looking up with a deadpan expression.

Beth didn't know how he managed to keep a straight face. She certainly couldn't. She burst out laughing, mortified that every person in the room knew she was pantyless — and could probably guess why. It was either laugh or cry.

Even Gabrielle had to fight a grin. "Go take your shower," she said to Beth, throwing the panties at her. "I'll put the kettle on for your tea."

Beth grabbed her robe and pulled a pair of clean panties out of her dresser drawer.

Shane looked up from his computer. "Need any help in the shower?"

"Um, I don't think so," she said, hastening out the bedroom door. She heard his chuckle as she escaped down the hall.

She'd had enough excitement for one morning.

Beth took the quickest shower ever, not wanting to leave Shane and Gabrielle unsupervised under the same roof for long. She was afraid they'd start brawling next.

Back in her bedroom, she hid in her small walk-in closet and dressed quickly in shorts and a t-shirt.

"I need to talk to Gabrielle," she told Shane when she came out. "Do you mind waiting up here? I'll bring you back some breakfast."

"Not a problem," he said, glancing up from his work. "Good luck, because I'm pretty sure she hates me."

Beth chuckled. "She doesn't hate you, Shane. She just — " To be honest, she wasn't sure how Gabrielle felt. "Let me talk to her."

Beth headed downstairs and found Gabrielle in the kitchen pouring herself a cup of coffee.

"The water's hot," Gabrielle said, pointing unnecessarily at the kettle whistling loudly on the stove.

"Thanks." Beth grabbed a mug and filled it with hot water, then opened the cupboard and grabbed her box of Lady Grey. "Gabrielle, why are you so hostile toward Shane?"

Gabrielle frowned as she glanced at Beth. "I'm sorry if I was rude."

"Why do you dislike him so much?" Beth said, dropping her tea bag into her mug to let it steep. "You hardly know him."

Gabrielle shrugged. "Beth, Shane's...." She stopped to pour a couple splashes of cream into her coffee and stir.

"Shane's what?"

"He's too old for you."

"That's what's bothering you?" Beth said. "He's too old for me? He's ten years older — so what? That's not the end of the world, Gabrielle. My dad was twelve years older than my mom, and they were very happy together."

Gabrielle shrugged. "He's still too old for you. And you know Tyler will throw a fit when he finds out."

"Since when do you care what Tyler thinks?" Beth said, checking her tea. "Gabrielle, I *like* Shane. He's been wonderful to me, even when I was difficult. He's never demanded more than I could give. He's kind, funny, patient, gentle... and he's a really good kisser." Beth grinned. "Gabrielle, I really like him. Please, give him a chance."

Gabrielle looked at Beth, her expression inscrutable.

"What?" Beth said. "What are you not telling me?"

Gabrielle's brow furrowed. "You must be hungry," she said, surprising Beth with the abrupt change of topic. "There are scrambled eggs and bacon in the warming tray, enough for both of you. I'm going to take my coffee out back."

And then Gabrielle walked through the French doors to the back patio, leaving Beth to wonder what her best friend wasn't telling her.

Beth made up two breakfast plates and poured a cup of Gabrielle's freshly-brewed coffee for Shane. She carried the tray up the back staircase, praying she wouldn't drop it. When she walked into her bedroom, Shane jumped up to take the tray from her.

"Thank you," he said, eyeing the food and coffee appreciatively.

"You can thank Gabrielle for both the breakfast and the coffee. All I did was pour."

"I'll be sure to thank her," Shane said.

As they leaned against the headboard and ate, Beth pondered possible reasons why Gabrielle was so dead set against Shane when she didn't even know him.

She didn't know him, right? She'd assumed they didn't already know each other, but maybe that wasn't true. Maybe they'd met before. That would explain a lot. For one second, she wondered if they'd dated before, but she dismissed that idea just as quickly. She would've remembered Gabrielle mentioning him. Maybe they'd just hooked up once. Feeling sick, Beth put down her fork. There was only one way to find out.

"Can I ask you something?" Beth said.

"Of course. Anything."

"Do you and Gabrielle know each other? I mean, from before yesterday? Have you met before?"

Shane paused a moment too long, and she knew the answer before he even said it.

"We met before, yes."

Beth looked at him, but his expression gave away nothing. Her heart started racing, and she realized she was dreading hearing the details. *At least he'd been honest with her.*

"Did you two date?" she said.

He seemed genuinely surprised by her question. "Date? No."

"Did you sleep with her?"

Shane nearly choked on his coffee. "God, no!" He looked askance at her.

"Don't look at me like that," she said. "I figured you two already knew each other somehow. It's the only explanation for her behavior that makes sense."

"I met her just once, at a business meeting. We never dated, and we sure as hell never had sex."

"What kind of business meeting?"

He was walking a fine line now. He couldn't divulge that he'd met Gabrielle through Tyler, and yet he refused to outright lie to Beth.

"Remember, I said Peter Capelli owed me a few favors? That's because I've done a lot of work for him."

"Security work?"

"Yes." Peter was the owner of Renaldo's, and Gabrielle worked at Renaldo's. He let Beth incorrectly connect the dots, and he felt like a bastard for doing it.

"So, you met her at the restaurant?" Beth said, trying to piece it together.

"No. It was in my office." At least that much was true. He was grasping at straws now, trying to minimize the subterfuge. He hadn't exactly lied to her, but he'd let her make an incorrect inference. But it was practically the same thing, and he knew it.

"Oh," she said.

He gave her as much honesty as he could afford at the moment. "Beth, sweetheart, I have no personal interest in Gabrielle whatsoever, beyond the fact that she's your roommate and friend."

Shane set his coffee on the nightstand on his side of the bed and turned to Beth, taking her hand.

"Please don't read anything into my having met Gabrielle before. It was at a client meeting. She attended *one* meeting, because she needed to be briefed on a case. I saw her only the one time."

"Then why is she so hostile toward you?"

He shrugged. "I think she may have disagreed with an opinion I expressed at the meeting. I really can't say more than that because of client privilege."

After they finished breakfast, Shane collected his things. "I'll be back to pick you up at six," he said, and then he gave her a long, lingering kiss.

Beth waved from the front window as he headed toward his car. When he was out of sight, she went in search of Gabrielle. Not surprisingly, she found her friend in the backyard tending the herb garden.

"Shane told me you two met before," Beth said, looking down

at Gabrielle, who was crouched at the edge of her garden, pulling weeds.

Gabrielle looked up at Beth. "Really?" She seemed genuinely surprised.

Gabrielle wiped her cheek with the back of her hand, leaving a smudge of soil on her face. Beth reached down and brushed it off.

"He did," Beth said. "I asked him if you two had met before. It was the only explanation that made sense for the way you've been acting around him."

Gabrielle sat back on her heels. "And what did he say?"

"He said you two met once before in his office, at a client meeting. Is that true?" If Shane had lied to her, she needed to know.

Gabrielle hesitated, and Beth held her breath as she waited for the reply. If Shane had lied to her about his connection to Gabrielle... she couldn't even bear to finish that thought.

But then Gabrielle said, "Yes. What else did he say?"

Beth released her breath and realized she was shaking. "He said you disagreed with his opinion on something. Is that true?"

"Yes, it is," Gabrielle said, ripping out a scraggly weed with more force than was necessary.

"And then, he said he couldn't say more because of client privilege."

Gabrielle nodded. "How convenient for him."

"But is it true?" Beth said, still half afraid to hear the answer. "Is what he said true?"

Gabrielle looked at her, frowning. "Yes," she said, sounding reluctant. "It is."

Beth's shoulders slumped in obvious relief. "I thought maybe you two had dated before," she admitted, starting to feel silly. Surely, if that had been the case, Gabrielle would have told her from the start.

Gabrielle scoffed, scratching the tip of her nose with the back of her glove. "No way! I don't date control freaks."

Beth grinned. "You think Shane's a control freak?"

Gabrielle looked askance at Beth. "You're kidding, right?"

She shrugged. "He seems pretty easy going to me."

Gabrielle laughed. "He would control when the sun rises and sets if he could figure out how to do it. He's trying to make a good impression on you, Beth. He doesn't want to scare you off."

"You don't like him, do you?"

Gabrielle sighed. "If you like him, I'm willing to give him a chance and see how it goes. Truthfully, Beth, he might be just what you need." She stood up and brushed the loose dirt from her pants. "You're seeing him tonight? At his place?"

"Yes."

Gabrielle's eyes narrowed. "Are you spending the night?"

Beth shrugged. "Maybe. I haven't decided."

"Are you ready for that?"

"I hope so," Beth said. "I want to be."

Gabrielle frowned, seeming far from convinced.

"He *knows*, Gabrielle."

"He knows what?"

"That I have issues. I haven't told him why, but he knows about the panic attacks. I chickened out on him last night at his apartment, and he was okay with it. He didn't get mad, and he didn't make me feel bad about it."

Gabrielle sighed. "If he treats you well, I'll be his new best friend," she said. "I mean that. All I care about is you. As long as you're happy and safe, I'm happy. But if he hurts you, I'll make damn sure he regrets it. I mean it, Beth. Text me tonight and let me know if you're staying overnight or not and when you'll be home."

"I will." Beth bit back a smile. Talk about control freak! Gabrielle was as bad as Tyler; she often suspected they were double-teaming her.

Gabrielle nodded. "Okay, then. We're good." She hugged Beth. "I need to take a shower and get ready for work. Call me tonight if you need me. You know I'll come running. And I'd be more than happy to kick his ass if need be."

They walked back into the house together. While Gabrielle

ran upstairs to shower, Beth started on the breakfast dishes. Shane wouldn't be picking her up until six that evening, and that meant she had plenty of time on her hands to fret about what she should wear and a hundred other things. She was too nervous to do much else.

14

At ten minutes before six, Beth set her overnight bag on the floor by the front door and went to the front parlor window to watch for him. From there, seated on the sofa, she had a clear view of the sidewalk out front.

She didn't know if she could go through with spending the night with Shane, but she wanted to be prepared just in case, so she'd packed a bag. She'd only known him for a little over a week, and she was already tied up in knots. She wanted this, she really did. She'd never been so attracted to a man in her life. But she didn't know if she could go through with it without freaking out — and that was the last thing she wanted him to see.

She'd taken her time getting ready that afternoon, trying to cover every contingency. She'd showered and shaved her legs and underarms. She'd taken time with her hair, arranging it in a loose updo that made her look more sophisticated. She'd applied a little bit of mascara and a pale smoky eye shadow that nicely complemented her eyes. She'd brushed her teeth and flossed to within an inch of her life.

When it came time to decide what to wear, she'd been at a complete loss. She wasn't a fashion hound by anyone's definition. She knew people who spent more on one pair of shoes than she spent on clothes in a year. She preferred to shop at thrift shops and consignment stores, and she loved vintage things.

Occasionally, she'd splurge and buy something from one of the indie boutiques in the city, but that was rare as she just couldn't justify the expense. After all, it was just clothes.

She settled on one of her favorite outfits — a sleeveless, pale blue linen dress with an empire waist and a low, square neckline that made her look like she might actually have some cleavage. Her bra and panties were plain white cotton, but there was no help for that.

She'd looked at the full-length mirror hanging on the back of her closet door and wondered what Shane would think. She was certain his usual dates wore slinky designer dresses and four-inch stilettos — like that woman they'd run into at Clancy's. Beth couldn't compete with women like that, and she didn't even want to try. If that's what he wanted, he was in for disappointment.

As she'd studied her reflection, she realized she liked the way she looked. If he was disappointed... well, she couldn't help that. She wasn't going to try to be someone she wasn't.

She was checking her purse for the necessities — inhaler, house key, credit card, phone — when she noticed movement out front. There he was. He'd double-parked in front of her house.

Her eyes widened as Shane got out of the car. "Oh, my God," she breathed.

He was stunning in a dark suit, white shirt, and black tie. His blue eyes were the only spot of color on him — well, his eyes and the bouquet of blue Forget-Me-Nots in his hand. He'd brought her flowers. It was such a simple thing, yet the tears welled up. No one had ever brought her flowers before.

Her hungry gaze followed him as his long legs ate up the distance between his car and her front stoop, his stride both controlled and graceful. He caught sight of her watching him through the window and gave her a small wave and a smile that made her belly do a somersault. She waved back, then jumped up from the sofa and ran to the front door to let him in.

His hot gaze swept over her as he stepped inside. "Beth."

His voice was low and warm, and it flowed into her like melted honey.

She smiled, her cheeks flushed. "Hi."

Shane closed the door behind him. "You look beautiful," he said, his voice a little rough.

The house was quiet, the only sound that of the steady tick-tock of the grandfather clock in the hallway. Shane stared down at her for much too long, which only made her more nervous. When the grandfather clock began to chime the hour, she jumped.

He smiled gently. "Are you okay?"

She nodded. "I'm fine. Just a little nervous, I guess."

He nodded as if he could relate. Then he handed her a bouquet of delicate blue flowers accented with Baby's Breath and tiny ferns. "For you. They match your eyes."

She smiled. "Thank you, Shane. They're lovely."

He followed her to the kitchen where she arranged the flowers in a crystal vase and set them in the center of the kitchen island countertop.

"Ready to go?" he said.

She nodded.

On their way out, she grabbed her purse from the hall table and reached down to pick up her overnight bag, but he beat her to it.

"I've got it," he said. And then he opened the front door for her.

"Tell me what you're thinking," Shane said, reaching for her hand as they rode the private elevator up to the penthouse. "I can see the wheels turning."

Beth shook her head, not wanting to go there. Her mind was a chaotic mess at the moment as her anxieties and inadequacies assailed her. Her heart was already racing, and she was trying hard to tamp it down before it got out of control. She took a deep, steadying breath. *Just keep it together and don't make a fool out of yourself.*

"Beth."

She sighed, recognizing the tone. He wasn't going to just give up. If she'd learned anything about him, it was that he was persistent. "I was thinking about the last time I was here."

Shane set her bag on the elevator floor and took her in his arms. She slipped her arms inside his jacket and around his waist, delighting in the strength and the warmth of his muscular torso.

"You don't have to do anything tonight you don't want to," he said. "You know that, right?"

When she didn't respond, he said, "Right?"

She nodded.

"I would love for you to stay the night, but if you want me to take you home after dinner, I will. No pressure. I want you to feel comfortable."

She looked up at him. "I don't want to run this time. Please, don't let me run."

He frowned. "Beth."

"Please, Shane. Promise me."

He shook his head, his expression a mix of conflicting emotions. "I'm not going to pressure you to stay," he said.

"I'm not asking you to pressure me."

"Then what are you asking?"

She shrugged, clearly frustrated. "I don't know. Just don't let me run. Promise me."

"All right, I promise." Shane turned her so that they were both facing the mirrored wall in the elevator. "Look at us," he said. He moved behind her, his hands on her shoulders as he drew her back against him.

She gazed at their reflection, mesmerized by the sight of the two of them together. The contrast between them was stark. She was pale in comparison to him, and her body was dwarfed by his height and broad shoulders. Just looking at him made her feel weak in the knees.

One of his arms snaked around her torso, just under her

breasts, holding her against him. He leaned down, putting his mouth to her ear. "You take my breath away, Beth," he said, his blue eyes glittering hotly as he looked up and met her gaze in the mirror. "Since the first moment I saw you, I've been a wreck. I want you more than I want my next breath."

Their gazes locked in the mirror, and the heat in his expression generated a corresponding heat low in her belly. She could feel his erection pressing against her lower back. His hand came up and played with a tendril of hair that hung down to her shoulder, coaxing the strand to wrap around his long index finger.

"I love your hair," he said, pressing his lips to the side of her neck.

Beth tilted her head to the side, giving him access to her throat. She shivered at the feel of his lips on her sensitive skin.

He released her hair and ran his fingers up into her loose updo, his fingers stroking her scalp. Tingles rippled through her. "I can't wait to take your hair down and feel it brushing against my body."

She closed her eyes and melted into him, and his arms tightened around her, providing some badly needed support. He could seduce her so easily. One hot glance, his mouth on her skin, his heated breath in her ear, and she was lost. It frightened her to think how easy it would be for him to simply take what he wanted from her.

The elevator came to a gliding stop, and Shane turned Beth to face him. "I meant what I said." He dropped a light kiss on her mouth. "It'll always be your call. Don't forget that."

The elevator doors slid open, and they stepped out into the foyer. Beth came to an abrupt halt when she saw a man standing in front of a door across the room. He had gray hair, cut short, and a handsome face with a strong jaw line and warm brown eyes framed by dark lashes. He was clean shaven, fit, with well-defined biceps and a lean abdomen. He was dressed in worn blue jeans and a black t-shirt that molded itself to his muscular torso.

The man straightened and smiled warmly at Beth. "Good evening, Miss Jamison," he said, with a faint southern drawl.

"Good evening," she said, feeling at a distinct disadvantage. She hadn't been expecting anyone else. She glanced at Shane.

"Sweetheart, this is Daniel Cooper. He shares the penthouse with me. He's my best friend and right-hand man."

"Somebody has to keep an eye on the big boss," Cooper said, winking at Beth.

She liked this man already, and she couldn't help smiling. "It's nice to meet you, Mr. Cooper."

"Just Cooper," the man said.

"Cooper, this is Beth Jamison," Shane said, completing the introductions.

Cooper nodded at Beth. "It's a real pleasure, ma'am," he said. Then he turned his attention to Shane. "The caterers are almost finished setting up."

"Thanks, Cooper," Shane said. He handed Beth's overnight bag to Cooper. "Would you mind putting this in my suite?"

"Sure thing," Cooper said, failing to suppress a knowing grin.

Beth blushed hotly. That man knew she was planning to spend the night!

Cooper opened the door to the apartment for them, and he followed them in. "I'll be in the office if you need me," he said to Shane, then he turned to walk away.

"Cooper."

Cooper stopped and looked back at Shane.

"Hold all calls this evening," Shane said.

"Understood," Cooper said, with a ghost of a smile on his face.

Shane led Beth into an open space of immense proportions, and she found it hard not to gawk. She'd thought her brother's condo in Lincoln Park was fancy, but it was nothing compared to this. There was so much space! She glanced around, finding it hard to take it all in.

As Shane led her further into the room, her gaze went straight to the exterior wall, which was floor to ceiling glass, providing an unimpeded view of Lake Michigan in the distance. The vista was breathtaking, the lake stretching out as far as the eye could see.

Despite its grand size and soaring ceilings, the apartment felt... cozy, thanks to the hardwood floors and the earth tones of the furnishings and area rugs. This apartment was a real home, not just a showcase with an astronomical price tag.

Shane led her to a sofa that sat facing a massive stone hearth. "Would you like to sit down and relax?"

"Yes, thank you." Sitting down right now sounded like a really good idea. She needed a few moments to collect herself.

The sofa faced a wood-burning fireplace, which was currently ablaze. The scent of the burning wood and the sizzle and pop of the flames were familiar and comforting. A large flat-screen television hung above the fireplace on the towering stone hearth that reached up to the high ceiling. The apartment was an unexpected combination of elegance and rustic charm.

"Your apartment is beautiful, Shane," she said.

"I'm glad you like it," he said. "But I can't take credit for it. My sister Sophie is an interior decorator. If I'd decorated the apartment, it would probably look like a bus station."

Beth's laughter was interrupted by the appearance of a striking young woman with a short bob of straight black hair and dark eyes. She looked tidy and professional in her black trousers and black dress shirt and tie. In her hands was a small tray bearing two slender wine glasses filled with a light golden bubbling wine.

"Good evening, Mr. McIntyre, Miss Jamison. I'm Danielle. Robbie and I will be serving you this evening. Would you care for an aperitif? We brought a lovely Prosecco, a Mionetto Rosé, compliments of Mr. Capelli. He thought Miss Jamison would like it."

Shane took both of the wine glasses from the tray and handed one to Beth. "Thank you, Danielle," he said. He took a tasting sip. "It's perfect. Please give Peter my thanks."

"I'll be sure to tell him, sir," Danielle said. "Dinner will be ready to serve in about ten minutes. If you'd care to relax, I'll come get you when we're ready." With a respectful nod, Danielle headed back to the kitchen on the far side of the open floor.

Shane took another sip of the wine. "I told Peter you weren't much of a drinker, so he said he'd send something special for you to try. It's sweet and fruity. I think you'll like it." Shane lifted his glass to hers. "To a memorable evening."

Beth touched her glass to his. "Cheers." She took a sip of the wine.

Shane watched her sip the wine. "If you don't care for it, there are plenty of soft drinks and fruit juices in the bar."

"No, no, this is fine," she said. She took another sip, hoping the wine would help settle her nerves a bit. "It's very good."

Shane picked up the remote control on the coffee table and pressed a couple of buttons. The quiet, soulful strains of old-fashioned delta blues filled the apartment.

Beth smiled. "Muddy Waters. You have good taste in music, Mr. McIntyre."

"You know Muddy Waters?" he said, clearly surprised.

She nodded. "My brother's taken me to a lot of barbecue joints. I know my blues."

"What type of music do you like?"

"I like just about everything," she said, taking another sip of wine.

"Mr. McIntyre, dinner is served," Danielle said.

Shane stood and offered Beth his arm. "Shall we?"

"I would be delighted, sir," she said, standing. "Should we bring the wine?"

He shook his head, setting her wine glass on the coffee table. "There'll be a different wine with the meal. I just need you."

Shane escorted Beth to the dining table where two place settings were laid out at one end. The lights in the apartment dimmed throughout the floor, and an elaborate crystal chandelier hanging over the dining room table came on, casting a golden light over the table setting. There were a half-dozen tapered candles already lit, randomly placed at their end of the table. The setting was beautiful and romantic, and she realized he'd gone to a lot of effort to make the evening perfect.

As soon as they sat, Danielle and a young man with short, curly blond hair came to the table carrying wide, shallow bowls.

"Italian Wedding Soup," Danielle said as she placed a bowl in front of Shane.

Her companion set the other bowl in front of Beth. "I'm Robbie," he said.

Danielle returned to the table with two salads. Robbie carried in a basket of sliced warm bread and another bottle of wine — a Chianti, he said — which he presented to Shane for inspection.

Robbie opened the bottle with a well-practiced flourish. "May I pour you a glass, sir?" Robbie said.

"Please," Shane said.

Robbie poured Shane a small amount of the dark red wine. Shane took a sip and nodded, and then Robbie filled both Shane's glass and Beth's.

Danielle and Robbie remained standing quietly at attention, and Beth wondered if they were going to stand there watching them throughout the entire meal.

Shane tasted the soup. "Excellent, thank you," he said, and Danielle and Robbie visibly relaxed.

Beth tasted the soup as well. "It's delicious."

Danielle smiled at the praise. "Thank you, ma'am."

"We have Pasta Bolognese for the main course and Tiramisu for dessert," Robbie said.

"Thank you both," Shane said. "Please, help yourselves in the kitchen."

That must have been the cue they were waiting for, because the two caterers retreated quietly to the kitchen, leaving Shane and Beth to enjoy their meal in private. Beth was relieved when they left; their attentive hovering was making her feel even more self-conscious than she already was.

When they finished their soup and salad, Danielle and Robbie reappeared as if on cue. Danielle cleared away the dirty dishes while Robbie set out plates of pasta. He poured Shane another glass of the Chianti and asked Beth if she wanted her glass topped off, but she declined and asked for a glass of water instead.

Once again, they were left to enjoy their meals. Beth was blown away by the delicious food and the beautiful table. It was like dining at a 5-star restaurant at home. She'd never experienced anything so extravagant.

"This is an amazing meal, Shane. Thank you."

He smiled. "I'm glad you like it. This is one of the perks of having friends in the restaurant business."

She took a couple bites of the pasta and thought it was delicious. But she was already feeling full. "I'll never be able to eat all of this," she said, looking at the bowl of pasta in front of her. There was enough food in front of her to feed a small army.

"Just eat what you want," he said. "We can have the leftovers tomorrow, if you'd like."

Tomorrow. As in, she was going to be an overnight guest?

And just like that, she lost what was left of her appetite. Butterflies began tumbling wildly in her stomach, and she felt a little queasy. She didn't want to stuff herself if what she thought might happen tonight actually happened. From the way Shane kept looking at her, she suspected that it just might happen. And the thought of being intimate with him made her so nervous it killed her appetite.

"The pasta's delicious, but I'd better stop now," she said, laying down her fork. She picked up a burgundy cloth napkin and discretely wiped her mouth, just in case she was wearing some of the delectable sauce.

He frowned at her plate. "You hardly touched your food. Would you rather have something else?"

"No! The food is wonderful. I'm just — I'm full. I can't eat any more."

She sipped her water while Shane finished his meal. When he laid down his own fork and wiped his mouth, Beth's heart rate kicked up a notch.

"You have to have some dessert, though," he said, giving her the most disarming smile.

As if on cue, Danielle carried in two dishes of Tiramisu and set one down in front of each of them.

"I'd better not," Beth said.

Shane picked up his dessert spoon and scooped up a small bite of his Tiramisu and offered it to Beth. "Just one bite?"

She opened her mouth, and Shane slipped the spoon between her lips. His gaze was fixated on her lips as they closed around the spoon.

"Oh, wow," she moaned, savoring the combination of sweet cream, chocolate, and espresso. The spongy cake literally melted on her tongue. "That's really good."

"Another bite?" he said, offering her another spoonful.

Beth grinned. "All right. Just one more." She opened her mouth, and he fed her another spoonful of the creamy confection.

"You have some cream on your lip," he said, reaching out to wipe her bottom lip with the pad of his thumb. He brought his thumb to his own mouth and licked it, never taking his eyes off her. He was watching her intently, and she was pretty sure it wasn't Italian desserts he had on his mind.

The glitter in his eyes was giving her a bit of desperately needed confidence, and she thought two could play this game. She used her own spoon to scoop up some of her dessert and held it out for him.

Shane reached out and wrapped his fingers around her hand, guiding her spoon to his mouth. He readily opened his mouth and drew the spoon inside, his gaze never once leaving hers. When she pulled the empty spoon back, he leaned forward and kissed her, and they both tasted like sweet cream and chocolaty espresso.

Shane growled as his hand slipped around to the back of her

head, and he held her still for a deeper kiss. "Hmm, dessert as foreplay," he said, shifting in his chair. "I don't think I can take much more. I'll tell the caterers we're finished." He rose from the table. "We can save the leftovers for tomorrow unless Cooper eats it all in the night. How's that?"

Beth nodded, and her nerves went into a sudden tailspin. Her face must have given her away because Shane looked down at her with a concerned expression. She'd never been any good at hiding her emotions.

"Relax, sweetheart," he said, reaching down to gently touch her face. "No pressure, remember?" He pulled her chair back from the table. "Why don't you go sit by the fire and relax?" he suggested. "I'll show Danielle and Robbie out."

Beth stood. "Thank you for a wonderful dinner," she said. "And please thank Danielle and Robbie for me."

"You're welcome, and I will." Shane leaned forward and planted a chaste kiss on her lips. "Go sit down before you fall down. I'll join you in a few minutes."

Beth headed back to the sofa, only too happy to escape. She sat in front of the fire, which was a soothing distraction. She leaned her head back on the sofa cushions and closed her eyes, focusing on the soft music coming through the sound system. She could just make out hearing Shane speaking with the caterers, thanking them as he walked them to the door.

A few minutes later, she felt the sofa cushions dip beside her as he joined her.

"They're gone," he said.

She opened her eyes and looked at Shane. He'd loosened his tie and unbuttoned the top button of his shirt.

"Are you all right?" he said.

She nodded. "I'm fine."

"You're very quiet."

She chuckled. "I think I'm in a 5-star coma."

He smiled. "I hope you mean that in a good way."

"I do," she said. "The food was amazing, especially the dessert."

Shane picked up the remote control and pressed a couple buttons. The soft blues segued into big band, and the air was filled with the unmistakable vocals of Frank Sinatra telling some lucky lady he had a crush on her.

Shane stood and offered Beth his hand. "Dance with me."

Despite the fact that her heart immediately took off at a gallop, she took Shane's hand and let him pull her up and lead her to an open area near the glass wall. She looked out at the early night sky, which was now a light shade of indigo. Out on the lake, lights from the chartered cruises had begun to sparkle like diamonds, and the stars twinkled faintly overhead in the clear night sky.

Shane pulled Beth into his arms.

"I'm not very good at this," she said, trying to follow his subtle movements without stepping on him.

"It's okay. Just relax and follow my lead."

Shane proved to be an excellent dancer, guiding her smoothly in sync with the music. His hand nearly engulfed hers, while his other arm wrapped around her waist, holding her close. She leaned into him, taking pleasure in his clean, masculine scent.

"Dancing is just an excuse to hold you, you know," he whispered in her ear.

His voice was low and intimate, and she shivered.

The music morphed to a favorite of hers as Sinatra crooned about some lovely lady flying him to the moon. Their pace slowed until they were practically standing still, simply holding each other. Shane tipped her face up toward his and kissed her gently. Then he pulled back and gazed down questioningly.

Beth lost herself in his gaze, in the heat and desire she saw there. This close, she could see tiny flecks of pale gold in his irises. She also saw a hunger that aroused her as much as it unnerved her.

"Will you stay with me tonight, Beth?" he said. His hand came up to cradle one side of her face, his thumb brushing her lower lip. "It's okay if you're not ready — "

She felt like a champagne bubble about to burst. All she knew was that she wanted this. For once in her life, she wanted to let go and experience the heat and the passion that she'd been living without. Before she could chicken out, she took a deep breath and stepped right off the cliff. "I'll stay. Yes."

15

Beth didn't remember how she got there, but all of a sudden she was standing in front of a closed door at the end of a long hallway. Shane opened the door, and she walked inside.

She was expecting a bedroom, of course, and a really nice one based on what she'd seen so far of the rest of the apartment, but this wasn't a bedroom by any stretch of the imagination. It was an entire suite of its own, an apartment within an apartment, with a sleeping area, a living and entertainment area, and a small gourmet kitchen and bar.

It was a masculine space, decorated in warm browns and blues, as cozy as the main room of the penthouse. On the hardwood floors were a number of large area rugs in browns, blues, and creams positioned about the room.

The ceilings were high in here, too, framed in crown molding with recessed lighting throughout, and the exterior wall was also glass from floor to ceiling, providing a panoramic view of the lake to the left and the city to the right. The nighttime scenery was magical, all flickering lights and towering glass, steel, and stone buildings. Long chocolate-brown drapes hung from rods over the windows that they could be pulled shut to block out the light when needed.

"Make yourself at home," Shane said, loosening his tie. "I'm going to lose the tie and jacket."

Shane disappeared through an open door, which Beth assumed led to a closet. She wandered around the suite and quickly discovered her overnight bag perched on a padded bench at the foot of a huge bed. She grabbed her toiletries from her bag and went in search of the bathroom to freshen up.

The en-suite bathroom turned out to be just as impressive as the rest of the apartment. The floor was brown travertine marble with flecks of gold. The walls were slate gray stone, and there was a stone hearth at the far side of the room. A fireplace in the bathroom? Really?

In addition to the large walk-in shower, there was also a hot tub big enough for half a dozen people. There were two private toilet stalls in the bathroom and a long marble counter with two sinks and a full-length mirror. Built-in cabinetry provided plenty of storage for linens and toiletries.

"I could live in here," she said, taking in the spacious and elegant space.

After making quick use of the facilities and brushing her teeth, she went in search of Shane and found him standing barefoot at the wet bar. He was dressed in his trousers and shirt. The top two buttons of his shirt were undone, and all she could think about was undoing the rest of them to discover what was underneath.

He turned to her and smiled. "Would you like a drink?"

"I've already had almost two glasses of wine, which is two glasses more than I usually drink. I'd better not."

"A little bit of whisky probably wouldn't hurt," he said. "It might help you relax."

"Do you think so?" She'd never had hard liquor before, but if it might help her relax, she was game to try it.

He nodded. "It's worth a try. Maybe then we could talk."

Talk? The irony wasn't lost on Beth. She was trying to get up the nerve to have sex with him, and he wanted to talk? "Talk about what?"

"You said you'd tell me about what happened to you. Maybe

we should start there."

She stepped back. "Oh, no," she said, shaking her head. "No."

Beth walked away from him and found herself standing in front of the glass wall looking out at an inky night sky. Feeling suddenly chilled to the bone, she rubbed her bare arms in a futile attempt to warm herself.

Shane came up behind her and placed his hands on her arms, stroking her. "You're shaking."

"I'm nervous," she admitted. And wasn't that a huge understatement. She knew she should tell him she was in over her head, but she couldn't bring herself to do it. She'd just have to muddle through the best she could. "It's been a while.... And it didn't go well."

His warm hands on her bare arms felt so good, she moaned. When she looked up, she saw his reflection in the glass in front of her.

"Beth, you panicked on me last night. I don't want to make the same mistake twice. If you confide in me, I'll be better prepared."

She shook her head. "No."

"Sweetheart, you said someone hurt you once. The last thing I want to do is hurt you, but if I don't know what happened — "

"No!" She moved out of his reach. "If I tell you, then tonight won't happen." He was right, but she also knew she'd be a wreck if she had to relive that nightmare. Already she was feeling panicked just thinking about it.

"Take your pick!" she said, fear and frustration taking over. "What do you want? Sex or my traumatic life story? But you can't have both. I can't handle both in one night." Her heart was thundering painfully.

Shane rubbed a hand over his face, clearly struggling with competing desires. He sighed. "Beth."

He had a way of speaking that grounded her, both commanding and comforting at the same time. When he said her name like that, in that steadying tone, her mounting anxiety simply deflated.

"Please, not tonight," she said, her voice no more than a whisper. She wrapped her arms around her torso. "I don't want to talk about it. I promise I will, soon, just not tonight. I want tonight to happen."

"It will happen," he said, coming toward her. He took her in his arms. "I just don't want to make any mistakes, Beth."

She looked up into his face. "On second thought, I will have that drink."

He looked at her, and for a moment she thought he was going to say no.

"All right," he finally said. He ran his hand through his hair and sighed. "But if I fuck this up, just remember who made the ultimatum here. It wasn't me."

"If anyone messes up tonight, it won't be you," she said.

He tucked a tendril of her hair behind her ear. "I promised I wouldn't let you run, remember?" He placed a gentle kiss on her lips, and then he took her hand and led her to the living area. "Come."

Shane sat Beth down on a soft leather sofa that stood facing yet another wood-burning stone hearth. He walked to the wet bar and pulled two tumblers from an overhead cupboard, along with a bottle of amber-colored liquor. Beth watched as he poured a scant half-inch of the liquor into one glass and a more generous amount into the other. Then he opened a bottle of spring water and added a dash to each glass.

"Have you ever had whisky?" he asked, picking up both glasses and gently swirling them.

"No."

He sat on the coffee table facing Beth and handed her the glass with the smaller amount of liquor in it.

After peering into the glass, she sniffed it and made a face.

"Sip it slowly," he cautioned her.

She took a hesitant sip of her drink and immediately began a violent coughing fit as the liquor burned the back of her throat on its way down. "You drink this on purpose?"

Shane laughed. "Yes." He took a sip of his drink. "I guess it's an acquired taste."

Beth took another sip, and this one burned just as badly. She swallowed with a scowl. "I don't think I've acquired it." She coughed again, gasping. "My throat's on fire."

He smiled at her. "You don't have to finish it, sweetheart," he said, reaching for her glass.

"No, I'll finish it." She looked dubiously at her glass. "I'm going to need it."

Shane set his glass down on the coffee table and stood. "Hold on." He retrieved a small bottle of Coke from the fridge and brought it and the bottle of whisky back.

"This will help," he said, filling her small glass with Coke. Then he poured himself a second shot of whisky, neat, and set the bottle on the coffee table.

Beth took a sip of her whisky and Coke. "That's much better." She could still taste a hint of the whisky, but it was greatly tempered by the sweetness of the soft drink. It didn't burn nearly as badly when it went down.

Shane chuckled, shaking his head. "I just mixed a 21-year-old Scotch with a soft drink."

She froze. "Is that bad?"

He savored a sip of his two-grand a bottle whisky and swallowed. "No, sweetheart," he said, smiling at her. "It's fine."

Beth returned his smile, feeling like her heart was being squeezed in her chest. He amazed her with his gentleness and patience. She hadn't known him very long, and already she trusted him more than she'd ever trusted anyone outside her family and Gabrielle. God, she wanted this to happen.

"Don't let me run," she said quietly.

Shane's gaze darkened as he knocked back the rest of his whisky. "I won't," he said in a gruff voice, wincing at the burn.

She laughed. "I thought you said to sip it."

"I'm way past sipping now."

Shane set his empty glass on the coffee table and leaned forward, cupping the back of Beth's head with his broad palm. He pulled her forward, and they met halfway. When his mouth came down on hers, it was hot and hungry. Their tongues clashed, and she tasted the sweetness of the Coke, the pungency of the whisky, and Shane. His mouth devoured hers hungrily. She thought she must be feeling the effects of the whisky now because her belly warmed, and she began to tingle all over.

"Lights, fifty percent," he said, and the room dimmed, leaving them in a cozy, twilight setting. He looked at her. "You said earlier that your previous attempts at intimacy didn't go well."

She nodded. *Oh, crap.* Her body was finally loosening up nicely and starting to buzz, and he wanted to talk?

"Tell me what happened," he said.

She attempted to pull back, wanting to put some distance between them, but he held her fast with a hand on the back of her head.

"I need you to tell me, Beth," he said, looking her directly in the eye. "Why didn't they go well? What went wrong?"

Mortified, she felt her face burn. She *so* didn't want to talk about this right now. It might ruin any chance she had of getting through the night.

"Beth, please," he said. "If you want this to turn out differently, you have to talk to me. I sure as hell don't want to make the same mistakes someone else made."

"I know," she said, frustrated. "It's just hard to talk about."

He watched her expectantly, waiting for an answer. Beth figured they would be here all night if she didn't tell him what he wanted to know.

"Okay, fine. I'll tell you. But can I have more whisky first?" She figured a little more of that fire in her belly couldn't hurt.

He didn't look overly happy about it, but he acquiesced. "Just a little bit." He poured another half-inch of whisky into her glass and added a generous amount of Coke.

She peered into her glass, frowning. "That wasn't very much whisky."

"It's enough," he said. "The goal is to help you relax, not get you drunk."

Copying him, she knocked back her drink in one swallow. Her eyes watered from the combination of the whisky and the carbonation of the soft drink.

"Jesus, Beth!" Shane took the glass from her and set it next to his on the coffee table.

They both started laughing.

Shane couldn't help himself. He leaned forward and kissed her, his lips clinging to hers. "Is the whisky helping?"

"I think so," she said, losing herself in his beautiful eyes. "I can't feel my toes anymore."

ꙮ 16

Shane moved to the sofa and hauled Beth onto his lap and turned her so that she was sitting sideways. He removed her sandals and tucked her bare feet up on the sofa cushions. "Now, talk to me."

When she didn't say anything, he made a frustrated noise that sounded an awful lot like a growl to her.

"You'd better start talking, Beth, unless you're ready to experience your first spanking."

She knew from the tone of his voice that he was just kidding about the spanking. Still, the idea of lying bare-bottom across his lap made her tingle from head to toe — and that had nothing to do with the whisky. For a moment, she thought about simply calling his bluff and taking him up on his offer.

She could tell from his resolute expression that he wasn't going to let her distract him, so she took a deep breath and let the words pour out of her. "I panic when I'm pinned down."

His entire body tensed, but his voice was calm when he said, "Go on."

"I can't bear to be pinned down or restrained. When I tried to have sex before, and... he was on top...." She shuddered. It was such a painful memory, and she'd been so humiliated.

"Jesus, sweetheart," he said, his lips in her hair. One of his hands came up and rubbed her back while his other arm settled around her waist. After a long pause, he said, "Have you ever tried being on top?"

"No."

"Would you be willing to try that?"

She chuckled nervously. "I'll try anything."

"Okay. What about the lights? Tell me about the lights."

"I'm afraid of the dark," she admitted, feeling ridiculous. Apparently, the whisky was loosening her tongue as well as warming her belly. *Good grief! What 24-year-old is afraid of the dark?*

But she figured she might as well lay it all out there, expose her dirty little secrets now and get it over with. He'd find it all out eventually, if he hung in there long enough.

"Can you tell me why?"

His voice was so gentle, so non-judgmental, it made her want to cry. She could feel the panic beginning to circle around her, like a vulture searching for easy prey, ready to swoop in and consume her at its first opportunity.

"I don't want to talk anymore, Shane." Her voice was small and tinged with defeat. She was trying so desperately to hold back the tears and tamp down the fear.

He was silent for a long moment. "All right. That's enough for now."

Shane helped Beth to her feet and led her by the hand to the bed. "Sit," he said.

The bed was clearly the focal piece in the room. It had a dark chocolate brown upholstered headboard and a pair of mahogany nightstands, one on each side of the bed, each holding a lamp. Like the rest of the room, the bed was decorated in neutrals. The comforter was brown, and the pillows echoed the browns and blue theme. A padded bench stood at the foot of the bed. Beneath the bed was a large plush rug in the same shade of dark chocolate. The wall behind the bed had been made from vintage red bricks, which added to the industrial-chic feel of the decor.

Beth climbed up on the high bed and sat watching Shane

warily. He seemed hesitant all of a sudden, and she was afraid he was going to change his mind about sex. Or worse yet, he might decide she was simply too much effort. She knew without a doubt that he never had to work this hard to get laid.

The fear that he was on the verge of changing his mind gave her the motivation to act. She slipped off the bed and walked toward him. "I want to do this, Shane."

When he didn't make a move toward her, she reached for the placket of his shirt and started unbuttoning it from the top down. Shane stood passively, watching her nimble fingers release each button. He did nothing to help her, and yet he didn't stop her either. Once she had the shirt unbuttoned, she pushed it off his broad shoulders and watched it slip to the rug at their feet.

As her eyes swept over his chest, her breath hitched in her throat, and she swallowed. His chest was ... beautiful. All sculpted muscles and hard planes, covered with a light dusting of brown hair that converged into a happy trail that disappeared beneath the waistband of his trousers. There were numerous scars on his chest, old and faded, undoubtedly souvenirs from his time in the military, but they only added to his attractiveness.

She unbuckled his belt and pulled it from his trousers, letting it drop to the rug with a dull thud.

His lips twitched, and he raised an eyebrow at her as if to say, Okay, now what? That little bit of encouragement was all she needed to reach for the button on his trousers. Damn, she should have insisted on having more whisky; this probably would've been a lot easier. As it was, she couldn't believe this beautiful man was just standing here, letting her undress him.

After unbuttoning his trousers, she pulled his zipper down gingerly. Shane let his trousers drop to the floor, and her gazed locked onto the magnificent erection tenting the material of his black boxers.

"You've come this far," he said, his voice suddenly rough as gravel. "For God's sake, don't stop now."

Beth felt her face go up in flames, but she wasn't about to

stop. She was pretty sure he was testing her, to make sure this was really something she wanted. Surprisingly, she found that she liked the feeling of control. Shane was letting her call the shots, and she liked it.

She took hold of the waistband of his shorts and eased it carefully over his erection.

"It won't break, you know," he said, chuckling. He helped just a little bit, just to speed things along. And then his shorts joined the rest of his clothing on the rug.

Beth had barely gotten a glimpse of his erection before he reached around her and knocked the throw pillows off the bed. He yanked the comforter and top sheet to the foot of the bed.

"My turn," he said. "Turn around." He motioned with his finger.

She turned her back to Shane, and he slowly unzipped her dress and pushed it off her shoulders. He caught it before it hit the floor and draped it neatly over the bench.

Beth felt chilled standing there in only her bra and half-slip. Her loose updo exposed the graceful curve of her neck, and Shane touched the small indent at the base of her skull with his index finger and dragged his finger down the center of her back. She shivered at his touch. Her slip soon joined her dress on the bench. And then she felt his warm fingers brush her skin as he unclasped her bra. He peeled her bra off slowly, and it, too, ended up on the bench.

"Turn around, Beth," he said, his voice low and rough.

As she turned to face him, her hands came up to cover her bare breasts. It was an automatic reflex. She'd always been self-conscious about her body.

Shane sat on the edge of the bed, less than a foot from her, and he seemed perfectly comfortable in his bare skin. He didn't seem the slightest bit embarrassed, and why should he? His body was a work of art. She glanced down at his erection, which was defying gravity as it strained eagerly upward. His penis was long and thick, flushed a deep, ruddy color in arousal. She forced herself to drag her gaze away from his erection and noticed that he was watching her.

"Put your hands down, sweetheart," he said, gently tugging her hands down to her sides. "There's no need to hide your body from me."

She dropped her arms and looked away, hating the feeling of being on display. She closed her eyes. When she felt Shane's finger trace the shape of her collar bone, from her left shoulder across to her right, she shivered.

"Are you cold?" he asked.

"No."

"Beth, look at me," he said quietly.

She shook her head.

His finger moved slowly down the center of her chest, following the valley between her breasts, down to her belly button where it traced a lazy circle around the little indentation. "I wish you could see yourself the way I see you," he said. "There isn't a single thing I would change."

Beth's eyes remained resolutely closed as his finger trailed back up her abdomen. His hand covered her left breast. "Your heart is pounding. So is mine. Here, feel."

He took her hand and placed it over his heart so she could feel for herself. "See? You're not the only one affected here," he said. "Feel what you do to me."

Beth opened her eyes and met his gaze, stunned by the mix of sincerity and hunger she saw in his eyes.

"You have the most beautiful skin I've ever seen," he said almost reverently, as he traced the meandering path of a fine blue vein down to her left breast. "It's almost translucent." His index finger slowly made its way to her nipple where it made a circle around her dusky pink areola. Her nipple puckered instantly, and she trembled.

He teased the tight little bud, brushing it lightly with the pad of his finger. Then he leaned forward and sucked her nipple into his mouth. When his lips closed over the plush pink tip and he sucked on her flesh, she felt a corresponding tug low in her belly. A liquid warmth swept through her in response to his wet pulls on her nipple. She grabbed his shoulders to steady herself.

As Shane continued to suck on her, his hands pulled her panties past the curves of her buttocks and down her long legs. When he released her breast and pulled back to look at her, she swayed toward him, and he caught her. He studied her body with blatant interest, finally reaching down and sifting a fingertip through the tuft of blond curls between her legs. He pressed the tip of his finger between her plump lips and found what he was looking for.

At the feel of his fingertip circling her slick clitoris, she jumped.

"I want you in my bed," he said in a hoarse voice. He scooted back on the bed, leaning against the headboard to make room for her. He sat watching her, waiting for her to take that last step.

She stood there trembling, wishing he hadn't left the decision up to her.

He opened the top drawer of the nightstand on his side of the bed and pulled out a strip of condoms, which he laid on top of the stand. He smiled at her. "I've been imagining you here in my bed for days now."

She took in the sight of him, the taut surfaces of his body, the ridges and planes of his tanned body. His erection stood straight up as if beckoning her. His suggestion that she be on top came back to her, and she couldn't help imagining herself climbing on top of him and straddling his hips, taking his erection into her body. Her belly quivered at the thought. Everything she wanted was right there in front of her, if only she had the courage to reach out and take it.

Shane patted the mattress. She clambered onto the high bed, feeling far from graceful, and knelt beside him. He reached behind her head to free her hair, letting it fall past her shoulders in soft, loose waves. He fingered her hair as it settled around her shoulders.

"I've wanted you since the first night I saw you at Clancy's. I haven't been able to think about much else," he admitted. "I've had a hell of a time concentrating at work. My coworkers all think I've lost my mind."

"I wanted to call you that first night," she admitted, looking at him. "I couldn't sleep for thinking about it. Every time I closed my eyes, I saw you."

"I didn't sleep much that night either." He tucked a strand of her hair behind her ear. "And I hope I won't be sleeping much tonight."

He held out his hand, silently beseeching her to take it. He was going to make her choose, she realized. She felt a cool draft of air on her bare skin, and she longed to press up against him and share in the warmth of his body.

She reached out and took his hand, and he gently pulled her close, laying her down beside him on the bed. Holding her gaze, he leaned over and lowered his mouth to hers, his lips gently settling on hers. He took his time kissing her, letting her get used to the feel of his mouth on hers. He coaxed her, teased her, tasted her. He let her taste him. His soft, firm lips eased hers open, and his tongue slipped inside, finding hers and gently stroking it.

"God, I want you," he groaned into her mouth.

Her hands came up and gripped his biceps, her fingers flexing on his muscles. She was shocked to realize he was shaking, too.

"Are you sure?" he said.

She squeezed his arms, loving the rock hard feel of his muscles beneath her fingers. "Yes. I want this."

17

Take it slow. And for God's sake, don't scare her.

The words were a mantra playing over and over in Shane's head. His balls had been aching for the better part of a week, and his cock was so hard it was well past the point of pain. He wanted desperately to spread her legs and sink balls deep inside her and ride her until he couldn't remember his own name. But he sure as hell couldn't do that. He had to get their first night together right. He wanted her to feel comfortable with him. He wanted her to feel safe. Damn it, he wanted her to want him as badly as he wanted her.

His mouth dipped down to hers once more, unable to resist kissing her. Her mouth was like heaven, silky and sweet, and he couldn't get enough. When she opened her mouth, he slipped his tongue inside and explored every inch of her. The soft sounds she made when his tongue stroked hers ratcheted him up that much higher. He honestly didn't know how much more he could take. The past week had been one long, extended session of foreplay. He wrapped her in his arms and held her against him, reveling in the feel of her soft breasts pressed against his chest.

All he could think about was getting inside her. He knew he should slow it down, but that was easier said than done at this point. He was about at the end of his rope.

He'd be as careful with her as he could. He knew taking his cock could be a challenge, so he'd give her time to get used to him. He nudged her legs apart with his knee and slipped one hand between her thighs. He gently drew his finger up the seam of her sex, skimming through her blond curls. Her entire body trembled when his finger sunk in, dipping into her hot core. She was so tight, her tissues clung to his finger. The thought of thrusting his cock through those tight, wet tissues almost made him lose it then and there.

"God, you're so wet," he groaned. Realizing how wet she was made his cock just that much harder, and the ache just that much worse. He could smell her arousal now, hot and earthy, and he wanted to taste her again. He wanted her scent, her taste, on his tongue. He scooted down her torso, his hands grasping her thighs and pushing them gently apart as he made room to settle between them.

"Shane?"

Her voice was barely audible over the roaring in his ears. Still, he picked up on the uncertainty in her tone. "Shh, it's okay," he said. "Just relax."

His tongue swiped along the seam of her folds, pushing past her swollen tissues, and he groaned when the taste of her hit his tongue. She was warm and wet, her earthy scent like an aphrodisiac. His tongue lashed her clitoris, and he was determined to drive her as crazy as he was. When he latched onto her clit with his lips, her hips bowed up off the bed.

She gasped, and then her fingers were in his hair, tugging the strands with urgent desperation. His long index finger gently pushed back inside her and began stroking the front wall of her channel. He could tell from her breathing and the loud, keening sounds she made that she was close.

"Shane!" she gasped, pulling hard on his hair. She stiffened under him, her body tensing as she cried out.

The force of her orgasm and the sound of her cries sent him into sheer overdrive. He surged up over her body, his mouth covering hers hungrily to drink in her sweet cries. Her eyes were closed tightly, and she whimpered through the residual waves of her orgasm.

All he could think about now was getting inside her. He wedged his hips into the open vee of her thighs and rocked himself against her heat, coating the fat head of his cock with her sweet wetness. He was desperate to feel her wet heat surrounding him, squeezing him, drawing him deep inside.

Condom! Damn it!

As he reached for a condom, he felt the first weak blow against his chest. He was so completely wrapped up in the demands of his body that it took him a moment to register the fact that she was pushing against his shoulders.

He glanced at her face, shocked at the utter panic he saw in her wide eyes. She shoved frantically at his shoulders, but he was too heavy for her to move. His brain started to come back online when he saw the tears streaming down her cheeks. Fuck!

"Beth?"

"No! *No no no no no!*" she wailed, pushing in vain to dislodge him. "Get off of me! *Get off! Get off!*"

He rolled off her, and she scrambled off the bed in a frenzy, crouching beside the bed as if to hide her naked body from him.

"Shit, Beth, I'm sorry!" He moved in her direction, but she scooted back blindly, falling on her bottom. Then she lunged to her feet and turned to run.

"Sweetheart, wait!" He went after her, but she turned back to face him and held up her hands beseechingly, as if to ward him off.

"No!" she sobbed, tears flowing freely now as she backed away from him. "I can't! I'm sorry! I can't do this!" She kept moving back, putting more and more distance between them. "I have to go now. I have to go!"

The pain of seeing her cringe from him was like a knife twisting in his gut. He'd done this to her! He'd fucking done this! How could he have been so careless?

He slowed his movements and approached her cautiously. "Easy, Beth," he said, his voice low and even. He held out one hand to her. "It's okay, sweetheart."

"It's not okay!" she cried. She hit the back of the sofa and couldn't go any farther. Tears streamed down her face as she was wracked with sobs. "I can't do this, Shane. I just can't!"

"You don't have to, baby." Her pleading gutted him. That, and the searing guilt that choked him, was more than he could bear. He sank to his knees in front of her, utterly devastated by what he'd done to her. To see such a beautiful, vibrant young woman reduced to pleading shook him to the core. Someone had once taken her free will and left her bound and gagged on a dirt floor. He thought of that innocent little girl who'd lain scared and alone in the dark for so many hours, and he felt sick.

Shane bowed his head, wondering how the hell he could have messed up so badly. When he finally looked up at her again, he found her standing frozen in place, visibly shaking, her wide eyes wet with tears. She looked like she was about to collapse at any moment. He went back for his discarded shirt and held it out to her as a peace offering.

"Let me put this on you, baby. Please. You're shaking."

He took a few steps in her direction, and her hands came up to cover her breasts. At that moment, Shane wanted to fucking kill Howard Kline. He vowed there and then that, one way or another, he'd end that bastard for what he'd done to this girl.

The sobbing had stopped, but she was still shaking. "I shouldn't have come."

The despair in her voice broke his heart.

He moved closer, holding the shirt in front of him like a shield. The last thing she needed right now was to see his flaccid dick. He needed to get some pants on ASAP.

"Let me cover you up, sweetheart," he said, coaxing her. "You're shaking."

When he was within arm's reach of her, he draped the shirt around her back and slipped her arms into the sleeves. His shirt was huge on her, the tails falling almost to her knees and the cuffs dangling past her hands. He buttoned the shirt quickly, and then he rolled the cuffs up past her wrists.

"That's better," he said, moving to her side so he could put a comforting arm around her trembling shoulders. "Come sit down on the bed, before you fall down."

He tried to lead her back to the bed, but when they got close, she pulled away from him and began frantically grabbing her clothes off the bench.

"What are you doing, Beth?"

"I'm getting dressed," she said, her voice shaky. Holding the wadded up clothing in her arms, she started for the bathroom.

His brow furrowed. He knew she was distraught, and she had every right to be. But he couldn't let her leave now, not like this. If she left now, she'd never be able to come back from this. "Why are you getting dressed? You can wear my shirt."

She looked back at him, her expression stricken. "I'm leaving. I'll call a cab."

Shane grabbed a pair of sweats out of a dresser drawer and hastily pulled them on, trying to think fast. If she left now, he might never see her again, and he couldn't let that happen. "I thought you were sleeping over. It's kind of late to be going home now."

She looked at him like he was a complete dimwit. "I can't do this, Shane," she said as if stating the obvious. "I'm sorry. I tried, but I can't."

"That was sex, Beth," he said. "I'm talking about sleeping over. They're two very different things."

She frowned at him. "You want me to stay anyway? To sleep with you? Just sleep?"

"Yes." He ran his fingers through his hair. "Please don't leave. I won't touch you, I promise. Just stay the night. I want to wake up with you in the morning, have breakfast with you. We can find something to do together tomorrow."

Shane approached her slowly and took the bundle of clothes from her. He returned her clothes to the bench at the foot of the bed, and then he brought her hands to his mouth and kissed them. "I'm really sorry, Beth."

Her brow furrowed, and she shook her head. "You didn't do

anything wrong."

"Yes, I did. I lost my damned head, and I scared you. Please, don't leave now. Let me make it up to you."

She looked at him warily. "I should go."

"It's late, and you're exhausted. You need sleep. That's all, just sleep. Come lie down with me and rest."

She stared at him, far from convinced that sleeping together was a good idea.

"Please," he said. "It's late and you're tired. Come lie down."

He pulled her gently by the hand to the bed. He was relieved when she lay down beside him, although she was careful to keep far enough away from him that there wasn't any risk of them touching. He straightened the bedding and covered them both.

She watched him, her gaze wary.

He grabbed a tissue from off his nightstand and wiped her cheeks. Then he brushed her hair back from her face. "Try to sleep."

Without a word, she turned onto her side, facing away from him.

Shane sighed. "Lights, thirty percent." He lay on his side facing her and watched her for a long time as she lay perfectly still. He could tell from the stiffness of her posture that she wasn't asleep.

She was shutting him out, and he fucking well deserved it.

⟲ 18

Beth lay still, wide awake and unable to block out the shame and embarrassment swamping her. It wasn't surprising, what had happened. It had happened to her every time before. Why had she expected it to be any different this time?

The bedroom was eerily quiet, although she knew without looking that Shane wasn't sleep either. Even with her eyes closed, she could feel the weight of his gaze on her. She tried not to think about what must be going through his mind. She'd flipped out on him like a total nut job, and he was probably wondering how he'd gotten involved with someone like her. Her first boyfriend's parting words came back to her: *You're such a fucking nut job!*

The panic eventually receded, only to be replaced with sorrow. Secretly, she was glad he'd asked her to stay the rest of the night. She hadn't really wanted to go, but she'd been afraid to stay. She hadn't wanted this night to be another one of her failures. She'd wanted him! She really had. She still did. The idea of running away from this was abhorrent.

The bedding rustled softly as he shifted behind her on the bed, and she thought he'd probably rolled to his back. She had no idea how long they'd been lying there, both pretending to be asleep, but she figured he was tired of watching her.

She turned to look back at him and saw that he was indeed

lying on his back. His hands were clasped on his abdomen, and he was staring at the ceiling, his jaw clenched and his lips flat.

Even after all the drama, looking at him still gave her butterflies. She'd never wanted someone so much in her life. If she couldn't do this with him, then she'd never be able to do it with anyone. And she'd be damned if she'd let some monster like Howard Kline steal this part of her life from her.

She rolled over and faced him, laying her hand on his chest. "I'm sorry, Shane," she said in a quiet voice.

When he looked at her, the mixture of sadness and resignation in his expression made her throat tighten painfully.

He swallowed hard and laid his hand on hers. "God, please don't apologize. You have nothing to be sorry for. I'm the one who fucked up. I'm the one who's sorry."

She rose up on her elbow and faced him. "I don't want to be like this," she said, her eyes tearing up. Her throat was so tight, it hurt to speak. "Can we try again?"

Shane closed his eyes, his expression pained, and Beth wondered if it was too late.

"You mentioned me being on top," she said. "Maybe that would help. I want to try again, but I'd understand if you don't want to."

He squeezed her hand. "It's not that I don't want to try again, Beth," he said. "I do. Believe me, I do."

"But?" she said, because there was definitely a *but* in his voice.

"I — I don't want to put you through that again."

"Can we try? Please?"

He looked at her, indecision warring on his face.

Her hand slipped out from under his and traveled down his body until she found his penis lying soft between his legs. Of course, he'd lost his erection. What did she expect, after all the ugly drama?

Shane gently removed her hand from his groin and returned it to his chest. "It's not permanent," he said, smiling at her.

She could tell from his expression that he wasn't willing to risk another catastrophe that night, so she shoved her fears away and took another leap of faith. She leaned forward and kissed him.

It was the first time she'd initiated a kiss with him, and she felt awkward doing it. Her lips moved hesitantly over his, and she hoped he would take over. At first he lay unresponsive, but when she licked the seam of his lips, his mouth opened beneath hers with a groan, and then he was lifting his mouth to meet hers, his lips clinging hungrily to hers.

When his hand cupped the back of her head, his fingers threading through her hair, she sighed with relief. *Thank god!*

He grabbed her hand and brought it back down to his penis, which was clearly back in the game, stirring and swelling rapidly. "Feel what you do to me," he said as he pressed her hand to his erection. His penis continued to stiffen, bucking beneath her fingers as he swelled. She gripped him through the sheet, and he growled deep in his throat.

Shane reached between her legs and touched her sex, testing her readiness, relieved to find her wet. "Straddle me," he said, ripping the sheet back.

Beth rose up on her knees and let him guide her onto his hips.

"How about we lose the shirt?" he said, unbuttoning the shirt he'd put on her earlier.

She blushed hotly, but nodded, as he undid the last button, baring her chest to his greedy gaze. When the shirt slipped off her shoulders, exposing her breasts, Shane grabbed it and tossed it to the floor. His erection had recovered fully and was once more defying gravity as it stood firm and demanding. He grasped her bottom and pulled her closer so that her sex was nestled right up against the thick root of his cock.

She looked down, captivated by the sight of her pale curls meshed with his dark, wiry hair.

"You're in control," Shane said, his eyes riveted to their sexes. "Take it at your own pace. If you want to stop at any time, just say so."

His heart hammered in his chest when he felt her trembling thighs grip his hips. He hoped like hell this would work, because he couldn't bear to see her fall apart again. Having her on top and in control was the only strategy he could come up with, other than simply getting her drunk, which he couldn't bring himself to do.

He reached between her open thighs and cupped her with his fingers, letting her get used to the feel of him touching her there. When she didn't baulk at that, he slipped a finger between her folds and began a slow exploration of her sex, reveling in her silky wetness.

When he pressed the pad of his thumb against her clitoris, Beth made an inarticulate sound, part groan and part cry. She rose up on her knees when his thumb began to work on her.

"Try to relax, sweetheart. Let me make this good for you."

Never in his life had Shane felt such anxiety in bed. He wanted this to be a good experience for her, the beginning of a relationship for the two of them. It wasn't just sex for him, and he knew it would never be just sex for her. Slowly and steadily, he massaged her clitoris, pressing and stroking, and he smiled when he felt her begin to relax and sink back down onto his thighs.

He kept up the stroking, ratcheting up the pressure, until he felt the muscles in her thighs tensing. But he didn't want her to come just yet. There was a hell of a lot more pleasure he could give her in the build-up to it. So he just kept stroking, alternately increasing and decreasing the pressure to keep her orgasm in limbo.

Beth's eyes drifted shut, and she started squirming against his touch, making soft whimpering sounds that made his cock even harder, if that was possible. Her thighs moved restlessly, and her hips began to rise and press against his hand as she sought to increase the pressure there. He slipped a finger inside her hot, flushed core.

"My God, you're so tight," he grated, loving the feel of her sex clinging to his finger. Her tightness was both a blessing and a curse. Being inside her was going to blow his mind — he already knew that. But his length and girth would make it harder for her to accept him comfortably.

She was slick with arousal, which gave him some reassurance. When her breathing became quick and shallow and her eyes widened in surprise, he knew she was close, and he backed off again.

With a frustrated cry, Beth glared at him, and that made him smile.

"Soon, sweetheart," he promised, knowing it would have to be soon. He was already so hard he hurt, and his balls were aching with the need to come. He knew he wouldn't be able to hold out much longer. "I want to make sure you're ready."

"I am ready," she groaned, pushing herself against his fingers, trying to find that wonderful pressure again.

Shane bathed her sex with her body's own wetness, priming her, making sure she was ready to take him. He knew she was in for some discomfort. There was no help for that. But he would gladly do whatever he could to minimize any pain she might feel.

He brought his thumb to his mouth and sucked off her juices, moaning with satisfaction. Then he ripped open a condom packet with his teeth and quickly sheathed himself.

"Rise up on your knees," he said, grasping her hips. She obeyed. He sat up and kissed her mouth, then dipped his head down and kissed the tip of each breast. "Now scoot closer." With his hands on her hips, he coaxed her forward on her knees. "Up and over me."

She did as he directed, but hesitated when she felt the broad head of his cock nudging against her opening. "Shane."

"It's okay," he said. "You're doing great. Lift up a little, sweetheart," he instructed, trying to position her over him. "Good. Now put me inside you. You do it." He grabbed her hand and brought it to his cock, then he grabbed the base of it and held himself steady, angled at her opening. "Use your hand to guide me in."

Beth edged into position up on her knees, awkward and unsure. His other hand gripped her at the waist to steady her.

"That's right," he said when she was finally in position. "Now sink down on me. Let gravity do the work."

She positioned the fat crown of his cock at the opening of her sex and pressed down a bit.

"That's it," he said. "Keep going."

"I'm trying," she said, her voice edged with frustration as she tried to work herself down onto him.

"It'll be easier once you get the head in," Shane said, and he bucked his hips upward, spearing the head into her.

Beth winced as the head of his cock breached her opening, and her eyes watered.

"You okay?" he said, his jaw tightening as he fought the urge to simply thrust himself deep inside her.

"Fine."

Shane let go of his cock and reached between her legs, stroking her clitoris again. "Work yourself down on me, slowly. Give your body time to adjust."

She pushed down, her body tensing.

"Relax your muscles," he said, teasing her clit with languorous little circles. He didn't want to rush her. He was grateful she'd made it this far, and he didn't want to risk a setback. But at this rate, he was certain he would die of blue balls before she was fully seated.

She kept advancing and retreating, a little bit at a time, until she started to make some progress. "Oh!" she gasped, when she slipped down a couple inches suddenly, pulling back up a bit in surprise.

"It's okay, sweetheart," he said, his hands squeezing her hips. "You're doing great."

She looked down at him, her eyes bright and unsure, her pupils dilated. Then she moved on him again and sank down a little farther. When he gave a tiny upward thrust with his hips, helping the process along just a little bit, her eyes widened.

"Okay?" he asked, his hands squeezing her hips.

"Yes," she said. "It's just... a lot... to take."

He had to bite his tongue to keep from chuckling. He was barely half-way inside her, and she thought this was a lot?

She shimmied herself down farther onto his length, and Shane thought he was about to lose either his mind or his load with all her wriggling. His gaze was locked on her sex, and he watched with fascination as her body swallowed his cock one slow inch at a time. Jesus, she was going to be the death of him!

The feel of her body enveloping him — so hot and silky wet — was trying his endurance. This would've been so much easier if she were beneath him. He cheated a little and rocked himself upward with tiny thrusts. Finally, when he was just about there, he gave one last desperate upward push which buried him to the hilt.

Beth winced again and grabbed hold of his wrists.

"Okay?" he said. God, finally he was inside her! He gritted his teeth as he struggled not to come.

She nodded. "Yes. It's just... a lot."

Shane noticed the tension in her expression and her death grip on his wrists. She looked rather uncomfortable. She was awfully small and tight, and while that was heaven for him, it probably wasn't so good for her. At least not yet.

"Beth, are you hurting?" he said.

She closed her eyes. "A little."

"Try to relax. Your body will adjust. Just give it a few moments."

Beth moved hesitantly on him, lifting up, and then inching back down again. She did that a few more times, finding it easier each time as her tissues softened and relaxed.

He bit back a groan. It had been a hell of a long time since he'd felt such a precarious hold on his climax. Her tight heat alone was enough to make him come. If she squeezed her sex, he'd undoubtedly lose it.

Beth was moving more freely on him now, and he saw her expression soften as she bit her bottom lip. She even smiled when she pulled up and then sank back down onto him, her wet flesh gliding easily along his rigid cock.

"Experiment with different angles, sweetheart," he said. "You'll find the right one. I want you to make yourself come on me. Just do what feels good and relax. It'll happen."

With her eyes closed, she began to move on him. She varied her angle, leaning forward, leaning back, changing her pace. She eventually let go of her death grip on his wrists and planted her palms on his shoulders instead, to steady herself. Before long, she'd found her rhythm as she worked herself leisurely on his cock.

"That's right, baby," he murmured as he watched her move on him. She likely had no idea how sensual she looked riding him. The lines of her body were exquisite, and her delicate breasts were sheer perfection as they gently bobbed up and down with her movements. A small smile appeared on her face as she concentrated on finding her pleasure.

Shane desperately wanted to start moving, to shove himself into her as deeply as he could, but he held back. There was no way he was going to ruin this for her. Tonight wasn't about him.

This was all for her. His sole objective was to show her how good it could be between them, to show her she could trust him to make things right for her. He clenched his teeth, keeping the urge to thrust in check, even if it killed him.

Gradually he felt her muscles begin to tighten. Her thighs clamped down on his hips, and he felt the tension climbing once again inside her. As she finally found what she was looking for, she whimpered.

"That's it, sweetheart," he whispered, stroking her thighs and trying to ignore the painful ache in his balls. "Just relax and do what feels good."

She must have found just the right angle because the languid pleasure on her face completely transformed her expression. She continued moving on him, right where she needed to be as she focused on that one spot.

"Shane!" she gasped, as her thighs tensed on him.

"I know," he said, his voice low. "Let it happen."

She worked herself on him, directing her body just where it

needed to be. When her climax hit, she cried out loudly.

Her sex clamped down on his cock, and now it was his turn to gasp.

"That's it," Shane said, his voice rough. And a heartbeat later, his cock erupted in a startling hot rush. His semen scorched his cock inside the latex, blistering him with heat. He wished they didn't need to use a condom. He wanted to fill her with his come and stroke himself mindlessly inside her hot, slippery channel.

When her tremors ceased, she collapsed onto his chest, and his arms came around her, holding her close.

"Beth." He kissed her temple. "Are you okay?"

She murmured something unintelligible as she pressed her face into his throat.

"I'll take that as a yes," he said, smiling into her hair.

They lay like that for several minutes, until she started shivering as the sweat on her skin began to dry in the night air.

Shane gently coaxed her to disengage from his cock and lay beside him.

He hated to leave her even for a moment, but he had to discard the condom. If it weren't for the condom, they could have fallen asleep like this, joined together with Beth lying on him. "I'll clean you up, and then we can talk."

Beth collapsed boneless on the bed and started to drift off to sleep. When Shane returned with a warm washcloth, he gently spread her thighs and wiped her clean.

He sat on the edge of the bed. "Beth?"

She was still reveling in the residual tremors of her climax. "Hmm?"

"Why didn't you tell me you were a virgin?"

When she didn't respond, he said, "There was blood on the condom, and there's blood on your thighs."

"It's not a big deal," she said.

"It kinda is," he said quietly.

She opened her eyes and looked at him. "Most of my friends

lost their virginity in high school, and the rest of them lost it in college."

"And you didn't. Beth, being a virgin is nothing to be ashamed of, you know," he said. "I wish you'd told me."

"Would it have made a difference?" she said.

"Yes. I would've been a hell of a lot more careful."

She yawned. "You were careful. Wonderfully careful. Can we go to sleep now? I'm so wiped."

He laughed. "Yes."

"Thank you," she said when he had finished bathing her.

Shane discarded the wet washcloth in the bathroom, and then he crawled into bed beside Beth. He drew the sheet and comforter over them and tucked himself up against her back, wrapping his arm loosely around her waist. When she nestled her bottom against his loins, he felt his cock twitch.

He lay there listening to Beth's gentle breathing, reeling from the fact that she'd been a virgin. In hindsight, it shouldn't have surprised him. She'd told him that her previous attempts at intimacy hadn't gone well. He'd assumed — incorrectly, obviously — she meant they hadn't been good experiences for her — not that the experiences had never actually happened.

He tried not to dwell on the fact that he'd just deflowered Tyler Jamison's little sister. That wasn't going to go over well when Tyler found out. Speaking of Tyler, now was as good a time as any to get her to start talking about Howard Kline.

"Beth?"

"Hmm?" She yawned.

It looked like their talk would have to wait until morning. She was clearly down for the count. "Never mind, sweetheart," he said, kissing the back of her head. "Go to sleep."

19

Beth may have fallen easily into a deep and restful sleep, but Shane lay wide awake, unable to switch off his brain. He was in serious trouble here. Not only had he fallen for Beth, hard, but he was deceiving her, and that didn't sit well. He knew he had to tell her the truth soon, but he wanted to build some level of trust with her before he confessed that he knew a hell of a lot more about her past than she realized.

He tightened his arm around her, drawing her close, struck by how strong his feelings had become so quickly. It wasn't just the sex — although her hesitant innocence had most definitely blown his mind. Watching her ride him had been exciting as hell. She couldn't have faked her reaction if she'd tried — everything she'd felt as they'd made love had been right there on her lovely face. Even with her lack of experience, she was the most naturally sensuous woman he'd ever been with. And they'd barely just scratched the surface. When he thought about all the things he could show her — teach her — about sex, he got hard again.

And it was more than just sex for him, too. He wanted to protect her. He wanted to keep her safe from Kline, or from anyone or anything in this world that threatened to hurt her. To hell with Tyler's contract. Beth was his to protect now. She was… his.

As soon as the thought entered his head, he knew he was entering new territory. He'd never felt this way about any woman. In the past, he'd dated one woman after the next, moving on after a few dates. It was better that way. He'd learned early on that if he dated one woman for very long, she started to get long-term ideas. And he'd never been interested in settling down like that. But now... the thought of moving on from Beth was repugnant.

After making sure she was indeed asleep, he let himself relax and drift off.

Shane had learned years ago to be a light sleeper, back in his days in the military when his life had depended on it. He'd learned to grab sleep when and where he could, whether it was in a cot in a military barracks or behind a rock or under a bush. He'd also learned to awaken fully alert at the slightest whisper of sound or movement.

Like now. He came instantly awake.

Beth.

He lay still, listening.

It wasn't anything overt really, but her breathing was shallow and fast. And even in her sleep, she had a death grip on his arm, which was still wrapped around her waist. Her legs shifted restlessly against his, and a small sound escaped her, barely more than a whimper. She was having a nightmare.

Her entire body shuddered, and she cried out in her sleep, a frightened, desperate sound that broke his heart.

Shane loosened his hold on her when she began to struggle against the invisible bonds that confined her. He wanted to hold her closer, tight to his body, but restraining her would probably make it worse. So he forced himself to remove his arm from around her waist. "Sweetheart?" he murmured, stroking her arm lightly. "You're okay."

She continued to struggle, and when she started crying, he couldn't take anymore.

"Beth, honey." He shook her shoulder gently. "Wake up."

She jerked suddenly and threw back her head, nearly hitting

him in the face. She was fighting in earnest now.

"Beth!" Shane rolled her to her back and shook her hard enough to startle her awake.

"What!" she cried, looking around with wild eyes.

"You were having a nightmare," he said.

"Oh. I'm sorry."

"Christ, there's no need to apologize," he said, brushing back her damp hair.

"What time is it?"

He glanced at the digital clock on the nightstand. "Three-thirty."

She groaned. "I'm sorry I woke you."

"It's not a problem." Shane rested his hand on her bare belly, stroking her.

"Mmm, that feels good," she said, turning toward him and snuggling into his chest. "You're so warm."

"That's me," he said. "I'm your private bed warmer."

Beth laid her hand over his heart. "Shane?"

"Yeah?"

"Thank you for last night. It was wonderful. I meant to tell you that last night, but I think I might have passed out."

"I thought it was pretty wonderful, too," he said. "And you did pass out on me, by the way, but that's all right. I took it as a compliment."

"It was a compliment," she assured him, stroking his chest. "I don't think I'd ever felt so good in my life."

His warm hand cupped her butt and he drew her closer. When he leaned down to kiss her soft pink nipple, she shivered.

"How do you feel?" he said.

"Fine." And when he sucked the taut little pebble into his mouth and leisurely bathed it with his tongue, she gasped, arching her back. "More than fine."

Shane lifted his head. "Are you sore?"

She moved a bit, not surprised to feel a tenderness deep inside. "Just a little."

"You know, there are other ways to have sex that don't involve you being pinned down." He rolled her over so that she was facing away from him, and he pressed up against her back.

Beth wriggled her bottom against his groin, smiling when she felt his erection prodding her.

Shane tucked her legs up a little and angled his pelvis. The hand that had been around her waist slipped down between her legs, and he touched her, his finger skimming through her curls to her core. His finger zeroed in on her clitoris and began to tease it, all while he was pressing a trail of kisses along her jaw and down her throat to her shoulder.

Beth squirmed in his arms. "Shane," she moaned, rocking against his finger.

"Yes?" he said, pleased to find her already wet.

"Why are you torturing me?"

"I'm not torturing you."

"Then what do you call that?"

"I'm stimulating you."

She chuckled. "I think I'm already stimulated."

"Do you want me to stop?" he said, his voice low and rough.

Beth had learned to recognize the subtle changes in his voice when he was aroused. She thrust her bottom back, pushing against his loins, thoroughly gratified when he groaned into her ear.

"No, don't stop," she said.

"What do you want me to do?" He pressed his face into her hair.

"I don't know. Just don't stop." She could feel herself growing hotter and wetter with each stroke of his finger.

Shane nudged her legs apart with his knees and inserted his finger into her core. "So hot and wet," he murmured, nibbling on her shoulder as his finger explored her sex.

"Shane!"

"What?"

"Do something!"

"I am doing something."

"I mean stop teasing me and make love to me."

"What, again?"

She laughed. "Yes, again!"

"All right."

He reached for another condom and quickly sheathed himself. Then he shifted his hips and pressed forward, spooning against her back. He lifted one of her legs and draped it back over his thighs, opening her. He tucked the head of his cock inside her warm wetness, reveling in her tightness and slowly pushed inside. "You mean like this?"

Beth pushed back against him. "Yes," she gasped.

Shane smiled as he pushed into her slowly, groaning when her silky wet tissues parted for him. There was no sign of anxiety in her this time. She was relaxed and aroused, and he felt pretty damn good about that. When his hips met her buttocks and he was fully seated, he sighed. "How's that?"

She rocked back against him. "Oh, God, that feels good," she said.

Shane chuckled. "Yes, ma'am," he said, pulling almost all the way out, then thrusting forward in a single smooth glide that buried him balls deep inside her.

"Ummph!" she gasped, clutching his arm, which had snaked around her waist to hold her to him.

He stilled. "You okay?"

"Yes!" she said. "It's just that you're really deep this way."

"Yes, I am," he said, not bothering to hide the gloating in his voice. And then he started to move, slowly at first in long smooth movements, and then a little faster and a little deeper. The feel of her, so hot and tight around him, threatened to steal his control, but he gritted his teeth and paced himself. He wanted this to be good for her. He wanted to give her time to build to her own climax.

"God, you are so tight, sweetheart," he said as her channel nearly strangled him in its tight grip. He kept up the measured slow and steady thrusts. He reached around and found her clitoris and began stroking the little nub with deliberate movements designed to fuel her orgasm. When his finger and thumb lightly pinched her clitoris, she cried out.

At the sound of her cry, he increased the pace of his thrusts, unable to help himself. The snug fit of her sex was driving him crazy, and he didn't know how much longer he could hold out. He felt his balls draw up, aching with the need to release. His tempo picked up, and his cock started battering her channel relentlessly, rocking them both in the bed. "Okay?" he managed to get out, breathless.

"Yes!" Her own voice was little more than a croak.

"Tell me if you're not."

'Oh, God, I'm fine. Please."

Shane began a relentless campaign against her clitoris, stroking and rubbing her flesh, driving her higher and higher. He could hear her panting in the dark, her breaths coming fast and shallow, and the small sounds she made deep in her throat. When he felt her muscles tense, he knew she was close. He angled his cock just so.

When her climax hit, Beth cried out loudly. Pleasure battered her body, radiating from her core outward like jolts of lightning. She shivered in his arms, and he held her close as the tremors coursed through her body.

His own body took its cue from hers, and he followed her, his body exploding in a hot rush as his hips bucked urgently against her body. "Fuck!" His guttural cry was hoarse in her hair as he emptied himself into her.

She could feel his hot breath on the nape of her neck as he tried to catch his breath.

"My God, Beth." He pulled gently out of her clinging sex and rolled her to her back so he could see her face. "Are you all right?" he said, brushing back her hair.

She nodded, a little short of breath herself. She was more than just fine as she reveled in the residual tremors of her orgasm.

He stroked her face, brushing the pad of his thumb along her cheekbone. Looking at her gave him such pleasure. He could lie there and stare at her for hours. He certainly wanted to, but he had a condom to dispose of. Once that was taken care of, he brought back another warm washcloth and cleaned her up. Then he slipped back into bed with her and spooned against her limp body.

"Go back to sleep, sweetheart," he said, kissing the nape of her neck.

They fell back to sleep, satiated and comforted by the warmth of each other's body.

Beth woke slowly, a little groggy and disoriented when she realized she wasn't in her own bed. Then it all came rushing back — she'd spent the night in Shane's bed. And after that first disastrous attempt, they'd had sex — twice! The relief she felt was staggering.

She was lying on her side, and Shane was pressed up against her back, his arm hooked around her waist. She could feel his erection prodding her bottom.

"Good morning," Shane said, kissing a spot on her shoulder. "Looks like I gave you a hickey last night. I'm sorry."

"I'm not sorry," she said, turning to face him. "Good morning."

"What's on the agenda today? Breakfast? A shower?"

"I'd like to take a shower first, if you don't mind," she said. "And then breakfast. I'm starving."

"That sounds like an excellent plan." He gave her a hopeful look. "Can I join you in the shower?"

Shane led her by the hand into the walk-in shower. With one push of a button, hot water sprayed out from multiple shower heads.

"Come on in," he said, pulling her into the water. "The water's fine."

Beth leaned her head back in bliss, letting the warm water rush over her. "Your shower is decadent," she said, pushing her hair back from her face as she wet it under the warm spray.

Shane poured some shampoo into his hands and massaged

the lather into her hair.

She groaned when his fingers began massaging her scalp. "That smells good," she said, inhaling the strong minty scent.

"It's my sister's. She uses this shower when she stays here."

"I don't blame her," she said, groaning with pleasure. "Which sister?"

"Lia, the youngest. She has an apartment in this building, too, but she often stays up here in mine. Lia works for me. She's a bodyguard."

"Your sister's a bodyguard? Really?"

"Yep. She often works undercover."

"Do your other sisters work for you, too?"

"No, just Lia. Sophie's an interior designer here in the city, and Hannah's in college. Lia's the only one crazy enough to work for me."

Shane positioned Beth's head under the warm spray to rinse away the suds. Then he reached for a bottle of body wash and lathered up his hands.

"This is a full-service spa," Beth said when he laid his soapy hands on her shoulders and began to work his way down her arms.

"I can't think of anything I'd rather be doing than running my hands all over your wet, naked body."

"You're waxing very poetically this morning," she said, smiling in bliss as his soapy hands massaged her body.

"Co-ed showers make me poetic. What can I say?" His hands came around her torso to cup her breasts, his thumbs swirling soap gently over her nipples. "I'm in a shower with a gorgeous woman who's naked and wet." He shrugged. "What can I say? I'm a simple man."

She chuckled. "You're easy to please."

He leaned down and kissed the side of her neck. "No, I'm easily pleased by you. All you have to do is crook your little finger, and you've got my attention. No other woman has ever had that effect on me."

Shane's hands traveled down her back to her waist and hips.

He soaped her buttocks, and then his hands moved around to her front where he soaped her belly and thighs.

When she was rinsed off, Beth turned in Shane's arms and reached for his shampoo bottle. "Now, it's my turn," she said.

Shane stood behind Beth as she brushed her teeth at the bathroom sink, a towel wrapped around his hips. He caught her gaze in the mirror. "There's an event next weekend I have to attend," he said, towel drying his hair. "It's a fundraiser for the Children's Hospital Foundation. I'm on the Board of Directors, so I have to be there. Will you come with me, as my date?"

Beth froze and looked at his reflection. A hospital fundraiser? That sounded like a very crowded event, and she didn't fare well with crowds. But still, she didn't want to pass up an opportunity to do something like this with him. "I'd love to," she said.

"It's a black-tie event," he warned. "And there's lots of schmoozing. It could be really boring."

"I don't mind," she said. Then she made a face. "But I'm pretty sure I don't have anything suitable to wear to a black-tie event."

"Why don't we go shopping then, after breakfast? I'd love to buy you a dress."

She made an effort to keep it cool. "I thought guys hate shopping."

"Well, as a general rule, I do," he said. "But if I get to watch you model sexy dresses, then I'm good."

Beth smiled at him. "Okay. But you don't have to buy my dress. It's nice of you to offer, but I can pay for it myself."

20

After dressing, they went in search of food. Beth followed Shane to the kitchen, where they found Cooper peering inside an industrial-size refrigerator with double glass doors. He was dressed in jeans, a t-shirt, and scuffed up boots. The air was redolent with the rich aroma of freshly brewed coffee.

"There are plenty of leftovers from last night," Shane said to Cooper. "We can have those, or we can make breakfast."

"*We* can make breakfast?" Cooper said, raising a sardonic eyebrow at Shane.

"Yes, *we*. I'll help."

"Shane, you're good at a lot of things, but cooking isn't one of them." Cooper smiled at Beth. "Don't let him fool you, Beth. He's just trying to impress you with his nonexistent kitchen skills."

Shane led Beth to a seat at the breakfast bar and kissed her. "What would you like to drink? Coffee? Tea? OJ?"

"I'll have some of that coffee," she said. "It smells divine."

Shane poured two cups of coffee and handed one to Beth. He brought her sugar, creamer, and a spoon, which he set on the granite counter in front of her.

Cooper turned to Beth, his arms crossed over his lean, muscled chest. "What would the young lady like for breakfast?" There was a smile on his face, and he seemed genuinely pleased to see her.

Beth smiled back. "Anything's fine, really," she said. "I can make it."

Shane put his hands on Beth's shoulders and gave her a light squeeze. "You relax and drink your coffee. Cooper and I know our way around a kitchen."

"Let's try this again," Cooper said, addressing Beth. "What would you like for breakfast? Eggs? Pancakes? Waffles? French toast?"

Beth's face lit up at the mention of French toast.

"Looks like we're having French toast," Cooper said. He opened one of the fridge doors and pulled out a carton of eggs. "And what you would you like with your French toast? Eggs? Bacon? Sausage? Hash browns?"

"Please don't go to any more trouble," she said. "The French toast is fine."

Cooper frowned. "French toast alone is not a sufficient breakfast, is it, Shane?"

"No, it's not," Shane said, sipping his coffee. He was leaning against one of the kitchen counters, watching the interplay between Beth and Cooper with an indulgent smile on his face.

"So, what'll it be, kid?" Cooper said.

"Bacon then, please?" she said, shrugging apologetically. "If it's not too much trouble?"

Cooper nodded, apparently satisfied. "And hash browns," he added. "Coming right up."

Beth watched in fascination as Shane and Cooper set about making breakfast. While Cooper cracked a half-dozen eggs into a shallow dish, Shane loaded a large griddle pan with enough bacon to feed a small army. The two men worked side-by-side, smoothly and efficiently.

"I thought you said you didn't know how to cook," Beth said to Shane, watching him fuss with the bacon.

"I don't," Shane said. "But I still remember how to follow orders. Cooper was my commanding officer in the military. Old habits die hard."

Cooper gave Shane a suffering glance. "Like you ever listen to a thing I say now."

"I do," Shane said, and he smiled at Beth.

While the bacon cooked, Cooper prepared the French toast and cooked the hash browns.

Beth couldn't help smiling as she watched the two men work. It was obvious they had a history of working together, as well as a deep mutual affection.

"She's not hard to please, is she?" Cooper said to Shane, as he used a spatula to turn the bread in the skillet.

"It doesn't seem so," Shane said, checking the bacon.

"She's easy to please and not very demanding," Cooper mused aloud. "Honestly, I think she would've been happy with dry toast. She has very nice manners, and on top of all that, she's drop dead gorgeous. Damn, Shane, where did you find her? Does she have an older sister who's single? A *much* older sister?"

Beth snickered as the two men discussed her as if she weren't sitting there listening to every word they said.

"Are we amusing you, young lady?" Cooper said, glancing back over his shoulder at her.

She grinned. "Yes. I don't have a sister, but my mom is single. And people have mistaken us for being sisters before. She's really nice. You'd like her."

Cooper delivered a plate of perfectly cooked French toast with butter and maple syrup, bacon, and hash browns to her place at the breakfast bar. Shane refilled her coffee cup.

"Need anything else, young lady?" Cooper asked as he stood at the counter.

"No, thank you. This is wonderful."

Shane and Cooper filled their own plates and joined her at the counter, one on each side of her.

"This is delicious, Cooper," Beth said, spearing a forkful of French toast. "Thank you."

"My pleasure, Beth," Cooper said, just before he shoveled a forkful of food into his own mouth.

When everyone had finished eating, Cooper cleared the dirty

plates from the breakfast bar. "So, what're your plans today?" he asked.

"We're going shopping for a dress," Shane said.

Cooper raised a skeptical eyebrow. "Really?"

Shane nodded. "Beth agreed to be my date to the hospital benefit next weekend, so we're going dress shopping. And then we'll grab some lunch downtown."

"I'll drive you," Cooper said. "Give me a heads up when you're ready to leave, and I'll bring the car around front."

When Beth excused herself to freshen up, Shane hung back in the kitchen with Cooper.

"What's the word on Kline?" Shane said once Beth was out of earshot.

"He was quiet last night, mostly surfed the Internet. Besides watching a lot of really bad porn, he found a video interview with Beth on the Kingston website that he watched repeatedly. He's obsessing over her, Shane."

Shane frowned, his expression tight. Then he pulled out his phone and called a number on his contact list. "Hi, Suzanne. It's Shane McIntyre. I need a favor. There's a video on your library's website featuring an interview with one of your employees, Beth Jamison. I need you to pull that video immediately. In fact, pull all media that contains an image or reference to Beth from the library website. Thanks. I appreciate it, and I owe you."

Shane hung up and looked at Cooper.

"Will you be armed on this little outing downtown?" Cooper said.

Shane shook his head. "No. It would be too easy for Beth to spot the gun, and I don't want explain that right now."

Cooper nodded. "I'll shadow you."

"Thanks."

"You knew Cooper in the military?" Beth said, as they stepped into the elevator.

"We were in the same unit," Shane said. "When I was discharged, I asked Cooper to come with me to start up a new venture. He was eligible to retire, so he agreed."

"You two seem very close."

"We are. Besides my brothers, he's my best friend."

The elevator doors opened to the front lobby, and they stepped out into a spacious, sunlit lobby. The exterior walls were all glass, which made for a bright and sunny space. There were numerous trees planted inside the lobby, and a tiered water fountain stood in the center of the room. As they approached the pair of glass doors that led to the front of the building, an older man dressed in a black suit and tie greeted Shane.

"Good day, Mr. McIntyre," the man said, smiling broadly at Shane.

"Hi, Eddie," Shane said, reaching out to shake the man's hand. "Eddie, this is Miss Jamison."

"How do you do, ma'am?" Eddie said, nodding his head at her.

"Eddie Rivers is one of our doormen," Shane said to Beth.

"It's a pleasure to meet you," Beth said.

They stepped through the automatic doors to a sunny, early Sunday afternoon. Beth waved at Cooper, who stood leaning against a black Lexus SUV parked in the circular drive. He looked pretty hot for an old guy in his worn jeans, t-shirt, and a well-loved black leather jacket. She had to wonder, though, why he was wearing a jacket when it was so warm out.

"Where to?" Cooper said, as he opened the rear passenger door. Beth scooted into the vehicle, followed closely by Shane.

"Sylvia's," Shane said, reaching for Beth's seatbelt.

Beth smirked at him as he buckled her in.

"Indulge me," he said. "You know I like to take care of you."

Thinking of how he'd taken care of her in the night — twice! — she smiled.

Shane's gaze locked on her mouth, and when he leaned closer his intent was obvious. He was going to kiss her, right in front of Cooper. Her gaze darted nervously to the front seat, to the back of Cooper's head.

"Don't worry about him," Shane whispered. His mouth was demanding as it covered hers, his lips parting hers so that his tongue could slip inside. When the radio came on, Beth jumped and pulled away from Shane. She glanced nervously at Cooper, and then back at Shane and shook her head.

Smothering a grin, Shane settled back in his seat and reached for her hand.

Cooper pulled the Lexus into a reserved VIP parking spot in front of a women's boutique in an exclusive section of N. Michigan Avenue.

"Don't wait around for us," Shane told Cooper as he helped Beth out of the car. "When we're done here, we'll walk to the restaurant for lunch. I'll call you when we're ready to be picked up."

Cooper nodded. "I'll leave the car here and walk a while. I have some errands to take care of."

As Cooper walked away, Shane took Beth's hand and led her to the front entrance of the boutique. She hesitated when she noticed the array of exquisite cocktail dresses and evening gowns on display in the shop's front windows. Apparently, Shane's idea of dressing up was a little different from hers. This place was way beyond her means.

"What's wrong?" Shane said, stopping when Beth held back.

"This place looks really expensive, Shane," she said, eyeing the displays. "I can't afford anything here. I know some nice consignment shops where we can find something pretty reasonable."

"Don't worry about the price, Beth," he said. "I'm paying for the dress. And shoes, too. It's the least I can do since I asked you to be my date."

Shoes? Of course, she'd need shoes. She had nothing to wear with a dress like this.

When Beth opened her mouth to object, Shane said, "The owner is my sister Sophie's best friend. Don't worry; she'll give us a good deal."

Shane tried to gently tug her forward, but she still resisted.

A woman dressed in a scarlet pencil skirt, tailored white blouse, and four-inch red heels caught sight of them through the windows and waved eagerly at Shane.

Shane waved back. "That's Sylvia Jackson. She's the owner."

Sylvia opened the door and waved them in. "Shane! How are you? Please, come in."

"Hello, Sylvia," Shane said as he ushered Beth inside with an encouraging hand on her back.

Beth tried not to gawk at the exquisite merchandise on display, from the clothing to the shoes to the accessories. She glanced at a rack of hand-painted silk scarves that were priced at $575. *Holy cow!* She was completely out of her element.

Sylvia Jackson was a strikingly beautiful woman. She had silky straight hair, black as ink, that hung to her jaw line in a sophisticated bob. Her red lipstick, perfectly matched to her skirt and heels, contrasted dramatically with her pale complexion. Her nose was slender, but it fit her oval face well. Her dark eyes were expertly outlined in kohl.

"What can I do for you today?" Sylvia said, assessing Beth with an interested gaze.

Shane pulled Beth close, tucking her against his side. "Sylvia, this is Beth Jamison, my... girlfriend. She needs a dress and shoes for the Children's Hospital fundraiser next weekend."

Beth didn't miss how Sylvia's perfectly sculpted eyebrows lifted when Shane called her his girlfriend. She was embarrassed to admit it, even to herself, but she'd felt a small thrill when Shane had said it. Was that really how he saw her? Was that what they were doing? The whole boyfriend/girlfriend thing?

Sylvia beamed. "I'm sure we can find something to Beth's liking."

"Something appropriate," Shane added.

Sylvia looked at Shane, her expression curious. "Appropriate?"

"Not too revealing," he said.

"I'm sure we'll find the perfect dress," Sylvia said. "If you'll both follow me, I'll show you to the private viewing room."

They followed Sylvia through a curtained doorway at the rear of the store and found themselves in a secluded room decorated in rich burgundy with gold accents. At one end of the room, a long, plush burgundy sofa was situated strategically to have a perfect view of the stage, which was surrounded by three tall, gilded freestanding mirrors.

"Help yourself to coffee, Shane, and have a seat," Sylvia said. She glanced from Shane to Beth. "Did you have any particular color or style in mind?"

Shane took a seat on the sofa and leaned back, crossing his leg and settling in. "Whatever Beth wants," he said.

"Why don't you come with me to the dressing room?" Sylvia said to Beth. "I'll bring you some selections to try on."

Beth followed Sylvia through a curtained doorway into an enormous dressing room lined with floor-to-ceiling mirrors.

"Size four" Sylvia said.

Beth nodded. "Yes."

"What colors do you like?"

Beth shrugged. "I like a lot of colors. I really don't have a favorite."

"Why don't you get undressed while I go grab some things for you to try," Sylvia said, heading for a door. "Hang your clothes on that rack there."

Beth removed her skirt and blouse and hung them up, standing self-consciously in her panties and bra. Sylvia returned quickly with a wheeled clothing rack that held at least a dozen dresses in a rainbow of colors and a variety of lengths and styles.

"Let's start with this one," Sylvia said, chuckling as she pulled a tiny red sequined dress off its hanger.

Beth could tell just by looking that the dress was a no-go, at least as far as she was concerned. Even if by some miracle the dress did fit her, she'd never wear it in public. Skimpy, slinky dresses just weren't her style.

Sylvia slipped the tiny sheath dress over Beth's head, and it felt about two sizes too small as Sylvia tugged it down her body. Sylvia stepped aside, and Beth gaped at herself in the mirror. Leaving absolutely nothing to the imagination, the dress was strapless, with an extremely low-cut neckline that blatantly displayed the inside curves of her breasts and a hemline that barely covered her buttocks. She wouldn't be able to bend over without indecently exposing herself, and the slit up one side would make it impossible to wear anything other than a thong underneath. She felt completely exposed, and she was certain it would fail Shane's 'not too revealing' edict.

"The red looks amazing on you, with your hair and complexion," Sylvia said. "Shane will love it. What man doesn't love a woman in a red dress, right? What do you think?"

"Well," Beth said, trying to find a polite way of saying she hated it.

"I'll go grab some shoes. I know just the pair. What size do you wear?"

"Nine," Beth said.

"I'll be right back."

Sylvia returned with a pair of champagne-colored shoes with four-inch heels. "Manolo Blahnik," she said. "We just got them in yesterday, and they're perfect with this dress. Here, slip them on, and then we'll show Shane."

Beth steadied herself against the back of the armchair as she slipped on the shoes, trying her best not to topple over. Once she had the shoes on, she looked at herself in the mirror, feeling like an absolute fraud. This was so not her.

"Sylvia, the dress is lovely," Beth said, striving for diplomacy, "but I don't think it's quite me."

Sylvia's brow furrowed. "But you look amazing! Own it, sister. Flaunt it."

Beth shrugged. "Thank you, but it's just not me."

Sylvia sighed. "All right. But let's at least show Shane, okay? It'll be fun to watch his reaction."

Shane was answering a text message when Beth and Sylvia walked into the room. When he heard them approach, he stowed his phone and looked up.

"Hell no!" he said, shooting to his feet. "Damn it, Sylvia! I said 'appropriate.' What part of that outfit is appropriate?"

Sylvia seemed genuinely taken aback. "What do you mean? This is perfectly appropriate for the hospital fundraiser. And she looks gorgeous!"

"That's not the point," Shane said. "When I said 'appropriate,' I meant appropriate for *her*."

"What's wrong with it?" Sylvia asked, clearly confused. "I admit it's a little on the skimpy side, but look at her, Shane. Not many women can pull off a dress like this, but she can. And you love red!"

"Yeah, what's wrong with it?" Beth said. Truthfully, she didn't like the dress either, and she had no intention of wearing it anywhere. But she was as baffled by Shane's reaction as Sylvia. And what did 'appropriate for her' mean, anyway?

Shane ran his fingers through his hair. "Come on, Sylvia!" he said. "That's a fuck-me dress, and those are fuck-me shoes. I'm not taking her anywhere dressed like that. I want something appropriate."

Sylvia crossed her arms over her chest. "Define 'appropriate' if you don't mind," she said, her voice tight.

"I meant something suitable for *her*. Something modest," Shane said.

"There's absolutely nothing wrong with this dress," Sylvia said, clearly frustrated. "And when did you become such a prude?"

Shane sent Sylvia a scathing look, but when he turned his attention to Beth, his expression immediately softened. "You look stunning in that dress, sweetheart," he said, laying his hands on her bare shoulders. "You really do. And if you like the dress, we'll buy it. But it's not the kind of dress I want you to wear to the fundraiser. Please choose something a little more... conservative. Something that, uh, covers more of you. And something not red. Anything but red."

Shane looked at Sylvia, and his expression hardened. "And Sylvia, lose the fuck-me heels."

21

Beth followed Sylvia back to the dressing room, trying hard not to fall flat on her face as she struggled to walk in the stilettos. She held still while Sylvia peeled the skin-tight dress off her body.

"You've really done a number on him, Beth," Sylvia said, shaking her head. "I've known Shane McIntyre since grade school, and I've never seen him like this with a woman. On any other woman, he would have gone for that red dress in a heartbeat. So what's your secret?"

Beth shrugged. "I just met him last week," she said, crossing her arms defensively over her chest as she stood there in her panties and bra.

"You're kidding me," Sylvia said, wrinkling her perfectly sculpted eyebrows. "You realize he's one of the most sought after bachelors in Chicago. I can't even count the number of women who've tried to snare Shane McIntyre. There's probably a support group out there for them. He's a serial dater, with one gorgeous woman after another on his arm. He treats his women well — no one has ever accused him of being stingy — but his heart's never in it. And now look at him! I thought he was going to throttle me out there for daring to put you in a slinky red dress."

Sylvia hung up the offending red dress. "How old are you?" she asked, glancing back at Beth.

"Twenty-four."

"You look young for your age," Sylvia said. "Maybe that's it. He usually dates women his own age, sometimes older. I'll bet he sees you as this young virginal princess who needs protecting. Dear God, you're not a virgin, are you?"

"Of course not," she scoffed, hoping it wasn't obvious.

Sylvia's expression changed abruptly, and her eyes widened. "Oh, my God. He's fallen in love." She looked thunderstruck.

"No," Beth said, laughing nervously. "We just met. We hardly know each other."

Sylvia shook her head. "Honey, there's no accounting for how and when people fall in love. Sometimes it just happens. He must have taken one look at you, and wham!"

Sylvia started pacing just as her face lit up with a huge grin. "I need to rethink this. He sees you as wife material, so he's not looking for a sexpot dress. We need something that is arguably modest, but still sexy. You'll want to keep him on his toes next weekend, trust me. I've been to these fundraisers. It's a meat market. Women will be crawling all over him, regardless of the fact that he's there with a date. I think I have just the thing," she said. "Wait here."

Sylvia returned a few minutes later with an ice blue chiffon dress slung over her arm and a pair of low-heeled, gold sandals dangling from her fingers.

"Here we go," Sylvia said, setting the shoes on the floor. "It's modest — demure, even — yet it's sexy as hell. Let's try it on you. It's not too low in the neckline, and it's certainly not too short, but it still screams 'sexy baby.'"

Sylvia slipped the dress over Beth's head, and it felt wonderful as it cascaded, loose and silky, over her body.

Beth glanced at her reflection in the mirror. "Oh, wow," she breathed. It was totally vintage. "I love it! It's beautiful."

"No, *you're* beautiful," Sylvia said, a very satisfied smile on her face. "The color goes perfectly with your complexion and hair, and the blue really makes your eyes pop. It's perfect."

Beth studied her reflection, stunned by the transformation. She barely recognized herself in the simple baby-doll style dress, sleeveless, with a modest, square neckline. With a high Empire waist, the dress hugged her breasts and hung halfway to her knees in loose, flowing layers of chiffon and silk.

Sylvia pulled Beth's hair up into a loose knot on top of her head and secured it with a pale blue ribbon. "You're going to turn every male head in the room," Sylvia said. "Your husband-to-be will have his work cut out for him just trying to keep them all at bay."

"Sylvia, he's not my husband-to-be," Beth said. "I told you. We hardly know each other."

"Fine," Sylvia said. "But when you find yourself with a freakishly huge diamond on your finger, come see me, and then we'll see who was right."

Beth smiled. "I do love the dress," she said, fingering the silky material. "I think this is the one." She searched for the price tag and found it pinned to the right side seam beneath her arm: $2900. "Oh, my god," she said. "It's nearly three thousand dollars!"

"Yes," Sylvia said. "Is that a problem?"

"I can't — " She was speechless. She couldn't imagine spending three thousand dollars on a dress. A used car maybe, but not a dress! "I'm sorry, but it's too much. Don't you have something less expensive? A *lot* less expensive? Do you have a clearance rack?"

Sylvia laid her hand on Beth's shoulder. "Honey, don't worry about the price. Shane's paying for it."

"I wanted to pay for it myself," Beth said. "I can't let Shane spend that much money on me."

Sylvia laughed. "You're kidding, right? Are you aware that Shane donates ten million dollars every year to the Children's Hospital fundraiser? Trust me, I don't think he's going to blink at spending three thousand dollars on a dress. He probably loses that much in his sofa cushions each week."

"He *donates* ten million dollars?" Beth said, suddenly feeling sick.

"Every year."

Beth sank into the armchair, feeling dizzy. She knew Shane owned his own company, but it had never occurred to her that he made that kind of money. She looked at the sandals dangling from Sylvia's fingers. "How much are the shoes?" she said, afraid to hear the answer.

"Eight thirty-five. They're Manolo Blahniks, and you *have* to have them with that dress."

Beth took a deep breath. "Eight *hundred* and thirty-five dollars?"

"Yes."

Beth thought of her favorite brown sandals, which she'd bought for twenty dollars at a sidewalk sale several years before.

Sylvia set the shoes on the floor at Beth's feet. "At least try them on. He can't accuse these of being fuck-me shoes."

Numb, Beth slipped on the dainty gold flats and stood, looking at her reflection. She did like what she saw, but what did she expect from an outfit that cost nearly four thousand dollars?

"Twirl," Sylvia said.

Beth turned in a circle, unable to suppress a smile. The dress seemed weightless as it swirled fluidly through the air, then settled around her. It really was a beautiful dress, and if it had been in her price range, she would have bought it. But, unfortunately, it wasn't.

"You're going to rock his world," Sylvia said.

Shane was on his phone with his administrative assistant when Sylvia reappeared, an enigmatic expression on her face. "Ready, Shane?"

"Diane, I'll have to call you back," he said, glancing up at Sylvia. "Thanks," he said, stowing his phone. He had a sinking suspicion that Sylvia was up to something, because she looked far too pleased with herself. His suspicions were confirmed when Sylvia motioned Beth to come forward.

The moment Beth stepped into the room, Shane stopped breathing. "Christ," he said, coming to his feet again. He took a step toward her and stopped.

"You don't like it?" Beth said, her expression falling.

"It's very modest," Sylvia said, practically gloating. "It's not too low in the neckline, and the hemline's not too short. And she *likes* the dress, Shane. Turn around and show him, honey."

Beth made one graceful turn in the dress and smiled when she saw her reflection in the mirrors.

Shane walked up to her and cupped his hands around her neck, gazing down at her with nothing short of awe. "You take my breath away," he said, his eyes burning. He leaned down and kissed her, his mouth languid and gentle.

"You like it?" Beth smiled up at him.

He could tell she loved the dress — he'd known the minute she walked into the room. Her beatific smile had given her away. While it wasn't a fuck-me dress, it was probably just as bad, perhaps worse. It was a sex kitten dress, and he knew every man at the fundraiser would take one look at her and think of sex.

"What do you think, Shane?" Sylvia said.

Shane cleared his throat. "It's a beautiful dress," he said, wondering what the hell he was going to do now. He didn't want anyone seeing her in that dress, but Sylvia had him on this one. It was a perfectly modest dress for a beautiful young woman, and he could tell from her expression that she wanted it.

He glanced at Sylvia, who had a don't-you-dare expression on her face. Sylvia knew exactly what he was thinking.

Shane looked at Beth. "Do you like it, sweetheart?" he said, knowing full well she did.

"Yes," she said. "But it's too expensive." Her smile faded. "I'll find something cheaper."

That killed him, right there. The fact that she was willing to forgo this dress just to save him a few dollars really touched him.

"We'll take the dress, Sylvia," Shane said. He'd just have to deal with the fall-out of a room full of men staring at her.

"And the shoes?" Sylvia said.

"And the shoes," he said, having resigned himself that this was the outfit Beth wanted.

When Beth heard the reluctance in Shane's voice, she went up on her toes and whispered in his ear. "The dress is nearly three thousand dollars, and the shoes are almost nine hundred dollars. It's too much. I can find something less expensive."

Shane smiled at her. "It's fine, Beth." If she wanted them, she'd have them. The price was irrelevant. He dropped a quick kiss on her lips. "Wrap them up, Sylvia."

They arrived at the sales counter and waited behind a woman who was paying for a handbag. Beth tried not to stare at the cash register display, but it was hard not to notice the sale price tag. Six thousand dollars for a purse? That almost made her dress and shoes seem like a bargain.

When the woman's transaction was completed, she turned to leave and caught sight of Shane. "Oh, my God, Shane!" she said, touching her hair. An ecstatic smile transformed her face, until she noticed Beth. Then her dark eyes hardened.

Beth felt like she was having some kind of déjà vu as she took in the darkly exotic woman. This one was tall with a slender build, with long hair the color of fine dark chocolate falling in thick waves past her shoulders. Her olive complexion complimented her dark eyes and thick, dark lashes. She wore an ultra feminine, sleeveless white sheath dress that flattered her perfect hourglass figure and a pair of taupe stilettos. Another gorgeous woman who clearly had some kind of past with Shane.

"Hello, Luciana," Shane said, reaching for Beth's hand.

"Hello, darling," Luciana said in a husky voice. "How wonderful to see you!"

The woman's midnight eyes ate Shane up with a proprietary hunger that shocked Beth.

"What brings you here, Shane?" But when the woman's gaze

drifted to Beth, her smile lost some of its luster.

Beth smiled perfunctorily, feeling self-conscious beneath the woman's intense scrutiny.

"I'm shopping with my girlfriend," Shane said. His hand slipped around Beth's waist, and he drew her closer. "Beth Jamison. Beth, this is Luciana Morelli."

"Girlfriend?" Luciana said, one slender eyebrow arching in astonishment as she took a second look at Beth.

"All ready!" Sylvia said as she approached the sales counter. She hung a garment bag on a stand and slipped the distinctive Manolo Blahnik shoebox into a shopping bag.

Luciana eyed the purchases. "Got special plans coming up?" she asked Shane.

"Yes," he replied. "If you'll excuse us." Shane steered Beth around Luciana and up to the sales counter.

"There's just one more thing," Sylvia said, her smile radiant as she presented an elegant gift bag to Beth. "Just a little gift from me, to make your evening extra special."

"Thank you, Sylvia," Beth said as she accepted the bag. She peered inside and found a package elegantly wrapped in cream tissue paper and tied with a matching silk ribbon.

"You're very welcome, Beth," Sylvia said.

Shane handed a credit card to Sylvia, and they completed the transaction.

When they left the shop, Luciana was waiting for them on the sidewalk out front.

"Will you be at the fundraiser next weekend?" Luciana asked Shane, pointedly ignoring Beth.

"Yes, we will," Shane said.

Luciana's smile faltered. "Good. I'll see you there." She reached out and touched his arm. "Be sure to save a dance for me, lover." Then she pivoted on her spiky heels and walked away.

Beth looked at Shane, who was frowning as he watched Luciana walk away. *Lover?*

"Shane, did you and she — "

"Yes," he said, looking down at Beth. "It was a mistake."

"She's very beautiful," Beth said. There was no use denying the obvious.

"She's a shallow, vain bitch." Shane took Beth's hand and led her to the Lexus. "And no, I won't be dancing with her at the fundraiser. The only woman I'll be dancing with is you."

22

As Shane opened the back hatch of the Lexus and stowed their purchases, he tried to push all thoughts of Luciana Morelli from his head. Luciana was a barracuda, with teeth just as razor sharp, and she'd nearly maimed him a time or two. He knew firsthand how vindictive she could be when she felt slighted, and the idea that she might set her vengeful sights on Beth gave him reason for concern. Given the opportunity, Luciana would tear Beth to shreds. He'd have to make sure she never had the chance.

"I wonder what's in here," Beth said, peering into the gift bag Sylvia had given her. She reached in and squeezed the package. "Whatever it is, it's very soft."

Shane grinned. "Why don't you open it?"

"I'll wait until we get back to your apartment," she said. She opened the rear passenger door and set the gift bag on the seat.

Shane pulled Beth into his arms and dropped a quick kiss on her smiling lips, reveling in her warm, feminine scent. As always, it made him hard, and he wanted her again, but he knew he had to pace himself. They made love twice last night, and she was likely sore.

The simple act of having her in his arms gave him such pleasure. He'd certainly dated more than his fair share of women — beautiful women, strong women, powerful women, alluring women, all types and shapes and sizes. There'd never been a shortage of women in his life, whether because of his looks — which women seemed to like — or his money. But he'd never felt like this before. He realized that simply being with Beth gave him pleasure.

Shane's mouth was at her ear, and he breathed in the scent of her hair. "How do you feel?" he murmured.

"Fine," she said.

"Are you sore?" he asked, clarifying his question.

She flushed. "A little."

He chuckled.

"Why?" she asked.

"I was just thinking ahead," he said. "There are other positions we could try, you know, where you won't feel pinned down. We've only just scratched the surface. I thought we might try some other positions when we get back to the apartment. But if you're sore — "

"I could probably manage that," she said.

He checked his watch. "Let's feed you first. Then maybe we can go back to my place and experiment."

They walked hand-in-hand along N. Michigan Avenue, and Beth took great pleasure in stealing surreptitious looks at him. She never got tired of looking at him, and each time she did, she felt a little jolt of pleasure. There was something about him that she found captivating. Even now, dressed down for a change in his ripped jeans and tee, he looked edible. His short hair was doing its own thing, probably because he'd run his fingers through it, and he was rocking a little bit of a bad boy image with his short beard.

It was amazing the difference a couple of days made. They hadn't known each other long, and yet, she already felt so close to him. Just holding hands with him as they strolled down the street gave her a thrill. She'd never imagined she could feel this way with someone.

"Can I ask you a question?" Beth said, finally drumming up the nerve to ask the question that had been on her mind since they'd left Sylvia's.

"Sure. What is it?"

"Have you taken other women shopping in Sylvia's boutique before?"

He hesitated. "Yes."

"A lot of them?"

"No, not a lot," he said. "Wait — how many constitutes 'a lot'?"

"More than three?"

"Then, yes."

"Did you object to any of their choices?"

Another pause. "No."

"Then why did you object to the red dress? Sylvia was sure you'd like it."

"I thought you said you didn't want the red dress."

"I don't, but that's not the point. Why did you object to it *for me?*"

Shane stopped walking and pulled Beth under a shop awning, turning her to face him. His hands came up to cradle her face. "Because the others didn't matter," he said simply, gazing down at her. "And you do. What did Sylvia say to you?"

"She said you were acting differently with me. She seemed... surprised."

"It is different with you," he said. "I didn't really care what the others wore. But with you, I do. I don't want other men seeing you in that red dress."

Beth looked into his eyes, trying to read him. She was so afraid of reading too much into what he was saying.

"It matters this time," he said. "*You* matter." And then he kissed her.

It was a hungry, scorching kiss, and before she knew it, he had her pressed up against the building, his hand cradling the back of her head to protect it from the rough bricks. She could feel his erection prodding her belly. His mouth ate at hers as he kissed her ravenously, his tongue stroking hers. Her arms went around his waist, and she held onto him tightly.

"Damn," Shane said, pulling back. He was breathing heavily, his eyes hot with arousal. It took him a moment to get himself under control, and then he pulled her away from the wall and tidied her hair, which he'd mussed pretty thoroughly. "Come. There's something I want to show you."

He took her hand, and they resumed walking.

"My office building is just ahead," Shane said a few minutes later.

He needed to tell Beth about Howard Kline. He needed to come clean. Showing her his building and telling her about his work would be a good way to lay the groundwork for a conversation he was dreading. And then, maybe over lunch, he could start to go down that road with her. The truth was, he was afraid to tell her. He was afraid she'd bolt.

"Here's my building," he said, pulling her to a stop in front of an office building situated on a busy corner.

Beth looked up at the modern glass and stone building, roughly 20 stories tall. The front of the building boasted a two-story glass lobby. Through the glass, she had a clear view of an impressive lobby, the front desk, and two banks of elevators.

"Nice building," she said, looking up. And then her eye caught the name engraved in stone over the entrance: THE MCIN-TYRE BUILDING.

"Oh, my god," she said. "Why is the building named after you?"

Shane chuckled. "Because it's my building. I own it."

"You own the building? *The whole building?*"

"Yes."

Beth looked at him, dumbfounded. "You own this entire building?" she repeated, peering up at the towering floors.

"Yes," he said, chuckling. "My company takes up the top half of the building. The bottom half is leased out to other businesses."

When she looked at him like he was crazy, he grabbed her hand and pulled her through the front doors to the reception desk, where an older man dressed in a security guard's uniform was seated behind a granite counter. The guard had salt-and-pepper hair and wore small, wire-rimmed glasses.

"Good afternoon, Mr. McIntyre," the man said.

"Frank, will you please tell Miss Jamison that I own this building?"

The man looked at Shane, his expression perplexed. But when Shane watched the man expectantly, clearly waiting for a response, the guard straightened in his seat and said, "Um, yes, sir." The man looked directly at Beth. "Mr. McIntyre owns this building, miss."

Beth glanced around the spacious lobby, noting the security guards positioned at all the doors. The floors were polished marble, and there was a seating area where a black leather sofa and several matching chairs were positioned around a coffee table. A credenza held a single-serve coffee maker.

The lobby's center aisle led to two banks of elevators. One of the elevators opened and two men dressed in jeans and t-shirts walked out, heading across the lobby for the main doors. They both greeted Shane by name as they passed, and Shane greeted them by name as well.

"All right," she said. "I believe you."

"Do you like Thai food? There's a great Thai restaurant just a block from here."

"I love Thai food," Beth said. "And all this walking is making me hungry."

Shane sent a quick text message, and they were off.

"You're awfully quiet," Shane said, squeezing her hand as they headed for the restaurant.

Beth looked at him. "It's a lot to take in."

"What is?"

She shrugged. "The whole weekend, I guess. Last night and

this morning. And now I find out you own a rather sizable chunk of downtown Chicago real estate."

"Is that a problem?"

"I don't know," she said, answering him honestly. She was just starting to realize how little she knew about him.

"Hey." He stopped her on the sidewalk and clasped her hands. "I know it's been a bit of a whirlwind weekend, but it's all good, right?"

She nodded, but Shane was far from convinced. She had trust issues. Maybe he was pushing her too fast, but the thought of backing off didn't sit well with him either. He wanted to push forward. He wanted to cement their budding relationship before she found out about his involvement with her brother. Before she found out about Howard Kline's parole. He wanted to be the one responsible for her protection, and for that to happen, she needed to trust him.

They stopped in front of a small hole-in-the-wall restaurant, and Shane opened the door for Beth. Inside, several couples sat on wooden benches waiting to be seated.

The young blond woman standing behind the host's podium waved at Shane. "Good afternoon, Mr. McIntyre." She grabbed two menus and waved them forward. "Your table is ready, sir. If you'll follow me."

"I texted ahead and made reservations," Shane explained, seeing the surprised look on Beth's face.

They followed their host to the rear of the restaurant, where she seated them at a small table for two in a quiet corner. Several potted trees and a freestanding wooden screen provided ample privacy. Beth picked up her menu and began studying it with an unwavering degree of concentration.

Shane watched her quietly for several moments, and she never once looked up. "Beth?"

"Hmm?"

He gently plucked the menu from her hands and laid it on the white damask tablecloth. "Talk to me. What's wrong?"

Beth shook her head. "Nothing's wrong." The truth was, she

was overwhelmed.

He reached across the table and took her hands in his. "You've hardly said a word since we left the office building. Talk to me."

She took a deep breath and shrugged. "I hardly know anything about you," she said.

"That's not true."

She looked around to see if anyone was within hearing distance. "You own a very expensive office building and a penthouse apartment in a very prestigious building, and you didn't even blink when you spent nearly four thousand dollars today on a dress and a pair of shoes. You're obviously rather wealthy. What else don't I know about you?"

Shane squeezed her hands. "I'm well off financially, yes," he said, frowning. "Is that a crime?"

"No, of course not," she said. "It's just... I'm not used to that, Shane. I was raised by a single mom. We had what we needed, and we were comfortable, but I just can't relate to that kind of money. I guess I should have realized how wealthy you are after seeing your apartment on Lake Shore Drive. That apartment is prime real estate."

He grimaced. "In the spirit of full disclosure, I should confess that I own that building, too."

She felt the bottom drop out of her stomach, and suddenly she was queasy. "You own the whole apartment building?"

"Yes. It's a very lucrative commercial investment," he said, sounding almost apologetic. "I reserve the top five floors for my employees, and the penthouse floor is mine. The rest of the units are leased out at full market rate. Two of my brothers and one sister also live in that building."

"Do you own other property as well?" she said.

"I also have a house in Kenilworth."

"Is that it?"

He nodded. "That's the extent of my personal real estate holdings. But the business owns a number of properties in the U.S. and abroad. We have a number of offices around the world."

Beth felt the blood drain out of her face. He was so out of her league.

Their server arrived at their table to take their drink orders. Shane ordered a bottle of beer, and Beth ordered her usual cola.

Beth pulled her hands from Shane's and dropped them in her lap.

Shane frowned as she looked away. "I'm not going to let you run, Beth."

"I'm not running," she said, looking at him. "I'm just — " She stopped, at a loss for words.

"You're just *what?*"

"I'm just trying to take it all in," she said. "It's a lot to process."

"You can have all the time you need, sweetheart, just as long as you don't run."

Beth shook her head. "I don't want to run."

But, in truth, that's exactly what she wanted to do. She wanted to go home and be alone with her thoughts. She needed time to make sense of the whirlwind past forty-eight hours.

Shane handed Beth her menu. "Let's eat, and then we'll go home. Back to my apartment."

Their server returned with their drinks, and they ordered a sushi sampler platter to share and two curried rice dishes. Beth sat quietly, preoccupied with her own thoughts as she sipped her soft drink.

Shane sat back in his chair and watched Beth intently. Her eyes were everywhere but on him, and that made him nervous. Actually, it scared the hell out of him, and that was an uncomfortable first. Nothing scared him. But the thought of losing her... damn it!

"Tell me about your job," he said, hoping to pull her out of her reverie. If the fact that they didn't know a lot about each other bothered her, then he'd rectify the situation.

She glanced up, seemingly surprised by his question. "I work in the library at Kingston School of Medicine."

"That's in Hyde Park, right?"

"Yes. It's not far from my home."

Of course, he knew where she worked. He knew just about everything about her, but he needed to get her talking.

"I'm a reference librarian in Special Collections," she said. "I manage the school's collection of rare and antique medical reference materials."

"Do you enjoy your job?"

She shrugged. "I love books. Working in a library seemed like a good fit for me. I couldn't afford to do what I really wanted to do."

"And what's that?" he said.

She smiled, her eyes lighting up. "I've always wanted to own a bookstore. That's my idea of heaven."

"Why don't you?"

"That's way beyond my means. I have college loans and a car to pay off."

Their server arrived with their appetizer and drink refills, and while they were sampling the assortment of sushi rolls, their entrees arrived.

"What about you?" she asked. "What's your dream job?"

"I have my dream job. I protect people and eliminate their problems."

"That's a very admirable profession," she said.

Shane kept her talking as they ate, encouraging her to tell him more about her job at the library. The more she talked, the more she seemed to relax. As they finished the meal, their server returned with the check, and Shane settled the bill. Then he texted Cooper and arranged for a pick-up.

On the drive back to Shane's apartment, Beth's curiosity got the best of her, and she pulled out the gift-wrapped package Sylvia had given her. She laid it on her lap, smoothing her hands over the soft tissue paper. She grabbed one end of the ribbon and pulled.

She stared in fascination at the exquisite silk and lace lingerie set in her lap, stroking the pale cream delicate fabrics. "They're beautiful!" she said, and then she laughed. "I guess Sylvia didn't think my plain old cotton bra and panties were up to par."

Shane picked up the dainty lace garter belt and held it up at eye level, admiring the dangling stocking clips. "Sylvia's trying to kill me."

Beth laughed as she snagged the garter belt from Shane's hands.

He turned in his seat to face her. "You could model all this for me at the apartment... just to be sure it fits."

Beth grinned at him. "Maybe I will," she said, fingering the silk undergarments.

Shane couldn't help but smile. Was she actually flirting with him? Unable to help himself, he leaned over and kissed her. He'd meant to keep it light, a teasing, seductive reminder of their previous night together, or a hint of what was to come. But the thought of seeing her in that lingerie made him slightly crazed.

He imagined peeling the sheer silk stockings off her long, coltish legs, and it made him hard. He imagined kissing his way up her legs to the apex of her silky inner thighs and nuzzling the crotch of those dainty silk panties. Then he wanted to strip those panties down her legs, spread her wide, and bury his face between her thighs.

His thoughts went somewhere dark when he realized she'd be wearing the lingerie underneath her fuck-me sex-kitten dress at the hospital fundraiser. Men would be looking at her in that dress, undressing her with their eyes and imagining what was underneath it. Just the thought made him a little crazy.

What had started as a gentle kiss quickly morphed into something hungry and slightly out of control. Shane abruptly released his seat belt and leaned into Beth, pressing her back in her seat. His mouth opened over hers, firm and insistent, and she gasped as his tongue pushed its way inside her mouth.

His hand went to her breast, cupping and kneading it through her blouse, and he reveled in the feel of the soft, pliant mound beneath his palm. His other arm wrapped around her waist, and he pulled her against him.

Beth was kissing him back just as eagerly, and soon they were both breathless. When his thumb and finger sought her nipple through her blouse and lightly pinched the little tip, she whimpered into his mouth.

Her eager response had the same effect on him as throwing gasoline on an already raging fire. His hand skimmed down her legs to the hemline of her skirt and burrowed up underneath it, skimming up her bare legs, seeking the warmth between her thighs.

He pressed his fingers against the damp crotch of her panties as he sucked at her mouth. Capturing her lower lip gently between his teeth, he gave her a tiny little bite, and then he licked the spot soothingly.

His index finger slipped inside her panties to find her already flushed with moist heat. When his finger delved into her damp curls and found her clitoris, she cried into his mouth, the sound startlingly loud in the enclosed space of the car.

"Shane!" Cooper barked from the front seat.

Shane froze as if he'd been doused with ice water. His mouth stilled on hers, and he withdrew his hand from beneath her skirt as if he'd been burned. He pulled back, abruptly releasing her. He'd been so caught up in the heat of the moment he hadn't realized he'd been practically crushing her into her seat, pinning her in place — and she hadn't seemed to realize it either.

"Fuck," he grated, his own face flushing hotly as he took in her dazed expression.

Beth's lips were swollen from his demanding kisses, and her pupils were dilated with arousal.

Shane reached up and touched her cheek, and her eyes widened when she detected the scent of her arousal on his fingers.

"We'll be home in fifteen minutes," Cooper said. "I honestly don't mind the show, but surely you two can wait that long."

Shane caught Cooper's gaze in the rearview mirror and nodded, silently offering his thanks. Cooper returned the gesture.

"I'm sorry, Beth," Shane said, searching her expression for

signs of anxiety. He gently brushed her lower lip, which was wet and not a little swollen from his kisses. "I got carried away."

Beth smiled tremulously because she was okay. In fact, she was more than okay. She'd loved every moment of his delicious assault. "I'm fine," she whispered, although her gaze kept turning guiltily to Cooper.

"I wasn't thinking," he said, his voice quiet. He straightened in his seat and buckled his seatbelt, facing forward.

Beth reached for his hand and gently squeezed it. "I'm fine," she reiterated, wanting to erase the self-reproving expression on his face.

And she did seem fine. He glanced at her and caught her smiling shyly at him, her cheeks pink and her eyes glittering.

She leaned over to him and pressed her lips to his ear. "I want you," she breathed, her voice barely more than air. Then she pulled back and looked at him, smiling at the answering heat in his eyes.

He was definitely on board with that.

23

They couldn't get back to his apartment fast enough, as far as Shane was concerned.

I want you.

She'd actually said that. Her words replayed in his head, over and over like a mantra. Right now, all he could think about was getting her home and into his bed. The image of her wearing the lingerie Sylvia had given her while sitting astride his cock was burning a hole in his brain.

Cooper dropped them off at the front entrance of the building, making some excuse about taking the car to get it fueled, which Shane knew was code for *You can have the place to yourselves for a while, idiot.*

The air in the private elevator was thick with anticipation, and it was all he could do to keep his hands off her. He was afraid if he touched her now, he'd end up taking her in the elevator.

He glanced at Beth's reflection in the mirrored wall, noting the high color in her pale cheeks. She was biting her bottom lip, and he realized she was excited. Her hair was still tied up in a loose knot with the ribbon Sylvia had given her at the dress shop, but it looked a bit worse for wear after he'd groped her in the car like a desperate teenager. She looked mussed and ready for bed, and he was only too happy to take her there.

Damn it, what had gotten into him back there in the car? It

was a miracle he didn't scare the shit out of her, pouncing on her like that. And surprisingly, she hadn't panicked on him, even though he'd pinned her to her seat like a sailor nailing a dock whore to a tavern wall.

Even now she was flushed, her eyes bright, and he could almost feel the excited energy radiating from her. He squeezed her hand, and she squeezed his back.

"Did I scare you in the car?"

Beth shook her head. "No."

The elevator door opened, and they stepped into the foyer. Now that they were home, Shane couldn't wait another second to pull Beth into his arms. Her mouth opened eagerly under his, her tongue shyly meeting his. She moaned sweetly into his mouth, and the sound of her eager pleasure made him even harder.

Shane pulled back. "Are you sure you aren't too sore?" He'd at least try to do the right thing. He'd give her an out, if she needed one, even if it killed him.

"I'm sure." Her arms went around his neck, and she went up on her toes to kiss him with a fervor that matched his own.

"Fuck," he said. "I can't wait." He lifted her skirt and picked her up. "Wrap your legs around my waist."

Shane carried Beth across the foyer to a console table set against the wall. He sat her on the table between a brass lamp and a vase of fresh-cut flowers.

"I want to fuck you right here," he said, breathing heavily as he shoved her skirt up past her thighs. He spread her bare legs and stepped between them. "Do you have a problem with that?" he said, pulling her hips to the edge of the table. *Dear God, please say no.*

"No," she said, looking up at him somewhat dazed.

When her gaze darted nervously toward the elevator, he strode to the elevator and punched a code into the electronic panel on the wall. "The elevator is out of service now," he said, coming back to her. "No one can use it without buzzing me first. We won't be interrupted."

Beth looked at him skeptically.

"Only Cooper can bypass the code I just entered," Shane said. "And trust me, he knows better than to come back here right now. There's nothing to worry about, I promise."

He pinned her with this hot gaze, painfully aware of the hesitation in her eyes. His hands came up to cup her face. "Sweetheart, I would *never* put you at risk."

She nodded, relaxing. "Okay."

Shane wasted no time reaching underneath her skirt with both hands to grasp the waistband of her panties and work them down her hips. Beth braced her hands on the marble table top and rocked her hips to help him. Once he got them off, he stuffed them into his back pocket.

Beth gasped when her bare buttocks came into contact with the cold marble tabletop.

Shane grinned at her expression. He reached up and caressed her face. "You are so beautiful. I look at you and lose myself, every time."

He unbuttoned her blouse and pushed it off her shoulders, leaving her sitting there in her bra with her skirt bunched up around her waist. He reached behind her to unclasp her bra, and then he very slowly peeled it from her body, watching hungrily as her nipples reacted to the cool air. Her hands came up over her breasts.

"Put your hands down, sweetheart," he said.

Beth couldn't stop shivering, and it had nothing to do with the temperature. She was sitting practically naked in Shane's foyer in the middle of the day while he was fully clothed. Even though she believed him when he said he'd taken the elevator out of service, she still couldn't help worrying that someone could walk in on them at any moment. And if that happened, she would die of mortification.

Shane watched her intently, probably looking for signs of anxiety. She was breathing hard, true, but it wasn't because of anxiety. She was excited, and he must have been able to tell that because he was pushing her a little bit.

"Beth. Hands. Flat on the table."

She dropped her hands to the table top and glanced up at him.

"Good girl." He brushed her lower lip with his thumb. "God, I want you. You want this? You want me?"

She swallowed hard. "Yes."

That was all the green light Shane seemed to need because he pulled her forward, right to the edge of the table, and dropped to his knees. When he pushed her thighs wide open and his gazed locked on her sex, her legs started shaking. She would have closed them if he hadn't moved between them, essentially pinning them open.

He looked up at her. "Okay?"

She nodded.

His eyes returned to her sex and he studied her, which she found very unnerving.

"Keep your legs open," he said, removing his hands. He reached between her thighs and opened her up to his hot gaze. "You're beautiful, so pink and glistening."

He stroked her from her core to her clitoris, and she shivered. Then he leaned forward and followed that same path with the tip of his tongue.

And then his mouth was on her, his lips and tongue teasing her clitoris.

"Oh, my God!" she cried, staring down at the top of his head, simultaneously shocked and aroused by the sight of him between her thighs. Her hands went to his head, but whether it was to push him away or pull him closer, she wasn't sure. In the end, her fingers sank into his thick hair, and she gripped his head tightly as she squirmed under his assault.

"That's right," he said, his growl muffled against her slick flesh. "Put me where you want me, baby." He ate at her like a starving man presented with a buffet, his tongue lashing at her clitoris. His held her thighs wide apart, and she leaned back, using her hands to brace herself on the tabletop.

Her legs trembled violently and her hips began rocking against his mouth. "Shane!"

Shane made an unintelligible sound between her legs, not bothering to lift his mouth from her sex. He licked at her, nibbling, stroking with his firm tongue. When he lifted her legs to open her even farther, his tongue pushed deep into her channel, and she bucked frantically against his mouth. As he stroked his tongue in and out of her, his thumb rubbed gentle circles on her clitoris.

The two-pronged attack was more than she could bear, and the pressure built steadily inside her. Breathing heavily, he pulled back and inserted his index finger into her wet channel, zeroing in on a spot deep inside her, while his thumb continued to tease and taunt her clit. Dueling sensations spiraled upward inside her, and she felt herself shaking uncontrollably as her impending release rose higher and higher.

"Shane!" she gasped, closing her eyes tightly.

"I know, baby," he said, peering up at her face. "Open your eyes and look at me. I want to watch you come."

She shook her head, panting as she fought against the inevitable.

"Look at me, Beth."

She opened her eyes, and they were a little bit wild as she met his gaze.

"Just let it happen, sweetheart," he said.

He was merciless as he stroked her sex, ratcheting her up until she came in a blinding rush, her cry a breathy, keening sound.

Shane shot to his feet, swiping his hand across his glistening wet mouth. The scent of Beth's arousal was strong in the air, and Shane's nostrils flared sharply. His hands went to the fastener of his jeans and yanked them open, and then shoved both his jeans and his boxers down to free his rigid cock, which protruded from his body like a battering ram.

Beth took in the sight of his cock, long and thick, and darkly flushed. Her eyes tracked the thick vein ran the length of him.

He fisted himself roughly, and a drop of glistening fluid seeped from the slit in the fat crown. Leaning forward, he teased her wet opening with the head of his cock, coating himself with her arousal. He stepped closer and wedged himself into her opening, then began pressing slowly and steadily inside her. His eyes were locked intently on hers as he watched her response.

They cried out simultaneously when his cock sank deep inside her. She gasped, partly in discomfort and partly from surprise, as his cock pushed ruthlessly into her silky, wet channel. It didn't hurt exactly, but the size of him stretched her wide, and she felt the burn as her body accommodated him. Her hands went to his wrists, gripping him tightly.

Shane started to move then, long, steady strokes, Beth gasping at the intensity of his thrusts. His mouth covered hers, drinking in her breaths and the keening sounds she made.

"God, you're so tight," he grated, his breath soughing in his chest as he stroked long and hard into her core.

Shane pressed his hot face into the curve of her neck, dropping kisses onto her pulse point and breathing deeply as he savored the scent of her damp skin. He couldn't get enough of her scent; he wanted to immerse himself in it.

Finally, he pulled back, his gaze going to his cock as he watched himself tunnel in and out of her body, his cock dragging through her wet tissues, creating the most exquisite friction.

"Watch us," he said. "Watch your body take in mine."

Beth looked down between them, mesmerized by the sight of his cock sliding powerfully in and out of her body. Her body had opened and softened, and now he could move comfortably inside her now. She watched his cock slam into her body, and then pull out, only to slam right back inside. With every stroke, the heat and the friction increased, stoking a fire deep inside her body.

Shane's heart was pounding so hard in his chest it was nearly choking him. His entire being was focused on the sensation of burying himself as deeply in her wet heat as he could. The act was more than just a simple coupling, and the realization stunned him. What he felt for her — the way his body roused for her, simultaneously wanting to dominate her and pleasure her — was something he'd never experienced.

The idea that this was something different for him, that this — that *she* — was something different, shocked him. He grabbed her face and held her still for his kiss, his mouth stealing her breath and drinking in her soft whimpers. When his cock exploded inside her and he filled her with his scalding heat, he shouted to the rafters, his rough voice filling the room.

Beth's mind reeled from the multitude of emotions and sensations hitting her all at once. Her sex burned from being stretched and pummeled, but it was a sweet fire that she reveled in. At the end, he'd taken her almost mindlessly, and she'd loved it. She'd always craved a physical union like this one, hot and fiery, all consuming, but it had always evaded her before now. Somehow, Shane made it all right. Right now he was buried so deeply inside her she couldn't tell where she left off and he began.

"Christ," he gasped, leaning forward to rest his forehead against hers, his chest heaving. "You're killing me, baby," he said to her, his voice catching.

As the tremors from his climax subsided, Shane's thrusts slowed to a gentle, gliding motion, and he relished the feel of his cock sliding in and out of her body. He stroked her slowly, gritting his teeth at the hypersensitivity of his cock.

Shane reluctantly pulled out of her body, and Beth looked down, captivated by the sight of his thick, ruddy cock coated with her body's juices and his semen.

They glanced up at each other simultaneously.

"Fuck!" he said, his eyes locked on hers. He gripped her thighs hard.

"I guess we got carried away," Beth said as she glanced down at the evidence.

Shane stared at her, dumbfounded. "I've never forgotten to use protection," he said. "Damn it, I'm sorry."

"It's okay," she said. In truth, she was reeling and didn't know what to think.

"No, it's not okay," he said, his voice tight. "I fucked up." Shane stepped back from the table and pulled up his boxers and jeans.

"I'm sure it'll be fine," she said, watching as his jaw clenched tightly. She reached out and grasped his hand. "It'll be fine, Shane. Don't worry."

Shane collected Beth's discarded clothing and threw them over his shoulder. Then he swept her up into his arms. "Come on, sweetheart," he said, kissing her sweat-dampened temple. "Let's get you cleaned up."

24

The apartment was eerily silent as they stepped through the foyer door into the hushed interior. Shane carried Beth to the master suite and laid her on his bed. After draping her blouse and undergarments carefully over the bench at the foot of the bed, he removed her skirt and covered her with the sheet, and then disappeared into the bathroom.

She lay on the bed feeling awkward as she felt his semen leaking from between her legs. She hadn't realized sex was so messy. Not really sure what the proper etiquette was in such a situation, she contemplated getting up and going to the bathroom herself to clean up when he returned with a warm washcloth.

"I think I'm making a mess on the sheets," she said.

Silently, he proceeded to wipe her clean, his actions gentle and methodical. He said nothing, his expression preoccupied.

His silence was starting to unnerve her. "Say something," she said when he'd finished and pulled the sheet back over her.

He looked down at her. "What do you want me to say?" he said, his voice harsh. "I already admitted I fucked up."

"No, you didn't fuck up."

"Yes, I did."

"It wasn't just your responsibility, Shane. Last I heard, it takes two to tango."

He looked far from convinced. "When was your last period?"

She shrugged. "I don't know. A couple of weeks ago, I guess."

He frowned. "You'd have nothing to worry about. You know that, right?"

She nodded. She might not know everything about Shane, but she knew without a doubt that he'd never shirk his responsibilities. "I know." She reached for his hand. "I'm not worried."

"I'll be right back," he said, releasing her hand as he headed for the bathroom.

After he'd gone, she sat up in bed, feeling suddenly bereft. She knew he was deeply shaken by what they'd done, but she couldn't help feeling like he'd shut her out. Afraid she'd worn out her welcome, she started crawling toward the foot of the bed to grab her clothes.

"What are you doing?" he said as he returned to the bed, his tone almost accusatory.

Startled, she turned to look at him. "I'm — " The words died in her throat. He was naked. She'd been expecting him to pack her up and send her home. Instead, he'd stripped naked.

"Getting dressed," she said, haltingly. "I should go."

"Now?" He looked disappointed. "Can't you stay a little while longer?"

Beth sat back down and tried to arrange herself in a somewhat demure pose, which wasn't easy as she'd been crawling naked across his big bed. "You want me to stay?"

"Yes, I want you to stay," he said, climbing onto the bed and reaching for her. He lay down and pulled her close. "You didn't get much sleep last night. I thought we could rest for a while, and then have dinner. There's plenty of pasta left over from last night. Or, if you don't want that, we can order something in. And there's more Tiramisu. You liked that."

"Okay," Beth said, grinning as she snuggled down beside him. His body radiated heat like a furnace, and she sighed. She could get used to this.

Shane kissed her forehead and slid one leg between hers,

the crinkly hair on his leg scratchy the tender skin of her inner thighs. "Are you warm enough?"

"Yes, thank you."

"I know it's no excuse," he said, his expression as grim, "but back there in the foyer, I couldn't have remembered my own name, let alone to use protection. I'm sorry, Beth."

"I didn't think about it either," she said, melting into his embrace. She laid her head on his chest, right over his heart, and she could feel his heartbeat against her temple. She loved this, being close to him, savoring his warmth and the security of his embrace. Now she knew what she'd been missing.

Shane began to rub his hand up and down her bare back, and she groaned from the pleasure.

"Have you ever thought about having kids?" Shane said off-handedly. "I don't mean now, of course, but someday. Do you want kids?"

"Sure," she said, measuring the steady beats of his heart. "I've always wanted kids."

Shane smiled. "I come from a big family. When I was growing up, there was always someone around to play with. I want that someday for my kids." He tipped her face toward his and kissed her gently. "You've had a busy weekend," he said. "Are you okay?"

She smiled. "I'm more than okay. I'm wonderful."

"Yes, you are," he said. "I've loved every minute we've spent together."

Beth frowned. "Well, maybe not all of it. Certainly not the drama and the hysterics last night. I'm sorry about that."

"Hey." He kissed her gently. "We got through it, though, didn't we? And we did all right in the end. There's absolutely no reason for you to reproach yourself."

"It's not going to be that easy," she said. "The panic attacks come without warning." She never knew when the next one would hit.

"I know," he said, stroking her hair. "One day at a time, right?"

Beth gazed down at their bodies lying entwined, marveling at the differences between them. His body was so different from hers, and not just in the obvious ways. Everything about him was bigger, rougher, darker. He was just so male. His skin was tanned a warm golden shade, his muscles so well defined.

She relaxed against him, her muscles turning to liquid, and her eyes grew heavy. She closed her eyes, *just for a minute.*

Shane smiled when he realized Beth had fallen asleep in his arms. She had to be exhausted. It had a been a whirlwind week-end, and she hadn't gotten much sleep the night before. And then they'd spent much of their day walking around downtown. He was glad she felt safe enough with him to drift off to sleep. That had to mean something.

He pulled her closer, practically wrapping himself around her body, and let himself take a cat nap.

The sun was starting to set when Shane woke. Outside, the sky was a light shade of indigo, and the buildings all around them were starting to light up the night sky. Inside his bedroom it was twilight, adding to the sense of intimacy.

"Lights, thirty percent," he said. He didn't want Beth to wake up in a dark room.

They were still wrapped in each other's arms, so it was an easy thing for him to lean close and nuzzle her temple. He breathed in the scent of her hair, and it made him instantly hard. He trailed kisses down her cheek to her jaw and ultimately to her throat, where he pressed his lips against her pulse point.

It was incredibly satisfying to have her in his bed. Before, he'd usually taken women to hotels for sex because he didn't want them getting too comfortable in his home, or expecting more than he was willing to give. In fact, he couldn't remember the last time he'd had a woman here at the penthouse, and he sure as hell never took a woman to his home in Kenilworth.

He'd always been upfront with women about what he wanted and what his intentions were. Sex was just a mutually satisfying encounter, where both parties got what they wanted and moved on. He was generous with his money when it came to women — because it was *just money.* Money was simply a tool to be used to accomplish an end. He'd gladly wine and dine them, take them to the best places, buy them clothes or jewelry or whatever it was they desired, and fly them to L.A., or New York City or even Paris for a weekend of sex. But his personal space — that had always been off limits.

Until now.

As he watched Beth sleep, he couldn't help wondering why this was different. He hadn't wasted any time at all getting her to his penthouse, in his bed. He'd been with a lot of women, and he'd always walked away afterward and never looked back. She was beautiful, yes, but he'd dated lots of beautiful women. He'd certainly dated women that were far more sophisticated and experienced. So why was it that every time he looked at her he felt like his next breath depended on her?

He stroked the bare skin of her arm with his fingertips and reveled in its softness. She was so soft, so defenseless. And she'd been hurt so badly. Once again, he felt a quiet, burning rage creep into veins, and he had to suppress the desire to end Howard Kline once and for all. He couldn't let that monster continue to roam free, posing a threat to Beth or to any other woman. Somehow, some way, he'd find a way to end that bastard. It was only a matter of time.

When Beth stirred, making sleepy sounds of annoyance from being awakened, he found himself grinning like an idiot. For God's sake, what was it about her that had him so tied up in knots? He only knew that every time he looked at her, his heart practically stopped. And for the first time in his adult life, he wasn't thinking about his next lay. Instead, he thinking ahead to a future he'd never given much thought to before. And that meant they needed to talk.

He dreaded opening up this can of worms, because he didn't know how she'd react to learning about Kline's release and the role Shane's company was playing in her life. But he had no choice, and now was as good a time as any.

"Hey, sleepyhead," he murmured into her hair as her eyes fluttered open. "Good evening."

She stretched, groaning like a noisy cat. "What time is it?"

"Almost six. Are you hungry?"

"Yes."

"I'm sure we can find something good in the kitchen. But first, can we talk?"

She turned toward him and buried her face in the crook of his neck. "No. No talking. Just eating."

He chuckled. "We need to talk, sweetheart."

"I thought guys didn't like to talk," she said. "Why are you the exception?"

"In this case, we need to. I need you to tell me what happened to you."

"No," she groaned, rubbing her face against him.

He'd known this wasn't going to be easy. She could be very stubborn. "Beth."

"Let's not ruin the afternoon," she said, her fingers meandering down his chest.

"We need to talk about it," he said, trying to ignore the pleasure of her touch. He could feel his blood flowing south to his dick.

Her hand continued its downward progress, moving past his belly button as she followed the trail of dark hair that arrowed down to his groin. Oh, hell. He shoved the sheet aside, shamelessly giving her access to his body.

"We don't have to talk right this minute," she said. "It can wait."

By the time her fingers reached the base of his cock, he was already erect. Beth smiled, thrilled with the effect she had on him.

"You're trying to distract me," he said as he watched her fingers gripped his cock.

"Is it working?"

He laughed. "Yes. You damn well know it is."

When she stroked the full length of him, he captured her hand and brought it to his mouth. He kissed the tips of her fingers, and then brought her hand to lay on his chest, where he held it to him.

"I know you don't want to talk about it, but we have to. I can help you, Beth. That's what I do. I help people, with... problems. I — my company helps keep people safe from threats. You told me someone hurt you."

"But that's all in the past, Shane." She pulled her hand out from underneath his. "There's no threat now. He's in prison." Beth went up on her knees and crawled toward the foot of the bed.

Oh, hell. "What are you doing?"

Hovering over him on all fours, Beth grinned. "It's my turn."

"Your turn to do what?" Although he knew damned well what she was up to.

She smiled as she wrapped her hand around the base of his thick cock.

"No you don't," he said, reaching for her. "You're not distracting me that easily. Come back here and talk to me."

Beth dodged Shane's reach, determined to go through with this come hell or high water. She'd never done this before, but she'd read about it enough that she should be an expert. Part of her did want to distract him from a serious conversation, but, mostly, she just wanted to do this, with him.

"You go ahead and talk all you want," she said. "Don't mind me." When her tongue came out to wet her lips and his eyes followed the movement, she couldn't help smiling. When her tongue darted out to touch the tip of his cock, his body bowed up off the bed.

"Fuck!"

She smiled, garnering sorely needed confidence from his reaction. He'd given her such incredible pleasure with his mouth, and now it was her turn. She leaned down and licked his erection from its base to its tip, her tongue coming up over the top of the crown, swirling around the sensitive head. Her tongue licked the slit at the tip of his erection, and she tasted something salty.

"Jesus, Beth!" he said, throwing his head back onto his pillow.

When she closed her lips over the head of his cock, sucking him deeply into the wet heat of her mouth, he fisted the sheets and groaned. And then she started to suck on him, her tongue and lips greedy as she drew on him.

"Oh, fuck!" he cried, raw and shameless as he clutched blindly at the bedding. "Beth!"

She wrapped one hand around the base of his cock and ran her tongue from root to tip, following the path of a thick vein that ran the length of him. The muscles in his thighs tensed as if stretched by taut wires, and his long, muscular limbs trembled. His breaths soughed harshly in and out of his chest. She licked her lips to wet them, and then opened them wide over the crown of his cock once more, sucking him into her mouth. His hips bucked, and he gathered her hair back from her face so he could watch her mouth on him.

As she worked his cock with her mouth and one hand, her other hand gently massaged the soft skin of his scrotum. She continued her gentle assault on his sac, astonished when she felt his balls draw up tight. His hands gripped at her head, almost painfully, but she reveled in his loss of control, thrilled that she was affecting him this way.

"I'm going to come," he rasped. "Beth, I can't — "

She lifted her mouth from his cock for a split second and took a breath, filling her starved lungs with much-needed oxygen. "Do it!" she gasped, swallowing him again. A moment later, his body shuddered violently as he bucked into her mouth, releasing himself.

"Jesus, Beth," Shane gasped, sitting up and reaching for her. He pulled her up the length of his body and wrapped her tightly in his arms. "I'm seeing stars," he said, his voice little more than a hoarse rasp. He lay boneless, his muscles twitching as his climax rippled through him.

Beth turned her head to catch his mouth and kissed him.

Shane smiled ruefully. "You did that to distract me," he said. "Mind you, I'm not complaining."

"I don't want to talk right now, Shane, please."

He gazed down at her beseeching expression and caved, even though he knew it was wrong. They needed to clear the air — *he* needed to clear the air. Putting it off was a mistake, but he found it hard to deny her.

Beth looked at the clock on the nightstand. "That pasta's sounding pretty good right now."

He kissed her. "All right," he said. "Let's eat."

Beth transferred the leftover pasta to a large casserole dish and put it in the microwave oven to gently warm. Shane set two plates for them at the counter, and then grabbed a cold beer for himself and a soft drink for her. They sat down together, sipping their drinks while they waited for the food to heat.

Shane's phone buzzed with an incoming message. "It's Cooper. He's on his way up. See, I told you he wouldn't interrupt us."

Beth felt her face heat up when she heard the elevator ping in the foyer, announcing Cooper's arrival. Surely Cooper knew what they'd been up to all afternoon, especially after that little show they'd given him in the SUV. Beth stifled a laugh when she realized Shane's apartment was essentially a very expensive bachelor pad, and Cooper was Shane's wingman of sorts.

"Hey, kids," Cooper said, walking into the kitchen holding two paper grocery sacks.

"Hi, Cooper," Beth said, giving him a little wave.

Cooper set the bags on the counter, and Shane stood up to peer into them.

"Thanks for doing the shopping," Shane said.

"There's more downstairs. Jake and Liam are carrying up the rest."

Shane glanced at Cooper, and a telling look passed between them.

"My brothers," Shane said to Beth.

"Oh, good," she said. "I'd like to meet them."

They heard the faint ping of the elevator. "And here they come now," Shane said, glancing pointedly at Cooper.

"I told them you had company, Shane," Cooper said.

Two men strode into the kitchen, apparently in the middle of an argument over baseball. One of them — a dark-haired, muscular man — carried two sacks of groceries. He looked rather intimidating in black jeans and a black t-shirt. Both of his arms were covered in complex patterns of swirling and geometric black tattoos. Beth couldn't decide if he was gorgeous or scary, and then decided he was both. The second man, who was blond and leaner than his brothers, was adroitly juggling four cartons of beer bottles.

Shane stepped forward and took two of the cartons of beer from the blond brother. "Hey, guys," he said, as his brothers set their packages on the kitchen counter. "There's someone I'd like you to meet."

The two brothers turned simultaneously and contemplated Beth. They didn't seem surprised to see her there.

"Beth, these are my brothers Jake and Liam," Shane said, pointing out which was which — the dark one being Jake, the blond one Liam. "Guys, this is Beth Jamison."

"Hi, Beth," Jake said, offering his hand to her. He gave her hand a firm shake. "It's a pleasure to meet you."

Beth smiled. "It's a pleasure to meet you, too."

She glanced at the blond brother. "Both of you," she added, extending her hand to Liam.

Liam shook her hand. "Nice to meet you," Liam said, holding on to her hand. "We heard through the grapevine that Shane had a *lady friend* over for the weekend, so we thought we'd come check you out."

"Okay, that's enough, Casanova," Shane said, liberating Beth's hand and pushing Liam back. "They're housetrained, Beth," Shane said, looking at her, "despite appearances."

Beth smiled. It was obvious that the three brothers were close.

Jake and Liam helped themselves to bottles of cold beer from the fridge and took seats at the kitchen counter.

The microwave beeped, announcing that the pasta was ready. Beth opened the microwave door, and the tantalizing aroma of Pasta Bolognese filled the air. She was glad she'd heated it all because she had a sneaking suspicion they'd need it.

"What smells so good?" Liam said, popping open his beer bottle. "Is there enough to share?"

⚘ 25

When it became apparent that his brothers hadn't come to torpedo him in front of Beth, Shane let himself relax a bit. They'd given him a few accusatory looks, but they'd been nothing but cordial to Beth.

While he and Cooper set the dining room table, Beth brought in the hot casserole dish, and Jake and Liam carried in cold drinks for everyone. Shane also brought out the bottle of Chianti they'd opened the night before, and they ended up having a pretty nice little impromptu dinner party.

He kept a close eye on Beth, afraid she might be overwhelmed by the unexpected company, but she seemed fine, smiling and talking — in fact, she seemed more than fine. She appeared to enjoy all the nonstop talk at the table about everything from the summer's gas prices to the Chicago Cubs to boxing.

Shane poured himself a glass of wine. "Would you like some?" he asked Beth.

She shook her head. "No thanks," she said, sipping her soft drink. "I'm good."

"To good food, and even better, to family and friends," Cooper said, raising his beer bottle for a toast, and they all joined in.

There was plenty of food to go around. Shane ate his fill, and then he leaned back in his chair to relax and sip his wine and watch Beth enjoying herself.

"So, Shane," Jake said, abruptly changing the topic of conversation. He leaned back in his chair and eyed Beth. "Have you told Beth about what you do for a living?"

Shane knew he could count on Jake to cause trouble. He eyed his brother sharply. *Shut up, Jake.* "Yes, I have."

"He showed me his office building when we were downtown this afternoon," Beth said, wiping her mouth on a napkin. "You work with him, right?"

"I do," Jake said. "So does Liam and our sister Lia. I just wondered if the topic had come up yet in conversation."

Shane tried to be subtle as he glared daggers at his brother. As usual, Jake knew how to push. Shane didn't like keeping Beth in the dark any more than the others did. And he knew Jake had a problem with Shane seeing Beth romantically when she was a client of theirs — even if she wasn't aware of that fact. *Talk about a conflict of interest.*

"We have dessert," Shane said, rising from the table. "Give me a hand in the kitchen, Jake."

Jake grinned at Shane as he stood. "I'd love to, Shane."

As soon as they were in the kitchen, Shane turned to face his brother, crossing his arms over his chest as he glared at Jake. "What the fuck are you doing?"

"You haven't told her yet," Jake said.

"No, I haven't. But I will, so back off."

"When?" Jake said.

"Soon."

Jake leaned against a kitchen counter. "You're playing with fire here, dipshit. If she hears it from someone else first, you're screwed. I'm just trying to do you a favor, man."

"I know that," Shane said, grabbing a serving spoon from the cutlery drawer. "But she doesn't like talking about her past. As soon as I bring it up, she shuts me down."

"*She shuts you down?*" Jake scowled, pointing at the dining room. "That little girl in there *shuts you down?* What are you, some fucking pansy? How did a tiny little piece of tail shut you down?"

Shane knew Jake was intentionally trying to get a rise out of him. But still. "Watch how you talk about her, Jake," he said, his jaw tightening.

"You're pussy whipped," Jake said, an ear-splitting grin on his face. But when Shane didn't rise to the bait, Jake stopped laughing. "No, you're in love. Good God."

As soon as the words were out of Jake's mouth, Shane thought his brother might be right. He'd never put those exact words together in his head like that, but he couldn't really dispute them. Everything was different with Beth, every look, every touch. She could bring him to his knees if she realized the power she had over him. There was no use denying it. "Jake, I'll handle this. Just keep your damned mouth shut."

"Look, man," Jake said, serious now. "Either you tell her, or I will."

Shane got up into his brother's face, his expression grim. "If you tell her, I'll beat you senseless, and I mean it," he said, gritting his teeth. "I'll tell her when the time is right."

Jake shook his head in disgust. "You're taking a hell of a risk here, and you know it. What's gotten into you? Did somebody hit you with a stupid stick?"

Both men turned when they heard a soft gasp across the room. Beth stood on the other side of the counter, her wide eyes on them. She glanced warily from Shane to Jake and back.

"I'm sorry," she said, her face burning. "I came to help... I'm sorry." She turned to go.

"Beth, wait!" Shane said. He reached her side and stopped her hasty retreat. "Sweetheart, wait."

She turned toward him, her expression guarded. "I came to help bring in the Tiramisu," she said. "The others are finished eating."

"I've got it right here," Jake said, holding the dessert dish and smiling at Beth. He gave Shane a quiet look — a peace offering. "I'll take it to the table."

Beth watched Jake walk past, and then she turned to Shane. "Is everything all right?"

"Yeah. Everything's fine. It was just a sibling squabble. We do that a lot." Shane observed Beth closely. She must not have heard much of their conversation, or she wouldn't be standing there so calmly. "Let's go have dessert."

After everyone had finished eating, and they'd cleared away the dirty dishes, Shane took Beth back to his suite. It was getting late, and he knew he'd have to take her home soon. He'd monopolized most of her weekend, and she probably needed some down time at her house. Besides, she had work in the morning, and he didn't want her staying up too late. But he wasn't quite ready to let her go.

"Come sit and relax," he said, leading her to the sofa.

"I'm stuffed," Beth said as she snuggled against him.

It was well into the evening now, and the sky had turned a deep, dark blue. The nighttime view through the windows was spectacular; it was like watching a million flickering fireflies.

"I like your brothers," she said, her arms slipping around his waist. "And Cooper, too."

He smiled as he wrapped her in his arms. "They like you."

"What were you and Jake arguing about in the kitchen?"

He shrugged. "Nothing important. We argue a lot. Don't you argue with your brother?"

"Tyler?" Beth said, sounding surprised. She shook her head. "Not really." She laughed. "Tyler tells me what to do, and I do it. Anyway, I'm not the arguing type."

Shane's expression grew dark. Tyler had a lot of influence on Beth. He had no idea what the man would do when he found out about the two of them. Tyler would undoubtedly be furious, and he'd probably try to stop Beth from seeing him.

"What's wrong?" Beth said.

Shane shook himself mentally and smiled at her. "Nothing's wrong." He brushed his thumb across her lips. "I won't be able to look at your mouth again without remembering what you did to me on that bed this evening. You blew my mind, sweetheart."

She grinned. "Good. That was the plan."

He leaned forward and kissed her. Then his expression turned serious. "Beth — "

"Don't." She pressed her fingertips against his lips, and his eyelids closed at the feel of her touch. "This weekend was wonderful, Shane. Please don't spoil it by bringing up my past."

He kissed her fingers, then gently pulled them away from his mouth. She'd guessed right, but now he couldn't bring himself to ruin the moment. "That's not what I was going to say."

Her relief was palpable. "Oh. Then what?"

"I was just going to say how much I enjoyed this weekend." He gave her a long and lingering kiss.

"Oh." She relaxed against him and smiled. "I did, too."

Shane pulled her close for a long, breath-stealing kiss. His hand covered her breast through her blouse, his thumb teasing her nipple until it pebbled beneath his touch. She shivered in his arms.

He made a rough sound deep in his throat and pulled back to look at her, shaking his head. He'd had her three times in 24 hours, and he figured that was enough. She had to be sore.

"What?" she said.

Shane looked at her, amazed. She made him feel all kinds of things he'd never felt before, and he wasn't sure he liked it. For a guy like him — someone who liked to be in control of himself and his environment — that sucked. But he realized he'd rather sit here and do nothing with her than do anything with anyone else. "When I'm with you, nothing else matters."

Beth rose up on her knees and scooted closer to him, her lips hovering over his. "That's how I feel, too," she whispered against his lips. She pressed her lips against his, and then opened her mouth. When her tongue stroked along the seam of his lips, he opened his mouth to let her tongue slip inside and tangle with his.

He kissed her back like a man drowning, and she was his lifeline.

"I should go home," Beth said.

It was nearly ten o'clock, and they'd been lying on the sofa making out like teenagers, all hands and lips as they indulged in each other. The only reason he hadn't taken it to his bed was because he didn't want her to be sore the next day.

"If I'm not home soon, Gabrielle will start to worry."

"All right," he said reluctantly, hating the idea of her leaving. He wanted her with him all the time because there was nowhere safer for her than under his roof. "Let's gather up your things, and I'll take you home."

Shane double-parked in front of Beth's townhouse, very much aware of an uneasy feeling in his gut. They had no plans to see each other again before the following weekend, when he'd be taking her to the children's hospital benefit. That was six days away — too long. Hell, one day was too long.

"Will you have dinner with me tomorrow evening?" he said.

Beth smiled. "I'd love to."

"Good. I can't stand the thought of going 24 hours without seeing you."

He carried her overnight bag as he walked her to the front door. She felt oddly bereft, knowing that they would be parting shortly. She'd spent pretty much the entire weekend with him, and now the idea of being separated from him left her feeling slightly depressed.

He followed her inside. "I won't stay," he said, his hands going to her shoulders. "I'm sure you're tired. I'll just kiss you good night."

He was right, of course. Still, she felt tempted to ask him to stay the night with her. How had she become so dependent on him so quickly?

When he walked her slowly backward until she came up against the wall and lowered his mouth to hers, she felt a tiny thrill. She opened her mouth to his, and his tongue swept inside and found hers.

Shane reluctantly released her mouth and sighed. "If I don't stop now, I won't stop at all," he said, reaching out to stroke her cheek. He glanced around, taking in the quiet house. "I guess Gabrielle's not home yet."

"She's still at work. She'll be home around midnight."

"I'll pick you up for dinner tomorrow after you get off work. Do you want me to pick you up at the library or here at your house?"

"Here, if you don't mind. I'd like to come home first and freshen up."

He tucked her hair behind her ear. "What time do you get home?"

"Six."

"I'll be here." He gave her a quick parting kiss. "I'll miss you until then."

Beth smiled. "Me, too." She missed him already.

After Shane left, Beth locked up. The house was dark and quiet. Usually she liked that, but not this evening. It was late, and she needed sleep because tomorrow was a work day. But she was way too wired to sleep.

As she ran up the stairs, she felt a slight twinge deep inside, but she welcomed the soreness. Finally, at the ripe old age of 24, she'd done something she thought she'd never be able to do. And not only had she done it, it had been spectacular!

She changed into shorts and a tank top in her bedroom, grabbed her iPod and ear buds, and then went to the spare bedroom to use the treadmill. She might as well put all this energy to good use. She walked hard and fast, listening to her favorite exercise playlist, hoping to burn off some of that excess energy as well as some of the decadent calories she'd consumed over the weekend.

Her mind raced as fast as her heart as she replayed their time together over the weekend. It didn't surprise her that she'd freaked out on him the first time they'd tried to have sex. No, the surprise had been in the way he'd handled it. He didn't ridicule her. He didn't call her a freaking nutcase, like someone else had. He'd been patient and understanding, and he figured out how to get around her defenses.

She felt a little thrill at the thought that they'd be seeing each other the next day after work. It was a little scary, how quickly she'd begun to rely on him. Was it possible to be in love with someone you'd known such a short time? Her parents had only known each other a couple of months before they'd gotten married, and their marriage had been a very happy one.

After a brisk two-mile walk on the treadmill, Beth felt herself start to lag. She washed up and got ready for bed, crawling between the cool sheets with her Kindle. She read for a few minutes, but soon her eyelids were too heavy to keep open, and she shut off her reader.

Beth turned on her side and cuddled with the spare pillow, wishing it were Shane. She flushed hotly when she remembered the sex they'd had in the foyer. She'd never been so excited in her life! She couldn't really fault Shane for forgetting to use protection when it hadn't occurred to her either. They were both to blame for that.

She tried to think back to the date of her last period, but she never bothered to keep track. It had to have been at least a couple of weeks ago, which put her in the ideal window of her cycle to conceive. She wasn't sure how she felt about that. She wasn't really scared, which surprised her. She slipped one hand underneath her nightgown and laid it on her belly, feeling its soft roundness. For a moment, she imagined it swollen with a child, her skin stretched taut. She imagined Shane lying beside her, his large hand caressing her distended belly. The idea wasn't as scary as it should have been.

It was a fanciful idea, she concluded. Her period would probably arrive as scheduled in a couple of weeks, and the incident would be forgotten. And after seeing how he'd reacted to the oversight, Beth doubted Shane would ever let such a lapse happen again.

$$\sim 26$$

Beth arrived at work Monday morning to find a new shipment of vintage medical journals that had arrived on loan from a medical college on the east coast. She got to work processing the items while Mary helped a pair of medical school students begin work on a new research project.

Beth's office phone rang, and she looked at the caller ID, not recognizing the number. "Special Collections. This is Beth."

"Good morning, sweetheart."

At the sound of Shane's voice, she felt a tingle race down her spine. "Shane!"

"I hope I'm not bothering you. I just wanted to say 'hi' and see how you're doing."

"You're not bothering me. It's great to hear your voice. But how did you get my work number?"

"I called the main campus switchboard. Did you sleep well last night?"

She chuckled. "Actually, yes. I did two miles on the treadmill after you left, and then I dozed off pretty soon after my head hit the pillow. It was a pretty busy weekend."

"It was indeed."

Beth could almost hear his satisfied smile through the phone line.

"I missed you in my bed last night," he said. "I could get used to having you there all the time."

Her heart missed a beat. "I missed you, too."

"Is everything all right?"

Beth knew exactly what he was asking, but it was far too soon to know anything. "Don't worry, Shane. I'm sure everything will be fine."

"I know it'll be fine, because we'll make it fine," he said. "I just wanted to be sure you were okay."

She chuckled. "You mean not freaking out, don't you?"

"Well, yes. I was more than a little concerned."

"I'm fine. Whatever happens, happens."

"Still, you know there's nothing to be afraid of, right? I'll take care of you. Never doubt that."

His words gave her all kinds of feels. "Shane, I'm not worried. Honestly."

"All right." He sighed heavily. "Hey, you promised to have dinner with me tonight, and I'm going to hold you to it."

"I wouldn't miss it for the world."

"Good. Where do you want to go?"

"I know a place in my neighborhood I think you'd like," she said. "And it's within walking distance of my house. Would that be okay?"

"That sounds great," he said. "I'll be at your place around six."

Beth hung up just as Mary walked into the office.

"What are you so happy about this morning?" Mary said, dropping into her desk chair.

"Oh, nothing."

"I saw that smile, Beth. That wasn't a 'nothing' smile. Out with it."

She shrugged. "I just got a phone call from... a friend. That's all."

"A friend?" Mary looked skeptical. "Or, a *friend*?"

Beth blushed as she turned her attention to her computer monitor and busied herself checking for new e-mails.

"Friends usually don't put smiles like that on a girl's face," Mary said.

"Well," Beth said, grinning. "I am sort of dating him."

"Sort of?"

"It's kind of new. I just met him."

"Ah, a new boyfriend. Those are the best kind," Mary said. "So, where did you meet this new boyfriend?"

"At Clancy's downtown. We've gone out a few times now, I guess you could say. And we have plans for dinner tonight."

"I take it, from the blush on your face, that you really like this guy."

"I do," Beth said. "He's... well, he's kind of wonderful."

"As long as he treats you well," Mary said. "That's what matters."

Beth had turned her attention back to cataloging the newly arrived periodicals, mostly to get her mind off Shane, when a text came through on her phone.

Looking forward to dinner tonight.

She smiled. So much for getting her mind off Shane.

Shane hung up his office phone and leaned back in his chair. He was pussy whipped — Jake was right. Just hearing her voice over the phone made him want to go straight to her workplace, drag her out of there, and take her back to his apartment. He knew Miguel was on duty outside the library at that moment, and he knew where Kline was at every minute of the day, but still it made him nervous to be separated from her. He'd feel a hell of a lot better if she had close personal protection when he wasn't with her. He'd have to talk some sense into Tyler.

"Hello? Earth to Shane?"

Shane looked up to see Jake standing in his office doorway, leaning against the door jamb and looking like a recalcitrant thug.

Jake often resembled the dark angel of death. Even now he

was dressed in all black: jeans, t-shirt, combat boots, with a pair of dark sunglasses hanging from the neck of his t-shirt. There was a gun holster strapped around his lean waist, sporting a .40 caliber semi-automatic pistol. His hair was thick and black as night, his eyes a deep, dark brown. He was the most ruthless of the four McIntyre brothers, often taking the bull by the horns and dealing with things head on, usually the hard way. Shane reasoned his way out of trouble. Liam charmed his way out. And Jamie... well, Jamie was smart enough not to get into trouble in the first place.

"What do you want?" Shane said, scowling at his brother. He knew what Jake had come to talk about. And the worst part was, Jake was right.

Jake sauntered into the office and dropped into one of the chairs in front of Shane's desk. "It's not what you think." Jake tossed a sheet of paper onto Shane's desk.

Shane picked up the print-out of an e-mail and read it, frowning as the words sunk in. "Fuck."

"My words exactly, brother." Jake leaned back and crossed one booted foot over his knee.

"Does he have the gun in his possession yet?" Shane said.

Jake shook his head. "No, but it's in the mail. He'll probably have it by Wednesday."

Shane ran his fingers through his hair, sighing. "Any asshole can buy a gun on the Internet these days, even a paroled kidnapper. Does Tyler know about this?"

"No," Jake said. "I just received this from the electronic surveillance team a few minutes ago. Do you want me to notify Tyler?"

"I'll do it," Shane said. "I want to talk to him about close personal protection again. I want someone in that room with Beth."

"Maybe this will be the leverage you need."

"I'm not holding my breath. Tyler Jamison is one stubborn S.O.B."

"I recommend we get Beth out of that townhouse, Shane," Jake said. "The security is pathetic. It took me less than three minutes to break into that house, bypassing the security system altogether. Now that Kline has a gun, the risk to her in staying there is too high."

"I'll talk to Tyler," Shane said. "But I doubt he'll agree to move her."

"We need to relocate the redhead, too. It's not safe for either of them in that house. It's either that or let me redo the security system in that building, and we can tie it into our own response center."

"I'm planning to ask Beth to move in with me at the Lake Shore apartment."

"Whoa. Don't you think that's a little premature?" Jake said.

"Yeah, but it's the only way I'll be able to relax. I'll worry if she's not with me."

"You're in love with her, aren't you?" Jake said.

Shane looked at his brother. "That has occurred to me."

"It's kinda soon, don't you think?" Jake said.

Shane shrugged. "I've been with a lot of women in my life, Jake, but I've never felt like this. I couldn't sleep last night because she wasn't in my bed. I came close to driving to her house in the middle of the night, just to sleep with her. So, there you go. If that's love, then I'm in it."

The rest of Beth's day moved at a crawl. She did her best to keep her mind on work and off of Shane, but that turned out to be easier said than done. When five o'clock finally rolled around, she grabbed her purse and sweater and headed out to the street. The weather was perfect — clear blue skies with a gentle breeze — so, instead of catching the bus home, she decided to walk. It was only a 30-minute walk, which would give her plenty of time to get home and freshen up before Shane arrived at six.

She'd barely walked a block from the library when someone called her name.

"Beth! Hey, wait up!"

She turned to see Andrew Morton jogging toward her.

"Hi, Beth," Andrew said when he reached her. He was breathless, his face flushed from his exertions.

Andrew was the last person she wanted to see, but good manners prevailed. "Hi, Andrew."

"Where you off to?" he said, panting for breath.

"Home," she said.

"I have class at six," Andrew said, adjusting his backpack. "But it's just a stupid ethics class. I can blow it off. Let's go grab a beer."

"I'm sorry, I can't. I have dinner plans tonight." And even if she was free, she wouldn't be spending her time with him.

"You at least have time for one beer. Let's go to Tank's. It's just down the block."

"I'm sorry, but I really can't. I have just enough time to get home and get ready for my date."

"Date?" He looked horrified. "You have a date?"

"Yes," she said.

"Surely you can make time for one drink," he cajoled, reaching out and snagging her wrist. "I'll buy."

"I'm sorry, but no, Andrew." She said it with a little more force than she had intended, so she smiled and tried to soften the blow. "Thanks anyway."

Why couldn't he just take 'no' for an answer? She tried to extricate her wrist from his grasp. He wasn't hurting her, exactly, but his hold was strong. He was a big guy, and he had a large hand. She would have to use considerable force to break free if he didn't willingly let her go.

"Andrew, please," she said, tugging on her wrist as she began to feel trapped.

"Just one drink, Beth," he said as if she were the one being unreasonable.

"Andrew, let go," she said, her anxiety rising. Her heart rate kicked up, and her chest tightened. Despite the fact that the sidewalk was crowded with students, she felt very much alone.

"Excuse me," said a deep voice from behind.

Andrew glanced up over Beth's head at the newcomer, and

his gaze hardened.

Beth glanced back and saw a stranger standing directly behind her. She sensed he was staring daggers at Andrew, although it was hard to tell because of the man's dark sunglasses. She guessed, from his lean, muscular body and smooth face, that he was about her age. He was taller than she was, but not as tall as Andrew, with short black hair and a warm brown complexion. He smiled, displaying even white teeth, somehow giving her the impression of a panther, poised and ready to pounce on Andrew.

He might have been a student at Kingston, but for some reason, Beth didn't think so. He was dressed like a college student — blue jeans, a t-shirt, and sneakers — but he wasn't carrying a backpack, and that was a quintessential accessory for a college student. He was also wearing a black leather jacket, which she thought was odd given the warm weather.

"What the hell do you want?" Andrew said, glaring at the stranger.

"Is everything all right, ma'am?" the new guy said, transferring his gaze to her as he ostensibly dismissed Andrew.

"Um, yes," Beth said, her voice shaking as she gazed up into the dark sunglasses. She really wished she could see his eyes. "I was just leaving." When she tugged on her wrist this time, Andrew let her go.

"Thank you," she whispered to her apparent rescuer.

Beth took full advantage of her freedom and put some space between herself and Andrew. She headed off briskly toward home, and when she glanced back a couple of blocks later, she saw her presumed rescuer standing toe-to-toe with Andrew, his arms crossed over his chest, blocking Andrew's way. Even from this distance, she could see that Andrew was glowering at the guy.

Beth hefted her purse strap more securely over her shoulder and started walking as quickly as she could. She couldn't help peering back every so often, as if she expected to see Andrew creeping up on her at any minute.

Shane arrived at Beth's house at five-fifteen. He rang the bell to make sure she wasn't home yet, but when no one answered, he sat on the top step to await her arrival. He hadn't even been there five minutes when a call came in from Miguel.

"Report," Shane said. Miguel was on guard duty. He wouldn't call unless it was pertinent to Beth.

"There was an incident as she was leaving work," Miguel said. "I had to step in."

That certainly got Shane's attention. Miguel wouldn't have stepped in without sufficient cause. "What kind of incident?"

"She was accosted on the sidewalk outside the library by some kid, a student, I think. He tried to strong-arm her into going somewhere with him. I had to step in and break it up."

"What did he do?" Shane said.

"He grabbed her wrist and wouldn't let go until I intervened. Once he let her go, I stayed with him to keep him from following her. Otherwise, he would have. This kid doesn't know how to take 'no' for an answer."

"How did Beth react? Did she seem okay?"

"She was a little shaken, but otherwise all right. She should arrive at your location any minute now."

"Were you able to ID this kid?"

"No. He eventually gave up and ran inside one of the buildings."

"Stay there and see if you can ID this guy," Shane said. "I want a full background report. I'll be with Beth for the rest of the evening and overnight. Let Miles know he's not needed tonight."

"Roger that."

"Thanks." Shane stowed his phone. Great. One more variable for him to worry about.

When Beth turned the corner onto her street, her eyes went right to the Silver Jaguar parked in front of her house, and her anxiety over Andrew faded instantly.

She spotted Shane almost immediately sitting on the step

outside her front door. He was dressed in a charcoal suit and white shirt, sans tie, the top button of his shirt undone. He looked relaxed and disreputably gorgeous sitting on her stoop waiting for her. Her stomach did a little flip.

Shane stood when she reached the steps and met her half-way, taking her in his arms for a long, hungry kiss. When he finally ended the kiss, he held her at arms' length and studied her. "Are you okay?" he said, frowning.

"Sure," she answered. "Why?"

His eyes narrowed. "You seem a little flustered. What happened?"

27

Beth smiled as she went up on her toes and kissed him. "I'm fine, Shane. I'm just excited to see you."

Shane hid his disappointment that she didn't tell him about the male who'd accosted her on her way home from work. He wanted her to come to him with stuff like this. He wanted her to rely on him.

When they broke apart a few moments later, he said, "Are you ready to go? I'm starving."

"Give me a few minutes to clean up first." She headed for the front door. "Come inside and have a seat. I won't be long."

Shane waited upstairs in Beth's bedroom as she freshened up in the hallway bathroom. He paced in her small bedroom as he read Miguel's follow-up text.

No sign of the perp. I'll keep looking.

It hadn't been a good day for Shane. First, the news that Kline had purchased a handgun, illegally, and now this. Beth had been practically assaulted on the sidewalk outside her workplace.

He knew what needed to be done to protect Beth. He needed her out of this townhouse and into his custody, 24/7. He could install her in the Lake Shore Drive apartment, but he'd prefer she go to his house in Kenilworth, just a half hour north of the city. She'd be safe there. No one could get onto the Kenilworth property uninvited. First, though, he'd have to deal with Tyler.

Beth swept into the bedroom, looking refreshed and energized. She'd put her hair back, and a few blond strands cascaded over her shoulders. She'd also put on a little pink lip gloss which made it even harder to stop looking at her mouth. She'd done something with her eyes, too, because her lashes seemed a tad darker and longer. Shane grinned at the efforts she'd made, knowing she'd done it for him. But she didn't need makeup.

"Just one more minute!" she said, disappearing into her tiny walk-in closet. She closed the door, and he heard the rustling of clothes.

A moment later, she hobbled out of her closet as she slipped on her sandals. She'd changed from the skirt and blouse she'd been wearing into a sleeveless dress and lacy, white sweater.

"Sorry to keep you waiting," she said, coming to a standstill, slightly breathless. "I'm ready."

Shane reached out and took her by the waist, drawing her to him. Her breasts pressed against his chest, and for a moment he wondered if they could skip dinner altogether and make good use of her bed instead. But no. She needed to eat.

"You look beautiful," he said, and then he leaned down to plant a kiss on her glossy, pink lips. One of his hands snaked up between their bodies to cover her breast through her dress, giving it a light squeeze. Pulling back from the kiss, he smacked his lips and licked the glossy residue from his lips. "Mmm, strawberry. I approve."

They left Beth's townhouse and walked hand-in-hand to the market district just a few blocks away. The area was bustling with early evening foot traffic as shoppers patronized a row of quaint shops.

"How was your day?" he asked as they strolled down the busy sidewalk. He wanted to know who had accosted her after work.

"It was fine," she answered, smiling at him. She seemed genuinely happy.

"You seemed a little flustered when you got home."

"Oh, it was nothing. I had a slight run-in with a student as I was leaving work. He can be a real pest sometimes."

"So, you know this guy? What's his name?"

Beth squeezed his hand. "It's nothing, Shane, really. Please don't worry about it."

"But you do know his name?" Shane persisted. This wasn't nothing.

"Well, yes," she admitted. "I know him. But he's harmless."

A shadow passed over Beth's eyes when she said this, and Shane knew he'd be having a private conversation with this kid soon, once they'd identified him.

They passed a jewelry boutique and an organic grocery before Beth stopped in front of a restaurant. The sign above the door said *Hal's Bar-B-Q.*

"It's not fancy," Beth said. "But the barbecue is really good. I think you'll like it. And they play blues."

She'd picked this restaurant just for him. He opened the rickety wooden door for her, and they were greeted with a blast of blues music and the aroma of sizzling barbecue as they stepped inside.

The restaurant was just a hole in the wall, sporting a collection of randomly placed tables covered with red-and-white checkered tablecloths and misfit wooden chairs. The wood floors were scarred and warped. Along one side of the restaurant was a long counter with bar stools, and behind the counter was a full-service bar. Classic Mississippi Delta blues was pouring out of the jukebox.

"I like it already," Shane said, squeezing her hand.

A middle-aged woman with her hands full of empty plates buzzed past them. "Sit wherever you like, folks," she said breathlessly. "I'll be with you in a minute."

They sat down at one of the few available tables and picked up their menus.

The woman who'd greeted them at the door arrived at their table with two glasses of ice water. "Welcome to Hal's. Do you know what you want?"

Shane ordered a brisket platter and a bottle of local beer. Beth ordered a grilled barbecue chicken breast and a Root Beer float.

Beth glanced at the door when a young couple with a baby in a stroller walked in. The couple sat at a table near them, and the father bounced the baby on his leg, entertaining him with silly faces while the mother looked on with a satisfied smile.

As she watched them, Beth felt a small, secret thrill. She knew the odds were against it, but, still, the idea was somewhat tantalizing. She wasn't ready to be a parent. She was only twenty-four; surely that was too young for her biological clock to start ticking. Still, she found the little family an appealing picture. She glanced at Shane, who was perusing the beer menu, and pictured him with a baby in his arms. It wasn't hard to do. She knew he'd take good care of their baby.

Their food arrived, and she shoved away her fanciful thoughts. As they ate and chatted, Beth's eyes kept wandering to the young couple with the baby. The baby had since gotten cranky, and now the mother was cradling him, nursing him beneath a strategically placed blanket. *Get a grip and quit staring.*

When their server brought Shane the bill, he paid her. "This was a great idea, Beth," he said. "Thank you."

They walked back to Beth's house holding hands. The neighborhood had started settling down for the evening. There were still some people out on foot, but the neighborhood had more of a small-town, relaxed vibe to it, far different from the frenetic energy of downtown.

When they reached her house, Shane pulled Beth into his arms and kissed her. "Can I spend the night?"

Her face lit up at his unexpected request. "Sure."

Shane smiled. "It just so happens I have my overnight bag in the car," he said. "I brought it, just in case."

She grinned at him. "Just in case?"

"Well, I am an optimist."

Shane grabbed his overnight bag from his car and followed Beth inside.

It was only eight-thirty, and since Gabrielle was at work, they had the house to themselves for the rest of the night. Shane took Beth's hand and led her upstairs to her bedroom, flipping on the light switch as they entered her room. He dropped his overnight bag on the floor.

Beth stood at the foot of the bed, smiling shyly at Shane, excited to have him in her bedroom again. The first time he'd been here, she'd felt so shy with him. Now she was a little more relaxed, and the idea of making love with him in her own bed made her stomach flutter. She sure hoped he'd brought condoms with him this time, because she hadn't thought to buy any.

"We're having a sleepover, on a school night," she said, grinning like a co-ed who'd just sneaked a boy into her dorm room.

Shane smiled at her, touched by her light-hearted enthusiasm. "So we are."

"It's early yet," she said. "What do you want to do?"

"You're asking me?" he said, as he slowly stalked toward her.

She took a few steps back as he neared, but he reached out and snagged her around the waist, pulling her close. His mouth closed over hers, his lips coaxing hers to open. His tongue slipped inside and found hers, stroking her. Her hands came up to grasp the lapels of his jacket.

"I know what I want," he said against her lips. "I want dessert."

"I'm sure we have some ice cream," she said, chuckling.

"That's not the kind of sugar I had in mind." Shane took a couple steps backward, drawing Beth with him. When the backs of his legs hit the mattress, he sat at the foot of the bed, pulling her between his legs. "Gabrielle's at work?"

"Yep," Beth replied.

Since he was seated, she stood a head above him. She put her hands on his shoulders and leaned down to kiss him. It was still sinking in that he was hers, and she had the right to kiss him and touch him, any time she wanted. He was hers. The notion gave her an unfamiliar sense of empowerment. Her hands slipped up into his hair, and she scraped her fingernails lightly along his scalp, ruffling his thick hair.

Shane groaned, closing his eyes as he leaned into her touch. "What time does she get home?" he asked, sounding a little distracted as Beth stroked his hair.

"Midnight." She pressed her lips against his temple, her tongue darting out to taste his warm, slightly salty skin.

Shane made a sound low in his throat and leaned into her chest, pressing his face against her breasts. His hands came around to grasp the backs of her thighs through her dress, squeezing her gently. "So, we have the house to ourselves all evening."

"We do." Beth felt her face heat. She had a pretty good idea where this was heading, and the idea of making love to him here, in her own bed, made her tingle from head to toe.

"Perfect," Shane said, pushing her back gently so he could rise to his feet. "Do you have any wine? Or better yet, something stronger?"

Beth blinked, thrown off guard by the swift change in topic. "Um, yes. Gabrielle has a well-stocked wine chiller in the kitchen, and my brother keeps a few bottles of liquor in a cabinet in the parlor."

Shane pulled Beth out the bedroom door and down the hallway to the stairs. "Let's check out the liquor cabinet. We're going to need a little liquid courage."

"We are?" she said, following him down the stairs. "For what?"

"You'll see," he said.

Shane opened the door to the liquor cabinet and made a dismissive sound as he surveyed its contents. "Your brother's taste in liquor leaves a lot to be desired. Bit of a cheapskate, isn't he?"

Beth chuckled, thinking that was an apt description of her beloved brother. "You could say that."

Shane selected the sole bottle of whisky in the cabinet and two tumblers. It was bottom shelf stuff, but it would have to do. He made a mental note to bring a decent bottle with him the next time.

"Kitchen," he said, motioning for Beth to lead the way. He followed her to the kitchen and set the bottle of whisky and the two glasses on the island counter. Then he headed for the fridge, where he located some Coke.

Beth watched as Shane poured whisky in both of the tumblers. He added a generous amount of Coke to one of the glasses.

"Drink up," Shane said, handing Beth her glass.

She looked at the contents. "Are you plying me with alcohol again?"

"Yes. Drink," he said, and then he took a sip of his own neat whisky, frowning at the less than satisfactory taste. "Your brother has absolutely no taste in liquor."

Beth chuckled at Shane's expression. Then she took a sip of her altered drink and made a face of her own. Even tempered with the sugary-sweet soft drink, she could still taste the alcohol. "This is awful," she said. "Even for whisky."

Shane knocked back the rest of his whisky in one swallow, grimacing. "How can your brother drink this stuff? He obviously doesn't come from good Scottish stock. No self-respecting Scot would ever touch this garbage."

Beth laughed. "Our mom's Swedish, and our dad was American, of English descent, I think," she said.

"Well, that explains it then. Drink," he said, pointing at her glass.

Beth took another sip. "Ugh. Honestly, Shane. How can you stand this stuff?"

"Amateur." Shane leaned down and kissed her.

She looked at him expectantly. "So, why do you think I need liquid courage? Because I know this isn't for your sake."

"Do you remember the night we met?"

"Yes."

"Do you remember what you were reading?"

Oh, God. Spanking stories. Her face flamed. "Yes."

He grinned at her. "We have the house to ourselves for almost four hours," he said. "That's plenty long enough for what I have in mind."

"Which is?" As if she didn't know.

"We'll christen your bed properly tonight," he said. "But first, somebody's going to get a spanking."

He gave her a salacious grin, catching Beth mid-swallow. She choked on her drink, coughing and spluttering so violently that Shane had to take the glass away from her and lay his hand on her back. "Are you okay?"

She looked at him through watering eyes. "Are you serious?" she gasped.

"I told you I'd meet all of your needs. You like to read spanking porn, so I'm going to give you a little taste of one in real life. Nothing too intense, just a little erotic paddling."

She wiped the water from her eyes with the back of her hand. "It's erotic romance, Shane, not pornography!" she said.

He shrugged. "What's the difference? It's still spanking. Honey, I saw the titles of some of those books you were eyeing at Clancy's. You're turned on by kink, and I'm going to give you some kink tonight."

"We can't actually do that!" she said, her face turning beet red.

"Why not?" He smiled down at her. "Sweetheart, there's nothing to be afraid of. I'm talking about some erotic kink. I'd never hurt you."

"But I can't," she said, completely flustered. No matter how enticing it might sound, she could never go through with it.

"Why not?"

"Because!"

Shane raised an eyebrow. "Because why?"

Beth shook her head. "I'm not even sure I want to," she said. "Reading about... spankings... is one thing, but actually doing it?

Shane, I don't think I can."

"Don't think about it, Beth. Let's just do it. You can always stop me at any time." Shane handed back her glass. "Finish it."

Beth gazed down at the dark amber liquid. "Liquid courage?" she said. "I can understand why I might need some, but why did you have a drink?"

"Maybe I needed it, too," he said. "I've never done this before."

"Really? You haven't?"

He shook his head. "I've done a lot of inventive things in my life, but spanking a woman isn't one of them. But hey, there's a first time for everything, right?"

After Beth had polished off the rest of her drink, Shane set her empty glass in the kitchen sink.

"Come," he said, taking her hand. "Let's go get our kink on."

"Oh, God," she moaned.

28

S hane closed Beth's bedroom door and dialed down the dimmer switch on the chandelier to a faint glow.

"Before we start, I want to make one thing clear," he said, turning her to face him. His voice was low and hushed, adding to the sense of intimacy in the dimly lit room. "This is an erotic spanking, just for fun. You know I'd never hurt you, right?"

Beth nodded, and a shiver coursed through her.

"I guess we need a safeword," he said. "Do you have one?"

Beth shook her head. She'd never needed one.

"I guarantee you won't need it, but still we should have one," he said. "How about... whisky?"

She smiled at his choice. "Whisky. Okay."

"If you say 'whisky,' we're done. Got that?"

Her insides were quaking, but she still managed to say it. "Yes."

Shane kissed her, tasting the sweetness of the Coke and the pungency of the whisky on her tongue. He smiled, then pulled back to look at her, his hand cradling the side of her face. "Have I told you that I'm crazy about you? Every time I look at you, I get weak in the knees."

She laughed. "No, you don't."

Shane shook his head in disbelief. "I don't think you comprehend your own allure." He led her to the foot of the bed, and then he sat down and gazed up at her.

When he sat there for the longest time, saying nothing, she started to fidget. "Oh, for goodness' sake!" she said, and she started to move away. Anything to hide her nervousness.

When he made a sound in his throat, Beth froze and looked back at him, captured by the searing heat in his gaze. "What?"

Shane pointed at the floor between his legs. He didn't say a word, he just pointed.

Beth felt a sudden rush of moist heat suffuse her body, starting low in her belly and radiating outward. She was practically melting inside, and he hadn't even said a word. How could he do that to her with just a look? Even now, she couldn't tear her gaze away from his.

Shane continued to point at the floor between his legs, his demeanor a mixture of patience and demand. Even though he hadn't said a word, his message was clear: *Come here.*

Beth walked back to him as if lured there by some invisible chain.

When she was within his reach, he captured her hand and pulled her between his legs. She was breathing heavily now, her slender nostrils flaring and the edges of her cheeks flushed with color. Her eyes were wide with both anticipation and trepidation.

The mixture of longing and fear in her gaze floored him, and he knew exactly what she needed from him. It wasn't a spanking she craved so much as the feeling of submission that went with it. The idea of smacking her didn't sit well with him, even if it was all in play. But the idea of getting her to submit to him, well, that had tremendous appeal.

"Take off your sandals," he said, his voice low and just a little bit rough.

Beth closed her eyes and took a deep, tremulous breath. She felt like she was standing at the top of a high dive platform, looking down at the water so far below. Did she dare jump? Did she dare step out into the open, knowing she would surely fall, and trust him to catch her?

She could say no. If she told him to get out of her house, he'd go. She knew that. And yet, she didn't want to do either of those things. Her heart yearned to take this chance, to take this leap of faith and trust him to catch her.

"Beth."

When he used that tone of voice, her insides melted. She took a deep breath, her heart pounding in her chest, and stepped off the platform.

Shane found himself holding his breath, his heart pounding in his chest like a jackhammer. They were at a crossroads, a defining point in their budding relationship. He was taking a hell of a gamble — what if he was wrong? What if it wasn't submission she was looking for?

He didn't release his breath until she placed her trembling hands on his shoulders to steady herself as she slipped off her sandals and nudged them under the bed. She stood between his legs with her eyes closed as if hiding from him as well as from herself.

But there was no hiding from this. "Look at me, sweetheart."

Beth's eyes fluttered open, and he watched her pupils adjust as she focused on him. Slowly, he reached out and removed her sweater, letting it slip off her shoulders. He caught it as it fell and laid it aside. Then he reached behind her and unzipped her dress. He drew her dress off her shoulders, so slowly, and laid that aside as well. She started trembling as she stood before him in her undergarments. He tugged the half-slip down her long bare legs, leaving her in her panties and bra.

He'd never felt such pleasure from the act of undressing a woman. He traced the top edge of one bra cup, his finger just lightly grazing her soft skin. She shivered at his touch, and he smiled.

"This is the bra Sylvia gave you."

"Yes." Her voice was little more than a whisper of breath.

He reached behind her torso and unhooked her bra, and then slowly pulled it off her body, watching mesmerized as her pink nipples puckered at exposure.

Putting his hands on her hips, he gently eased her to the side and closed his legs, creating a perfect platform for her to lie across. He shifted a little, sitting at an angle so that when she lay across his lap, her torso would be supported by the mattress.

"Lie across my lap, Beth."

She looked down at his lap, and then she looked him in the eye.

"You know the safeword," he reminded her. "It's whisky. You can say it at any time. But trust me, you'll never need to."

Beth felt a curious mixture of fear and giddy excitement. She was afraid of the unknown, but, at the same time, she felt weak-kneed with anticipation. Shane was offering her an experience she'd only read about, something she'd fantasized about for so long. And now, here was her chance to experience it firsthand for herself.

She took a deep breath and stepped forward, unsure how to accomplish what he'd asked without looking like a total klutz. His hands came up to guide her into position, and she moved over him so that her pelvis rested on his lap, and her chest rested on the mattress.

"Are you comfortable?" he asked, laying a gentle hand on her back.

"Yes." She lay her head on the quilt, her face turned away because she couldn't bear to look at him.

She shivered when he caressed the twin mounds of her bottom through the fabric of her panties.

Shane fingered the silky lace, his hand curving over one butt cheek, squeezing it gently. "Sylvia would be glad to know you're wearing her gift."

"I doubt this is what she had in mind," she said.

"Oh, I wouldn't be too sure about that." Shane moved his hand to her other cheek, smoothing the creamy fabric.

She tensed when Shane's fingers slipped between her thighs.

"Spread your legs a bit," he said, nudging her thighs open. He pressed his fingers against the damp crotch of her panties. "You're so warm here and already a little wet."

His index finger slipped inside her panties and teased the slick opening of her sex. "Hmm, very wet."

Beth made a noise deep in her throat, something between a moan and a whimper. She tried to close her thighs, but couldn't because his hand was wedged between them.

"It's okay, Beth. Relax." His finger pressed inside her opening and he collected some of the silky fluid and brought it to her clitoris. He worked the little flesh, stroking it, applying just the right amount of pressure to make her squirm. She pressed her hot face into the quilt and moaned.

Shane withdrew his finger and started working her panties down over her buttocks and past her thighs. He pulled them off completely and dropped them on the floor. Beth closed her legs.

He made a disapproving sound. "Open your legs, sweetheart," he said. He nudged her legs apart once more, and then his finger was there again, searching. He teased her clit until she was squirming, and then his long index finger pushed into her heated core.

She gasped, grabbing hold of the bedding.

"My God, you're so wet," Shane said, his finger sliding deeper inside her. Already she was swollen from her body's heated flush. Her wet tissues clung to his finger as it sank deeper. He began to move his finger inside her, thrusting it slowly in and out. His finger curled, hitting the sweet spot inside her body as he stroked her, driving her desire. The squirming was now accompanied by breathy whimpers.

"Do you want me to spank you, or do you want me to make you come like this?"

"Shane, please," she moaned, her hips moving in tandem

with his relentless stroking.

"Please what? You have to say it, baby."

"Make me come," she pleaded, her hips rocking shamelessly against his touch.

Beth closed her eyes and surrendered to the mind-numbing sensations Shane was creating as he teased her. Her entire being was focused on his long finger as he stroked it in and out of her in a steady, coaxing rhythm. Her hips rocked against his touch, and she couldn't have stopped if she'd wanted to. At that moment, all she could think about was what he was doing to her body. She forgot everything else — all her fears, all her anxieties. She lost all sense of shame as her body surrendered to his touch.

She pushed back against his hand, opening her thighs wider to give him better access to her body. The sensations continued to escalate, stealing her breath and making her heart race. Her breaths turned into audible gasps. Higher and higher he drove her, knowing just where to touch her, just how much pressure to use, until the conflagration inside her ignited, setting off an explosion that ricocheted through her body.

She let out a high, keening wail that nearly brought the ceiling down on them as her orgasm swept through her. She grasped the quilt with both hands and buried her face in the soft fabric to muffle her cries.

Even before her cry had stopped reverberating in the room, Beth found herself wrenched up off his lap and positioned on her hands and knees on the bed. Her arms were too shaky to hold herself up, so she promptly found herself face down on the mattress, her bottom shamelessly propped up in the air. Her hands grasped at the bedding as she searched for something to hold onto.

She heard the rasping sound of Shane's zipper, and then his hands landed surprisingly hard on her hips, hot against her bare skin as he pulled her to the edge of the bed. When she heard him tear open a condom package, her belly clenched with anticipation.

A moment later, the blunt head of his cock was at her opening, demanding entrance. He pushed himself inside her slick channel, relentlessly surging forward as he thrust into her wet heat. He made a low, guttural sound as he pushed deep, and Beth gasped when his cock was fully seated. He held still for several moments, letting her get used to him, and then he began a slow retreat, the drag of his cock stoking her fires with sweet friction.

He thrust back inside to the hilt, and she rocked forward from the momentum. She gasped, unaccustomed to having him at this angle. He was a lot to take all at once, and she must have made a sound of distress, because he froze.

"Are you okay?" His voice was a deep rasp.

"Yes!" she gasped, rocking backward, reveling in the feel of him sliding through her slick flesh. "You're bigger this way," she panted.

"I'm all the way in," he said.

Shane began to move then, slowly at first, giving her time to adjust to the fullness. But then his rhythm picked up, and soon he was thrusting into her with considerable strength. "Is this okay?"

"Yes!" she gasped, her breaths coming fast and shallow as she surrendered to the increasing power behind his thrusts.

Shane barely heard her breathy reply. He was balancing a fine line, caught between wanting to fuck her hard and senseless, and fearing he'd overwhelm her. So far, this position hadn't triggered her fears. He wasn't on top of her, and he wasn't holding her down. She could easily pull free or roll away from him if she needed to.

"Remember your safeword," he grated as he thrust into her. "Use it if you need to."

"I'm fine," she panted, as his thrusting rocked her forward on the bed. She had to brace herself.

He knew he could be a demanding lover, and he was used to being with women who welcomed his fierce nature in bed. With Beth, though, he was afraid of taking things too far, pushing her too much. But the welcoming wetness of her sex, and the incredible sounds she was making, spurred him on. He reached around for her clit and began stroking her again, maintaining just the right pressure to bring her along with him.

"I can't!" she moaned. She couldn't possibly come again so soon.

"Yes, you can."

But her body seemed to have a mind of its own, and she began to whimper as another climax neared.

"That's right, baby," he said, as her sex tightened. "Come with me."

When her sex clenched hotly on his erection and she cried out, he surrendered to the needs of his own body. When his climax hit him, Shane shouted loud enough to wake the dead as he emptied himself inside her, reveling in the mind-numbing pleasure.

When the tremors of his climax eased, he rolled them to their sides and rested behind her, still locked deep inside her. "Give me a minute to get my breath," he said, wrapping his arm around her waist.

He enveloped her in his arms, and she snuggled back against him. "I've got to get rid of this condom," he muttered. "But I don't want to move."

When Beth giggled, Shane squeezed her, relieved to know he hadn't completely traumatized her. "So much for your first spanking," he said, realizing he'd never actually gotten around to it.

"That's okay," she said, her voice drowsy. "What you did was even better. I'm certainly not complaining."

Beth lay against Shane's furnace-hot body, absorbing the heat radiating off her own personal electric blanket. Eventually he stirred, gently disengaging from her body to dispose of the condom.

He returned quickly and climbed back into her bed, spooning behind her. "I'm really glad Gabrielle's not home. Otherwise, I'm pretty sure I'd be a dead man. Your neighbors probably heard me."

Beth chuckled as she snuggled back into him, drowsy and sated. Her bones were liquid, and she could barely move a muscle.

Shane covered them with the bedding. "You okay?" he said, reaching for her hand and linking their fingers together.

"I'm perfect," she said, yawning.

A faint noise brought Shane out of a deep sleep in an instant. He lay perfectly still, assessing his surroundings. *In Beth's bed.* She was beside him, asleep.

He glanced at the digital clock on her nightstand; it was just after three o'clock in the morning. Something had awakened him, so he lay quietly, listening. He heard the grandfather clock ticking downstairs in the foyer. He heard Gabrielle in the next room as she muttered something unintelligible in her sleep and rolled over in her bed. He heard a car door shut in the alley behind Beth's house, and a dog barked somewhere off in the distance.

Beth's breathing was shallow and quick, too quick. She made a small sound in her sleep, a pained whimper. That's what woke him. She was having another nightmare. His suspicions were confirmed when she jerked violently in her sleep and started gasping.

"Beth!" His hand went to her shoulder, and he found her bare skin chilled. He shook her gently. "Sweetheart, wake up."

Her breathing grew more erratic, and she moaned. Then she cried out sharply as if she were hurt.

He shook her more forcefully. "Beth, wake up!"

She shot up into a sitting position, gasping for air, and she raised her hands as if she were warding off an assailant.

"Beth!"

She looked at him, her eyes wide and unfocused. "What?"

She glanced around the room to get her bearings. "It was just a dream," she sighed.

Shane sat up and turned her to face him. "Sweetheart, *enough!*" he said. "You have to tell me."

↪ 29

Shane felt, as well as heard, the sob that came out of Beth as she lay back down. She was breathing erratically, in short gasping breaths.

"Do you need your inhaler?" he said, already reaching across her for the nightstand drawer.

"No. I'm okay," she said, clutching at him as if he was her lifeline.

"No, you're not okay, Beth." His voice sounded harsh, tinged with frustration. To soften the blow, he leaned down and gently kissed her. "I need you to tell me."

Beth sighed and pulled Shane down beside her, turning into him. She wrapped one arm around his waist and snuggled into his warm body, and immediately she felt the fear begin to dissipate. Lying with him like this soothed her more than anything else ever had.

"Beth."

She buried her face against his chest. "You're using your bossy tone," she grumbled. *The one that made her insides melt.*

"You haven't heard bossy yet, Beth, but you're about to if you don't start talking."

"I know," she groaned, squeezing her eyes shut.

"I can't help you if you don't talk to me," he said, making her look at him. "Who hurt you, Beth?"

She looked into his eyes, those steely blue orbs that looked rather impatient at the moment. She hated talking about it.

Once more, she stepped off that high-dive platform, trusting that he would catch her. She took a deep breath, filling her starved lungs with air, and then released it as she blurted it out. "When I was six years old, I was kidnapped."

Shane made a rough sound as he tightened his hold on her, simultaneously relieved and pained. He'd been prepared for those words; he'd known they were coming, but, for some reason, hearing them hit him unexpectedly hard. He cleared his throat. "Go on."

"I was playing in my front yard, riding my bike on the sidewalk. My mom was inside cooking dinner."

When she stopped talking, Shane found one of her hands buried under the bedding and linked their fingers, squeezing her hand for encouragement.

"Someone grabbed me from behind and pulled me off my bike. He threw me into the back of a van, then climbed in behind me and shut the doors. It was dark in the van — I couldn't see anything. He taped my wrists and ankles so I couldn't move."

She fell silent again.

"Then what happened?" Shane's heart was hammering in his chest, but he had to keep her talking. They were finally getting somewhere.

She cleared her throat. "The man who took me — his name is Howard Kline — he lived out on a farm. There was an old cellar, just a big hole dug deep into the earth, with wooden steps and a metal trap door. There were no windows and no electricity; it was pitch black down there. That's where he put me, in that cellar. My wrists and my ankles were taped so I couldn't stand. He cut my clothes off, and then left me lying on the dirt floor in the dark. I was so scared I couldn't stop shaking, and I was too afraid to sleep. I just lay there crying all night.

"The next morning, the trap door opened. I remember the sunlight hurt my eyes. My eyes were tearing from the bright light, but I could see the police coming down the stairs, with their guns and flashlights. Tyler was the first one down the steps. He cut the tape from my wrists and ankles, and then he wrapped me in his jacket and carried me outside to an ambulance."

As he kissed Beth's forehead, he thought about how easy it would be to simply end Howard Kline's life. A simple shot to the head, and it would all be over. He'd never in his life been so tempted to take matters into his own hands — to play the vigilante — and seek retribution where it was due. He shook at that moment with the need to do just that. It was a line he'd never crossed, but this situation... Beth's situation really tested him.

"So, what happened to the kidnapper?" Shane said, to keep her talking.

"There was a trial, and he was convicted on all charges. The judge sentenced him to 30 years."

"Did he hurt you, Beth? Did he sexually molest you?" He had to ask her that, even though he was loathed to even say the words. The thought of what Kline could have done to her made him physically ill. He knew from the police report that Kline hadn't molested her, but he needed to hear her say it.

She shuddered, and he tightened his arms around her. "No," she said. "He hardly touched me. Once he put me in that cellar, I never saw him again."

"You must have been terrified."

She didn't say anything more, and he felt her body growing heavy against his as she started to relax back into sleep.

"I just want to sleep, Shane," she said, her voice weary. "Please."

He heard in her voice an echo of the pain she must have suffered as a child, and it tore at him. "Okay, sweetheart."

She was using sleep to avoid the topic, but it was the middle of the night, and she did have to go to work in the morning. So he let her sleep. There would be time for further conversation, for there certainly was a lot more to be said.

When Beth's alarm clock went off at a quarter after six, she groaned as she hit the snooze button.

Shane stirred beside her and stretched. "What time do you have to be at work?"

"I usually leave at seven-thirty to get there by eight," she said, pressing against him. She rubbed her nose against his shoulder and inhaled, relishing the scent of him. "It's a half-hour walk."

"I'll drive you," he said, brushing back her hair. "I'd like to see where you work."

"You want to come in?"

"Yes. If that's okay?"

"Of course it is," she said. "I'd love for you to come to my office."

Shane's hands slipped beneath the covers and sought her soft, sleep-warmed body. He came up on one elbow and pushed the bedding down to her waist, uncovering her breasts and belly.

"Good morning," he said, smiling down at her as he ran his hand down her abdomen to her belly.

"Good morning."

He bent down and took one of her nipples into his mouth, suckling it. He laved the peak with his tongue, and when it puckered into a tight little knot, she shivered. Shane's hand cupped her breast, plumping it for his mouth to feast on. Her hands clutched his arms, kneading the heavy muscles. His mouth released her nipple with a wet pop, then his mouth drifted to her other breast, and he treated that one with the same attention.

He released her breast and began to trail kisses down her torso to her belly button, which he nuzzled and kissed. She was squirming now, her legs moving restlessly. He chuckled, then moved lower still.

"Um, what are you doing?" she said.

"I'm saying 'good morning,'" he said.

When his teeth nipped gently at her pelvic bone, she jumped.

"Oh! I like how you say 'good morning.'"

Then his mouth drifted farther down, to the nest of blond curls covering her sex. As his nose brushed her hair, he inhaled her scent and gave a little growl.

"Shane? Are you sure you want to do that now?"

He glanced up at her. "Yes. Why?"

"Look at the time. Besides, I should shower first."

"I can be quick," he said, shoving the bedding aside and scooting farther down the bed.

She chuckled as her hands fisted the sheet beneath her. "Maybe I don't want you to be quick."

"Then you can be late to work," he said, nudging her legs open and sliding between them. "I can't think of a better way to start our day."

Beth's fingers went to his hair, alternately stroking and tugging the strands.

"Gabrielle might hear me," she said as Shane pried open her folds, and then tickled her clitoris with the tip of his tongue.

"Then be quiet," he said against her warm, moist flesh. He began lapping at her clit with lazy strokes of his tongue. When he inserted one finger inside her core and began stroking her deep inside, she started squirming in earnest.

"Shane! I can't be quiet!" she hissed, when he started tormenting her clit with rapid flicks his tongue.

He lifted his head and looked at her. "Do you really want me to stop?"

She made a face at him and then closed her eyes in embarrassment. "No."

"Then use my pillow to muffle the noise."

Beth grabbed the spare pillow and pressed it to her face just as Shane's mouth returned to her sex. It was a wicked one-two punch, his long finger stroking her inside as his tongue battered her clit. Her hips lifted off the mattress as she pressed herself against his mouth. She held the pillow to her face, her loud whimpers only partially muffled.

Shane showed no mercy, using all of his considerable skill to drive her crazy. He assaulted her clit with delicious intent, while his finger stroked her mercilessly. She was practically thrashing now as her orgasm loomed in front of her. She was close, *so close*, almost there, just a little more, when Shane's tongue abruptly abandoned her and his finger withdrew from her wet, swollen channel.

"Shane!" she cried into the pillow, feeling desolate at his retreat.

When Shane's slick finger slipped down to gently tease her anus, Beth made a choked sound behind the pillow — part surprise and part shock — and Shane chuckled when she squirmed out of his reach.

"Beth, do you have any lube?"

She set the pillow aside and eyed him suspiciously. "Yes. Why?"

"Where is it?"

"I don't know," she said, looking up at the ceiling.

He grinned. "Is it in here?" He reached over and opened the top nightstand drawer, where he quickly located a small bottle. He squirted some of its contents onto his finger. "Has anyone touched you here before?" he said, the tip of his finger rimming the tightly puckered opening.

"No!" she said, half-heartedly attempting to roll away from him.

It wasn't much of an attempt, and he held her in place easily. "Do you remember your word?"

"Yes!" she hissed.

"What is it?"

"Whisky!"

The tip of his finger teased her hole. "Relax, sweetheart," he said. "It's just my finger. It'll slip right in if you let it. It won't hurt, I promise. In fact, I promise you'll like it."

Beth brought the pillow back over her face and produced a string of incomprehensible words.

He chuckled. "I didn't understand one word of that. You'll have to move the pillow."

Beth lifted the pillow from her hot face and glared at him, gasping for breath. "Do you really have to do that?" she hissed.

Shane smiled. "Yes, I do. Now be quiet, or you'll wake Gabrielle." He glared back at her mulish expression, raising his eyebrow. "If you really want me to stop, say the magic word."

Beth scowled at him, and then laid her head back down and covered her face with the spare pillow. She didn't want to use the damn word. What he was doing to her was alternately thrilling and terrifying, and she didn't want him to stop. The bottom line was, she trusted him. He wouldn't do anything to hurt her.

Shane chuckled. "Relax your bottom, sweetheart," he coaxed. "Take a deep breath, and then slowly let it out and relax. I promise this won't hurt if you relax."

Beth's belly rose as she sucked in a lungful of air, then fell slowly as she exhaled.

"Now relax your muscles," he instructed. "And push out a little bit."

He chuckled at her muffled response from beneath the pillow. But she did what he said, and he slipped his finger inside her.

"Good. Now stay relaxed, and don't be afraid."

Once he'd slid his finger past her body's tight ring of muscles, he gently glided his finger in deeper, stroking the interior lining of her body. As soon as his finger was sliding easily in and out of her backside, his tongue resumed tormenting her clitoris. Her body had already been well primed for an orgasm, and the combination of his finger stroking her backside and his tongue battering her clitoris sent her immediately crashing right over the edge. She squirmed and bucked against his mouth, her limbs trembling as she whimpered and squealed into the pillow. When a devastating climax tore through her body, she screamed bloody murder into the pillow, her hands pressing it tightly to her face to muffle the sound.

As her keening wails subsided, Shane surged up and pulled the pillow from her face. He reached for a condom packet and ripped it open. A moment later, his thick cock was sheathed, and his hips were cradled between her thighs, pushing forward.

Beth was still reeling from the most tumultuous orgasm she'd ever had when Shane lodged the head of his cock inside her wet opening and pressed deep inside. She was so slick he had no trouble burying himself completely in one thrust. He covered her with his big body and leaned down to take her mouth with his. He kissed her voraciously, his greedy kisses matching the demanding thrusts of his cock. He slammed into her hard, over and over. Her hands came up to grasp his straining forearms as he held himself suspended above her. His mouth ate at hers, swallowing the exquisite sounds she made.

When his climax hit, he shouted to the rafters. A moment later, they heard a loud thud as something heavy hit the wall that Beth's bedroom shared with Gabrielle's.

"Do you mind!" came an annoyed shout from the other bedroom.

Beth shrieked with embarrassment, and Shane collapsed on Beth, breathing heavily. They both had to bite back their laughter.

"So much for not waking up Gabrielle," Shane said.

It wasn't until Shane had rolled off Beth and lay beside her, his chest heaving as he tried to catch his breath, that he realized he'd been on top of her, his weight pressing her into the mattress. And she hadn't even seemed to notice. They were making progress.

He smiled.

～ 30

After a quick shower together, which they tried to accomplish with as little laughter as possible, they dressed and headed downstairs to the kitchen for an even quicker breakfast of coffee and bagels with cream cheese. They slipped out of the house without further arousing Gabrielle's ire and headed for the Kingston campus.

Shane found an open parking spot in a guest lot not far from the library.

"It's a beautiful campus," Shane said, as he reached for her hand.

The 2- and 3-story brick buildings were early twentieth century, Georgian style architecture, covered with ivy. The lawns were well maintained, green and lush from the summer rains.

Shane squeezed Beth's hand, and she looked up at him. "If you see the student who harassed you yesterday after work, I want you to point him out to me."

"All right," Beth said. But, honestly, Andrew Morton was the last person she wanted to run into.

Shane opened one of the two large mahogany doors for Beth and followed her inside the library.

Devany looked up from the reception desk and her eyes widened when she saw that Beth wasn't alone. "Beth! Hi!"

"Hi, Devany," Beth said, pulling Shane with her to the front desk.

Devany eyed Beth's hand linked with Shane's. "Good morning, Beth," Devany said, her curious dark eyes glued to Shane.

Shane offered his hand to Devany. "Shane McIntyre," he said, as they shook hands. "I'm Beth's boyfriend."

Shane looked at Beth, assessing her reaction to his pronouncement in front of her co-worker. Her startled expression quickly morphed into a smile.

"This is my friend, Devany Ross," Beth said to Shane.

"It's a pleasure to meet you, Devany," Shane said, smiling down at the young woman, whose dark eyes darted back and forth between Beth and Shane.

"I'm going to take Shane up to the Special Collections room," Beth said. "I'll see you later, okay?"

"Okay," Devany said. "Beth, do you want to do lunch today?"

"Sure."

"It was nice to meet you, too!" Devany called, as Shane followed Beth up the wide, curving staircase to the second floor.

Now that he was inside the library, Shane began scanning the environment, noting the entrances and exits, mentally mapping the locations of the stairs and elevators. Most importantly, he looked for visible signs of a security presence. So far, he was not impressed.

Miguel had been in the library several times, going through the same process, and they already had an accurate map of the interior of the building. By Shane's standards, the security was far too lax. Granted, it was a library, not a bank. Libraries weren't known to be hotbeds of violent acts. Still, he thought they could do better than what they were doing now with just a few modifications.

Shane made note of the security guard seated at the front entrance, near the reception desk. The guard had been playing a game on his phone and didn't once look up as they'd entered the building. A second security guard was seated at a counter in the lobby, not far from the front reception desk, but he, too, had paid them no mind as they'd entered and approached the reception desk.

It was clear that the library administrators weren't expecting any kind of threat and weren't taking security seriously. That was unacceptable. He'd be having a private conversation with the university's president very soon.

Beth led Shane to a door marked "Special Collections" and entered a code into an electronic keypad to unlock the door. Shane opened the door for her, and they walked into a spacious, well-lit room.

"This is where the students do their research if they need access to historical reference materials," Beth said, indicating the tables. They she pointed at rows and rows of bookcases. "And, of course, there are all the books and periodicals. Our desks are in there," she said, pointing to the glassed-in office. "And that's Mary, my coworker." Beth waved at Mary, who seated at her desk. Mary waved back.

"Introduce me," Shane said.

"Sure." Beth headed toward the office, Shane right behind her.

Mary's gaze was fixed on Shane with a great deal of interested speculation.

"Mary, this is Shane McIntyre," Beth said as they entered the office. "This is my co-worker, Mary Reynolds."

"It's a pleasure to meet you, Mary," Shane said, shaking hands with the woman.

Shane guessed Mary to be in her early 50's, even though her hair was entirely white. She was petite — not much over five feet tall — and quite fit, as Shane surmised by the strength of the woman's grip on his hand. Her hair was cut in a short, boyish style, giving her an appealing elfin appearance. When she smiled, her brown eyes crinkled at the corners.

"So, you're Beth's new admirer," Mary said to Shane. "I'm happy to meet you."

"Likewise, ma'am," Shane said.

Mary held on to Shane's hand with a tight grip as she eyed him intently, a blatant challenge in her steely gaze. *Don't you dare hurt this girl.*

Shane squeezed Mary's hand in return, acknowledging the unspoken message. Mary Reynolds would make a good ally inside the library.

The inner office was situated against a solid wall, the other three sides made of glass, giving the occupants a clear view of the rest of the Special Collections area. Shane made note of the usual office paraphernalia: two desks situated facing each other in the center of the room, two desktop computers, two office phones, a fax machine, a printer. There were a few filing cabinets in the room and some plants. It was a quiet, cozy space.

He was pleased to see that there was a lock on the office door, but with three glass walls, the office couldn't offer much in the way of protection under true duress.

"Where does that lead?" he said, pointing at a door in the one solid wall in the office.

"That's our packing room," Beth said. "We pack and unpack shipments of books and other materials in there."

Shane walked to the door and opened it, peering inside. He flipped on a light switch and surveyed the room — it was little more than an oversized closet with a work counter, two metal shelving units filled with flattened cardboard boxes, and countless rolls of packing tape. The room itself was a dead-end, which was good. There was no way into the Special Collections room other than through the electronically secured door. The only problem was that the door to the workroom didn't have a lock — he'd have to see about rectifying that. If it had a good lock, the packing room would make an excellent panic room, if the need arose.

Shane closed the door to the packing room and returned to

Beth, where she stood by her desk.

"I guess I'd better let you get to work now," he said, reaching out to cup the back of her neck. He pulled her close and kissed her. His mouth might have lingered a little longer, and a little deeper, on hers than appropriate in front of a perceptive audience, but he wanted to make sure Mary Reynolds understood he was far more than simply an "admirer" of Beth's.

When he ended their kiss, Shane glanced at Mary, who was eyeing them keenly. She obviously felt some affection for Beth, and perhaps a bit of maternal protectiveness.

Shane fished a business card out of his wallet and handed it to Mary. "Here's my contact information," he said. "In case you ever need to reach me. Program it into your phone."

Mary nodded.

"Would you give me your cell number?" he said, handing her his phone.

"Sure," Mary said, keying in her number, then handing back his phone.

"Thanks. Don't ever hesitate to call me if Beth ever needs anything," he said.

Shane turned to Beth. "Have a good day, sweetheart," he said. "I'll call you later."

He kissed her one last time, and then he let himself out.

"I didn't realize things had gotten so serious between you two," Mary said, propping her hip on the edge of Beth's desk. "The last thing you said was 'we're just friends.'"

Beth dropped onto her desk chair, looking a little shell-shocked as she powered on her computer. She glanced up at Mary, who was eyeing her expectantly. "I guess things have progressed a little since then."

And wasn't that an understatement, considering what he'd done to her a little more than an hour ago in her bed. That wasn't something 'friends' did to each other. She squirmed in her seat as if she could still feel the residual tingles from the startling pleasure his finger had generated in her backside. Jeez. She'd had no idea that was an erogenous zone!

"I like him," Mary said, returning to her own desk. "You have my approval, not that it matters." Mary shook her head. "I'll bet he's amazing in bed. All that controlled intensity. And, my God, he's hotter than hell."

When Beth's face turned bright red, Mary smiled at her. "Don't ever play poker, Beth. You'll lose every time."

31

The rest of the week passed in a blur for Beth. Shane called her a couple of times each day just to say 'hi' and tell her he was thinking about her. They texted and e-mailed each other, and Beth enjoyed feeling connected to him. He slept over with her on Wednesday night, and he took her to Clancy's Friday evening for some quality book browsing time.

"You know not to judge a book by its cover, right?" Beth had said when he pointed out to her a couple erotic romance novels he thought looked interesting.

"They look pretty damn good to me," he'd said, eyeing the scantily clad couples on the covers.

After the visit to Clancy's, they went back to Beth's house for another sleepover. Shane left her house Saturday morning to go to his office for the day to catch up on work before their big evening at the hospital fundraiser that night.

They'd decided to go back to his apartment to get ready together for the benefit. She'd had all day Saturday to worry about what could go wrong, so she was a nervous wreck by the time Shane picked her up at five-thirty.

"You look beautiful," Shane said when he stepped through the front door. "Who did your hair? Did you do this?"

"Gabrielle did it."

Shane reached out and gently touched one of the curling tendrils that fell to her shoulder, letting it wrap around his finger. The rest of her hair was up in a simple, yet sophisticated braided twist.

"I'm going to enjoy messing that up later," he said, planting a kiss on her lips.

When the elevator arrived at the penthouse floor, they stepped out into the foyer where Cooper stood waiting for them. He was dressed in all black, trousers and a button-up shirt, with an empty gun holster strapped to his chest. He was leaning against a wall, using a pair of chopsticks to fish out the last bite from his carton of Chinese take-out.

"Hey, Beth," Cooper said, smiling as she stepped out of the elevator.

She returned his smile. "Hi, Cooper."

Cooper looked at Shane. "What time do you need to be there?"

"We should arrive at the hotel at seven-thirty," Shane said. And then to Beth, he said, "Cooper's driving us tonight."

"If you're getting all gussied up, we'll take the Mercedes," Cooper said. "It's gassed and ready to go. We leave in one hour."

"Cooper has a gun?" Beth said, as they walked down the hallway to Shane's suite.

"Yes. All of my employees carry guns. Being armed comes with the territory."

"Oh. Do you carry a gun?"

He nodded. "Usually."

"Why haven't I ever seen it?"

"I keep it out of sight when I'm with you."

"Do you have one on right now?"

"Yes."

She looked at him, perplexed. He was wearing trousers and a button-up shirt, which was tucked in. Where could he possibly hide a gun? "Where is it?"

"I have a small caliber handgun in an ankle holster."

Her eyes widened. "Really?"

He nodded. "Yep, really."

When they reached his suite, Shane set Beth's overnight bag on the bench at the foot of his bed. "I had your dress dry cleaned for you," he said.

Beth glanced at her dress, stockings, and garter belt laid out neatly on Shane's bed, and the butterflies in her belly took flight. She started to feel queasy. Crap! What had she been thinking when she agreed to go to this thing with him? She hated crowds! Like really, really hated them. She avoided crowds like the plague, and now she was about to attend a very high-profile social event. What if she had a panic attack at the benefit? The last thing she wanted to do was embarrass Shane in public.

"What's this?" Shane said, indicating the small tote bag she held with a death grip.

"My shoes." She pulled out the pair of Manolo Blahnik flats and set them on the floor beside the bed. "I've been wearing them a little bit each day to break them in." She glanced down at the shoes.

"Sweetheart, is everything okay?"

She looked up at Shane, not sure how to answer that. It was a little late for her to be getting cold feet. They were due to leave within the hour.

"Hey, what's wrong?" he said, taking her into his arms. "Would you like a drink?"

She wrapped her arms around his waist and laid her forehead on his chest. "Yes. A little liquid courage sounds good."

"Come with me." Shane led her over to the bar and fixed a drink for each of them. He handed her a glass. "Here, sit down before you fall down."

Beth sat on the sofa and sipped her drink.

Shane sat on the coffee table facing her, his own drink in his hand. "Now, tell me what's bothering you."

Her eyes were glued to her glass. "It's nothing." *I'm scared.*

He reached out and tipped her face up. "Beth."

"I've never been to anything like this," she said. "I won't know how to act."

"Just be yourself," he said, stroking the edge of her cheek.

She leaned back in the sofa, pulling away from his touch. "I don't do well around a lot of strangers, Shane. I freeze up. I might have a panic attack."

"I'll be right beside you the entire time," he said. "There's nothing to worry about, I promise."

Beth took a long drink, her eyes watering when she finally caught her breath.

Shane set her glass on the coffee table beside his and took her hands. "You don't have to go tonight if you don't want to," he said, kissing her knuckles. "You can stay here and relax, and I'll be home as soon as I possibly can. Cooper can stay here with you, to keep you company."

Beth looked at him, searching his beautiful eyes, wanting so desperately to take him up on his offer and stay at the apartment. But she couldn't bail on him now. He'd gone to such trouble buying her the outrageously expensive dress and shoes, and she didn't want to disappoint him. "I'll go."

"Are you sure?"

"Yes." No.

Shane leaned forward and kissed her, his lips gentle as they clung to hers. "You don't have to go," he breathed against her lips. "Honestly."

She straightened, mentally berating herself for being a coward. "I'll go."

"Then let's get dressed before Cooper comes looking for us."

Beth had showered before Shane picked her up, so all she needed now was a quick trip to the restroom to freshen up before slipping into her outfit. They both went into the bathroom and brushed their teeth. Beth fiddled a little with her hair, until Shane came up behind her, put his hands on her arms and planted a kiss on the nape of her neck.

"You look beautiful," he said.

Beth rolled her eyes at him and made a dismissive sound.

"I can't wait to see you in your dress." He played with a tendril of her hair, wrapping it around his index finger. "Come, let's get you dressed."

Shane led Beth to his bed, where her garments waited. He glanced dispassionately at the pale blue chiffon dress. "I still think it looks like a nightgown. Every man there's going to take one look at it and picture you in his bed."

She slipped her arms around his waist. "I think you're a little biased."

"I'm not. I'm a man. I know how men think."

Shane pulled off Beth's top and helped her out of her shorts, leaving her in the lace panty and bra set Sylvia had given her. He ran his index finger along the top edge of the bra cups, and she shivered.

"Remind me to thank Sylvia," he said. "I owe her for this."

Shane picked up the garter belt and held it up to Beth. "I've been fantasizing about seeing you wear this since Sylvia gave it to you." He helped her don the garter belt, and then held each sheer stocking for her to slip on her legs, clipping each one to the garter belt.

Shane stared at her legs. "This evening is going to be sheer torture."

Then he slipped the dress over her head and watched the soft layers of fabric cascade fluidly down her body.

Beth slipped into her shoes. "I'm ready," she said. "Now it's your turn."

Shane held up his index finger. "Not quite. I have something for you." He grabbed a small red gift box off the top of the dresser and handed it to her.

Beth gazed down at the box, her eyes going right to the Cartier logo.

"Open it," he said.

She opened the box and stared in awe at the necklace inside, a delicate gold chain with a diamond and pearl pendant. She touched the luscious pearl topped with a gold cap inlaid with dozens of tiny diamonds. It was simple and elegant, and it complemented her dress perfectly. She smiled up at him. "It's beautiful."

He removed the necklace from the box and clasped it around her neck. "I chose this because it's delicate and lovely," he said. "Like you."

Beth turned in his arms and went up on her toes to kiss him, her arms going around his neck. "Thank you, Shane."

"You're very welcome, sweetheart."

"Now it's your turn to get dressed, and I get to watch," she said, grinning.

Shane's closet was larger than Beth's entire bedroom at home. It was an organizer's dream with all its racks and shelves and drawers. The closet was vastly underutilized, though, she quickly realized. Shane didn't seem to be much of a clothes horse. There was a rack of suits, perfectly pressed white dress shirts and ties, as well as one of jeans, casual shirts, sweatshirts, and t-shirts. She saw two pairs of sneakers on the floor, a couple pairs of black loafers, and several pairs of scuffed boots.

She watched from the doorway as he quickly shrugged off his shirt and tossed it into a laundry basket. Her stomach did a little flip when his hands went to the fastener of his trousers and he pulled them off. Sure enough, right above the cuff of his black crew socks, a small black gun was tucked into a holster attached to his ankle. The sight of him standing there in his black boxers, lean muscled and long limbed, with a gun attached to his ankle, took her breath away. She took such delight in looking at his body, a finely-chiseled assemblage of muscles and bones and powerful sinew. As she studied him, his penis roused to attention, lengthening and thickening within the confines of his boxers.

Shane glanced down at his burgeoning erection. "I can't help it," he said. "Not if you're going to stand there staring at me."

Beth's face flushed hotly, and she looked away, busying herself studying his array of dark suits.

Shane went to her and wrapped a hand around the back of her neck. "I like it when you look at me," he said, his gaze burning hers. "Don't stop." He drew her close for a kiss. When she moaned, he pulled her into his arms and kissed her hungrily.

A sharp rapping on Shane's bedroom door broke them apart.

"Fifteen-minute warning!" Cooper yelled through the door. "How long does it take two people to change clothes?"

Shane chuckled as he released Beth. He dressed quickly in black trousers, a white undershirt and a freshly pressed white dress shirt, a charcoal gray cummerbund and matching bow tie. Before he donned his tuxedo coat, he strapped an empty gun holster to his chest.

"You're going to carry a gun?" she said.

Shane nodded. He strode to a safe embedded in the wall and punched a code into an electronic panel. The door to the safe swung open and Shane withdrew a black handgun. With a few swift moves, he checked the gun, then slipped it into the holster.

After he put on his jacket, he checked his watch. "Ten minutes to spare," he said, smiling at her.

She smiled back, feeling weak in the knees. As enjoyable as it had been watching him get dressed, all she could think about was watching him undress later.

As they stepped outside the lobby doors, Beth immediately caught sight of Cooper leaning against a black Mercedes-Benz sedan parked in the circular drive. He'd donned a black leather jacket, presumably to conceal the gun he carried.

"You're late," Cooper said as he straightened. But the grin on his face belied his gruff tone.

Shane checked his watch. "We're right on time."

Cooper looked at Beth. "You look gorgeous, young lady."

"Thanks, Cooper," she said.

"Stop flirting with my date," Shane said, as he opened the rear passenger door for Beth.

She scooted inside the vehicle, and Shane slid in beside her.

Beth laid her purse on her lap, her fingers nervously fiddling with it.

"You have your inhaler?" he said, nodding at her purse.

"Yes. I'm ready for anything."

When they arrived at the hotel, Cooper joined the queue of cars waiting to approach the front entrance.

"Don't go far," Shane told him, laying a hand on the man's shoulder. "I'm not sure how long we're staying."

Cooper glanced at Beth, then at Shane, and nodded. "Call when you're ready," he said. "I'll be here."

A hotel usher opened the rear passenger door, and Shane stepped out of the car. He turned to help Beth out.

The event organizers had spared no expense. A red carpet led from the curb to the entrance of the hotel lobby. The walkway was roped off, and numerous reporters and photographers stood outside the red velvet ropes, snapping photos and soliciting statements from the guests. Couples strolled through a veritable gauntlet of photographers rapidly firing off shots. A male photographer stepped up to the rope and snapped a candid shot of Shane and Beth. She flinched at the bright flash.

Shane tucked Beth's hand into the crook of his elbow and gave the photographer a quelling look. The photographer smiled apologetically and shrugged before moving on to the next couple.

The crowd outside the hotel was growing quickly as more and more couples arrived. Cameras flashed left and right, and reporters shouted to be heard over the growing din.

Beth had a death grip on Shane's arm, and she felt his lips at her ear.

"Any time you want to leave, just tell me," he said.

She glanced at Shane, so very debonair in his black tux. The photographers seemed to follow his every move, taking shot after shot of him. He took all the attention in stride, seemingly unfazed by the scrutiny. He answered the questions of a few of the reporters, smiling congenially.

He attended this event every year, and she was sure he'd never doubted that he'd make it through the evening before tonight. His previous dates had probably relished all the attention. She was a huge inconvenience to him, and the least she could do was suck it up and pretend she was having a good time.

"Mr. McIntyre!" yelled one of the reporters. "Who's your date?"

Shane glared at the reporter. "She's a friend."

A friend? Shane McIntyre and friend. For some reason, that cut right through Beth. She certainly hadn't expected him to announce to all and sundry that they were dating, but she'd never expected him to withhold her name. Maybe she'd been reading too much into his attention all along.

Shane didn't miss the flash of hurt on Beth's. But there was no way in hell he wanted her name plastered all over the Chicago newspapers and social media sites the following morning. The media tended to jump all over his dates like sharks at a chum fest, and most of them loved the attention. But Beth wouldn't appreciate being the center of attention, and he sure as hell didn't want to make it easier for Kline to glean more information on her. He'd hurt her, and he couldn't explain why. Still, he felt compelled to say something.

He reached for her hand. "I was protecting your privacy, Beth."

She smiled at him. "It's fine," she said. "You don't have to explain."

Fuck.

They finally made their way into the crowded hotel lobby where dozens of couples milled around, most of them middle-aged and

older. She tried not to stare at the ostentatious displays of diamonds and pearls.

Shane directed her to a reception table in front of the ballroom entrance.

"Shane!" A tiny woman with a cloud of short, white curls on
her head reached out and grabbed Shane's hand, squeezing it
hard. "It's so good to see you, dear!"

"Hi, Dottie," Shane said, smiling at the woman as he pressed
a kiss to her soft, wrinkled cheek. "Dottie Patterson, may I pres-
ent my girlfriend, Beth Jamison."

"Girlfriend!" Dottie clasped her thin, bony hands in delight.
"Good Lord, I can't believe it."

"It's a pleasure to meet you," Beth said, smiling to mask her
confusion. One minute she was a *friend*, and now she was his
girlfriend again.

Dottie cast her pale blue eyes on Beth and smiled with approval. "I thought he'd never settled down."

"Dottie's husband is a retired pediatric cardiologist," Shane
said. "He and my father worked closely together for decades."
Shane smiled down at the woman with genuine affection. "Dottie, where's Gene?"

"Oh, he's running around here somewhere," Dottie said.
"When I see him, I'll tell him you're here. I know he'll want to
see you, dear."

Inside the ballroom, magnificent crystal chandeliers hung from
the ceiling, and in the center of the room stood dozens of large,
round tables covered with white damask tablecloths. The tables
were set with fine crystal and silver place settings. At one end of
the ballroom was a stage where several chairs had been arranged
in a line behind a podium. A bar, orchestra, and dance floor were
at the other end. Many of the male guests were already in line
at the bar, while the women were scattered in small groups at
the edge of the dance floor. Servers dressed in black pants, dress
shirts, and ties wandered through the ballroom carrying trays of

hot hors d'oeuvres and champagne flutes.

A smiling brunette dressed in a teal suit and white blouse approached them. "Good evening, Mr. McIntyre."

"Good evening, Cheryl," Shane said. "This is my guest, Miss Jamison."

The woman consulted her clipboard. "You're seated in the front, sir. If you'll follow me." She led them to one of the tables near the stage, where she pointed out their name cards.

Shane was seated to Beth's right. He checked to see who'd be sitting on her left. "Would you please seat Dottie Patterson on Beth's immediate left, and then Dr. Patterson beside Dottie?"

The woman made a quick notation on her clipboard and nodded. "Yes, sir."

"Let's check your purse at the cloakroom," Shane said. "And then we'll find you something to eat. It'll be at least an hour before supper is served."

"Sounds good," Beth said, pasting a smile on her face. She'd hardly eaten anything all day, and she was starting to feel the effects. She should eat something before she ended up in a puddle on the floor.

They wandered over to the cloakroom to check her clutch.

"I'll keep your inhaler," Shane said, holding out his hand. Beth handed him her inhaler, and he slipped it into his inside jacket pocket. "Just in case," he said.

After they checked Beth's clutch, Shane flagged down a server with a tray of hors d'oeuvres. Beth selected a bite-sized quiche filled with spinach and an herbed cream cheese and popped it into her mouth. It melted in her mouth, and she moaned with delight.

Shane chuckled at her reaction and handed her two more of the tiny quiches. A moment later, he snagged another waiter and handed Beth a mini skewer with tiny cherry tomatoes and fresh mozzarella balls garnished with small pieces of fresh spinach leaf.

"Thank you, Shane, but that's enough. If I eat much more, I won't have any room for supper."

Shane accepted two flutes of champagne from a passing server as he led Beth to a quiet spot out of the flow of traffic. He handed one of the glasses to her.

"To us," he said, tilting his glass toward hers. "To a memorable evening."

"To us." She tipped her glass against his, and then took a sip of champagne.

The orchestra struck up a lively waltz and couples eager to dance took to the floor. Beth watched couples flocking to the dance floor and hoped that Shane wouldn't get any ideas along those lines.

It didn't take her long to realize that Shane attracted a lot of attention. Even out of the way, as they were standing against the wall, a steady stream of people stopped by to talk to him. He was unfailingly polite, and he introduced her to almost everyone who stopped by. Eventually, it all became one big blur to Beth.

"I sincerely hope there won't be a test," she said during one of their rare moments alone. "I can't possibly remember all these people's names."

"There's no test, I promise," he said, chuckling as he drew her close for a quick kiss. "Did I mention how lovely you look tonight?" he murmured, kissing her cheek.

"I think you did mention it." She blushed at the blatant heat in his eyes.

She'd been doing a lot of that — blushing — throughout the evening. Many of the guests had ooh'd and ahh'd over her to Shane — particularly the older guests — as if she were a pet poodle he was showing off. She had received more than her fair share of compliments on her dress, her hair, her face, and on her eyes.

Dottie Patterson, one of the more welcome faces that Beth recognized, had dragged her very congenial husband, Gene, over to say hello. But not everyone had been quite so welcoming. A few of the guests — women, to be precise — had been courteous, but aloof, when Shane had introduced her. Those happened to be the younger women, relatively speaking, the ones under the age of 50, who eyed Shane with a directness Beth found inappropriate. They didn't even bother trying to hide the fact they were undressing him with their eyes. Always polite, Shane seemed not to notice their fawning, but it had annoyed her to no end.

Shane had long since drained his champagne flute — and half of Beth's as well — and was in the mood for something a little more substantial. They made their way through the throng of people chatting, networking, and dancing to the bar, where Shane ordered a whisky neat for himself and a Coke for Beth.

"Would you like to dance?" he said, when they'd finished their drinks.

Beth frowned as she glanced at the packed dance floor. "Shane, I don't know how to dance."

"It's easy, sweetheart. All you have to do is follow me." He wrapped his arms around her waist and drew her close. "Just one dance, please," he said. "I'd really like to hold you in my arms right now."

"All right," she conceded. "But only if I can visit the ladies room first. My bladder is about to burst."

32

Beth's trip to the ladies room wasn't entirely a ploy to avoid dancing. After a partial glass of champagne, water, and a soft drink, her bladder really was about to burst. She also needed a break from the crushing crowd of well-wishers and curious onlookers. She'd lost count of how many people had stopped to speak to Shane and, out of politeness, to her. Most of them had been friendly enough, but a couple of the women had practically glared daggers at her.

To her surprise, Shane came inside the ladies' room with her and did a quick sweep of the room. It was a large restroom, designed to support a large facility. There were two long rows of stalls separated by an equally long counter with a black marble top and a half-dozen sinks. On the counter stood elaborate flower arrangements and silver bowls of tiny, individually-wrapped soaps. Crystal chandeliers and velvet wallpaper with intricate gold highlights added to the upscale ambiance.

The restroom wasn't empty. Beth could hear the tell-tale, quiet sounds of women using the facilities. But Shane had been discreet as he'd made his round.

Smothering a chuckle, Beth shooed him toward the exit. "What in the world were you looking for?" she whispered, as he was halfway out the door.

"You'd be surprised what goes on in public restrooms," he

whispered back.

A young woman in a housekeeping uniform tried to enter the restroom just as Beth pushed Shane out the door. The attendant, whose long black hair was pulled back in a ponytail, gaped at him.

"I was just leaving," he said in a low voice. Then, to Beth, he said, "I'll be right outside. Holler if you need me."

"I think I can manage," she said wryly.

Shane paused beside the restroom attendant and spoke quietly in her ear. The girl stared up at him in surprise and nodded. And then he was gone.

Beth heaved a sigh of relief, grateful for a brief moment of solitude, even if it was just in the bathroom. As an introvert, she found huge crowds exhausting. After nearly an hour of mingling, she was reaching her limit.

She claimed a vacant stall and took care of business, using the temporary timeout to rest and recharge her batteries. She tried to block out everything around her and concentrate on slowing her heart rate and taking deep, even breaths. After hearing a couple of women come and go from the room, she figured she'd dallied long enough. She wouldn't put it past Shane to come checking up on her.

When she finished washing her hands and turned off the faucet, the bathroom attendant gave her a hand towel.

"Thank you," Beth said.

She was halfway to the door when a voice stopped her in her tracks.

"Well, if it isn't the jailbait," a woman said in an acerbic voice.

Beth turned, recognizing the woman they'd talked to in Sylvia's boutique. The woman Shane admitted he'd slept with. The woman's expression was openly hostile, but surely she hadn't heard her correctly. Beth smiled. "Hello. You're Luciana, right?"

Shane's words came back to her. *She's a vain, shallow bitch.*

Luciana sneered at Beth. "You're a fucking genius, you know

that?"

Immediately, Beth's internal alarm bells started ringing, and her pulse rate skyrocketed as a wave of heat flashed through her. Her chest tightened painfully. No, she hadn't misheard the woman. Beth glanced at the attendant, surprised to see her gaping at Luciana.

Luciana Morelli was dressed in a short, skin-tight, red sequined dress that barely covered her thighs. Her rich, dark hair was styled in a sophisticated chignon, and her wickedly long fingernails were painted red, as were her pouty lips. The woman's face was flawless, with artfully made up eyes, impossibly long lashes, and perfectly sculpted brows. On her feet were four-inch spiked heels.

Beth decided the prudent thing to do was simply ignore the woman, so she turned toward the door and resumed walking.

"I have to give you credit, though," Luciana continued. "The whole virginal act is brilliant."

Beth turned back. "Excuse me?"

"What man could resist this?" Luciana gestured at Beth. "You look like a virginal sacrifice. How old are you anyway? Shane's too smart to fall for jailbait. But sweetie, you're about as close as a man can come to robbing the cradle without ending up in jail."

Beth looked away from Luciana, partly to mask her embarrassment, and partly hoping that someone else would come along, and Luciana would stop talking. But there was no one else in the room, except for the attendant who hung back silently, her dark eyes huge as she listened to the exchange.

The attendant glanced apologetically at Beth and muttered something under her breath before scurrying out of the restroom.

"You've got the high-and-mighty Shane McIntyre so twisted around your little finger he can't see straight," Luciana said. "What's your secret?"

The woman's tone was so blatantly bitter that Beth couldn't help but feel sorry for her. Whatever had happened between Luciana and Shane must have been unpleasant.

"That's enough, Luciana!"

Beth jumped at the sound of Shane's voice. She glanced back and found him standing just inside the restroom, his furious gaze locked on Luciana.

"Shane!" Luciana said, brightening instantly as she pasted a beatific smile on her face.

At least she had the grace to blush.

"Get out, Luciana," Shane said, his voice brittle.

This wasn't his master-of-the-universe tone, Beth realized. He saved that tone for people he cared about. This was something completely different; this tone said, *I'll give you five seconds to do what I said, or you'll wish to hell you had.*

Apparently, Luciana was familiar with that particular tone, because she stalked right past Beth without another word and left the restroom.

Shane released a heavy sigh. "I'm sorry, sweetheart," he said, pulling her into his arms. "I had no idea she was in here, or I wouldn't have left you. Luciana dislikes me, in case you hadn't noticed, and that's putting it mildly."

"I think she dislikes me even more," Beth said, melting into his embrace.

He scoffed. "We dated for a couple of months about a year ago. She wanted more. I didn't. She wasn't happy about it."

"I can tell." Beth looked up at him askance. "Have you dated every woman in Chicago?"

He chuckled. "Not hardly. Besides, it's my net worth they're interested in, not me personally."

"I don't believe that for one second." Beth's hands came up to smooth the lapels of his tuxedo. "It's not your money women are interested in, Shane."

The restroom door opened, and three women walked in, chatting excitedly. They stopped dead in their tracks when they noticed Shane.

"If you'll excuse us, ladies," Shane said, taking Beth's hand and leading her out of the restroom.

Out in the hallway, the attendant stood wringing her hands.

"Thank you," Shane said to her.

The young woman blushed, her smile completely transforming her anxious face. "You're welcome, sir," she whispered, and then she headed back into the restroom.

"Did she come out here to get you?" Beth said.

He nodded. "I asked her to watch out for you."

Beth smiled, rising up on her toes to kiss him. "It's not your money, Shane. It's you."

When they reentered the ballroom, the orchestra had just struck up a waltz by Mozart. The dance floor was still crowded with eager — if not entirely skilled — couples showing off the fruits of their expensive dance lessons.

A small group of men standing by the bar caught Shane's attention, and they waved him over.

"You go ahead and talk to your friends," Beth said. "I'll wait here and watch the dancing. I need a minute after Luciana."

"Are you sure?"

"Yes, please."

"Okay. I won't be far. And I'll be right back."

After he'd gone, Beth moved back against the wall, well out of the flow of traffic.

"Beth!"

She turned, surprised to hear someone calling her name. She was even more surprised to see Andrew Morton eagerly striding toward her. "Andrew? What are you doing here?"

"I came with my dad," he said. "My mom's out of town, so he dragged me along with him. He's around here somewhere."

Like every other male at the benefit, Andrew Morton was wearing a black tuxedo. With his artfully disheveled blond hair and handsome face, he was undeniably pleasant to look at. Too bad he gave her the creeps.

"What are you doing here?" Andrew asked, a tad breathless.

"I'm here with my... boyfriend." It was the first time she'd publically referred to Shane as such.

"Boyfriend?" Andrew frowned.

Beth saw the disappointment on Andrew's face, followed by a flash of anger.

"Who? Where is he?" Andrew demanded, grabbing her wrist. "Point him out."

"Andrew, that hurts!" Beth cried, and she yanked her wrist free from his tight grip. The identity of her boyfriend wasn't any of his business, and she was about to tell him that when she felt Shane's presence at her back.

He hadn't said a word. He hadn't made the slightest noise, but Beth knew he was there. She could feel a wall of charged electricity at her back. When Andrew's gaze went over her head and turned stony, it only confirmed her suspicions. Shane's hands landed proprietarily on her bare shoulders.

"Introduce me, sweetheart," Shane said in a deceptively mild tone.

"This is Andrew Morton," she said. "Andrew, this is Shane McIntyre. He's... my boyfriend."

A myriad of emotions flashed across Andrew's face — astonishment, anger, resentment.

"You're Richard Morton's kid," Shane said. He pulled Beth back against him. "How do you know Beth?"

Andrew bristled. "From school. I go to Kingston Medical. Beth works in the library."

"I know where Beth works," Shane said, his voice cold. That quickly, the pieces fell into place. This was the kid who'd accosted Beth outside the medical school library earlier in the week. Miguel had given him a detailed description of the kid — it fit Andrew Morton perfectly.

Shane turned Beth around to face him, dismissing Andrew. "How about that dance now?"

Andrew stepped forward. "I was going to ask her to dance."

Shane glanced at Andrew, his expression hard. "Go find your own dance partner, kid. She's mine."

Shane offered his arm to Beth, and she took it. "You okay?" Shane said as he led her to the dance floor.

She sighed. "I'm fine. I was just surprised to see him here."

"Richard Morton is a big donor to the Foundation. He also has a big ego and, apparently, it's hereditary."

When they reached the dance floor, Shane swept Beth into his arms. "Just relax and follow me," he said, when he felt her tense up.

Beth took her first halting steps with Shane, her heart beating triple time. She stumbled a couple of times, and once she stepped on his toes. "I'm so sorry!"

"You're doing great. Just relax," he murmured into her ear. "And don't worry, these shoes have reinforced steel toes."

Beth laughed, not sure if he was joking or not.

They were off and moving, flowing through the throng of dancers as if it were second nature. Shane made it seem effortless. His arm around her waist kept her steady, and his other hand guided their movement deftly through the crowd. She was eventually able to relax a bit in his arms, trusting him to keep her upright and heading in the right direction.

They finished the waltz without further mishap — no more stumbling, no careening into other couples, no more stepping on anyone's toes. Shane talked her into a second dance, and Beth laughed when Shane suggested she take over and lead him in the next waltz.

"I don't think that would be a good idea," she said, chuckling. "We may end up in the coat closet or something."

They were well into their third dance, and Beth was actually starting to have fun, when Shane came to an abrupt halt, catching Beth as she stumbled.

"I'm cutting in," Andrew said, coming out from behind Shane to reach for Beth.

When he felt Beth tense in his arms, Shane forced himself to tamp down his anger and keep calm. "Go away, Andrew."

"I said, I'm cutting in." Andrew's hands latched onto Beth's waist.

Shane made to pull Beth away from Andrew, but Andrew tightened his grip on her waist, and for a split second they were actually playing tug of war over Beth.

Shane abruptly released Beth, and she stumbled for a moment before regaining her balance. In a deft move, Shane grabbed hold of Andrew's hands, and when he applied just the right pressure, the boy immediately let go of Beth. Shane took hold of one of Andrew's arms and twisted it up behind the kid's back, and marched him off the dance floor. Beth hastened after them, following them through an unmarked door into a service corridor.

Shane had already shoved Andrew face first into a wall, Andrew's arm still pinned behind his back.

Beth gasped at the tightly controlled fury on Shane's face. He looked like he wanted to kill Andrew. "Shane?"

"I told you to stay away from her," Shane grated into Andrew's ear. "Don't talk to her. Don't even look at her."

Shane kicked Andrew's feet apart and quickly frisked the boy's pockets with his free hand. "Stay the fuck away from her, kid. If you bother her again, I will personally make you regret it."

Shane released Andrew, and Andrew pushed away from the wall, his chest heaving as he turned toward Shane and glared at him, his hands fisted at his sides.

"Consider this a friendly warning, kid," Shane said. "I don't want to see your face anywhere near Beth again. Is that clear?"

Shane turned away from Andrew, leaving the kid gasping and sputtering in outrage, and gently led Beth by the hand back into the ballroom. She was visibly upset by what had happened, so he led her straight to their assigned table and sat her down. He turned his seat to face hers and sat down, leaning forward and taking her hands in his. "You're white as a sheet," he said, squeezing her hands.

Beth shook from adrenalin. "I'm fine."

"Tell me about Andrew Morton."

"He's a first-year student at Kingston," she said, gazing at Shane. Even now, she could tell he had a tight rein on his anger.

"Does he come to the library?"

"Yes."

"Does he come to your office?"

"Yes."

"Has he been harassing you? Causing you any problems at work?"

Beth looked at Shane, surprised by his questions. She nodded. "He comes to the Special Collections room a lot, oftentimes on flimsy excuses. Mary thinks he might be coming there just to see me."

"I think Mary's right," Shane said, nodding as if she'd confirmed something he already suspected. "Andrew Morton is a narcissist," Shane said. "He's a spoiled rich kid who thinks he can have whatever he wants."

A woman's voice came over the ballroom sound system at that moment, announcing that the servers would be bringing out the first course of the meal shortly.

Beth was still shaking, her heart beating too fast, and her breaths were becoming increasingly labored. She closed her eyes and tried to take a slow, deep breath, but her lungs felt starved. She started coughing.

Shane reached inside his jacket for her inhaler and handed it to her. She smiled with gratitude and quickly administered the medication.

Dottie and Gene Patterson arrived at their table then and took their seats, delighted to see that they were seated with Beth and Shane.

Shane caught Dottie's eye. "Dottie, I need to take care of something. Will you stay with Beth, please?"

"Sure, honey," Dottie said, reaching out to pat Beth's back.

Shane stood. "Thanks, Dottie. Don't leave her side until I get back."

"I won't," Dottie said, waving him off. "Don't worry."

Shane kissed Beth. "I'll be right back," he said. "Stay with Dottie."

"Where are you going?"

"To have a talk with Richard Morton."

Shane found Richard Morton standing beside a table, deep in conversation with the CEO of the children's hospital. Although it galled him to do it, Shane waited for a break in the conversation before he spoke. "Excuse me, Susan," he said, nodding at the CEO. Then he turned to Andrew's father, his expression hardening. "Richard."

Richard Morton turned to look at Shane. "Shane," he said, surprised. "What brings you to my door?"

"Your son does," Shane said. "Can we talk? In private."

Richard Morton's brows furrowed at the mention of his son. "Andrew? What about him?"

"Not here," Shane said, nodding toward the double doors. "Let's go out to the lobby."

Shane turned and headed for the hotel lobby, not bothering to see if Richard followed him or not. If Richard didn't care enough about his son to hear what Shane had to say, then Shane didn't care either.

But sure enough, as soon as Shane stepped out into the hotel lobby, Richard spoke up.

"What the hell is this about, Shane?" Richard said, clearly irritated by the interruption. "I don't appreciate your high-handed — "

Shane stopped and turned to face Richard Morton. "I'll make this quick, Richard. Your son has an unhealthy interest in my girlfriend."

"Oh, come on!" Richard said, grinning. "How in the hell would Andrew know your girlfriend?"

"She works at the Kingston library."

"Oh," Richard said, frowning. Then his expression cleared. "Well, I'm sure it's harmless. He's just a kid! So he has a crush on your girl?" Richard scoffed. "What, you can't handle a little competition?"

"I don't care what it is, as long as it ends." Shane jammed his index finger into Richard's chest. "Talk to your son. Tell him to stay the hell away from Beth. I've warned Andrew, and now I'm warning you. If Andrew bothers her again, I'll put a stop to it, *my way*. Am I being clear?"

Richard glared at Shane. "You don't scare me, Shane," he said, scowling. "And you stay the hell away from my son."

"Cut the crap, Richard. I'm giving you the chance to handle this your way. If I have to handle it — handle *him* — I guarantee you won't like the results."

When Shane came up behind Beth and laid his hands on her shoulders, she jumped. "Sorry," he said, kissing the top of her head. He took his seat beside her. "What did I miss?"

"I was just telling Beth about our Alaskan cruise," Dottie said.

Shane reached out and squeezed Beth's hand. She gave him a surreptitious smile.

The meal progressed quickly as the servers brought out course after course. There was soup and salad, followed by the main course. A parade of dessert carts offering a fantastic assortment of decadent sweets rounded out the elegant meal. Shane passed on dessert, opting for a glass of red wine instead. Beth selected a plate of strawberries dipped in dark chocolate.

Sipping his wine, Shane leaned back in his chair and watched Beth eat her strawberries. He reached out and snagged one of the lush berries from her plate and held it out to her. She grinned at him as she opened her mouth and took a bite, moaning appreciatively as she bit into the piece of fruit. When she glanced at Shane, she was startled by the blatant heat she saw in his eyes as he watched her.

"Want one?" she asked with a teasing smile on her lips. She held a strawberry out to him.

He leaned forward and took the entire strawberry into his mouth. After he'd eaten it, he leaned forward and whispered in her ear. "What I really want to eat is you, as soon as we get home."

As soon as we get home. That had such a nice ring to it, Beth thought.

33

I t was well after midnight when Shane led Beth outside to the line of waiting cars. All of the awards had been bestowed and all the speeches made, to resounding applause, and Beth was exhausted.

Shane had gone up on the stage to hand out several awards to top donors. He received an award himself — the last one of the evening — as Benefactor of the Year for donating $12 million to the pediatric oncology department so they could purchase some ground-breaking new equipment.

Beth had watched him accept the award. He'd looked debonair in his tuxedo, and he'd appeared confident and relaxed in front of the huge crowd. His remarks had been brief, yet poignant. He said the impetus behind his donation to the Pediatric Oncology Department was the memory of big brother, who'd died at age six from a brain tumor. His hope was that with this new equipment, other families might not endure the same tragic loss his family had.

Beth was shocked by his pronouncement. He hadn't mentioned anything about having lost a sibling. He finished his brief speech, then left the stage to a resounding round of applause. When he returned to his seat, he reached blindly for her hand and held it tightly as the applause died down. After saying their goodbyes to the Pattersons and to a few other friends of Shane's, they'd collected Beth's purse from the cloakroom and left the hotel.

Beth caught a glimpse of Andrew Morton and his father standing beside a limousine. A chauffeur opened the rear passenger door, and Richard climbed inside. Andrew paused to look at Beth, his expression hard. After a moment, he climbed in after his father.

"There's Cooper," Shane said, leading Beth down the sidewalk to the Mercedes.

Even though it was summer, the late night air was a tad cool. Shane put his arm around Beth's shoulders to keep her warm. "Let's get you home and into bed."

Seated in the back seat of the Mercedes, Beth closed her eyes and sighed as she leaned into the soft leather seat. She kicked off her shoes and stretched her legs. "Oh, that feels so good."

Beth reached across the seat for Shane's hand. "Thank you for this evening. I had a lovely time."

"Liar," he said affectionately, and he squeezed her hand. "You were accosted by one of my bitter exes in the ladies room and nearly assaulted on the dance floor. I wouldn't blame you if you said it was the worst night of your life."

"And you rescued me both times," she said. "So I can't complain."

The three of them rode the elevator up to the penthouse floor.

"Good night, Cooper," Shane said, as he and Beth turned down the hallway that led to his private suite. "Hold down the fort tonight, will you? No interruptions, please."

"I hear you," Cooper grumbled, chuckling as he headed for the kitchen.

By the time they reached the bedroom, butterflies had taken up residence in Beth's stomach. She had an agenda tonight, and the thought of carrying it out scared her to death. Shane had been wonderful all evening, and she wanted to do something special for him. She knew what she wanted to do. She just wasn't sure how well she could pull it off.

"I'm going to lose the tux," Shane said, heading for the closet.

Beth nodded, heading in the opposite direction. "I'll just freshen up."

She stood looking at herself in the bathroom mirror, trying to give herself a pep talk. Her dress truly was lovely, but it wasn't the dress that Shane wanted to see her in. It was the lingerie. So she stripped off the dress and hung it on a hook on the bathroom wall. Then she quickly brushed her teeth, touched up her hair, and walked back into the bedroom.

"Lights, thirty percent," she said, and the lighting dropped to a seductive level.

She had no experience with seduction. Looking around the room, she searched for the best spot to wait for him. Should she stand somewhere? Should she lie on the bed and strike a seductive pose? Crap! She had no idea how to do this. She was afraid she'd look silly no matter what she did.

Shane walked out of the closet dressed only in his boxers and stopped in his tracks when he saw Beth.

"Say something!" she said, feeling foolish and overexposed.

"I'm speechless." His eyes glittered hotly as he took in the sight of her in the lingerie he'd been fantasizing about for the past week. The sexy lace bra and panties showed off the sleek lines and gentle curves of her body. But the garter belt and sheer thigh-high stockings were probably going to give him a heart attack. "You take my breath away."

There was no hiding his physical reaction, since his erection strained eagerly against the material of his boxers. He started toward her with a determined glint in his eyes. Steeling herself, Beth took a deep breath and met him halfway. She laid her hand on his bare chest, right over his heart, and was surprised to feel it thundering beneath her palm. She smiled and slid her hand slowly down his muscled torso, brushing her fingers through the crisp dark hair that arrowed downward. Her fingers kept going, slipping down to trace the stark outline of his erection through his boxers.

Shane reached for her, his hands sliding down her torso to her waist. His fingers skimmed along the top edge of her garter belt, then slipped underneath it to stroke the soft skin of her belly. "I can't wait to strip this garter belt off you."

She stepped back out of his reach, a hint of a teasing smile on her lips. "Not so fast, mister."

Shane cocked an eyebrow at her, his expression a mix of disappointment and anticipation as he wondered what she was up to.

She walked around him in a slow circle, her fingertips trailing across his abdomen and around his back. Standing behind him, she dragged her fingernails gently down his spine and was thrilled to see him shiver in response.

After completing her slow circle around him, she sank to her knees on the rug and ran her hands up his muscular thighs.

At the sight of her on her knees, Shane closed his eyes and let out a long, heavy breath followed by a groan. "Beth."

"Yes?" She ran her hands around to the back of his thighs, urging him closer.

He looked down at her. "Sweetheart, you don't have to do this."

"But I want to," she said.

He looked down at her skeptically.

"I do!" She gazed up at him, stunned by the blatant desire in his glittering blue eyes. He might be trying to give her an out, but his eyes told a different story. Yeah, he wanted this. Badly. And she was going to give it to him.

She leaned forward and pressed her lips against the hard ridge of his erection, right through the silky fabric.

His stance faltered. "You're trying to kill me, aren't you?"

Smiling, she opened her mouth on the ridge of him and exhaled. Her hot, moist breath made his cock buck violently.

"Jesus!" Shane cried.

She gripped the backs of his thighs, her nails lightly scoring his flesh through the fabric.

"Beth."

Grinning at the rough pitch of his voice, her hands went to the waistband of his boxers, and she peeled his shorts down, carefully freeing his erection from the material. She let his shorts drop to the floor, and he stepped out of them and kicked them aside.

Shane stood at Beth's mercy, watching her with avid interest. His arms were stiff at his sides, his hands clenched as he resisted the impulse to reach for her. This was her show; he'd let her call the shots, even if it killed him.

Peering up at Shane's tense expression, Beth leaned forward and licked the head of his cock.

His hands went to her head, cradling her face. "God, baby," he choked out.

Taking badly needed courage from his reaction, she licked the length of his cock, from root to tip, marveling at the velvety smoothness of his skin. How could he be so hard and so soft at the same time?

"Sweetheart?" he said, his voice uncharacteristically hesitant as he stroked her hair. "I should shower first."

"No," she said. "I want you like this."

Shane closed his eyes as if in pain, and his hands gently gripped the sides of her head.

Holding his cock firmly, she traced the path of a thick vein with her tongue. When she reached the tip of him, she opened her mouth and enveloped the head of his cock, licking the droplets of moisture she found here. Her tongue swirled around the crown, stroking the sensitive glans. Then she pushed him deep into her mouth, as far as she could take him, enclosing him in wet heat.

"Oh, God," he groaned, his hands tightening in her hair.

When she began to suck on him, her mouth working him, he made a rough sound deep in his throat. She bathed the glans with her tongue, teasing the ridge until his groans grew louder.

Shane lost his balance and stumbled, catching himself. "Fuck!" His breath came fast and harsh now, and his hips began to move of their own accord. Unable to help himself, he held her head as he began to thrust into her wet mouth. "Beth." Her name came out as a low, ragged groan.

She licked and sucked him, her mouth and tongue and hand working in concert to drive him crazy. She must have been doing something right, because he was holding onto her like a drowning man holding on to a life preserver. He started making low growling noises in his throat.

"Beth," he grated. "I can't hold out much longer."

He hissed loudly when she gently scraped her teeth along this length. "Fuck!" He grabbed her beneath her arms and hauled her to her feet.

"I wanted you to come," she said, frowning against his lips, as he kissed her hungrily.

Shane swung Beth up into his arms and carried her to the bed. "I want to come inside you," he said, his chest heaving. He kissed her again. "I need to be inside you. Now."

Shane fell back onto the mattress, bringing Beth down on top of him so that she straddled his hips. He scooted toward the head of the bed, taking her with him. Grabbing a condom packet, he ripped it open with his teeth and quickly sheathed himself.

"Get your panties off," he said, breathing hard as he reached for her. "Lift up."

Beth went up on her knees, and Shane quickly realized he couldn't remove her panties with the garter belt and stockings still in place. He fingered the straps from the garter belt. "Damn, these are sexy," he said. Then he reached for the crotch of her panties and gently pulled it way from her body and ripped it.

"Shane!" Beth cried, clearly outraged. "Those are new!"

"I'll buy you more," he growled. His gaze locked on her inner thighs, his hands stroking the tops of her stockings as she positioned herself over him. He reached between her legs to test her readiness and found her sex drenched and ready for him. With a fist at the root of his cock, Shane held himself steady as she brought herself down over him. She gasped when he wedged the fat head of his cock into her opening.

"Ride me," he said, his voice hoarse.

Beth lowered herself onto him slowly, rocking her hips as she slowly sank down. She was so aroused, her sex so wet and slick, she had no trouble working him inside. Once fully seated on him, she lifted up a bit, testing their fit, and her tissues clung to him, dragging against him to create the most delicious friction.

"Come on me," he said, leaning up to kiss her. He sucked on her lips, on her tongue, and he bit her lower lip gently. Then he bucked his hips up into her, causing her to bounce on his loins. "Come, baby, please," he said, arching his head back as he raised his hips, thrusting himself deeper until their bodies were flush together. He laid his head back and closed his eyes tightly as he reached between her legs and began stroking her clit.

Beth closed her eyes and leaned forward, her hands pressed into his pillow, one on each side of his head. She started to move, slowly at first, until she found her rhythm, and then with more confidence. She varied her angle until she found just the right one, the one that caused his cock to drag along the sweet spot deep inside her.

She moved languidly on him, her eyes closed as she navigated his body using only her sense of touch. She rocked herself on him with increasing abandon, gasping when she found what she was looking for.

"That's my girl," Shane said, his hands clutching her waist as he watched the myriad of emotions cross her face. "Ride me, baby," he said. He grit his teeth, struggling to hold back his climax until she'd found hers.

Beth rocked herself with sensual abandon, lost in her own pleasure as she rode the length of him, his cock sliding easily through her wetness. She felt hot all over.

Shane reached up and unhooked the front clasp of her bra. The two halves fell open, revealing the sweet mounds of her breasts to his hot gaze. He slipped his hands inside the cups of her bra, his thumbs brushing her nipples. He gently rolled both nipples between this thumbs and index fingers, lightly squeezing them. She groaned loudly.

She was so close to coming — she could feel it gathering inside her, just waiting to be released. She focused her movements on just the right spot, letting his cock drag back and forth over her tender, sensitive interior. That tantalizing sensation deep inside her rose higher and higher, and she couldn't help the soft, desperate sounds coming from her throat. She was so close now. So close!

"Shane!" she gasped as her muscles clenched down on his cock.

He reached for her hips and his jaw clenched. He was desperate to take over and ram himself into her, but he wanted her to take what she needed from him first. "Look at me, Beth. I want to watch you come."

Beth opened her eyes, stunned by the intensity of his gaze. When her climax hit, her eyes locked helplessly on his, and she cried out. Shane leaned up and kissed her, swallowing her cries.

When the residual tremors of her climax eased, he began thrusting himself hard and fast into her sex.

"I want you on top," Beth said.

"Are you sure?" he said, breathing hard. "We don't have to."

"I want to. I want to feel you like that." She rolled to the side of him, and he moved with her, still buried deep inside.

Shane rolled Beth to her back and came up over her. He held himself up, careful to keep as much of his weight off her as possible, and began moving in carefully measured thrusts.

"Harder!" She pulled him down to her. "Please!"

Shane couldn't resist giving in and letting go. He'd fought the urge to do just that, but with her giving him a green light, he couldn't hold himself in check any longer. He thrust himself into her body, sinking balls deep into her luscious, wet heat. He braced his arms on either side of her and began a steady, fierce rhythm. His mouth dropped to hers, devouring her and drinking in her loud, keening cries as his hungry cock devoured her sex.

"Shane, stop!" she gasped against his lips.

When she started pushing frantically against his chest, he rolled smoothly to the side, taking her with him so that they stayed joined, face to face. He thrust one last time deep inside her, and his hoarse cry reverberated through the room as his climax ripped through him. He held himself still, deep inside her, as his body erupted. When the tremors finally stopped, he pulled out, his chest heaving as he drew in a shaky breath.

"I'm sorry," she said.

Shane turned to look at her, a pleased smile on his face. "Are you kidding? You were amazing!" He pulled her close and wrapped his arms around her, kissing her soundly. She curled into his side, reveling in his warmth and the masculine scent of his body. They lay quietly together as their heart rates stabilized.

Once he had recovered somewhat, Shane removed the condom. "I'll be right back," he said, rising from the bed. When he returned, he cleaned her up, then crawled beneath the covers with her, pulling her close and kissing her.

"That was incredible," he said.

"I panicked."

He shrugged. "That's all right." He kissed her on the forehead. "You did really well. Baby steps, sweetheart. Baby steps."

They settled into the bed, their bodies sated and their muscles relaxed. Shane stretched and groaned in pleasure. "You haven't started your period yet," he observed, as Beth lay drowsily against him.

"No," she murmured. She yawned, completely wiped out. "Anytime now," she said.

"Sweet dreams tonight," he said, kissing her forehead. "I'll chase the nightmares away."

34

Beth walked into her kitchen Monday morning and found Gabrielle standing at the sink rinsing out a coffee mug. "Gabrielle, can I talk to you?"

"Sure." Gabrielle put the mug in the dishwasher. "What's up?"

"It's about Shane."

Gabrielle closed the dishwasher door and straightened, her arms crossing over her chest. "What about him?"

Beth took a deep breath. "I think I'm in love with him."

Gabrielle's expression fell. "Don't say that, Beth."

"Why not?" Beth said, taken aback. "Why would you say that?"

Gabrielle simply stared at Beth, her jaw clenched tightly.

"Gabrielle, you're not being fair to him. He's a wonderful guy!"

"He's lying to you, Beth!" Gabrielle said, throwing up her hands. "Okay? He's lying to you. He's not who you think he is."

Beth's eyes narrowed in confusion. "What are you talking about?"

"Do you honestly think you just *accidently* met him at Clancy's? Please tell me you're not that stupid."

Beth recoiled as if her best friend had slapped her.

"Oh, God, I'm sorry, Beth," Gabrielle said. 'I didn't mean that. But it's true, sweetie... it wasn't a chance meeting." Gabrielle pushed her long hair back in exasperation. "Tyler will kill me for telling you this, but you need to know. Tyler *hired* Shane's company to protect you. You have bodyguards watching you 24/7. Tyler's *paying* them. This is just a job to Shane, Beth. He's taking advantage of you."

Beth shook her head, her thoughts reeling. "That's ridiculous."

"It's not ridiculous. In fact, there's someone outside watching our house right now. He'll follow you to work, and then either he or someone else will follow you home in the evening. There are bodyguards watching you around the clock."

"Gabrielle, that's insane! Why in the world would Tyler hire bodyguards to protect me?"

"Because of Howard Kline."

At the mention of Kline's name, Beth felt a stabbing pain in her chest as her heart missed a beat. "Howard Kline?" she said, shaking her head. "Howard Kline's in prison."

Gabrielle shook her head. "He was released a couple weeks ago on parole."

"No! They can't do that!" Beth cried. "The parole board would have notified me if they were releasing him early. There are rules about that. They can't just release someone early without notifying the victim."

"They did notify you. Tyler knew ahead of time that the notification was coming, and he intercepted it."

Beth's eyes began to tear up. "Why would he do that?"

"Because he didn't want you to worry. He hired Shane's company to protect you. They're also monitoring Howard Kline's movements around the clock as well, trying to determine if he's a threat to you now or not. And based on what I've heard from Tyler, he might be."

Beth began pacing. "Gabrielle, do you hear how crazy this sounds?"

"It's easy enough to prove. Go outside and meet one of your bodyguards. His name's Miguel, and he's parked out front in a black Mustang. Shane's been deceiving you all along, Beth. That's why I don't like him."

Beth's vision blurred as her eyes filled with scalding tears. "That's not possible, Gabrielle." She wiped her eyes with the back of her hand. "Shane would never — "

Gabrielle grabbed Beth's hand and pulled her toward the front door.

Beth tugged on her hand. "What are you doing!"

"I'm going to prove that Shane's lying to you." Gabrielle opened the front door and pulled Beth outside.

Beth yanked her hand free. "This is crazy!"

Gabrielle pointed at a black Mustang parked across the street and three houses down from theirs. "There's Miguel. Go see for yourself."

Beth stared at the Mustang. "Oh, my God," she said. It couldn't be true. What Gabrielle was saying couldn't possibly be true. Shane wouldn't have lied to her like this. He wouldn't have.

She glanced back at Gabrielle and saw her best friend's eyes filled with tears, too. That's when Beth knew it was true. Gabrielle looked as gutted as Beth felt.

"I'm so sorry," Gabrielle said, reaching for Beth's hand. "Sweetie — "

Beth jerked her hand out of Gabrielle's and marched across the street, making a beeline for the Mustang. The windows were darkly tinted, but as she neared the car, she could tell there was someone in the driver's seat. She walked up to the driver's door and rapped on the window. The window came down, and Beth gaped at the dark-haired young man seated inside.

"I remember you!" she said, pointing at him. "You saw you on the Kingston campus last week. You helped me. Are you following me?"

The young man removed his dark sunglasses and laid them on the dash. Then he looked up at Beth.

"Who are you?" she said.

He scowled at Gabrielle over Beth's shoulder, and then he turned back to Beth. "Hello, Miss Jamison," he said, nodding at Beth.

"Oh, my God!" Beth said. "You *are* following me."

"I'm providing you with protection, yes," he said.

"Do you work for Shane McIntyre?"

He hesitated a moment, then nodded. "Yes."

Beth wrapped her arms tightly around herself. "What the hell is going on?"

Miguel sighed, then pushed a button on a dashboard panel.

Through the open window, Beth heard a woman's voice coming through the car speakers.

"Hi, Miguel," the woman said. "What can I do for you?"

"Diane, I need to talk to Shane."

"I'm sorry, but Shane's in a meeting right now."

"Interrupt his meeting. I need him on the phone, STAT."

"Certainly. Hold, please," the woman said.

A moment later, Beth's stomach dropped when she heard Shane's voice over the car speakers. "Miguel, what's wrong?" His voice was an odd mix of urgency and caution.

"Shane, I'm on speaker, and I'm not alone."

There was a moment of silence, and then Shane said, "All right. Who's with you?"

Before Miguel could reply, Beth leaned through the open car window and said, "Shane? Is that you?"

Beth heard a muffled curse over the speaker.

Then Shane said, "Yes, Beth. It's me. What's going on, sweetheart?"

"Maybe you could explain that to me!" she said, her voice rising. "Gabrielle told me about Howard Kline. And about you. I want to know what's going on!"

There was another moment of silence, and then Shane spoke. "Miguel?"

"Yeah, Shane?"

There was an audible sigh over the phone line. "Please bring Beth to my office," Shane said. "If that's agreeable to her."

Beth was already moving around the front of the car to the front passenger door. Miguel disengaged the door locks, and Beth slid inside. She buckled her seatbelt and looked expectantly at Miguel.

"We're on our way," Miguel said, and then he ended the call.

"Don't blame Shane," Miguel said. "He wanted to tell you everything from the beginning, but Tyler refused. If you want to blame someone, blame your brother."

Beth glanced at Miguel, then turned her gaze forward. It was all she could do at the moment to maintain her composure. She wanted to scream. She wanted to cry. But she wouldn't do either in front of a stranger.

She felt sick when she recalled what she and Shane had done together in his bed just two nights before, after the hospital fundraiser. She'd given him everything. She'd put herself out there, risked everything, despite her fears, and made herself vulnerable to him in ways she'd never done with anyone. She'd exposed her deepest self to him, her deepest fears, her deepest needs. And now she felt utterly betrayed. All this time, he'd known who she was and said nothing. All this time, he'd pretended to be someone he wasn't.

Their time together had all been a lie, and now it was all crashing down around her. The knowledge that he'd just been using her was like acid, burning a hole in her gut. She felt sick.

On top of all this was also a gut-wrenching sense of betrayal by Tyler. How could he have kept Howard Kline's parole from her? It was *her* life! She had a right to know that Kline was a free man. How long had that monster been loose on the streets without her knowledge? She knew her brother was controlling, and that he wanted to protect her, but this was going too far!

And then there was Kline to think about, but Beth couldn't even allow herself to go there yet, to even contemplate him being free. To think about Kline would require reliving the horror that had spawned her nightmares, and she could not do that right now.

Beth hardly paid any attention to where they were until they arrived at the brick-and-glass office building downtown. She looked up at the words **THE MCINTYRE BUILDING** engraved in stone over the front doors and felt sick.

Miguel pulled into the building's underground parking garage and parked near a bank of elevators in a slot marked Reserved. He slipped a chunky, black handgun into a holster strapped to his chest, and then pulled on a black leather jacket before getting out of the car. Beth got out and followed him to the elevators.

"Did your roommate tell you?" Miguel asked her as they rode up in the elevator car.

"Yes." The admission burned. It hurt that her brother had confided in Gabrielle, but not in her. This was her life they were talking about, and yet she'd been intentionally kept in the dark. It seemed like everyone she cared about had deceived her.

Miguel made a sound of disapproval right before the elevators opened.

"Don't blame Gabrielle," she said as she stepped out of the elevator. "At least she finally told me the truth."

Beth followed Miguel through a set of double glass doors. Inside was a reception desk, where a woman with white hair and soft blue eyes sat. The nameplate on her desk said *Diane Hughes.*

"Good morning, Miss Jamison," the woman said cheerfully, the corners of her eyes crinkling as she smiled warmly at Beth. Then Mrs. Hughes looked at Miguel and said, "Go on in, honey. He's expecting you."

Miguel walked up to a closed wooden door and rapped sharply once, then pushed it open wide and held it for Beth. Miguel followed her in and closed the door behind them.

Beth walked into a spacious, sunlit corner office, with breathtaking views of downtown Chicago, and came to an abrupt stop when she saw Shane seated behind a large desk. She glanced around the room, taking in the sleek furnishings. This was a Shane she didn't know. This was the corporate CEO who sat up in his fancy office and managed the lives of thousands of employees. She really didn't know much about the man she'd let into her life — into her body — did she?

She'd taken a risk and shared her heart with him. She'd let him inside, deep inside, and now she realized he'd shared only a small sliver of himself with her.

Shane rose from his chair and came around the desk. "I can explain, Beth," he said, his wary gaze locked on her.

Beth swallowed hard, nearly choking on the lump in her throat. She'd tried so hard on the way over to keep it together, but seeing him here in this unfamiliar setting was too much. He seemed much more a stranger to her now and less like her patient, teasing lover.

To her utter shame, her eyes filled with tears. She glared at him. "You lied to me," she said, her voice breaking.

"No, sweetheart," Shane said, his expression pained as he came forward and laid his hands on her shoulders.

She twisted away from him. "Don't call me that!"

Shane winced, and a flare of regret crossed his face. "I'm sorry, Beth. I should have told you before now. I wanted to, but the time never seemed right. You weren't ready to hear it. But that's no excuse. I know that."

Beth took a step back, wrapping her arms around herself. She looked at him through a blur of tears, her throat so tight it hurt to speak. "Gabrielle told me Tyler hired you," she said hoarsely. She took a shaky breath, trying to maintain control. "You lied to me, Shane."

"I didn't lie to you, Beth," he said, parsing his words carefully. "I withheld information, yes. I admit that. But it was for your own safety. I had every intention of telling you when the time was right, but I never lied to you. If you believe anything, believe that."

"I don't know what to believe anymore!" The world was falling in on her from all sides, crushing her with its weight. When she looked at Shane, she saw a stranger, and the loss of the Shane she'd known — her Shane — was devastating.

Shane watched the myriad emotions flit across her face — none of them good — and felt his own anxiety spike. "Sweetheart," he said as he reached for her.

"I told you not to call me that!" She stepped farther out of his reach.

Shane ran his fingers through his hair, fighting the urge to go to her. The farther she moved away from him, the more desperate he was to reel her back in. "Please don't pull away from me, Beth. Let me explain."

Her chest grew painfully tight, and each breath became a struggle. She shook her head, feeling light headed. "Our meeting at Clancy's wasn't an accident, was it?"

He shook his head, his expression remorseful. "No."

"You were there because of me."

"Yes."

"You were *working*. It was just a job for you."

He grimaced. "I was filling in that night for one of your bodyguards, yes. But it was never just a job for me. It stopped being a job the minute I laid eyes on you."

She stared at him like he was a complete stranger.

"Beth, please," he said, taking a few steps in her direction.

"I defended you to Gabrielle! I told her you'd never do something like this to me. I told her she was crazy! But she wasn't, was she?" The blood drained from her face, leaving her feeling chilled. "Oh, God," she said, squeezing her eyes shut. Her arms tightened on her abdomen as if she could hold herself physically together while her insides felt like they were coming apart.

"I trusted you!" she cried, sobbing now. Her breaths came in rapid, shallow pants, and the dizziness grew. Her vision started to dim.

Shane rushed toward her and caught her as her knees buckled.

35

Shane carried Beth across the room to a closed door. Miguel was already there, and he opened the door for them.

"Where are we going?" Beth said.

Shane carried her through the open doorway into ... an apartment? He laid her down on a tan sofa and tucked a small sofa pillow under her head. Then he pulled off her sandals and dropped them on the floor.

"How many apartments do you have, Shane?" she said.

"Just breathe, Beth," Shane said, as he sat down beside her. He brushed her hair back with gentle hands. "Try to relax."

Beth closed her eyes against the dizziness and tried to rein in the panic, but her mind was like a runaway train careening out of control. She tried to block it all out, and still the tears came. When she felt a light touch on her cheeks, she opened her eyes to see him dabbing gently at her tears with a tissue.

"I wanted to tell you everything from the beginning," he said in a quiet voice. "Even before I met you. But Tyler was adamantly against it. He didn't want to scare you."

He looked her in the eye, and she was struck by the bleakness she saw there.

"But to be completely honest," he said, his fist crushing the damp tissue, "I was afraid to tell you."

She couldn't imagine Shane ever being afraid of anything.

"Afraid of what?"

"Of this. Of your reaction. I was afraid you'd run."

She made a pained sound, squeezing her eyes shut. "It was just a job for you."

Shane shook his head. "No. It stopped being a job the minute I laid eyes on you. I took one look at you, Beth, and knew I wanted you. It was never a job after that. I was biding my time, waiting for the right moment to tell you."

She remembered her giddiness at seeing him that second time at Clancy's, and the memory made her feel sick. How could she have been so damn gullible?

She started shaking, and Shane grabbed the fleece blanket that lay along the back of the sofa and covered her.

"I know this is a shock," he said, stroking her hair. "Jesus, I'm sorry, honey. The last thing I wanted to do was hurt you."

"I need to go," Beth said, shoving the blanket aside and struggling to sit up. She felt far too vulnerable grieving here in front of him as pieces of herself were ripped away. She needed to put as much space between them as possible, so she could grieve in peace.

"You're not going anywhere right now," Shane said, gently pushing her back down.

"I'm supposed to be at work. Mary will be wondering where I am," she said as if he hadn't said a word.

Shane pulled out his cell phone and pressed a button. "Diane, call Mary Reynolds and tell her Beth will be late to work."

"She doesn't know where I work," Beth said, eyeing Shane suspiciously when he ended the call.

"It's our business to know things, Beth. Diane will figure it out," he said.

"I really do need to leave," she said, sitting up and swinging her legs to the floor. She grabbed her sandals and slipped them on.

"You're not leaving, Beth. We need to talk."

"There's nothing to talk about."

"The hell there isn't!" He took a deep, steadying breath. "We need to talk, not just about us, but also about Howard Kline."

Beth's face blanched at the mention of Kline's name.

Shane leaned back in the sofa and drew her close. "Please don't worry about Kline. I have people watching him around the clock. He can't take one step in your direction without my knowledge. And if he did make a move, I have people in place to intercept him before he gets anywhere near you. I swear to you, Beth, Kline won't get within a mile of you."

"How did he even get out of prison?" she said. "He was supposed to serve 30 years. It's only been... what? Eighteen?"

Shane shrugged. "I've never claimed to understand how the parole board works. The bottom line is they approved him for parole, and he's out."

Beth shuddered, and Shane tightened his hold.

"He can't get to you, sweetheart," he said, kissing her temple. "I won't let him, I swear to you."

"I woke up this morning on top of the world, and now in less than a couple of hours, everything has crashed and burned."

"No, it hasn't," Shane said. "Granted, you didn't know about Kline, and I know that's a huge shock. But nothing else has changed. We just spent an amazing weekend together — damn it, you know how I feel about you. Nothing has changed."

"Shane." Now it was her turn to use *that* tone.

"Beth, please. You asked me not to let you run, and I'm going to keep my promise. I'm not letting you run."

"This is different," she said. "This isn't running."

"Bullshit! You run when you feel threatened. I'm not a threat to you, Beth. I love you."

Her eyes widened at his declaration. "This morning I told Gabrielle I was falling in love with you. That's why she told me Tyler hired you."

"Nothing between us has changed, Beth," he said, turning to face her.

Shane leaned forward slowly, giving her plenty of time to pull away. She eyed him warily as he moved closer. Her eyes drifted shut when his mouth covered hers, his lips coaxing hers open.

And then he was kissing her, his tongue making love to hers. She clutched at his shirt with trembling fingers.

His mouth lifted, hovering over hers. "The first time I saw you, I wanted you," he admitted. "And the first time I had you, I knew you were mine."

"Shane — "

She was interrupted by a knock at the door.

"What is it?" Shane barked, annoyed at the interruption.

Miguel opened the door. "Do you need me to stay?" he said.

"No, you can take off. Thanks, Miguel," Shane said.

Miguel turned to leave.

"Miguel, wait!" Beth said.

Miguel paused.

"Would you mind giving me a ride back to my house? I need to get to work."

Miguel looked to Shane.

"Beth — " Shane said.

"I'm leaving," Beth said, as she stood and put several feet between herself and Shane.

Shane glanced at Miguel and reluctantly nodded.

"I'd be happy to drive you to work," Miguel told her.

"Thank you," she said.

Shane glanced at Miguel. "Give us a minute," he said tersely.

Miguel nodded, then stepped back into Shane's office and shut the door behind him.

As soon as they were alone, Shane turned to Beth. "I know you're upset, and you have every right to be. But give me a chance. Be mad at me all you want. Yell and scream at me if you need to, but don't shut me out."

"I'm not mad at you," she said in a calm voice.

His stomach clenched. She should have been railing at him, screaming. Instead, she was calm. Too calm. She'd checked out already, he could sense it. She'd already made up her mind.

He felt a swift flare of anger that she would give up so easily on what they had. "If you're not mad at me, then what the fuck are you?" he said, his expression tight.

She flinched at his tone.

Shane knew her answer before she said the words.

"I'm not mad," she said, her voice brittle. "I'm done." She headed for the door and paused before opening it. "It was a mistake from the beginning. I should've known better."

Beth found Miguel waiting for her in Shane's office. "I'm ready."

Miguel glanced over Beth's head at Shane, who stood silently behind her in the open doorway to the suite, his expression tense.

Beth was numb as she followed Miguel on shaking legs. She just hoped she could make it out of the building before she collapsed. Right now, more than anything, she just wanted to curl up in a ball and give in to the agonizing pain in her chest.

They passed the desk of Shane's executive assistant — Mrs. Hughes — whose bright, friendly smile faltered when she saw Beth's face.

"Have a good day, Miss Jamison," Mrs. Hughes said in a subdued voice.

The woman's gaze bounced back and forth between Beth and Miguel, and Miguel give the woman a quick shake of his head.

The hallway leading to the elevators seemed interminably long, and Beth was quickly running out of steam. She was operating on sheer adrenalin now, in complete flight mode, and she didn't know how much longer she could keep it together. Her chest felt like it was being squeezed in a vise, and her throat was so tight it hurt to swallow.

When they passed a women's restroom, Beth made a sudden detour and pushed her way through the door. Inside, the four stalls were empty. She was alone in the room.

She leaned shakily against the nearest wall, afraid she wouldn't be able to stay upright much longer. Her heart thundered painfully, and the vise around her chest tightened to the point she could barely breathe.

As the realization of what she'd done hit her — *oh, God, she'd left him* — the pain overwhelmed her, and she slid down the wall to the cold tile floor. It came rushing at her, wave after wave of excruciating pain. Now that she was away from prying eyes, the tears flowed unchecked. There was no stopping the wracking sobs that took her over.

A draft of cool air against her overheated skin was the only indication she had that someone had come into the bathroom. And then he was there on the floor with her. Wordlessly, Shane gathered her up into his arms and settled her on his lap. She pressed her wet face into the front of his shirt and sobbed.

Shane rocked her, his lips in her hair. "I'm sorry, Beth. I'm so sorry."

Beth was silent on the drive back to Hyde Park. She sat in the front seat of Miguel's car, staring blindly out the passenger window at the passing scenery.

She'd left him. She'd left the man who'd held her on the bathroom floor as her heart broke into a million pieces. He hadn't seemed to care that she ruined his shirt, soaking him through to the skin with her tears. He'd just held her, his lips in her hair, murmuring unintelligible words. When she'd finally cried herself out and climbed awkwardly to her feet, she'd noticed that his eyes were wet, too. She wouldn't let herself even think about that — about what he might be feeling. She couldn't.

Without a word to Shane, she'd wiped her face and nose on a tissue, and then walked out of the restroom to find Miguel and Mrs. Hughes waiting in the hallway.

"Let's go, please," she'd said to Miguel, continuing down the hall toward the bank of elevators, trusting that he would follow.

She kept walking, even though she felt sick inside. She'd just walked out on the only person she'd ever loved, the only person she'd ever trusted enough to let inside.

"Beth?"

She glanced at Miguel, blinking as if coming out of a daze. He looked as awful as she felt. "I'm sorry, what?"

"I've known Shane a long time," Miguel said. "He's — "

"Please don't," she said. "I don't want to talk about it."

"He's a good guy, Beth. Maybe he screwed up, but that doesn't mean — "

"Miguel." She gave him a quelling look.

"Just think about it, okay?" Miguel said. "Don't make any hasty decisions."

"It's too late for that," she said.

Miguel stopped at Beth's house so she could grab her purse. Then he drove her to the library, pulling up to the main entrance to let her out.

She opened the car door. "Thank you for the ride."

Miguel shrugged off her gratitude. "No need to thank me."

Her anger flared anew. "Right. You're just doing your job."

Miguel frowned. "I would've done it anyway, Beth."

Beth instantly regretted taking her anger out on him. He'd been nothing but kind to her, and he didn't deserve her animosity. She should direct her ire at the people who deserved it, namely her brother and Shane. "I'm sorry."

He smiled at her. "No problem. I'll see you around."

Her brows wrinkled in surprise. "You're not still going to watch me, are you?"

He nodded. "Yes. Until Shane tells me otherwise."

Beth's eyes teared up again as she got out of the car. As she approached the main entrance to the library, she surreptitiously wiped the tears from her face and pasted a thin smile on her face.

Devany greeted her from behind the front reception desk with her usual wide smile.

Beth waved at her friend, but couldn't muster the energy to do much more. She headed toward the staircase, but stopped when Devany called her over.

"What's wrong?" Devany said.

"Nothing," Beth said. "I'm fine."

Devany shook her head. "You're not fine. You look awful. What happened?"

Beth's throat tightened painfully. "I broke up with Shane this morning."

"What!" Quite a few heads turned their way at the outburst, so Devany lowered her voice. "Why?" she hissed.

Beth shrugged. The situation was far too complicated and far too personal to explain, so she gave her friend the short version. "He lied to me."

Devany frowned. "Was it a big lie or a little one?"

"Does it matter?"

"I guess it depends on the lie," Devany said. "But you were so happy! I can't believe you broke up with him. Are you sure?"

"Yes, I'm sure." *No, I'm not. I probably just made the biggest mistake of my life.* "I'll see you later, okay, Devany? I'm already late."

"Sure," Devany said, frowning. "See you later."

As Beth took the stairs up to the second floor, every step seemed more and more difficult as if she were trudging through quicksand, sinking deeper with each step. She keyed in her access code and let herself into the secured room, relieved to find it empty. She headed straight for her desk and dropped into her chair, grateful for the opportunity to be alone for a few moments.

For a badly needed distraction, she turned on her computer and watched the monitor flicker to life. When her cell phone chimed with an incoming message, she dug her phone out of her purse and checked the screen. It was a message from Shane.

Did you get to work okay?

Surely, he could have asked Miguel; he didn't need to hear it from her. When she realized it was just an excuse to contact her, part of her was elated that he was reaching out to her even after what she'd done. But the other part of her knew it was futile. Prolonging the contact between them would only make it harder on them both.

Beth silenced her phone and returned it to her purse, and then she stowed her purse in the bottom drawer of her desk. Needing to put some space between herself and that text message, she rose from her chair and paced in the small office, looking for something to do to keep her mind off Shane's message. Her eyes fell on the pot of fresh coffee on the credenza, and she poured herself a cup. She wasn't a big coffee drinker, but this gave her something to do. She sat down at her desk and had just taken her first sip when the door to the Special Collections room opened, and Mary came in carrying a small plate with two bagels and packets of flavored cream cheese.

"I come bearing carbs!" Mary said, smiling triumphantly.

Mary laid the plate on Beth's desk. "Someone left a bag of bagels in the employee lounge this morning. Here, have one."

Beth took a plain bagel and a packet of cinnamon-flavored cream cheese. "Thanks."

"Beth? What's wrong?" Mary said.

"Nothing."

Mary sat on the edge of Beth's desk. "I hope you never plan to go into the spy business, because you'd suck at it. Your face is an open book. Now, tell me what's wrong."

Beth sighed. "I broke up with Shane this morning."

"Why?" Mary said.

Beth tore off a piece of the bagel and stuck it in her mouth. "I don't want to talk about it."

"Did he cheat on you?"

"No!" Beth said, indignant that Mary would accuse Shane of cheating.

"Then what? What could be so egregious that you'd dump a mega hunk like him? That man is sex on a stick."

Beth suppressed a grin at Mary's words. Then she sobered. "He lied to me."

Mary frowned. "Lied about what?"

Beth sipped her coffee as fresh tears started. "Please, I can't talk about it right now."

"Oh, honey, I'm so sorry," Mary said, reaching out to tuck Beth's hair behind her ear.

36

He was officially a stalker now. Shane had sent Beth four text messages in the past hour and called her cell twice, and she hadn't responded once. Miguel had assured him she was in the library. He said he'd dropped her off at the main entrance and watched her walk in, and he hadn't seen her leave — at least not by the front entrance. But still, Shane needed confirmation that she was there and that she was okay. He couldn't stop thinking about how she'd looked when she left. Gutted. She'd been absolutely gutted. And it was his God damned fault.

He wanted to go see her for himself — just to be sure she was okay — but he didn't think she'd appreciate that just yet. She was probably still reeling from what she'd learned this morning. She needed time to process everything, and then time to start thinking more clearly. Yes, he'd fucked up, but surely this was something they could get past. What they had was far too amazing to lose because of one well-intentioned screw-up.

Short of going down to the campus himself, though, or sending Miguel inside to find her, he figured his most expedient way to find out what he wanted to know was to contact Mary Reynolds. He dialed Mary's cell phone, hoping like hell she'd answer. Otherwise, he'd have no choice but to head there himself.

Mary answered on the fourth ring. "Mary Reynolds."

He could tell from the wary tone of her voice that she already knew. Good, that would simplify things. "Mary, this is Shane McIntyre. Please, don't let Beth know it's me on the phone."

"Okay. How can I help you?" she said.

"Is Beth there with you?"

"Yes."

"Is she all right?"

"I'm not too sure about that," Mary said, her voice clipped.

Shane sighed. Of course she wasn't all right. "Did she mention that we had a falling out this morning?"

"Yes, something along those lines."

"I take it she's right there," Shane said. "You can't speak freely?"

"That's right."

"The reason I called you was to make sure she's there and that she's all right. She was upset this morning when we parted, and she won't reply to my texts or take my calls. I just wanted to be sure she's all right."

"I guess you could say that," Mary said.

"Thank you," Shane said. "Please call me if there's a problem."

"I'll do that. Thanks for calling." And then she ended the call.

Shane was debating whether or not to send Beth another text message when someone rapped sharply on his office door.

"Come in," he said.

"Hey, Shane." Jake walked into Shane's office, shutting the door behind him. He made himself comfortable in one of the chairs in front of Shane's desk. "So, what's new?"

"Cut the crap, Jake," Shane said, amazed at how quickly bad news travelled. "Miguel called you?"

"No. Miguel called Liam, and Liam called me. Something about the Jamison girl finding out about the protection order and about Kline. Do you have any idea what Tyler will do to you when he finds out?"

"I can only guess," Shane said. "But Tyler is the least of my concerns right now. I'm worried about Beth. She thinks I lied to her."

Jake crossed his arms over his chest. "You did lie to her,

knucklehead."

Shane ran his hands through his hair. "I mean intentionally. Jesus, can this day get any worse?"

Jake chuckled. "All right, tell me. What the fuck have you been doing with our client's little sister? Pardon the pun."

"It's simple," Shane said, leaning back in his chair. "I fell in love with her. End of story."

Jake grinned. "I knew it! I told you so!"

"Well, this morning she told me she was through with me, and now she won't talk to me."

"How'd she find out?"

"Gabrielle."

Jake nodded his head. "I knew the roommate was a weak link. It was only a matter of time before she squealed."

"It's not Gabrielle's fault. She was just trying to protect Beth. But now Beth won't take my calls or respond to my texts. I'm completely in the dark, and it's driving me nuts."

"What are you gonna do? Cut your losses and run before Tyler gets wind of this?"

"Hell no. I'm going to get her back."

"Seriously?" Jake said. "Since when have you ever chased after a woman?"

"Since now. I'm not going to lose her, Jake."

Jake grinned. "Oh, this is going to be interesting, especially once Tyler finds out."

The rest of Beth's morning passed uneventfully. She had two student appointments, she answered some e-mails, and she packed up a collection of periodicals that were due to be shipped back to Johns Hopkins Medical Center. It was noon by the time she made it back to her desk. She was dying to check her cell phone, but she was afraid of what she'd find. The problem was, she didn't know which would be worse... if he'd continued trying to contact her, or if he'd given up.

"Did you bring your lunch today?" Mary asked.

"No," Beth said. With all the excitement that morning, she'd forgotten to bring lunch.

"You need to eat something," Mary said. "Let's walk over to the cafeteria and grab something. Or we could go off campus if you'd prefer."

Beth didn't feel like eating anything, but she knew she'd feel even worse if she skipped lunch. Her body wasn't very forgiving when it came to skipping meals. The last thing she needed today was to pass out from low blood sugar.

"The cafeteria's fine," Beth said. She really didn't have the energy to go anywhere else.

As soon as she stepped out of the library, Beth noticed Miguel's black Mustang parked in the visitor lot in front of the library. When she and Mary headed toward the Student Union, Beth glanced back and saw Miguel following on foot. Funny, he must have been following her all over campus before and she'd never noticed. What surprised her now was how oddly comforting it was to know he was there.

The Student Union was a quick 10-minute walk from the library. It felt good to be out in the sunshine and fresh air, and, for a few minutes, Beth tried to convince herself that she was handling all of this just fine.

She bought a bowl of vegetable soup and a fresh baguette, and Mary got her customary chicken wrap and chips. They sat at one of the window tables.

"Your soup's getting cold," Mary said after a while, as Beth stared out the window watching birds squabbling over a birdfeeder.

Beth hadn't touched her soup. She just didn't feel like eating. Her body might be here with Mary in the cafeteria, but her heart and mind were elsewhere. "I'm just not hungry," Beth said. She was also very conscious of the fact that Miguel was seated on the other side of the dining room eating a sandwich. Now that the cat was out of the bag, so to speak, he wasn't trying to be invisible.

"It might help if you talked about it," Mary said. "I'm a good listener."

"I can't — " What could she tell Mary without revealing more of her past life than she wanted to? She didn't like people knowing about what had happened to her. Whenever she told someone, they'd always ended up treating her differently, so she'd stopped telling people. "He withheld some important information from me," she finally said.

"You said he wasn't cheating on you," Mary said.

Beth shook her head. "No, he'd never do a thing like that. He has too much integrity." And then she realized what she'd just said. Shane was an honorable man. He'd always been honest with her about so many things, about his personal life, about his fears for her, about what he wanted them to be to each other. He'd been honest for the most part, and yet he'd kept such vital information from her. It didn't make sense.

"Okay," Mary said. "So he didn't cheat. Is he married?"

"No! It's nothing like that."

"Did he intentionally try to mislead you?"

Beth shook her head. "No. It wasn't intentional. He was just... waiting for the right time to tell me something."

"So, what happened?"

"Someone beat him to it."

Mary leaned back in her seat and crossed her arms. "Beth, I've never seen you as happy as you've been these past couple of weeks. Are you sure you want to end it with him because of some withheld information? Maybe he would have told you himself when he thought the time was right. When I met Shane, he struck me as a pretty honorable person."

"He is," Beth said, closing her eyes. She covered her face with her hands and groaned. "Oh, God. I don't know what to think."

"Think carefully, Beth. Guys like Shane don't come around every day."

The rest of the day dragged. Beth had several afternoon student appointments, she cataloged some new arrivals to the collection, and she took several phone calls. One of them was from Gabrielle.

"Are you okay?" Gabrielle said.

"No, not really."

"I'm sorry about this morning," Gabrielle said. "I shouldn't have told you like that. I just — well, when you said you were falling in love with him, I guess I just lost it. I thought you should know the truth about what you were getting into. I'm really sorry, Beth. I feel terrible."

"It's okay. I don't blame you. It's Tyler who kept the information from me. Tyler and Shane."

"I can take the evening off from work tonight and stay home with you. I'll make you whatever you want for dinner, and we can just hang out and watch a movie."

"No, that's okay. Thanks for the offer, but I don't want you to miss work on my account. I'll be fine."

"I'll do the mailroom run," Mary said late in the afternoon. "I'll be back."

After Mary left, Beth dug her cell phone out of her purse and checked her messages for the first time since the morning. There were ten texts from Shane, as well as three missed calls. A glutton for punishment, she scrolled through the texts.

Did you get to work okay?

I'm sorry.

Beth, please talk to me.

I was going to tell you. I was just waiting for the right time. There was no easy way to tell you.

I was afraid you'd bolt when I told you, so I kept putting it off.

Please don't punish me like this. I'm sorry.

Would you at least send me a message, so I know you're okay?

Would it kill you to throw me a god damned bone? Just say something. Anything.

Okay, I'm officially groveling now. Tell me what you need from me and I'll do it. I can fix this.

I love you.

Beth could barely finish reading his messages for the tears obscuring her vision. She put her phone back in her purse and closed her desk drawer. There was no way she could listen to his voice messages. If she heard his voice right then, she'd lose it completely. Right now, it was all she could do to make it through the last hour of the day. And then she could go home and have a melt-down in private.

Beth walked home from work. The weather was fine, and the exercise would do her good. It might help her think things through and clear her head a little. She was just a couple of blocks from the library when Miguel pulled up alongside the curb and lowered the front passenger window.

"Want a ride home?"

She smiled sadly at him. "No, thanks. I could use the walk."

He nodded, then continued to follow her at a discreet distance.

She found it odd to think that people — strangers — had been following her around for weeks and she hadn't known. Good God, how much was Tyler paying for this protection? She couldn't even begin to imagine what this cost, and how could Tyler afford it. He made a pretty decent salary, yes. But this had to be costing him a fortune. And that wasn't even taking into account the cost for conducting surveillance on Howard Kline.

She'd need to talk to Tyler soon about all this crazy security stuff. She also needed to find out what they knew about Howard Kline. So far, she hadn't given him much thought. She'd been too distraught over Shane's betrayal to even think rationally about

Kline.

Shane's betrayal. That's what it had felt like. Since the moment she met him, he'd been lying to her. Granted, he hadn't been doing it to be malicious, but still, he'd been deceiving her. How could she ever trust him now?

He said he'd meant to tell her, and Beth figured that much was probably true. Shane couldn't have continued his charade for much longer before Tyler got wind of it. In fact, Beth realized it was just sheer luck on Shane's part that she hadn't yet told Tyler about her new so-called boyfriend. But then she realized she'd been putting that conversation with Tyler off, because she'd been afraid of how Tyler would react. Shane wasn't the only one who hadn't been forthcoming. She was guilty of that, too.

Beth waved at Miguel when he parked across from her house, and then she went inside. She thought it was really unnecessary for Miguel to sit outside her house. She didn't need a babysitter. She really needed to talk to Tyler. He needed to put a stop to these bodyguards. She thought about picking up the phone and calling Tyler, but she just wasn't ready for that conversation.

Skipping dinner because it just seemed like too much effort, she went upstairs and changed into lounging pants and a t-shirt. She tried watching one of her favorite rom-coms downstairs in the parlor, on the big TV, but her mind kept wandering back to her meeting with Shane that morning.

Halfway through a movie she wasn't really watching, she checked her phone and saw one new text message from Shane.

Please reply. I'm worried about you.

By the time the movie ended, she was lying on the sofa clutching a throw pillow as the tears fell unchecked. The loss of Shane was like a gaping wound in her chest, open and raw. Her heart ached. She didn't have the energy to go upstairs to her own bed, so she pulled an afghan over herself and closed her eyes.

Shane walked into the kitchen at Renaldo's at ten-thirty that evening.

Peter Capelli glanced up from an enormous stock pot of sauce he was inspecting. "Hey, Shane. What brings you here?"

"Actually, it's a personal matter," Shane said, his sharp gaze sweeping the kitchen. He spotted Gabrielle standing in front of a stove. Her back was toward him, and she hadn't seen him yet, but he saw her. Her red hair was a giveaway. Shane nodded in Gabrielle's direction. "Do you mind if I have a word with Gabrielle?"

"No, of course not," Peter said, eyeing Shane in bewilderment. "How do you know Gabrielle?"

"She's my girlfriend's roommate." Shane clapped Peter's shoulder. "Thanks, man."

Shane walked through the crowded, bustling kitchen to Gabrielle. When she pulled a skillet off an open flame and passed it to a colleague, she turned, jumping when she realized who was standing behind her.

"What are you doing here?" Her expression was tense as she glared at him. She glanced at her boss across the room, who was watching the two of them with keen interest. "You shouldn't be here," she hissed. "I'm working."

"I need your help, Gabrielle."

Gabrielle frowned in surprise. "You need my help? Why?"

"Because Beth won't take my calls, and she won't return my texts."

Gabrielle flushed. "I see."

"You didn't see her this morning, Gabrielle," Shane said, his voice tight. "I found her on the floor of the ladies' room in my office building, sobbing."

Gabrielle blanched. "Oh, God."

"Yeah," Shane said, his tone bitter. "I'm worried about her. She's hurting, and it's my fault. I'm trying to give her some space, but not knowing if she's okay is killing me."

"What do you want me to do?"

"Call me tonight after you get home. Let me know how she's

doing."

Gabrielle nodded. "All right. I'll call you."

"Hey, you," Gabrielle said, coming to sit by Beth on the sofa. "What are you doing down here? You should be in bed."

Beth opened her eyes, blinking at Gabrielle. "I didn't feel like going upstairs."

"Beth, I'm so sorry," Gabrielle said. "I shouldn't have told you like that."

Beth shrugged. "Everything you said was true." She took a deep, shaky breath. "I broke up with him this morning."

"I know. He stopped by the restaurant tonight and asked me to check on you when I got home. I'm supposed to call him."

"Was he angry with you?"

"No. He just seemed worried. He said you weren't returning his messages."

"I don't know what to say to him," Beth said, a lump in her throat. She was so tired of crying.

"What do you want to say?" Gabrielle said.

Beth shrugged, and then the tears started. "It hurts so badly," she sobbed. "It's killing me. I don't think I've ever cried this much in one day."

"Oh, sweetie." Gabrielle's eyes filled with tears. She pulled Beth into her arms and held her tightly. "This is all my fault."

"It's not your fault," Beth said, wiping her eyes on her t-shirt.

Gabrielle pulled the afghan off Beth. "I'll walk you up to bed. Come on."

Beth followed Gabrielle upstairs. After a quick trip to the bathroom, Beth crawled into bed.

"Try to get some sleep," Gabrielle said, covering Beth. "Things will look better in the morning. They always do."

It was nearly 1 a.m. when Shane's cell phone rang. He was sitting in the Escalade outside Beth's townhouse because he'd wanted to be close by in case she changed her mind about seeing him.

When the phone rang, he picked it up and checked the caller ID. It was Gabrielle Hunter, thank God. "Gabrielle, how is she?"

"She's devastated, Shane," Gabrielle said. "I've never seen her like this. I'm really sorry. I should have kept my damn mouth shut."

"No, don't beat yourself up for this. It's my fuck-up. I should have told her sooner."

"What are you going to do?" Gabrielle said.

"I'm not sure yet. But I'm not giving up. I'll give her some more time — one more day. If she doesn't contact me by tomorrow evening, I'll come to her and make her talk to me. I know I can fix this if she'll just let me."

"I hope you can fix this," Gabrielle said. "I really do. I've never seen her like this. I think she really loves you."

Shane's phone rang an hour later. "What is it, Jake?" he said, surprised to be getting a call from his brother at this hour.

"Kline's out trolling for hookers."

"Fuck, you're kidding me."

"Nope. Really skanky ones, too," Jake said. "That's probably all he can afford. Plus, they're the only ones who would have him. Have you seen this guy? Prison wasn't kind to him."

"Where are you?" Shane said, starting the Escalade's engine. "I'm coming."

Shane called for an immediate back-up to take his place outside Beth's townhouse. Then he drove to Jake's location. He parked a couple blocks away and walked up to the front passenger door of Jake's black Bronco Raptor. He rapped sharply on the window, and Jake unlocked the door.

"Where is he?" Shane said, settling into the front passenger seat. He'd seen plenty of surveillance photos of Kline since they'd started watching him, but he'd never seen the man in person. He'd been too focused on Beth. But now, feeling edgy and restless because Beth wasn't talking to him, he had a burning

VULNERABLE   337

need to see Kline in the flesh.

Jake pointed down the block as he handed Shane a pair of night vision goggles. "There, on the north side of that liquor store."

Shane trained the goggles on the two people in the shadows of a run-down brick building. He could barely make out the shape of a man leaning against the building. Another figure, presumably a female, was on her knees in front of the man.

"She's a meth addict," Jake said. "I got a good look at her face, or what's left of it."

Shane swore as he watched the man ramming his cock deep into the woman's throat. Kline had a hold of the woman's long, stringy hair, and he was using it to restrain her as he fucked her mouth. It made Shane's gut twist to think that this prick had once had his hands on Beth. And the thought that he might try to get his hands on her again made Shane sick.

Kline bowed his body sharply as he came in the prostitute's mouth, shoving himself so deeply down her throat that she gagged. When Kline finally released her, she leaned over and vomited on the ground.

"Jesus," Shane muttered. He watched Kline zip up his pants and begin walking in the direction of Jake's vehicle. It was pitch black outside, and all of the street lights on the block were broken, so there was little risk of Kline seeing them. As Kline neared the Raptor, Shane made note of the man's long greasy comb-over and his flabby belly hanging out from beneath his stained t-shirt.

As Kline neared, Shane laid down the goggles and reached inside his jacket for his gun.

"What the fuck are you doing?" Jake said.

"I can end this once and for all," Shane said, pulling the slide back on his handgun to load a round into the chamber.

"No, Shane." Jake clasped the barrel of the semi-automatic and forced it down, so that it was pointed at the vehicle floor. "I won't let you do it. Not like this."

"This fucker wants to hurt Beth!" Shane hissed.

"She's not in any immediate danger, Shane. We're watching them both 24/7. Kline can't get within a mile of her, and you know it."

"Yeah, but as long as he lives, he'll continue to be a threat to her." Shane eyed his brother. "One way or another, I'm going to remove the threat."

"Fine. But you'll do it right, when the law's on your side. If you do it this way, it's cold-blooded murder, plain and simple, and I won't let you do that. Now, stand down and holster your weapon."

Shane locked gazes with his brother, blue eyes glaring hard at dark ones. Finally, Shane relented and holstered his gun. The two men sat perfectly still as Kline ambled drunkenly past, well hidden behind the darkly tinted windows of the Raptor.

"You'll get your chance, Shane," Jake said. "Just be patient. It has to be done right."

✒ 37

The next morning, Beth was even more desolate than she'd been the day before. She'd tossed and turned all night, unable to stop replaying the confrontation with Shane over and over again. Every time she closed her eyes, she could feel his arms around her as he'd sat holding her in the ladies' room floor. She couldn't get the memory of his expression out of her head. He'd looked... gutted.

Shane's text messages had started up again that morning. Beth had to keep her phone on silent because knowing he was reaching out, and not responding to him, was killing her.

Before she left for work, she ate half a bagel and drank a cup of hot tea. She ended up driving to work, because she didn't have the energy to walk. And now that she knew Miguel was following her during the day, she found herself watching for him. She rolled her eyes when she spotted his Mustang two cars behind her on her drive to work. After she parked in the employee lot and got out of her car, she spotted him in the visitor lot and waved to him as she walked up to the front entrance to the library. He waved back, and that had made her smile.

She helped a couple of students in the morning, then cataloged some new materials that had come in the morning's mail. But she had no energy, and her lethargy was compounded by an overwhelming sense of loss.

To make matters worse, her period still hadn't started yet. It was overdue now by at least a couple of days, and she was starting to get nervous. She'd never really given much thought to the idea that she might be pregnant. It had just seemed so unlikely that they'd get pregnant after just one episode of unprotected sex. But now she was officially late, and if it turned out that she was pregnant, well, she'd just broken up with the father of her hypothetical baby. Talk about rotten timing! If her period didn't come by the end of the week, she'd have to take a pregnancy test. But right now, it was the last thing she wanted to think about.

She found herself sneaking peeks at her phone and reading his incoming text messages. Some of them were pleas for a second chance, some were declarations of love, and some were apologies. A few of them were frustrated and even angry. But the ones that got to her the most were the ones that simply asked how she was doing.

Please tell me you're okay.

She supposed some might consider the constant stream of messages creepy, but she found them comforting. At least she knew he was still out there, still thinking about her.

"Beth, talk to him," Mary said. Mary was sitting at her desk, answering e-mails, but her attention kept wandering to Beth.

Beth just shook her head.

"I have to run to the restroom," Mary said, rising from her chair. "I overdid it on the coffee this morning, and my bladder's about to burst. Will you be okay alone for a few minutes?"

"Of course," Beth said.

"I'll be right back."

Beth checked the time. It was just a few minutes before her next student appointment at 11 a.m. She checked her calendar and saw the student's name: Maggie Swenson. She remembered Maggie from previous visits — a small, sturdy blond, very intelligent and highly-driven. Good. Working with a dedicated student like Maggie would help her focus.

The bell to the Special Collections door chimed, and Beth got up to let Maggie in. She opened the door and saw Maggie standing there with a bright smile on her face.

"You look happy," Beth said, returning Maggie's smile.

"I *am* happy," Maggie replied, showing a matched set of dimples. "I got an 'A' on my anatomy midterm!"

Beth chuckled. "Congratulations! Come on in, and let's get started."

A hand shot out of nowhere, shoving Maggie sideways, so hard she toppled to the floor, shrieking loudly as she landed hard on her backpack.

"Maggie!" Beth cried, reaching for the young woman.

Beth had barely taken a step toward Maggie when Andrew Morton appeared in front of her. He shoved Beth back into the Special Collections room with a palm to her chest, and Beth stumbled backward, fighting to keep from falling, too.

"Andrew!" Beth cried, catching herself on the edge of a study table. "What are you doing?"

Andrew stalked into the room and slammed the door behind him. "You stupid bitch!"

"Andrew!" Beth gasped, shocked by his fury, both in his voice and in his expression. He was absolutely livid.

"Thanks to you and your fuckwad boyfriend, I'm screwed! My dad took away everything! My car, my credit cards! Everything!"

Andrew advanced on her, his hands fisted at his sides. His face was bright red, his eyes screwed up in rage, and there was saliva on his chin.

"Andrew, I'm sorry!" Beth cried, edging around the table as she tried to keep some distance between them. "I never meant — "

"Shut up, bitch!" he yelled. "Your God-damned boyfriend thinks he's so fucking hot! He thinks he owns you, and no one else can have you. Well, he's wrong!"

Andrew kept coming, moving faster now with intent. Beth scooted backwards, not wanting to turn her back on him. When he started gaining on her, she had no choice but to turn and run for the inner office. She'd made it inside the room and was trying to shut the door, but he'd managed to wedge his big black boot in the opening already, so she couldn't close it. So she turned and ran for the phone on her desk to call campus police, but as she was dialing their extension, Andrew ripped the phone cord out of its jack. He yanked the phone out of her hands and threw it across the room where it bounced off one of the glass walls and hit the floor with a loud ringing thud.

Andrew grabbed Beth's arms and shook her hard, her head rocking forward and back. His fingers squeezed her arms hard, so hard she feared he would tear the flesh from her bones.

"Andrew, please!" she gasped as she tried to catch her breath.

Andrew released her abruptly, and she dropped to the floor like a stone, striking the back of her head against the metal leg of her desk. She rolled over, attempting to get up on all fours, but just as quickly, he hauled her back upright and struck her in the face with his fist, knocking her right back down to the floor.

"No one tells me what I can or can't do!" he screamed down at her. "No one! Certainly not you and your prick of a boyfriend!"

Beth lay on her side gasping as she struggled to breathe. Her chest tightened painfully, signaling an asthma attack in progress. But her inhaler was in her purse in the desk drawer, and there was no way she could reach it.

"Let's see how much your boyfriend likes you with your pretty face all messed up!" Andrew hauled his booted foot back and kicked Beth in the side of the head.

Her ears rang on impact and blinding pain shot through her skull, then ricocheted down her spine. She lay on her side and curled in on herself, bringing her arms over her head for protection when she saw the boot coming at her again. Andrew kicked her, this time striking her left forearm as it lay protectively over her face. She felt the bone snap under the force of Andrew's steel-toed boot, and she screamed when a burning streak of pain shot up her arm and blasted her skull.

Repeatedly his boot came at her, and he kept changing his

angle, trying to get at her face. Try as she might to cover herself, he managed to get one kick straight into her face. Pain exploded in the center of her face, and her vision started to waver. She saw bright pinpricks of light, sure he had broken her nose. She tasted blood now — a lot of it — running down the back of her throat and filling her mouth, so much she nearly choked on it. Her lips stung, and she realized her bottom lip was split open. She could feel blood trickling down her chin. Her face was swelling, and she found it increasingly difficult to breathe. She gagged on the blood pooling in her throat and turned her face to the floor to spit it out.

She was dizzy now, short of breath and unable to focus her eyes. The boot just kept coming at her as he relentlessly hammered her arms, head, and chest. She was gasping, desperate for air and trying not to choke. When her vision grew dim, she thought that passing out might be a blessing. At least then she wouldn't feel this burning torrent of fire and pain.

"Beth!"

She heard Mary's horrified scream and saw Mary grab Andrew's arm and attempt to haul him away from her. Andrew kept kicking frantically at Beth, trying to connect with some part of her body.

"Stop it!" Mary screamed as she tried to drag Andrew back from Beth, pummeling him with her small fists. "Get away from her!"

Andrew's boot struck Beth twice more in the abdomen, knocking what little breath she had left from her, before Mary managed to drag him back several feet.

"Beth, can you call for help?" Mary cried, struggling with all of her might to hold Andrew back. "Use my phone!"

Beth rolled up onto her knees, coughing and gagging on blood and saliva, and then collapsed back onto her side.

"Can't ... breathe," Beth wheezed, her breath rattling in her throat.

At the sound of Beth's ragged voice, Andrew froze. No longer struggling, he stood still as Mary held onto him, staring down at Beth in horror. Beth lay on her side, her arms cradled around her abdomen. She struggled for breath, and her face had begun to turn colors as dark, bloody bruises formed. Her battered nose was beginning to swell, and her bottom lip was swollen and split wide open.

"Oh, God," Andrew whispered, gaping at Beth's ruined face. His gaze bounced frantically back and forth between Beth and Mary.

Beth coughed, spitting up blood, and whimpered like a wounded animal.

Andrew made a gagging noise, then wrenched free of Mary's hold and ran for the door.

Mary dropped to her knees beside Beth, her hands hovering over Beth's body, not sure where to touch her or what to do.

"Inhaler," Beth gasped, her voice barely audible.

Mary wrenched open the desk drawer and grabbed Beth's purse. With shaking fingers, she fumbled to locate Beth's inhaler. She shook the inhaler, and then held it up to Beth's torn mouth.

"Can you inhale?" Mary asked her as she held the device in place.

Beth wrapped her bloody lips around the mouthpiece and sucked in as Mary depressed the inhaler. When Beth fell back, losing contact with the inhaler, Mary dropped it, and then reached for the phone on her own desk. With shaking hands, she dialed campus police.

"Hold on, honey," Mary said to Beth after making the call. "The police are coming."

Mary crawled to the front of her desk and opened the top drawer, pulling out her cell phone. She crawled back to Beth's side and dialed Shane's number with shaking hands.

"Hang on, honey," Mary said, laying a gentle hand on Beth's shoulder, wanting to offer comfort, but afraid of hurting her in the process. "Help is coming."

Beth's body shook violently, and she didn't respond. Her eyes were closed, and Mary feared that she'd lost consciousness.

Shane answered on the second ring. "Mary? What is it?"

"It's Beth!" Mary cried into the phone starting to lose her composure in the aftermath of such violence. "She's hurt! Badly! I've called campus police, and they've called 9-1-1. They're coming."

"Hurt how? Where are you? What happened?"

"We're in our office. She's on the floor. She's not responding. I think she's unconscious. It was a student. Andrew Morton," she said, her voice shaking. "He attacked her! He beat her, Shane! He kicked her face and her chest. She's bleeding and having trouble breathing. He ran off, and then I called campus police."

"Have you administered her inhaler?"

"Yes. Well, I tried to. I'm not sure how much of the medicine got in her. Her face is so swollen. Her nose is probably broken, and she's wheezing badly. There's a lot of blood in her throat. I can hear it gurgling."

"Listen very carefully, Mary," Shane said, his voice eerily calm. He was a little short of breath as if he was running as he talked. "Roll her to her side to prevent her from choking. My guy Miguel is right outside the building. I'll send him up to you."

"Okay." Mary's voice broke on a sob, and she started crying. "How could he do this to her?"

Shane cursed over the phone, then said, "Mary, I have to hang up now to call Miguel. He'll be at your door in three minutes. Let him in."

"Okay. Are you coming?"

"I'm heading to my car now. I'll get to her as quickly as I can."

Mary ended the call and wiped her face on her sleeve. She rolled Beth to her side and rubbed her back gently. "Help is coming, honey. It's going to be all right."

But there was no response from Beth.

Mary stayed at Beth's side, stroking her hair and talking to her, trying to offer comfort. In almost no time, she heard a deafening pounding on the door. Mary jumped, and then she remembered that Shane was sending someone to them.

Mary ran to the door and yelled, "Who's there?"

"Miguel Rodríguez! Shane sent me! Open the door, Mary!"

Mary opened the door, and Miguel pushed inside, a black gun in his hand.

"Where is she?" Miguel demanded, quickly scanning the room.

"In there." Mary pointed toward the inner office. "She's unconscious."

"Andrew Morton did this?" Miguel asked Mary as he holstered his gun. He knelt beside Beth and checked to see that she was breathing. Her breaths were short and shallow, accompanied by the sound of fluid rattling in her throat. He checked her pulse, then the reactions of her pupils.

"Yes, it was Andrew," Mary said.

"Did someone call 9-1-1?"

"Yes," she said. "The ambulance is on its way."

Miguel nodded, continuing his inspection of Beth.

The door opened and two uniformed campus police officers rushed in, a man and a woman. They came right to Beth, and the woman radioed the dispatch operator, who confirmed that the paramedics had arrived on campus, their ETA five minutes.

"I'll wait for the paramedics downstairs," the female officer said.

"She's unconscious," Miguel told the male officer. "Pulse is fast, breathing is fast and shallow. She's asthmatic."

"I used her inhaler on her," Mary said, "but I'm not sure how much medicine went into her. That's when she passed out."

"Who are you?" the male police officer asked Miguel.

Miguel pulled out his wallet and showed his identification to the officer. "Miguel Rodriguez, private security. I work for McIntyre Security. Miss Jamison is one of our clients."

The officer looked at Miguel's identification, and then nodded. "Do you know who did this?" he said, kneeling beside Beth.

"Andrew Morton did it," Mary said. "He's a student here."

"Were you a witness, ma'am?" the officer asked.

"Yes. I pulled him off of her."

"Do you know where he is now?"

Mary shook her head. "He ran off."

Miguel had pulled out his cell phone and was making a call when the paramedics arrived. He stepped back, speaking into his phone as the paramedics assessed Beth's vitals and prepared to load her onto the gurney.

"No, she's unconscious," Miguel was saying into the phone. "They're taking her now." Miguel glanced at the paramedics. "Where are you taking her?"

"University of Chicago Medical Center," one of them said as they strapped her onto the gurney.

"U.C. Medical," Miguel said. "Right. I'll see you there." Miguel ended the call. "I'm riding in the ambulance with her," Miguel told the paramedics as they began to wheel her to the door.

⁀ 38

Shane took a deep breath, steeling himself before entering Beth's curtained unit in the ER. He'd been warned ahead of time by Mary Reynolds that it was bad. But nothing could have prepared him for the sight that met his eyes. Beth lay unconscious on the bed, small and battered, covered with an obscene amount of blood on her face and chest. Just looking at her made his chest hurt as if a giant fist was squeezing the life out of him. His hands balled into fists at his sides as he watched a nurse gently wash Beth's face with a damp cotton ball.

He must have made a sound, because the nurse looked up expectantly. "Hello. And you are?"

"Shane McIntyre." He swallowed hard. "I'm Beth's boyfriend." He approached the foot of the bed, his gaze riveted on Beth.

"She's been in and out of consciousness," the nurse said, looking at Shane with sympathy. "She has a concussion, but her vitals are stable. She'll be okay."

Shane nodded, relieved, but not trusting himself to speak. His throat had closed up on him. A movement in his peripheral vision drew his attention to the corner of the room where Miguel stood against the curtain, a dark and silent guardian angel.

Shane nodded his gratitude at Miguel. Miguel smiled sadly

at Shane and clapped him on the shoulder as he quietly left the unit.

"The doctor will be back any moment," the nurse said. "He went to write up some orders for Miss Jamison."

Shane glanced at the nametag on the nurse's uniform. "Thanks, Kelly," he said. That was about all he could manage at the moment. He'd gotten a good look at Beth's face. At the moment, she was... unrecognizable. Her face was grotesquely swollen and discolored. Her nose was swollen, possibly broken, and her bottom lip was split open. There was dried blood on her face and chin and neck. Even her hair — her beautiful hair — was matted with dried blood so dark it almost looked black.

She lay as silent and still as death.

For a moment, he stopped breathing, his jaw clenched so tightly he feared it might shatter. He wanted to kill Andrew Morton. And he could have. At that moment, if he had his hands around the kid's throat, he'd crush it without a second thought.

"Can I touch her?" he asked the nurse as he walked around to the other side of the bed.

"Yes, just be careful," the woman said. "We won't know what, if anything, is broken until after the x-rays. And watch her IV. We're giving her pain medication."

Shane glanced down at Beth's left arm. Hell, he didn't need an x-ray to know it was broken. If he had to guess, he'd say she had some broken ribs, too, and maybe a broken nose.

Shane reached out a tentative hand, surprised to see it shaking. He'd handled plenty of explosives in his career. He'd held a sniper's rifle as steady as a rock. But, right now, his hand shook.

A young man wearing a white lab coat swept into the curtained room. His dark eyes went right to Shane, and he smiled. He picked up the medical chart hooked to the foot of the bed and methodically scanned the stack of papers with sharp eyes. "I'm Dr. Prakash," he said, reaching out to shake Shane's hand.

"Shane McIntyre. I'm Beth's boyfriend."

"I'd like to examine Miss Jamison now," Dr. Prakash said. "If you wouldn't mind waiting outside?"

"Actually, I would mind," Shane said, a mulish expression on his face. "I'm staying."

Dr. Prakash nodded. "Very well," he said.

Shane stepped back from the bed to allow the physician access to Beth. As the doctor examined her, Shane studied her face. Practically every inch of it was bruised and battered. Both eyes were swollen and dark with bruising. There were lacerations on both cheeks and on her forehead. And her mouth... dear God, her mouth.

Dr. Prakash peeled back the two halves of Beth's hospital gown, uncovering her chest and abdomen. There were bruises already forming on her chest, over her breasts, as well as over her ribs.

Shane stepped closer to see the damage for himself. Dear God, that little fucker had kicked her breasts. Her sweet, beautiful breasts. Shane fought for control as his gorge rose, threatening to choke him. The knowledge that someone had hurt her made him want to lash out, but, at the moment, there was no one to lash out against.

Dr. Prakash uncovered Beth's left forearm and gently palpated the purple and red knot the size of an egg that was located halfway between her elbow and wrist.

When he realized he was holding his breath, Shane forced himself to take a deep breath. He didn't know which was worse: his rage at Andrew Morton, his anger at Tyler for not following Shane's recommendations to have someone there in the library with Beth, or his own crushing sense of guilt at having failed her.

No matter how he looked at it, the assault on Beth was his fault. He was the one who'd provoked Andrew Morton at the hospital benefit. He'd thought to scare the boy away from Beth. Instead, Andrew had retaliated against Beth. He'd completely underestimated the danger that Andrew Morton posed. The bottom line was this was *his* fault.

He'd fucked this case up from the very beginning because he'd let his emotions get in the way of his judgment. He should have told Beth up front that Tyler had hired his company. He should have assigned close protection inside the library from the very beginning, despite Tyler's objections. It killed him to think that if Mary hadn't intervened when she did, Andrew might have killed Beth, whether he'd intended to or not.

He was done playing nice with Tyler. He was going to do things his own way now.

The sound of Beth coughing, choking on her own saliva, yanked Shane out of his own dark thoughts. He rushed forward just as Dr. Prakash gently grasped Beth's shoulders and rolled her to her side, steadying her.

"You're okay, Beth," Prakash said, his voice warm and sympathetic. "Beth, can you hear me? You're in the hospital. You're going to be okay."

Beth's eyes flickered open, and she cried out.

"Beth." Shane moved into her line of sight, his hand hovering over her head. He wanted to touch her so badly, to comfort her and let her know he was there, but he didn't dare touch her face. Instead, he laid his palm gently on the top of her head and leaned close.

"Sweetheart, it's Shane," he said. "I'm here. You're in the hospital. You're safe."

Beth started crying then, horrible gut-wrenching sobs that nearly tore Shane apart. His eyes stung with tears.

"Shane!" Her gasp was hoarse and so weak he almost didn't hear her.

"I'm here, sweetheart," he said, his face hovering over hers. He wanted desperately to put his lips on her, but there wasn't a single inch on her face that was unmarked. Finally, he laid his lips gently on her hairline, just the faintest brush of his lips. "I'm here, baby."

Her entire body went limp as she lost consciousness again.

"We'll be sending her for x-rays and a CT scan soon," the doctor said. "For now, stay with her. Call for the nurse if she wakes up again. We need to monitor her concussion closely."

Shane nodded as he pulled a chair up beside her bed.

"I'll give the order to have her admitted," Dr. Prakash said.

"She'll be here with us for a little while."

Shane stayed by Beth's side. He wanted to hold her hand, but both of her hands were battered. She must have tried to protect her head with her hands, because her knuckles on both hands were cut and bruised.

The nurse returned a few minutes later to resume gently washing the blood from Beth's face and neck. Shane stared at the water in the basin as it changed from pink to bright red to a deep, dark red. Beth's blood. Andrew Morton had shed Beth's blood. The fucker could have killed her.

Shane heard a discreet noise from the curtained entrance to the unit. He looked back and saw Cooper standing there, stiff and silent. The man's gaze was glued to Beth's still form.

"How is she?" Cooper said.

"Her vitals are stable," Shane said, "but she's in a hell of a lot of pain."

"Has she regained consciousness?" Cooper asked.

"They said she's been in and out of consciousness. She came to once since I've been here, for about a minute or so. She was distraught."

Cooper scrubbed a hand over his face, grimacing. "I called Tyler and Beth's mother. They're on their way."

"What about Andrew Morton?"

"He's in custody at the county jail," Cooper said.

"Good. Call Gabrielle Hunter," he said. "She'll want to be here."

"Troy Spencer's here," Cooper said. "He wants to know what you want to do about Morton."

Shane's jaw clenched tightly. "Send Troy to the courthouse. Tell him I want Andrew Morton charged with everything we can throw at him. Assault, battery, unlawful imprisonment, and anything else Troy can dream up. Oh, and call Richard Morton. Tell him just what his sick bastard of a son has done."

"Richard knows," Cooper said. "Chicago PD arrested Andrew

at his parents' house. Andrew lives with his parents." Cooper glanced once more at Beth, frowning, and then he slipped away as quietly as he'd come.

Shane stroked Beth's hair with a feather-light touch. On the surface, he was afraid of hurting her. But deep down inside, he was afraid she might rebuff him if she woke and found him here. He couldn't bear it if she turned him away now.

He had no idea what to expect when she finally regained consciousness, and that scared the shit out of him.

39

The first thing that registered in her mind was pain — bright, blinding pain. She hurt all over. Her head was throbbing, and every breath she took felt like a knife stabbing her in the chest. She was cold one minute and hot the next. When she felt a pinch on the inside of her right elbow, she opened her eyes and discovered an IV line taped to her arm.

At first she was confused, disoriented. She didn't know where she was or what had happened. She only knew that she hurt. She started gasping as panic set in.

"Beth, it's all right," Shane said, looming over her. "It's me, sweetheart. It's Shane. Can you hear me?"

She squinted at him, blinking several times to bring him into focus. "Shane?" Just trying to speak hurt. Her lips stung.

"Yes, sweetheart," he said, laying his palm on the crown of her head. "I'm here. Try not to talk. I know it hurts."

"Everything hurts." Her voice sounded odd to her own ears, her words slurred.

"I know, baby. You're in the hospital, but you're going to be okay."

"What happened?"

"Do you remember Andrew Morton coming into your office? He hurt you."

She shook her head and then cried out in pain.

"Try not to move, baby," he said, his hands going gently to her shoulders. "Lie still."

Images flickered rapidly through her mind as if her memories were just now coming back online. *Andrew.* He pushed her. He hit her. And he kicked her, over and over. Why would he do that? And then Mary came, and there was screaming and yelling. And then everything went dark.

"Mary," she said, frowning as she tried to make sense out of the cascading images. "Mary made him stop."

"Yes, she did."

Beth glanced up at Shane, shocked by how wrecked he looked. "What's wrong?"

"Andrew hurt you in your office at the library. But you're going to be all right."

But that wasn't what Beth had meant. She wondered what had happened to Shane to make him look so devastated. But she didn't have the energy to explain herself. Her eyelids were too heavy, and the darkness pulled her under once more.

When Beth opened her eyes again, the bright overhead lights blinded her. She blinked, trying to clear her vision. She heard movement at her side, and turned her head just a bit and saw Shane seated in a chair beside her bed. He was watching her closely, his expression wary.

"Shane," she said, and she found that it hurt even to speak.

"I'm here, Beth."

She felt his fingers lightly stroking her hair and she closed her eyes in an attempt to block out the pain. Even her hair hurt. But she didn't say anything to him, because she didn't want him to stop. She didn't ever want him to stop.

Shane watched Beth close her eyes, shutting him out, and he felt her rejection like a swift kick to the gut.

"Beth, listen to me," he said, leaning close, his voice low. He knew this wasn't the time or the place for this, but he couldn't wait. The possibility that he might actually lose her seemed all too real.

"When Tyler came to me, asking us to protect you, you were just a name on a piece of paper. When I accepted the job, I had no idea what you would come to mean to me. And then, after I met you, and we talked, I couldn't stay away." He stroked the tip of his index finger across her brow.

"Beth, please. Don't punish me for what happened before we met. Yes, it started off as a job, but it quickly became more than that for me. I'm sorry I didn't tell you sooner. I was afraid of scaring you away. I wanted you to get to know me — learn to *trust* me — before I told you the truth about how we met. I know I fucked up, sweetheart. But I *never* meant to deceive you. I swear. Please believe that."

She began weeping, so quietly.

Shane's stomach dropped as he watched the tears stream down the side of her battered face. He swallowed hard, trying to tamp down his own panic. He wasn't going to let her give up on them so easily. Damn it! He knew he should leave her alone and let her rest, but he felt an overwhelming fear that, if he lost her now, he'd never get her back.

Shane leaned closer, and Beth felt his warm breath on her cheek.

"Shh, baby," he said. "Please don't cry."

"I'm sorry I ran," she said, her words barely intelligible. "I was hurt."

His lips hovered over her brow. "Don't cry, Beth, please. You'll hurt yourself."

She made a faint chuckling sound, but quickly choked it off, groaning. "I already hurt," she whispered. "I don't think this will make it any worse. I need to say this. I'm sorry I walked out, Shane. I was just so hurt, I didn't know what else to do. I regretted it later, but I was afraid it was too late."

"Jesus, Beth, it's never too late," he said.

She felt his lips in her hair, and his tenderness made the ache in her heart even sharper.

"I'm the one who's sorry," he said, his voice tight. "I should have told you everything sooner. I was waiting for the right time, but I guess there never is a right time."

"It doesn't matter now, Shane. None of it matters. I love you."

He had to clear his throat. His fingers trembled as they touched her brow. "I love you, too."

Beth reached out with her right hand and searched blindly for his hand. When she found it, she latched onto it. "I'm cold."

"Hold on," he said. He released her hand and poked his head outside the curtained doorway, where Cooper was standing guard. "We need a warm blanket in here."

When Shane returned to her bedside, he took her right hand gingerly in his, cradling it. "I wanted to hold your hand earlier," he told her, "but they look pretty badly injured. I didn't want to hurt you."

Beth shook her head, grimacing at the pain. "I don't care if it hurts. I want to hold your hand."

Shane linked their fingers together, careful not to put any pressure on her torn knuckles.

Every little touch hurt, but Beth tried not to show it. Her ribs were on fire, and her head felt like someone had split it open with a tire iron. She was sure he wouldn't touch her at all if he knew how much it hurt. And right now she wanted him touching her more than she wanted the pain to stop. If things were right between them again, she knew she could get through this.

A moment later, Kelly entered her unit, holding a white cotton blanket. "Here you go, sweetie," the woman said. "A warm blanket." Kelly unfolded the blanket and laid it gently over Beth.

Beth sighed as the warmth from the blanket seeped through the sheet into her body. "Thank you."

"You're welcome, honey," the nurse said. Kelly looked at Shane. "After we take her for x-rays and a CT scan, we'll move her into her own room."

"Thanks," Shane said. "Can we increase her pain medication? She's really hurting."

"I'll ask Dr. Prakash."

Beth finally drifted off to sleep, to Shane's utter relief. The knowledge that she was in so much pain was killing him, because there was nothing he could do about it. Every gasp and whimper had felt like a serrated knife twisting in his gut. He would gladly have taken her pain for her if he could have.

The nurse returned every so often to check on Beth, but no one else came in. Cooper hovered outside the curtained unit on guard duty, peering in at them every so often. A steady stream of people came to Beth's unit — Jake, Liam, Mary Reynolds, Lia — but Cooper intercepted everyone, murmuring quietly to them outside the curtain before sending them away. No one came into the little cubicle except for the nurse and Beth's doctor.

Shane sat in a chair beside Beth's bed, cradling her right hand in his. Her breathing had stabilized, and he was glad for that. Right now she appeared to be sleeping deeply, a little more comfortable thanks to some additional pain medication.

Shane's attention was diverted when he heard Cooper speak sharply outside the curtain. There was a brief scuffle, and then the curtain was pushed aside as Tyler Jamison strode in. His hard gaze went right to the bed as he took in his sister's still form.

Shane watched the blood drain from Tyler's face, and the man's eyes filled with tears. Cooper followed Tyler into the room, standing right behind the man, looking to Shane for a signal.

"It's okay, Cooper," Shane said, nodding.

Cooper stepped back from Tyler, but remained inside the curtained area.

"Dear God, what happened?" Tyler said, coming to stand at the foot of the bed. He looked at Shane. "Who did this to her? Kline? All I was told was that she'd been assaulted."

"It wasn't Kline," Shane said. "It was a student at the medical school. Someone she knew. He attacked her in her office."

"What the hell are you doing here?" Tyler hissed, glaring at

Shane. "What if she wakes up and sees you?"

If looks could kill, Shane figured he'd be a dead man.

Tyler stared down at his sister, his expression grim as he catalogued her many visible injuries. His entire demeanor radiated burning anger, but whether it was directed at Shane or at Andrew Morton, Shane wasn't sure. Probably both.

Tyler swallowed hard. "Was she raped?"

"No," Shane said quickly, coming to his feet.

"How bad are her injuries?"

"She has a concussion. One of the bones in her left arm is broken. She may have cracked or broken ribs. She's been in and out of consciousness. She's going for x-rays and a CT scan soon. Then they'll admit her and put her in a room."

Tyler glared at Shane. "Why are you here, Shane?" he said, his voice low. "You shouldn't be here. What if she wakes up?"

Shane heaved a sigh, knowing it was time to face the music. He noticed Cooper take a step closer to Tyler.

"I'm here, Tyler, because she needs me here," Shane said.

"What the fuck does that mean?" Tyler grated.

Beth made a pained sound in her sleep, and Shane reached down and gently stroked her hair.

Her eyelids fluttered open, and she blinked under the bright lights. "Shane?"

"It's all right, sweetheart. I'm here," Shane murmured, glancing down at her.

At the sound of Shane's voice, Beth focused her gaze on him. "Don't leave me," she said.

"I won't, honey. I promise."

And then her eyes drifted shut again.

Shane glanced at Tyler, prepared for anything. Tyler stood rigid and silent, his hands clenched, his entire body radiating fury as he glared at Shane. Shane knew that if it weren't for Beth's presence, Tyler would have been at his throat already.

Tyler's voice was as flat and hard as black ice when he spoke in a low voice. "I hired you to protect her, Shane, not seduce her."

Shane admired the man's restraint. He didn't think he would've been quite so calm if he'd been in Tyler's place. "We're not doing this here, Tyler," he said, his own voice tight with emotion. "Not in front of her. She's been through enough."

"Thanks to you!" Tyler hissed. Then his eyes narrowed. "You bastard! Are you fucking my sister?"

Shane knew Tyler was burning to tear him apart. "I said not here, Tyler," Shane said, striving to keep his cool. "She doesn't need to hear this."

"Oh, she'll hear it all right," Tyler said, his voice rising. "Maybe not right now, but she'll hear it."

Beth stirred, and her eyelids fluttered open. "Tyler?"

Tyler's gaze shot to Beth's face, and he smiled at her, his expression instantly softening. "Hey, kiddo," he said, his voice gentle as he walked around to the far side of the bed, opposite Shane. "How are you? Not so good, huh?"

"Everything hurts, Tyler," she said.

As Tyler got a closer look at her battered and bruised face, his jaw clenched tightly. Then he leaned down and gently kissed the top of her head. "I know it hurts, kiddo. I'm so sorry, Beth," he said. "Mom's on her way. Gabrielle's coming, too."

Beth tried to smile at her brother, but she grimaced instead.

"It's okay," Tyler said, reaching out to touch her, but hesitating, afraid of causing her more pain. "Don't try to speak."

Beth's eyes drifted shut, and she sighed.

Cooper's phone buzzed with an incoming message, and he checked his phone. "It's from Jake. Morton's been booked at the county jail. The police are on their way here to take statements."

Shane nodded. "Have them start with Mary Reynolds. She's in the waiting room. She's an eye witness. They'll need to talk to Miguel, too. He didn't see Andrew, but he saw Beth on the floor right after the attack. Tell them Beth won't be able to make a statement right now."

"I want to know everything," Tyler said, glancing at Shane, then at Cooper. "The perp's in custody?"

"He is," Cooper said.

A young man dressed in scrubs entered the cubicle, a clipboard in his hand. "We're ready for Ms. Jamison in Radiology," he said.

The young man looked at Shane and then at Tyler, apparently unsure who he should be addressing. "Is there any chance Ms. Jamison could be pregnant?" he asked.

Shane looked at Tyler, whose expression had hardened. "Yes," Shane said, meeting Tyler's gaze directly. "There is."

Tyler glared at Shane with barely restrained fury.

The young man made a notation on his clipboard, then hung the clipboard from a hook at the foot of Beth's bed. "Is someone going to come with her?" he said, looking from Shane to Tyler and back again.

"I'm coming," Tyler said in a firm voice. "I'm her next of kin." Tyler glared at Shane, daring Shane to challenge him.

Shane nodded. "Stay with her," he said to Tyler. "I'll go speak to the police."

Tyler eyed Shane. "You and I are going to have a talk later."

Shane nodded. "I'm sure we will." Then he gently kissed the top of Beth's head. "I'll see you soon, sweetheart. I won't go far."

Cooper followed Shane to the ER waiting room, where they found a small crowd gathered, waiting for word. Jake, Liam, Miguel, and Lia were seated together in one corner of the room, along with Mary Reynolds. They jumped to their feet when Shane entered the room.

"How is she?" Mary said.

"She's in a lot of pain, but she's stable. Her brother's going with her to Radiology for X-rays and a CT scan. Then she'll be admitted to the hospital and taken to a regular ward." Shane looked at Jake. "Have the police arrived?"

"Not yet, but they're en route," Jake said.

Shane nodded. "Mary, they'll need a statement from you. And one from you, as well, Miguel. Beth won't be making a statement any time soon."

Cooper looked up from a new message on his phone. "Morton's been charged with assault and battery, for starters," he said. "Troy's down at the County jail, overseeing the charges. He's going to push for a denial of bail. The kid's father is also at the jail."

Shane nodded. "Beth's mother, Ingrid Jamison, is on her way here. So is Beth's housemate, Gabrielle Hunter. Watch for them and give them Beth's room number, once we know what it is."

Shane looked at his sister. "Lia, I'm assigning you to Beth full time. Close personal protection, effective immediately."

"Sure thing," Lia said, coming to her feet.

Shane glanced at Cooper. "Once we get Beth's room number, I want someone posted outside her door 24/7."

"You got it," Cooper said.

"I'll go talk to the nurse and see if I can find out which room they're moving her to," Shane said. "We might as well relocate to her new location."

Shane and Lia were seated in Beth's new room, and Cooper was standing guard at the door when the orderly brought Beth and Tyler back from Radiology.

Shane jumped to his feet when the orderly wheeled Beth's bed into the room. She was awake, and she smiled tremulously at him.

"Hi, sweetheart," he said, gently brushing his hand over the top of her head. "How'd it go?"

"Okay," she said. Her expression grew wary. "My brother's here."

"Yes," Shane said, smiling at her. "I saw him earlier."

Tyler remained rooted in the open doorway, his eyes locked on Shane. When Tyler motioned for Shane to come out into the hall with him, Shane nodded.

Shane kissed Beth's forehead. "How did the scans go?"

"Okay," she said, cradling her left arm. "My arm's broken."

Shane nodded. "I'm sorry, sweetheart. They'll cast it soon,

and that should relieve some of the pain." He stroked her fore-head. "I'm going to step out into the hallway for a few minutes." Shane pointed at a petite blond seated in a chair across the room. "Beth, that's my sister Lia. She's going to hang out with you for a while."

"Oh, okay." Beth glanced uncertainly at Lia, who was sport-ing a lot of facial hardware, not to mention facial tattoos.

Shane had to bite back a smile. Lia — who was currently in her punk-gothic guise — was certainly an eyeful. "You couldn't have changed first?" he said, glancing wryly at his sister.

"Hey, I came as soon as I heard," Lia said, shrugging. "I was working."

Shane smiled reassuringly at Beth. "Don't worry. Lia doesn't bite. I'll be right back, sweetheart."

Shane stepped out into the hallway and faced Tyler, who was standing ramrod stiff, his hands on his hips. Tyler's entire body was rigid with restrained violence, his expression tight. Cooper stood off to the side, leaning nonchalantly against a wall, his eyes locked on Tyler.

"If we weren't standing outside my sister's hospital room," Tyler hissed, "I would beat the living shit out of you!"

"You could try," Shane said, crossing his arms over his chest.

Tyler fisted his hands at his sides. "Don't push me, asshole. I'm only holding it together for Beth's sake."

"Hey, you'll get your chance, I'm sure. If you want to meet me in the ring after this is over, I'm more than game."

Tyler shook his head at Shane. "I hired you to protect my sis-ter, not seduce her. How the hell did this happen?"

"I didn't seduce her."

"Bullshit! I saw the way she looked at you!" Tyler lunged for-ward and grabbed Shane's shirt collar, slamming him up against the wall.

Cooper made a move toward Tyler, but Shane held him off with a hand gesture.

"She's just a kid, Shane!" Tyler growled. "She's no match for you, and you know it! I'm sure you had her eating out of your hand in no time."

"Tyler, I'm sorry," Shane said, not resisting because he knew full well that Tyler was right. "I have sisters. I know how I'd feel if I were in your place. But trust me, I never set out to seduce her."

"Then what the fuck did you set out to do, Shane? No matter how it happened, you ended up in my sister's bed, didn't you? She's too young for you, too vulnerable, and too traumatized. Your conduct is entirely unethical and unprofessional."

"We are lovers, yes," Shane said. "But it's not — "

Tyler's hands went to Shane's throat, and he squeezed. And still, Shane didn't fight back. He wasn't about to lay violent hands on Beth's brother if he didn't have to. But apparently, Tyler didn't have the same scruples.

"She's too God damn young for you, Shane!" Tyler seethed. "She's just a kid!"

Shane, his face turning red, couldn't have replied even if he'd wanted to, not with Tyler cutting off his air.

"That's enough, Tyler!" Cooper growled, grasping one of Tyler's wrists, applying pressure in a strategic spot, causing Tyler to instantly let go.

Tyler threw up his hands and stepped back, breathing hard.

Shane came away from the wall, sucking in a lungful of air. "My behavior was unprofessional only because I didn't tell Beth the truth up front, and because I didn't end the protection contract with you first. I'm ending it now."

"What!" Tyler looked aghast. "You won't protect her anymore? Kline just bought a gun!" Tyler's eyes widened with what could only be described as fear. "Shane, I can't protect her around the clock by myself."

"I didn't say I wasn't going to protect her, you idiot," Shane said. "I said I'm ending my contract with you. As her boyfriend — as her lover — I'm taking over her protection. I'm going to do things my way now."

"Your way!" Tyler ground out. "Look at her in there!" he

growled, pointing toward Beth's room. "Some asshole just beat the shit out of my baby sister!"

"That never would have happened if you'd let me put a body-guard in the library with her!" Shane hissed back. "I wanted someone in the room with her from the very beginning, and you shot that down, every time. My biggest mistake was abiding by your wishes. If I'd followed my own instincts, she never would have gotten hurt."

"You can't know that," Tyler said. "The kid might still have gotten to her."

"No, he wouldn't have," Shane said. "If Lia had been in there like I wanted, she would have knocked Morton flat on his ass the instant he even looked at Beth wrong."

"Lia? You're kidding me, right? That little psycho-punk sister of yours? Give me a break!"

Shane scoffed. "I'd like to see you go five minutes with Lia in the ring. She would hand you your ass, you arrogant prick."

At that moment, the psycho-punk herself stuck her blond spiky-haired head through the open doorway and glared at both of them. "Keep it down, assholes," she said. "Princess can hear you."

Shane glared at his sister, who disappeared back into Beth's room.

"Look, Tyler," Shane said. "I plan to be around for a long time. You and I are going to have to learn to live with each other, for Beth's sake. I won't have you upsetting her."

"Me!" Tyler grated. "I'm not the one who seduced her!"

"It wasn't like that, Tyler!" Shane said stiffly.

"Then what was it like, Shane?" Tyler glared at him. "Tell me."

"I love Beth," Shane said. "Signed, sealed, and delivered."

Tyler looked stunned. "What?"

"You heard me," Shane said. "Get used to the idea. I'm not going anywhere."

"How does she feel?" Tyler said.

Shane frowned. "We had a bit of a setback earlier this week. But it's nothing I can't fix. I'm sorry, Tyler. This isn't how I wanted you to find out."

"She's too young for you, Shane," Tyler said, his anger abating. "She's too... fragile for you."

Shane shook his head. "She's young, yes. But she's stronger than you think."

Tyler leaned against the wall for support as he contemplated the fact that Shane and his sister were intimately involved.

"Tyler, I'm taking over Beth's protection, effective immediately. As soon as she's released from here, I'm moving her to my home in Kenilworth. She'll have everything she needs there to recuperate."

"She doesn't need to move in with you," Tyler said. "If she moves in with anyone, it should be with me or our mother."

Shane shook his head. "Tyler, understand this: Beth is mine. I will personally ensure her safety. The best way for me to do that is to move her to my estate in Kenilworth. It's a secure location, monitored and patrolled 24/7. She'll be perfectly safe there, and she'll have everything she could possibly want."

Tyler eyed Shane suspiciously. "And after she's recuperated?"

"That will be up to her," Shane said, "but I'm hope she'll agree to stay."

"So, where were we?" Lia McIntyre said as she dropped back down into the visitor's chair beside Beth's bed. "Sorry about your face. It must hurt like a bitch."

"It does," Beth said, struggling not to smile. She was also trying hard not to stare at Lia, but it was difficult. Lia's tongue was pierced, Beth realized, when she caught a glimpse of the silver ball attached to it. Beth wondered how much it had hurt to have that done. And she'd done it *on purpose*. Why? Why would someone do that to themselves?

"You're Shane's sister?" Beth said, highly skeptical. They looked nothing alike, and they couldn't be more different in personality. Lia McIntyre was completely outrageous. She was nothing at all like her poised, restrained brother.

"One of them," Lia said.

"I think Shane said he has three sisters?"

"Yeah," Lia said. "Besides me, there's Sophie and Hannah. I'm the cool one. Sophie's a stuck-up princess, and Hannah's a science nerd."

Beth grinned at that, but quickly wished she hadn't. Any facial movement was agonizing.

Lia's blond hair was short and spiked with gel, the tips dyed purple. She wore an extraordinary number of tiny diamond stud earrings in both ears and a sapphire stud in her left nostril. She was dressed in black cargo pants that hung low on her lean hips and a black, cropped t-shirt bearing the logo "Parental Advisory" that showed quite a lot of midriff. Lia was a couple inches shorter than Beth, lean, and muscled.

Lia's belly button also sported some bling — a gold hoop with a charm dangling from it — was that a mermaid? On her feet were chunky, black combat boots that looked like they'd seen better days. And then there was the most striking feature of all — the tribal tattoos on her lovely, heart-shaped face. Above and below her eyes, on her nose and cheeks, were dots and squiggles, triangles and slashes. The tattoos were surprisingly beautiful really, if not extremely unconventional, like Lia herself.

Lia looked at Beth's arm, which was immobilized in a temporary splint. The swollen lump on her arm was an angry mixture of dark purple and red. "Aren't they going to do something about that?"

Beth nodded. "I'm getting a cast once the orthopedic doctor reads the X-rays."

"You don't need an X-ray to tell that arm's broken," Lia said.

Lia propped her boots up on the footboard of Beth's bed and crossed her arms, trying to get comfortable in the less-than-comfortable chair. "The cops arrested the fucker who beat you. I thought you'd want to know."

"I didn't know," Beth said. "Thanks."

"I hope they throw the book at the asswipe. If Shane's attorney has anything to say about it, they will. Troy Spencer's a beast in the courtroom. He'll make sure the guy rots in prison for a long time."

A nurse came into the room and introduced herself to Beth — her name was Susan. The woman had brought Beth a pitcher of ice water and a plastic cup with a lid and straw. She took Beth's vitals, then administered the next scheduled dose of pain medication through Beth's IV. She also showed Beth how to operate her bed and the television set, and how to call for a nurse. Beth noticed that the nurse's curious gaze kept sliding over to Lia.

After the nurse left, Beth finally had to ask. "Are those tattoos on your face real?" Lia had such a lovely face. Beth couldn't understand why she'd want to mark it up like that. The tattoos were mesmerizing, yes, beautiful actually, but still... were they permanent?

"Nah, they're fake. Shane won't let me have real tats on my face. I do a lot of undercover work so I can only have tats in places that people generally don't see. You know, like on my ass."

"Oh." Beth nodded. "Lia, do you mind if I ask how old you are?"

"Twenty-two," Lia said.

"I'm 24," Beth said.

"I guess we'll be seeing a lot of each other now, since my brother is freaking nuts about you."

Beth smiled. "I guess so."

40

S hane stepped into the waiting room, and a small crowd of
people jumped to their feet. It was after 5 o'clock, and a few
more faces from the office had appeared, including AJ and
Frank from IT and Shane's executive assistant, Diane.

Diane walked up to Shane and wrapped her arms around his
waist, tears in her eyes. The top of her head barely came halfway
up his chest. "I'm so sorry, honey," she said. "Is she all right?"

Shane nodded as he returned Diane's embrace and patted her
back. "She will be. She's in a lot of pain, but her injuries aren't
serious."

"That poor child," Diane said, wiping her wet eyes on her
sleeve. "How could someone do that to such a sweet girl?"

The elevator across the hall opened its doors, and two women
stepped out. Shane recognized one of them — Gabrielle Hunter. The other woman was an older blond. Both women seemed
a little bit lost.

He knew immediately that the other woman had to be Beth's
mother, Ingrid Jamison. The resemblance between them was obvious. Ingrid Jamison was a beautiful woman. In her mid-sixties,
she was tall and slender, like her daughter. Her face was shaped
like Beth's, and she had clear blue eyes. Ingrid's pale blond hair
fell to her shoulder blades. When she smiled hesitantly at Shane,
her face lit up with a smile that was identical to Beth's. The sight

of it made his heart contract.

"You must be Beth's mother," Shane said as he approached her.

"Yes," she said, looking hesitantly at the small crowd assembled in the waiting room. "I'm Ingrid Jamison."

Shane offered his hand to Ingrid and they shook. "It's a pleasure to meet you, Mrs. Jamison. I'm Shane McIntyre."

"How is my daughter?" Ingrid said. "Can I see her?"

"She's in Orthopedics right now, having her arm casted," Shane said. "Tyler's with her. Beth's ribs are bruised, and she has a concussion. Her face is pretty badly battered, but her doctor said she should heal fine. She's going to be fine, Mrs. Jamison. You can see her as soon as she gets back to her room. I'll take you there now, so you can wait for her."

Shane glanced at Gabrielle, who looked very ill at ease. "Hello, Gabrielle," he said. "I'm glad you came. Beth will be happy to see you."

Gabrielle glanced at Ingrid Jamison, then back at Shane. "Shane, I'm sorry for telling Beth like I did."

Shane shook his head, dismissing her apology. "There's no need to apologize, Gabrielle. I understand why you did it. It's okay."

Cooper was standing guard outside Beth's room when Shane and the two women approached.

Shane nodded at Cooper, and then ushered Mrs. Jamison and Gabrielle inside the room. The center of the room — where Beth's bed would be when she returned from Orthopedics — was conspicuously empty. Lia got up from the guest chair she'd been sitting in and hopped up on the windowsill.

"Mrs. Jamison, this is my sister, Lia McIntyre," Shane said. "She'll be helping me look after Beth. Lia, this is Beth's mother and Beth's roommate, Gabrielle Hunter."

"Hello, Mrs. Jamison," Lia said.

"Call me Ingrid, please," the woman said. "Do you mind if

I sit?" Ingrid sank gratefully into one of the two chairs in the room. Gabrielle took the other.

Ingrid's gaze went to the doorway. Shane glanced behind him to see what she was looking at. It was Cooper standing in the open doorway.

"I beg your pardon," Shane said, smiling apologetically. "Mrs. Jamison, this is Daniel Cooper. Cooper, this is Beth's mother, Ingrid Jamison."

"Ma'am," Cooper said, tipping his head at Ingrid.

"Hello," Ingrid said, a small smile on her face.

"Can we get either of you something to drink?" Shane said to Ingrid and Gabrielle. "Coffee? A soft drink? Water?"

"I would love some coffee," Ingrid said, looking at Shane with a hopeful expression on her face.

"I'll get it," Cooper said. "How do you take your coffee, ma'am?"

Ingrid smiled at Cooper. "Thank you, that's very kind. And please, call me Ingrid. Sugar and cream, if it's not too much trouble."

"Not at all... Ingrid," Cooper said. Then he looked at Gabrielle. "Anything for you, miss?"

"Water, please," Gabrielle said.

After Cooper left, Ingrid looked imploringly at Shane. "Please tell me what happened to my baby. Tyler was very vague when he called me."

Shane frowned. "Beth was attacked earlier today in her office. It was a pretty brutal beating, and she's in a lot of pain, but none of her injuries are serious."

"Do they know who did this to her?"

"Yes," Shane said. "He's a student at the medical school. He's been arrested and is in the County jail now, awaiting arraignment. My attorney is investigating what charges we can bring against him. For starters, he's charged with assault and battery. I expect there will be more charges coming."

"Your attorney?" Ingrid said, taken aback. "Why yours? Why not Tyler's?" She eyed Shane suspiciously. "Pardon me, I don't mean to be rude, but what business do you have with my daughter?"

Shane hesitated, painfully aware that this wasn't the best time or place to tell Ingrid he was involved with her daughter.

"I'm Beth's boyfriend," Shane said. There was that god-awful word again. It didn't do their relationship justice.

"Boyfriend?" Ingrid eyed Shane skeptically. "Beth didn't even tell me she was dating anyone, let alone that she had a boyfriend."

Ingrid looked at Gabrielle for corroboration of Shane's claim.

Gabrielle nodded. "Beth's been seeing Shane for a couple of weeks."

Ingrid looked back at Shane. "No offense, but aren't you a little too old for my daughter?"

"No, ma'am, I'm not," Shane said.

She frowned at him. "Where did you meet Beth?"

"I met your daughter through Tyler," Shane said. "Your son hired my firm to provide bodyguards for Beth."

"Bodyguards!" Ingrid said, sitting up in her chair, completely astounded. "Whatever for?"

Just then, Cooper walked through the door carrying a cup of coffee and a bottle of water. He handed the bottle to Gabrielle.

"Here you go, Ingrid." Cooper smiled at her as she took the coffee cup from his hand. "Sugar and cream."

"Thank you, Daniel," she said, returning his smile.

Shane wasn't absolutely sure, because Cooper had a pretty healthy tan, but he suspected Cooper was blushing.

Cooper looked at Shane. "I passed Beth and Tyler coming out of the elevator. They'll be here any second."

Ingrid Jamison jumped to her feet as the orderly wheeled Beth's bed into her room. "Oh, my God, Beth!" she cried, horrified by the cuts and bruises on her daughter's face.

"Mom!" Beth cried.

Cooper intercepted Ingrid as she rushed toward Beth, taking the cup of hot coffee from her hand. She smiled gratefully at him.

"Oh, my sweet baby," Ingrid said, as she moved to Beth's side and reached for her daughter.

"Careful!" Shane barked, and Ingrid froze, a stricken look on her face. "I'm sorry," Shane said. "Just be careful where you touch her."

Ingrid looked from Beth to Shane to Tyler, her hands hovering uncertainly over Beth. "Where can I touch her?" she said. Her gaze went automatically to Tyler, who stood looking grim beside Beth's bed. "Tyler?" Her voice cracked.

"She'll be okay, Mom," Tyler said, putting his arm around his mother.

"The top of her head's okay," Shane said. "Avoid her chest and face. They're the worst."

Ingrid laid gentle hands on her daughter's legs, sliding them up carefully to her waist. "My poor baby," she said, crooning in a way only a mother could.

"I'm okay, Mom," Beth said. "Please, don't worry."

Ingrid moved up to the head of the bed and leaned over to stroke the top of Beth's head gently. Then she leaned down and kissed her daughter there. "It's okay, baby," Ingrid said. "We'll take very good care of you."

Cooper pushed a chair toward Ingrid, and she sat down beside Beth's bed.

Gabrielle sat in the other visitor chair. "Wow, you look awful, Beth," she said.

Beth chuckled, then whimpered in pain. "Hurts... to... laugh," she said, gasping each word.

"Then don't laugh," Gabrielle said, unable to refrain from smiling.

"I can't... help it. Everyone... keeps... telling me... how terrible... I look."

"You always look beautiful, honey," Ingrid said, brushing Beth's hair back. "Even now."

A young woman arrived with Beth's dinner tray.

Ingrid surveyed the dinner plate. "Chicken broth, mashed potatoes, and Jello. Looks like you're on a soft food diet."

Ingrid jumped to her feet and arranged the tray for Beth.

"Here, honey, let me help you. Let's raise up your bed a bit, so you can eat. I'll feed you."

Shane watched Ingrid Jamison go into full mother mode and smiled. Having Ingrid here was just what Beth needed.

As Ingrid offered Beth a spoonful of broth, Shane glanced at his sister who was sitting on the windowsill with her knees drawn up. "Why don't you go grab some dinner? I'll be here."

Lia hopped down from the windowsill and walked past Shane toward the door. "Text me when they're gone," she whispered to Shane. "I can only take so much family time."

Tyler glanced at his mother and Gabrielle, who were busy helping Beth manage her dinner. Then he caught Shane's gaze and cocked his head toward the hallway, motioning for Shane to join him.

"I'll be right outside in the hallway, sweetheart," Shane said to Beth. Then he followed Tyler into the hall.

"Does Beth know you want to move her into your house in Kenilworth?" Tyler said.

"No," Shane said. "I haven't had a chance to tell her. I will once things quiet down a bit."

Tyler shook his head. "Don't bother. I want her to come live with me for the time being," Tyler said. "At least until the issue of Kline has been resolved. The last place she needs to be is under your roof. She needs to be with her family."

Shane stood with his arms crossed. He'd been expecting this. "She's not a child, Tyler. She can make up her own mind."

"Not under these circumstances, she can't," Tyler said. "She's been traumatized, and she's overwhelmed. Her mother and I will make this decision. She'll be fine in my condo. I live in a secured building. She'll be safe there."

"Like I said, Tyler, she can make up her own mind."

"We'll see about that. But what about tonight?" Tyler said. "How late are you staying?"

"I'm staying all night," Shane said. "I'm not leaving her. I'll spend the night with her, here in her room. A few of my people will be staying overnight, too. We've got it covered."

Tyler frowned. "Jake told me Kline bought a gun."

"He did," Shane said. "And this morning he bought ammo at a local gun shop. We're monitoring his PC and phone 24/7. There's not much Kline can do that we don't know about. Don't worry. We won't let him get anywhere near her."

Ingrid and Gabrielle left at 8 p.m., when the nurse popped in to remind everyone that visiting hours had officially ended. Tyler hung around for a little while longer, reluctant to leave Beth. There'd been such a stream of people in and out all day that he hadn't had a chance to really talk to her.

"I'd like to be alone with my sister for a while," Tyler said to Shane.

Shane nodded. "We'll go get some coffee," he said, referring to himself and Lia, who was back up on her window perch.

Tyler had been taking care of Beth, one way or another, for her entire life. That wasn't about to change just because Shane was in the picture now. He knew it had to be hard for Tyler to adjust to having another man claiming rights where Beth was concerned. Besides, Shane wanted his own private time with Beth, and he knew that wouldn't happen until Tyler finally left for the evening. And Tyler wouldn't leave until he'd tried his best to talk her into staying with him.

Lia followed Shane out of the room.

"I'll stay here," Cooper said outside Beth's door. "You two, go get some coffee."

"Forget coffee," Lia said as she and Shane headed to the elevator. "Is there a bar nearby?"

"I could sure use a drink," Shane said, punching the button to summon the elevator. "It's been one hell of a day."

They took the elevator down to the basement. The cafeteria

was closed for the night, so they each grabbed a cup of coffee, and Shane got a sandwich, from vending machines. They found a table and sat.

Shane watched Lia dump half a cup of sugar into her coffee and shook his head in dismay.

"What?" she said.

"Nothing." He took a sip of his coffee. "Beth broke up with me yesterday morning," Shane told Lia.

Her eyes shot up at him. "Why?"

"Gabrielle told her that Tyler had hired us. She was... hurt," he said. "I was trying to give her some space, waiting for an opportunity to talk to her — to work things out — when the attack happened this morning."

"Oh, God. Poor Beth."

Shane grimaced. "Yeah, she's had one hell of a week, and it's only Tuesday."

"What are you going to do now? About Beth, I mean."

"I'm going to talk to her as soon as Tyler leaves," Shane said. "We did talk a little bit earlier today, but she was in no shape to discuss our relationship. Honestly, she still isn't, but I can't put it off any longer."

"So, you hadn't told her you were the hired help?" Lia surmised, smirking at her brother.

"Gabrielle beat me to it. Beth was devastated, to say the least."

"Well, you can't blame her, can you?"

"No," Shane said. "I can't. I admitted to her that I'd fucked up, but she was hurt. Really hurt. She has trust issues to begin with, and this didn't help. But I'm not giving up on her. I love Beth. I'm not going to lose her."

"Well, if this evening was any indication, I don't think you have anything to worry about. She couldn't keep her eyes off you. She doesn't want to lose you any more than you want to lose her. It'll work out."

"I certainly hope you're right," Shane said.

"Let's just hope her brother doesn't fuck things up for you. God, he's such a prick."

41

Tyler closed the door to Beth's room and dropped into one of the empty visitor chairs.

"I love you, Beth," he said, his eyes pained as he studied her face. He reached out with his index finger, just barely skimming the surface of her face, taking care not to put any pressure on the multitude of bruises. "When I got the call that you'd been hurt, I swear my heart stopped in my chest."

Beth's eyes started watering. "I love you, too, " she said, attempting a small smile. It hurt.

She was exhausted. Every bone in her body ached, her face was a minefield of pain, and her muscles had turned to mush. More than anything, she just wanted to sleep, but she knew she and Tyler needed to talk. Surely he knew about her relationship with Shane by now.

She tried to sit up. "Tyler, I — "

"No, lie down," he said, reaching out to gently ease her back down. "It's okay. I know about you and Shane." A muscle flexed in his jaw as he clenched his teeth. He swallowed hard, and his eyes glittered like diamonds.

She knew he was upset, but he was holding it in for her sake.

"He told me he loves you," Tyler said, watching Beth's face for her reaction.

A small smile made the corners of her mouth curve up. Shane

said that to Tyler? Well, that made it official. "I love him, too," she said, heaving a deep sigh. It felt good to say that aloud.

"You don't sound very excited about it," Tyler said.

"I am excited. But it's just so new," she said, her fingers nervously playing with her blanket. "And so unexpected. I never thought I could feel like this with someone. I never thought that someone could feel this way about me." She wiped her eyes with the back of her right hand. "Tyler, he knows everything about me. He knows how I am, and he still wants me. He's so patient and considerate. He's never made me feel that I'm less than what I should be."

Tyler chuckled, his voice harsh. "Shane McIntyre is a lot of things — arrogant, controlling — but he isn't stupid. He knows a good thing when he sees one and you, kiddo, are a good thing." Tyler squeezed her hand. "How did you meet him?"

Beth grinned. "At Clancy's a couple of weeks ago. He was there on a Friday evening. We spoke, and then he asked me to join him in the cafe."

"You couldn't have known who he was."

She shook her head. "No. I thought it was just a random meeting. That he was... you know, picking me up." She felt her face heat.

Tyler shook his head, clearly displeased. "It wasn't random, Beth. He knew exactly who you were."

"I know," she said. "We've... talked about it."

"How did you find out?"

"Gabrielle told me yesterday morning. I spent most of last weekend with him. When I told her I was falling in love with him, she... well, she told me everything. She thought I should know the truth."

"I'm sorry, Beth," Tyler said.

"It was... difficult. He'd lied to me the entire time we'd known each other. That was hard to take."

Tyler sighed. "I've known Shane for a long time, Beth. I may not always see eye-to-eye with him, but I'll admit he's an honorable man. He didn't set out to deceive you. He was ethically bound to silence, because of our... business arrangement. And, to be honest, he wanted to tell you everything from the beginning. I wouldn't let him."

Beth nodded. "I just wished he'd told me himself before I heard it from Gabrielle."

Her gaze sharpened as she eyed her brother. "Shane's not the only one who kept things from me," she said, unable to completely mask her resentment. "You kept Howard Kline's parole from me. That was wrong. And you told Gabrielle, but not me! I had a right to know."

Tyler frowned. "I'm sorry, but I didn't want you to worry."

Beth shook her head. "You can't keep information like that from me, Tyler. It's my life."

"You'd been through so much already. I wanted to protect you from all that." Tyler's expression turned serious. "Shane's going to ask you to stay with him until we get Kline back behind bars. I think that would be a mistake. I want you to come live with me, at least until it's safe for you to be on your own again."

Beth gave her brother a melancholy smile. "Don't you think that should be my decision?"

There was a quick rap on Beth's door, and then Shane walked in. He was alone — there was no sign of Lia. Beth hoped Lia had better things to do than hang around her hospital room all evening.

Tyler stood as Shane approached, the two men glaring at each other across the foot of Beth's hospital bed. Beth looked at one and then the other and rolled her eyes. They were worse than two junkyard dogs fighting over a bone.

"Were you listening?" Tyler said.

"Yes," Shane said unabashedly. He crossed his arms over his chest. "Anything that concerns Beth concerns me."

Tyler scowled at him. "You presume a lot, Shane. I think it's in Beth's best interest for her to come stay with me, and I'm sure our mother would agree."

"That's Beth's decision to make, not yours. She's an adult, Tyler."

"Guys, stop!" Beth raised a placating hand as she glanced from one to the other. She couldn't help grinning at the novelty of the situation. There were two men in her life now. "Can you at least be civil to each other? Please?"

Beth reached for Shane with her good hand. He smiled at her, relaxing his stance, and pulled one of the chairs around to his side of the bed and took a seat. "Sorry, sweetheart," he said. "I'll try to behave." He kissed her hand. "So, is everything okay?" He looked from Beth to Tyler and back.

"All good," she said, smiling at him.

Shane looked up expectantly at Tyler, who stood glowering over them both. "It's late, Tyler," he said. "She needs to rest."

Shane knew this had to be hard for Tyler. Tyler was used to being the only man in Beth's life. Now he had to share that role, and Shane knew that couldn't be an easy adjustment.

"You said you're staying the night?" Tyler said.

"I'll be here all night, as will Cooper, Lia, and Miguel. One of us will be with her at all times."

Tyler nodded. He leaned down and kissed the top of Beth's head. "I'll be back in the morning, kiddo. Call me if you need me."

"I will." Beth looked at the two men flanking her. They were so different from each other, and yet they were so much alike. She loved them both, and the fact that she had both of them in her life filled her with a degree of contentment she'd never known. "Tyler?"

"Yeah?"

"I love you."

He smiled. "I love you, too."

The nurse on the evening shift stopped in Beth's room and took her vitals. Then she helped Beth walk to the restroom to take care of business. Beth's ribs burned, making standing very difficult, let alone walking. With the nurse's help, Beth used the facilities and brushed her teeth and hair before shuffling back to her bed.

"Don't get out of bed during the night without help," the nurse told her. "Don't even stand up without help. You could easily fall."

The nurse looked at Shane. "Are you staying the night?"

"Yes."

"Good. Don't let her get out of bed by herself."

When they were finally alone, Shane dialed the lights in the room down to a low, twilight setting. He didn't want Beth to wake up in the dark in a strange place and panic. A movement in the partially open doorway caught his attention. It was Jake, standing there with his hands on his hips, looking like business.

"I'll be right back," he told Beth. "I need to have a quick word with Jake out in the hall."

Shane stepped out into the hallway. "What is it?"

Jake frowned. "Well, it's not good news." He closed the door to Beth's room. "Kline's been looking at bus routes that service Hyde Park, specifically the Kingston campus."

"Fuck."

"Yep. That's what I said. He has a gun, ammo, and now he's planning transportation to her workplace. He's going for her."

Shane nodded. "Good."

"Excuse me?" Jake said, raising a cynical brow.

"I want him to go after her. That'll give me the justification I need to take him out."

"Shane, I know you want to put an end to this guy. We all do. But you've got to be careful."

Shane nodded. "I'm not going to let this asshole hang like a black cloud over Beth's head for the rest of her life. I just have to figure out how to do it without putting Beth at risk and without breaking any laws."

"All right," Jake said. "I'll start working on something."

"Jake, make sure there's absolutely no risk to Beth. I won't tolerate that for a second."

Jake nodded. "I kinda figured that out on my own, Papa Bear."

Shane walked back into Beth's room, closing the door behind him, and took a seat beside her bed. "We need to talk, sweetheart," he said, taking her hand.

"Hmm?" she said turning to face him.

"You look like you're about to pass out. Never mind. It can wait until morning. You need sleep."

As if on cue, Beth yawned, and they both chuckled. She sighed deeply. "I'm so tired. I can't keep my eyes open."

Shane lowered the head of the bed to a comfortable sleeping position. "Go to sleep," he said, stroking her hair.

"You'll stay with me?" she said.

Beth's question sounded an awful lot like a plea, and he felt his chest tighten. A horrifying thought resurfaced in his mind — a thought he'd been trying to keep out of his head since her attack. *What if Mary hadn't been there to stop Andrew Morton?* There was no telling how this day might have ended.

He smiled at her. "Wild horses couldn't drag me away."

Smiling, she closed her eyes, letting her muscles and bones relax for the first time that day. "Shane?"

"Yes?"

"I regretted walking out on you," she said. "When I realized what I'd done, I was miserable, but I didn't know how to fix it."

"It was my fault, Beth. All of it. I should have told you the truth sooner." He kissed her hand. "And I was beyond miserable; I was devastated, terrified I'd lost you."

She made a sleepy sound. "Never," she said, her voice drowsy. "Can we start over?"

"I would love that." Shane stood and leaned over her, his mouth hovering over hers, just short of touching her. "I would give anything to be able to kiss you right now," he whispered against her lips.

His warm breath on her lips made her shiver. "Do it," she whispered. "Kiss me."

"I can't," he said. "Not until your lips are healed."

"Do it," she whispered against his lips. "Please."

He made a sound, part frustration and part resignation, and then he touched his lips to hers, barely making contact.

Beth sighed. "I love you."

"I love you, too, sweetheart." He sank back into his chair and sat there, watching her drift off to asleep.

Lia came quietly into the room and laid a hand on Shane's shoulder. "Do you want the cot?" she whispered, indicating the narrow bed the nurse had rolled in for them.

"No, you take it. I'll sleep here."

Beth's scream rent the air in the dead of night, wrenching everyone in the immediate vicinity fully awake.

Shane, who'd fallen asleep with his head resting on his arms at the edge of her bed, shot to his feet, sending his chair crashing to the floor. In that split second, he'd already scanned the room, looking for a threat. Cooper burst into the room, his Beretta steady in a two-handed grip. After a quick scan of the room, Cooper lowered his gun.

Lia sat up in the cot and glared at the two men. "Good God, what was that awful sound?"

Shane looked down at Beth's restless figure in the bed, and then glared at his sister. "She was having a nightmare."

Lia lay back down with an annoyed huff and turned on her side facing away from Beth's bed. Cooper holstered his gun as he quietly slipped out of the room.

Shane righted his chair and sat back down. It was four-thirty in the morning, but he was surprisingly wide awake after only a few hours of restless sleep. He wouldn't sleep well here. He wouldn't sleep well again, not until he had Beth safely ensconced in his Kenilworth house. She'd be safe there — he just needed to get her to agree to the move.

"Shane?"

He almost didn't hear Beth's whisper. He leaned forward.

"What is it, sweetheart?" he whispered back.

"I need to go to the bathroom."

He smiled. "Okay. I'll help you."

"No, that's all right. I can do it myself." Beth attempted to sit up on her own, but she groaned at the burning pain in her torso and fell back against the pillows.

"Your nurse gave strict instructions that you're not to get out of bed without assistance."

"Shane!" she hissed. "I don't want you taking me to the bathroom!"

He sighed. "Then Lia can help you. Or, I'll call for a nurse."

"No, don't wake Lia."

"Too late, Princess," Lia muttered. "I'm already awake. I'll do it."

"Thank you, Lia, but that won't be necessary." Beth glared at Shane. "And you're not doing it either."

"How about Cooper, then?" Shane suggested. "I'm sure he'd be happy to help you."

"No!" Beth hissed.

"I'm sorry, sweetheart," Shane said. "You have to allow one of us to help you." He leaned toward her, his mouth near her ear. "Why not me? I've seen and tasted every inch of your delectable body. What's the big deal?"

"Okay, you," she said, sounding resigned. "But just to the bathroom door. Once I'm inside, I can manage on my own."

He chuckled. "We'll see about that."

Shane helped Beth sit up and swing her legs to the side of the bed. He helped her stand, careful of her broken arm, and then supported her as she shuffled across the room. When they reached their destination, he pushed the bathroom door open. "Do you want the light on?"

"No, thank you. I can manage from here," she said.

Shane partially loosened his grip on her, and she immediately began listing to the side. "I'll just help you over to the toilet," he suggested, tightening his grip on her. "Then you can hold onto the handrail for support."

"Okay," Beth said, realizing just how weak she was. If Shane had let go of her, she would have landed on the floor.

When she reached the toilet, Beth grabbed the handrail with her good hand, holding on for dear life. Her broken arm, which was strapped in a sling, was of course no use. She simply stood there, realizing she couldn't do this alone. She couldn't lift her gown and sit down and hold onto the railing at the same time, not with just one functioning hand and hardly any strength at the moment. It was mortifying to be so weak and unable to do the most basic thing by herself.

Shane stood behind her, holding his tongue.

"I can't do it," she finally said, her voice sounding thick with defeat.

"I'll lift your gown," he said gently. "You sit down."

When she was seated, he said, "I'll wait outside. Call me when you're done."

Beth managed to take care of business, albeit a bit slowly. Once she was done, she figured if she could keep her gown from falling into the toilet, she could stand and shuffle to the sink on her own. It was just a few feet away. Surely she could manage that on her own.

She tucked the ends of her gown inside her sling and stood carefully, holding onto the hand rail for support. A wave of dizziness hit her, and she closed her eyes for a moment.

She looked over at the sink and wondered if she could walk those few steps without assistance. It wasn't that far. Keeping her hand on the support rail as long as possible, she shuffled on her feet from the toilet to the sink. Once there, she leaned against the sink for support while she used her right hand to turn on the water.

As she waited for the water to heat up, she glanced in the mirror and saw her reflection for the first time since the assault. Dear God, she looked half dead. She must have made a sound, because the door opened, and Shane was suddenly there behind her, his hands on her waist to steady her.

He frowned, meeting her eyes in the mirror. "You were supposed to call me."

Beth's eyes filled with tears as she stared at her reflection. She barely recognized herself. Her face was mottled with a hideous array of red and purple splotches, angry and dark. Her nose was swollen, as were her lips, and she had two black eyes. There was no way she could go back to work looking like this, even if she could move on her own.

Shane felt his throat tighten at the sight of her tears falling silently down her battered cheeks. He hated that she was hurting. His arms snaked around her waist from behind, and he gently pulled her against him, his lips in her hair. "I will never let anyone hurt you again, I swear it."

She met his gaze in the mirror, feeling as fragile as she looked.

"It will all heal," Shane said, as he reached around her and held her palm under the soap dispenser. He squirted some soap into her hand and lathered it for her. "Dr. Prakash said you'll be as good as new in a couple of months," he said as he rinsed her hand under the warm water.

"A couple of *months?*"

"It'll take at least that long for the discoloration to go away and for your ribs and arm to heal."

"How could someone do this to another person?" she said, scowling at her own reflection.

"Andrew Morton is sick," Shane said. "I spoke to his father on the phone today. Andrew's been in therapy for years for mental health issues. But don't worry about him; he'll never get the chance to hurt you again."

Beth lost what little strength she had mustered and sagged weakly against Shane. He dried her hand with a paper towel, and then gently scooped her up and carried her back to her bed.

"She okay?" Lia said from the cot.

"Yeah, she's fine," Shane said, as he tucked Beth back into bed.

42

E arly Wednesday morning, Shane was sitting beside Beth's hospital bed, helping her with breakfast, when Cooper cracked open the door to her room.

"Police are here to take Beth's statement," Cooper said.

Shane looked at Beth. She was wearing a pale blue fuzzy robe from home over her hospital gown, and her hair — which Shane had brushed for her that morning — was in a ponytail. At least she looked respectable.

"Are you ready to talk to them?" he said.

Beth shook her head. "I really don't want to do this. I don't want to think about it." The moment Cooper had mentioned the police, her pulse rate had started to climb. The last thing she wanted to do was relive what Andrew had done to her.

"I know. But you have to give the police a statement, sweetheart," Shane said. "We might as well get this over with. They'll just keep coming back."

She sighed. "All right," she said, sounding far from enthusiastic.

Shane nodded at Cooper. "Let them in."

Cooper pushed the door open, and two uniformed officers walked into the room. They were both middle-aged men, one tall with graying hair and the other stout with dark hair. They approached the bed, the tall one came to stand at the foot of the bed. The other officer took the empty guest chair.

The one standing at the foot of the bed spoke. "Good morning, Miss Jamison. I'm Officer Markham, and this is Officer Jenkins. We're here to take your statement about the attack on you yesterday."

Shane stood. "Shane McIntyre." H shook hands with both officers. "I'm Beth's boyfriend."

Cooper had also stepped into the room and was standing just inside the door, his hands on his hips, looking very much like a guard standing at attention. He had his jacket on, hiding his gun holster, and Beth couldn't help wondering if it was legal to carry guns inside a hospital.

Beth smiled at Cooper, and he smiled back. Cooper reminded her of a Rottweiler guarding his territory. This Rottweiler was gray around the edges, but he was, nonetheless, ferocious. The realization that he was here on her behalf sent a wave of warmth through her. He wouldn't let anything happen to her; neither would Shane.

"We're sorry to bother you, Miss Jamison," Officer Markham said as he pulled a small notepad and pen from his pocket. "We have statements from Mary Reynolds and Maggie Swenson already, but we need your statement, too."

"Please sit, gentlemen," Shane said. He rose from his chair and pushed it to the foot of the bed for Officer Markham. Shane sat beside Beth on her bed, taking her hand and giving it a gentle squeeze.

"Who's Maggie Swenson?" Shane said, looking at Beth.

"She's a student at Kingston. She was there when Andrew arrived." Beth looked at Officer Markham. "Is Maggie all right?"

"Yes, she's fine," Markham said. "Ms. Swenson said she was standing at the door to your office when Andrew Morton came out of nowhere and shoved her to the floor. Is that correct?"

"Yes. She hit the floor really hard."

"And then what happened?" Officer Markham said.

"Then I saw Andrew standing in front of me. He looked... furious. His face was red, and he was breathing hard. He pushed me back inside the Special Collections room and closed the door behind us."

Officer Markham jotted down some notes on his notepad, then looked up at her expectantly. "Did Andrew say anything to you?"

"He pushed me, and I fell against one of the tables. He yelled something at me."

"Can you remember what he said?"

"He called me something. I think he called me 'a stupid bitch.'"

"Did he say anything that would explain what had set him off?"

Beth grimaced, trying to think back to something she would have rather forgotten. When Andrew's words came back to her in a blinding rush, she made a pained sound.

"What?" Officer Markham said.

She looked at Shane, her expression stricken.

"What did he say, Beth?" Shane said.

"He was angry about the benefit," Beth said, looking at Shane. "He was angry at you."

"What benefit?" Office Jenkins said.

"There was a charity benefit for the Children's Hospital Saturday night, at the Hilton," Shane said. "Andrew Morton was there. He harassed Beth on the dance floor, so I removed him physically and had a talk with him in the hallway." Shane's expression grew tight as he looked at Beth. "Do you remember what he said?"

Beth swallowed hard. "He said something about his dad taking away his car and, I think, his credit cards."

Beth watched Shane's face grow pale.

Shane cleared his throat. "I told Andrew's father — Richard Morton — what Andrew had done. I warned Richard to keep his son under control. Richard must have taken those things away from Andrew as punishment." He was talking to the officers, but his eyes were on Beth. "It was my fault. Andrew attacked Beth in retaliation against me."

"It's not your fault, Shane!" Beth said, tightening her grip on his hand. "You couldn't have known what Andrew would do."

"Miss Jamison?" Officer Markham said. "What happened then?"

"I ran," she said. "I tried to get to my office, but he blocked the door, and I couldn't close it. So I ran for the phone to call for help, but he grabbed me and ripped the phone cord out of the wall. I fell and hit my head. And then he started kicking me." She shuddered. "I don't remember anything after that."

"We have Ms. Reynolds' statement," Officer Jenkins said. "She came into the office as he was kicking you. She pulled him off of you, and then he fled the scene. Ms. Reynolds called campus police."

"She also called me," Shane said. "One of my employees, Miguel Rodriguez, came to Beth's location and waited with her until the EMTs arrived. Miguel said Beth was unconscious by the time he got there."

Officer Markham made some notes. "Can we speak with Mr. Rodriguez?" he said.

"Of course," Shane said. He glanced at Cooper.

Cooper nodded. "I'll take care of it."

"If that's all, Officers?" Shane said. "Beth's tired."

Officer Jenkins rose from his chair. "We'll be in touch if we need anything more."

"It's not your fault, Shane," Beth said after the officers left.

"Actually, it is," he said, his countenance bleak. "I underestimated Andrew Morton."

Ingrid Jamison and Gabrielle Hunter arrived shortly after the police left, planning to visit with Beth for the rest of the morning.

Shane left Beth in her mother's very capable hands, with Lia lurking unobtrusively in the background and Miguel on guard duty. He drove to his apartment to take a shower and change clothes. On the way back, he stopped at a fast food drive-thru to grab food for himself, Lia, and Miguel, as well as something he thought Beth might be able to eat. He figured she was ready for a change of pace after eating hospital food for 24 hours.

When Shane got back to Beth's room, Ingrid was brushing Beth's hair and generally fussing over her daughter, who seemed to be soaking up the maternal attention. Tyler was there now, too, appearing a little more relaxed than he had the day before. He was even wearing jeans, which was a first as far as Shane knew. He'd never seen the man in anything other than his typical men-in-black suit and tie.

A delegation of Beth's friends from the library — Mary Reynolds, Devany Ross, and a couple other young women — stopped by to see her, bringing flowers and balloons. Devany gave Beth a musical get-well card that played *The Chicken Dance*. Shane thought Lia might blow a gasket on the third playing of the card.

Even Richard Morton stopped by briefly, to see Beth's injuries for himself. He stood at the foot of her bed, studying her face with a deep scowl on his face.

"I'm very sorry, Miss Jamison," Richard Morton said, his voice nearly as stiff as his posture. "I... " He cleared his throat and looked around the room as if he were completely at a loss. "There's nothing I can say, really," he said. "I can't undo the damage my son caused. I'm very sorry."

Beth smiled sadly at the man. "Thank you."

Shane walked Richard down the hall to the elevator.

"Shane, I don't know what to say," Richard said.

Shane nodded, thinking Richard looked awfully pale. He'd never really cared for the man — Richard Morton had arrogance down pat — but right now, he felt sorry for the man.

After Beth ate her lunch, Shane finally managed to get everyone out of her room. Lia took off to go grab a shower and a change of clothes at the Lake Shore apartment. Tyler escorted his mother and Gabrielle down to the cafeteria so they could get some lunch. Shane gave Miguel instructions to keep everyone out of the room for the next half-hour, short of an emergency.

Shane sat in the chair beside Beth's bed, facing her. He leaned toward her, his elbows on his knees. "Beth, we need to talk."

Beth looked at him warily. "Okay," she said. "What do you want to talk about?"

Shane couldn't take his eyes off the bruises that stood out starkly on her pale face. Her lips were still swollen, but the cuts were starting to heal. At the moment, he struggled with a burning need to hunt down Andrew Morton and exact revenge on Beth's behalf. But there wasn't time to indulge in that kind of thinking right now. The need to settle things with Beth was eating at him.

"I want to discuss your security arrangements," he said. "I've canceled Tyler's contract. I'm going to personally oversee your safety now."

"I thought Andrew was in jail," she said.

"He is. And after the court hearing, I expect he'll be remanded to a mental health facility for evaluation and treatment. And then he's either headed for prison or a psychiatric hospital. Either way, he's not getting out anytime soon. But frankly, Andrew's not my main concern. Kline is."

Beth frowned. "What about him? Tyler said you weren't sure if he was still a threat."

"He is a threat, sweetheart," Shane said. "He recently bought a handgun over the Internet — illegally — and he purchased ammunition. We also know he's been scouring the Internet for information on you — where you live, where you work, anything he can find. And, he's been shadowing you on social media sites. He's a serious risk, Beth."

She paled.

He interlaced their fingers. "I want you to move into my house in Kenilworth. You can recuperate there while we deal with Kline."

"But what about my house?"

"Beth, your house isn't secure. My estate in Kenilworth is," he said. "No one can get on that property without permission. I want you to come stay there with me."

"For how long?"

He shrugged. "Beth, I'm asking you to move in with me. Not just because of the security issue — although that's a big part of it — but because of us, as well. To be perfectly honest, I want you under my roof."

"You'd be living there, too?"

"Yes. I usually stay there only on the weekends, but with you there, I'll live there full time. I can even work from there if need be. The house has everything you could possibly want, plenty of space and amenities. There's an indoor pool, a movie theater, a library. I'll make sure you have everything you need. I'm going to ask Gabrielle to pack up your personal belongings this afternoon, and I'll have them delivered to the Kenilworth house this evening."

"But Kenilworth is a bit of a drive from Hyde Park. With morning traffic, it would take me more than an hour to get to work."

"Beth, I don't want you to go back to the library."

"What?"

"I want you to quit your job."

Her brow wrinkled. "I can't quit!"

"Why not?"

"Because! I have bills to pay. I have a car payment and school loans. And I pay half the utilities on the townhouse."

Shane sighed. "Beth, money isn't an issue. I'll take care of your bills. I'll provide everything you need."

Beth stared at him like he'd grown a second head. "I can't just take your money, Shane."

"You won't be taking it. I'm giving it to you."

Shane rose from his chair and sat on the bed beside Beth, putting his arm around her shoulders. She melted into him, wrapping her good arm around his waist.

"Beth, you can't go back to work right now anyway — certainly not until your injuries heal, and that's going to take some time. You can't even walk across this room on your own without risking a fall. Please, come home with me. You'll have all the support and care you'll need to recuperate there. How about this?

Take short-term leave from work while you're healing. Then you can think about it, see how you like the house, and then make a decision about the long-term. If you still want to return to Kingston when you've healed, then all right. We'll make it work."

"I need time to think about this."

"There isn't much time. Dr. Prakash has said you can be released this evening," Shane told her. "I want to take you home with me tonight. You can't go back to the townhouse. For one thing, you wouldn't be able to negotiate the stairs. Besides, the townhouse isn't secure."

"What about Gabrielle? If it's not safe for me, it's not safe for her either." Beth shifted on the bed and gasped at the stabbing pain in her side. Of all her injuries, it was her ribs that was causing her the most problems. Shane was right. She couldn't walk across the room on her own right now, let alone take care of herself at home. She wouldn't be able to go up and down the stairs. Gabrielle had to work; she couldn't just stay home for days to take care of Beth.

"Don't worry about Gabrielle," he said. "I'll move her to the penthouse."

Shane sat watching Beth, not saying a word. He was used to simply telling people what to do, and they did it. He'd had plenty of women, and they'd all tended to cater to him. But he'd never had a girlfriend before, especially one with a stubborn streak.

He bit back a chuckle. He fully intended that she would be coming home with him that evening; he just thought it would go more smoothly if she thought it was her decision. And if she flat-out refused to come home with him, then he'd have to move in with her in her townhouse. There was no way in hell he was letting her go anywhere without him.

"You're right," she said. "I can't go home. I wouldn't be able to go up and down the stairs on my own."

"Stairs aren't a problem at my house," he said quietly. "There are elevators."

"You have elevators in your house?" she said, incredulous. "Plural?"

He nodded. "Two."

Beth shook her head in disbelief.

"Your mom can come stay with us, too, if you want. Or Gabrielle," he offered, playing one of his wildcards. "Whatever you want. It's a big place. There's plenty of room."

"All right," she said, rolling her eyes. The bottom line was she couldn't take care of herself at home. "I'll come. Just until my injuries are healed.

43

"You're free to go, sweetheart," Shane said, as he strode into Beth's hospital room holding a sheaf of papers. "Dr. Prakash signed your discharge paperwork."

Beth was dressed and seated in one of the guest chairs.

"It's about time," Lia said, hopping down from the window-sill. "This place blows."

"I'll get the car," Cooper said, heading for the door.

Shane and Lia walked with Beth as a hospital staff member wheeled her down to the front entrance. When they got there, Cooper was waiting outside with the Mercedes.

Shane helped Beth transfer from the wheelchair into the back seat of the sedan. Then he walked around to the other side to climb in beside her. Lia rode up front with Cooper.

As they headed north on Lake Shore Drive, Beth leaned back into the soft leather seats and watched out her window for glimpses of Lake Michigan. Water stretched out to the horizon as far as the eye could see.

"You like the water, don't you?" Shane said, watching her watch the lake.

Beth nodded. "When I was little, Tyler and my mom would bring me to the beach, and I'd play for hours in the sand, building sand forts and hunting for shells."

"My house is right on the lake," he said. "I'd love to take you out on the lake when you're feeling better. We have a private beach; you can hunt for shells and build sand forts to your heart's content."

Beth regarded her cast. "I won't be playing in the sand for the next six-to-eight weeks, at least."

She went back to staring out her window, watching the smaller boats as they entered the marinas. Watching the boats helped her keep her mind off Andrew Morton. One minute she'd be fine, and the next she'd remember the sight of his boot coming right at her face and she'd flinch. She couldn't stop the instant replays. She grabbed hold of the armrest.

"What's wrong, Beth? Talk to me," Shane said, his voice low. He reached across her to peel her fingers off the door handle and interlaced them with his.

She looked at him, her eyes tearing up. "It happened so fast. One minute I was fine, and then he — I can't stop thinking about it. I keep reliving it over and over in my head."

Shane released his seat belt and shifted closer to Beth, putting his arm around her. He tried to pull her close, and at first she resisted, far too tense to relax, but eventually she leaned into him. He felt her silent tears as they wet his shirt.

"I keep ruining your shirts," she muttered.

"That's all right. You've had one hell of a week, sweetheart," he said. He looked up and caught Lia's concerned expression from the front seat.

Beth was shaking now, as if all the adrenaline in her system had crashed and her body was responding by going into shock. She closed her eyes and pressed her wet face into his shirt, the fabric soaking up her tears like the thirsty ground soaks up rain. His scent permeated her consciousness, a tantalizing combination of warm male skin and something else, something elusive, maybe his faint cologne. Shane's hand was in her hair, gently stroking, and it felt so good. She closed her eyes and let the motion of the car lull her to sleep.

When the car slowed, Beth lifted her face and looked around. They were on a quiet, residential street. At least, she assumed it was a residential street because they passed the occasional lamp post and mailbox.

"Where are we?" she asked.

"We're in Kenilworth," Shane said. "My house is just down this road."

Through gaps in the trees, she caught fleeting glimpses of huge houses set well back from the road, with acres and acres of lush green woods and lawns in front.

After another mile, Cooper slowed the car and turned onto an unmarked two-lane road. When they came to a towering wrought iron gate, Beth realized it was a private lane.

Cooper stopped the car at the gate.

"Good evening, Mr. Cooper," said a smooth, deep voice coming through the car's speaker system.

"Charlie, open the gate," Cooper said.

"Welcome home, Mr. McIntyre, Miss Jamison," the voice said. "Miss Lia."

"Cut the theatrics, Charlie, and open the damned gate," Cooper said.

Almost instantly, the gate began to move, swinging inward in a wide arc. Cooper drove through the opening and continued along the drive. Beth glanced back and watched as the gate swung shut behind them.

They must have driven for another half mile or so as the paved lane carved its way through the trees. As they exited the woods, the landscape on both sides of the road opened up to lush pastures.

When they came to a second gate, Cooper stopped the car.

"Driving a bit fast this evening, Mr. Cooper?" said the voice through the speakers. "You made the second checkpoint eight seconds early."

Beth chuckled, earning a dirty look from Cooper in the rear view mirror.

"Are you tired of your job, Charlie?" Cooper replied.

"No, sir." The gate promptly swung open.

After a few more minutes, they passed a small lake surrounded by cattails waving in the breeze and inhabited by a multitude of ducks and geese paddling around in wild abandon. A half-dozen Adirondack chairs were positioned on a long floating dock that extended over the water. A number of small boats were tied at the dock.

"Can we go canoeing?" Beth asked Shane.

"That depends. Can you swim?"

She chuckled. "Are you kidding? Tyler wouldn't let me get within ten feet of the water until I'd passed all of the Red Cross swimming classes at our rec center. I'm a certified lifeguard."

"Really?" he said.

Beth elbowed him. "Yes, really. Don't sound so surprised."

"Then, yes," he said. "You can go canoeing. And if I fall in and get knocked unconscious, I expect you to save me."

Beth turned her gaze forward just as the lane merged with a wide, circular drive in front of the house. In the center of the drive was a towering water fountain rising up from a white marble pool.

"Oh, my God," she said, her right hand grasping Shane's thigh as she leaned forward to gape through the front windshield at the massive structure in front of them. "I thought you said this was a house! This isn't a house; it's huge!"

He chuckled. "It's not that big."

"How many bedrooms are there?" she said.

"Twelve."

"It reminds me of a ski lodge I visited once with Mom and Tyler."

Cooper followed the circular drive and parked in front of the wide, wooden steps that led up to the main entrance. Shane got out and walked around to open Beth's door.

"Welcome home," he said, and then he leaned in and kissed her lightly on her lips. "Fair warning… there are some folks here who are dying to meet you."

Just as he said that, the front doors opened and out walked

a tall, sturdy man. He was dressed in muddy thigh-high boots and coveralls, his face deeply weathered and his silver hair cut in a severe flat top. Right on the man's heels was an exuberant, Black Lab puppy, prancing as he followed the tall man out of the house.

"Gus, sit," the man said, and the puppy's haunches dropped to the ground like a stone, although his tail continued wagging with tremendous enthusiasm. "Good boy."

The man walked down the front steps to the car and peered inside at Beth. "Pleased to meet you, Miss Jamison," he said, dipping his head.

"Sweetheart, this is George Peterson. He's the foreman. He manages the property."

"Hello, Mr. Peterson," Beth said.

The man's wrinkled, craggy face was instantly transformed by a wide, welcoming smile. "Welcome, young lady," he said. "And you should call me George."

A woman with a long braid of silver and white, with keen dark eyes and broad cheekbones, stepped outside the house and stood on the front steps. She wore a beaded peasant blouse over a pair of gray trousers and a pair of scuffed, brown riding boots. She glanced down at the small crowd gathering around Beth's open car door, her gaze eventually coming to light on Beth.

"This is Elly," Shane said. "George's wife. She runs the house."

Elly Peterson walked down the steps and approached the car. She frowned as she studied Beth's face. "My God, Shane. Who did this to her?" the woman said in a quiet voice, glancing sharply at Shane.

"He'd better be behind bars," George said, straightening to his full height.

"He is," Shane said, as he lifted Beth out of the car.

Elly smiled at Beth. "Come inside, darling," she said, reaching out to pat Beth's cast.

Shane carried Beth through the open doorway into a spacious, well-lit foyer with a soaring ceiling.

"I'm taking her straight up to bed," Shane said to Elly. "She's exhausted." Shane walked across the foyer and pressed a button on the wall. Immediately, a paneled door slid open to reveal an elevator car.

44

"Here's our room," Shane said, coming to a closed door at the end of the second floor hallway. He opened the door and carried Beth inside.

Her eyes swept the neat, masculine room. It wasn't nearly as big as his suite at his Lake Shore apartment, but it was nonetheless impressive. The wall to the left was made entirely of stones, with a wood-burning fireplace carved into it and a huge flat screen television mounted on a wooden mantel. A king-sized bed covered with a chocolate brown comforter and piled high with pillows stood against the opposite wall, which was formed from massive logs. Recessed lights in the ceiling bathed the room in warm light. Overhead, ceiling fans spun lazily, stirring the air.

The most impressive feature was straight ahead, at the far end of the room. A pair of glass doors led to a covered balcony that faced Lake Michigan. It was nearly dark outside, but even from this distance, Beth could see the reflection of the moonlight on the surface of the lake.

"This is a beautiful room," Beth said.

"It's yours now, too," he said. He set her carefully on her feet. "The bathroom's through there, and the closet is through that door. Miguel brought all your clothes and personal items from your bedroom. You'll find everything organized in the closet."

"Personal items?" Beth said, going pale. She kept her vibrators in the bottom drawer of her nightstand, not to mention her collection of erotic paperbacks.

"Is something wrong?"

"No, nothing's wrong." She could feel her face turning pink.

"Here, let me help you." Shane's hands went to her waist. "Where do you want to go?"

"To the bathroom. I need to get ready for bed."

"I asked Elly to stock up on everything you might need. You'll find it all in the bathroom cupboard."

Shane helped her walk to the bathroom, but she stopped him at the threshold with a hand on his chest.

"I can manage from here," she said, grinning at him.

"But you're exhausted," he said.

"Shane, I think I can handle this on my own."

"All right," he said, releasing her reluctantly. "Call out if you need help."

She entered the bathroom and flipped on the light switch. As she started to close the door behind her, he blocked it and poked his head inside.

"I'll grab you a nightgown from the closet," he said.

"Thank you."

She walked into the bathroom, moving slowly because everything was sore. Her muscles ached, and her bones felt like lead. Her gaze went right to the sunken Jacuzzi, and she wished she had the energy to soak in a tub of hot water, but she was simply too tired. Maybe tomorrow. All she wanted to do right now was crash in Shane's big bed.

She found an impressive supply of toiletries in the cupboard — toothbrushes, toothpastes, soaps, shampoos, lotions and creams — not to mention an assortment of other personal hygiene products a woman might need. There was even a box of jumbo condoms. Oh, my God. Elly was certainly thorough.

She selected a toothbrush and brushed her teeth at the double sink. Shane stepped inside the bathroom carrying a pair of her panties and a nightgown. He was barefoot and shirtless, dressed just in his trousers, which hung enticingly on his lean hips. Just looking at him half-dressed made parts of her wake up and take notice. He looked absolutely edible.

"Thank you," she mumbled around her toothbrush.

"You're welcome," he said. He pointed at his own toothbrush, which stood in a ceramic holder beside the sink. "Do you mind?"

"No, go right ahead."

Shane quickly brushed his teeth and used the facilities. "Call me when you're finished," he said when he'd finished, and then he walked out and closed the door.

Shane was standing out on the balcony looking at the lake when he saw movement out of the corner of his eye. Beth was walking slowly toward the bed, in obvious discomfort. He met her halfway and carefully lifted her into his arms and carried her to the bed. He laid her down gently, and then covered her with the sheet and blanket.

"It's kind of early for bed," she noted, glancing at the clock on the nightstand. It was just half-past nine. She yawned. "I doubt you go to bed this early."

"I don't," he said. "But it's our first night cohabitating, and I have you in my bed. I'm not going to miss out on this."

"It's only temporary, though, right?" she said. She didn't want to read too much into his motives for having her move into his house.

He shrugged. "Let's take it one day at a time. Who knows, maybe you'll like it here so much you'll decide you want to stay."

Shane had been hoping to stave off this conversation for a while. He didn't think she was ready to contemplate moving in with him permanently. When they'd discussed it at the hospital, she'd agreed, but with the premise that it was temporary. He'd agreed at the time, for the sake of getting her here. But the truth was, he wanted this to be a permanent arrangement.

He removed his trousers and draped them over the back of an armchair in front of the hearth. Then his hands went to the waistband of his boxers. "I normally sleep naked. Is that a problem?"

Beth blushed, her eyes following the trail of hair that ran down his muscular abdomen, disappearing beneath the waistband of his boxers. "I don't mind."

He shucked off his boxers and strode toward the bed, completely comfortable with his nakedness. Beth's eyes widened at the sight of him, his penis rousing right before her eyes, lifting from the thatch of dark hair at his groin.

"Sorry," he said, glancing down dismissively at himself. "Ignore that."

Ignore it? Impossible!

He turned off the overhead lights, and then he walked over to the lamp on her side of the bed and switched it to a nightlight setting. "Is that enough light?"

Beth nodded, unable to speak. He didn't judge her for her fear. He just took it in stride. Gabrielle was the only other person, besides her mom and Tyler, who didn't chide her for her fear.

Shane crawled into bed beside her and pulled the covers up to his waist in an attempt to hide his burgeoning erection. He snuggled up beside her, taking care not to jar her ribs, and kissed the top of her head. "Are you comfortable?"

"Mmhmm," she murmured, feeling her eyelids grow heavy.

"Good. Try to sleep, sweetheart. Your body needs rest to heal. I'll be right here if you need anything in the night."

Beth's body did indeed crash as soon as she closed her eyes, but her mind wasn't cooperating. Every time she was about to drift off to sleep, she'd flashback to the attack. The mental image of Andrew's boot coming at her face was so realistic she'd actually flinch, waking herself up. Twice she'd been half asleep when she jerked awake.

"Beth?"

"I keep seeing his boot coming at me."

He leaned close and kissed her temple. "Do you want something to help you sleep?"

"No. I don't want to take anything."

"Do you want a drink?"

"No."

"What will help, then? What do you need?"

"You. I need you." She reached over and laid her hand on him, surprised to find him still hard.

"Sorry about that," he said.

"Don't be." She gripped him through the blanket.

"Beth, no," he said, gently removing her hand. "We can't."

"But that's what I need."

"I can give you what you need without having sex. Sex isn't an option right now, not until you're healed."

Beth felt Shane's fingers slip beneath her nightgown.

"Don't move a muscle," he said. "I mean it. Lie still."

"That's easier said than done," she said, squirming when his fingers started traveling up her thighs.

He chuckled. "What happened to the panties I brought you?"

"I left them in the bathroom."

"And why is that?"

"When you came into the bathroom wearing just your pants, it gave me ideas, so I left them off."

"You're quite an optimist, sweetheart," he said. "But there's no way in hell we're having sex anytime soon."

He came up on his elbow and gazed down at her. "There are other ways to distract you, though."

She reached up and caressed the side of his face, and he pressed his face into her hand, kissing her palm. He kissed the side of her throat, right over her pulse. It was one of the few places that was unmarked.

Then his left hand slipped between her thighs. "Open your legs," he said.

And she did.

His index finger brushed across the top of her mound, skimming through her curls. He traced the lips of her sex, and then his finger dipped inside, searching for the wetness collecting inside her channel. She started trembling from the anticipation alone. She wanted him, inside her.

"Do you like this? My fingers on you?"

"You know I do," she breathed, closing her eyes as she reveled in his touch.

"Open wider," he said, his hand nudging her thighs farther apart.

Taking his own sweet time, he explored her sex, his fingers sliding through her wetness, drawing it up from her core to bathe her clitoris. Her body began to tremble when his finger applied the lightest pressure on that tiny bundle of nerves. Gently, so very gently, he stroked her clit. Her hips began to rock and lift as she pushed against his touch.

"You have to lie still, Beth," he said, his voice low.

"Lie still?" she said, incredulous. "Are you kidding?" Yes, her ribs were killing her and every little movement hurt, but there was no way she could hold still.

"I mean it. You have to lie still, or I'll stop."

"Don't you dare!" she hissed.

And then she gasped because his thumb had replaced his finger on her clit, and now his long index finger was sliding inside her wet channel and pushing deep, searching.

He began a slow and methodical stroking inside her body, as the pad of his thumb tormented her clit. It wasn't long before she felt it, that elusive sensation building deep inside her, spiraling as he kept up the slow stroking. She whimpered with frustration as desire blossomed closer.

"Look at me, Beth," he said. "Keep your eyes on mine. I want to watch you come."

She looked at him, and the intensity in his gaze took her breath away.

Shane watched Beth's face as he stroked her, mesmerized by her expression. He could tell she was close. She gasped and pressed herself against his hand.

"Hold still, baby," he said, his voice rough, the low rasp unrecognizable even to himself. He was the one torturing her body, and yet he found himself just as aroused as she was. He was pretty sure his cock was hard enough to drive nails.

She did this to him. It was as if she held some intangible power over him, and his body recognized it and responded. He'd never in his life felt this with anyone, this desperation to be near her, to be needed by her. When she'd walked out of his office, his world had stopped spinning. Now all was right again because she was back. God help him if she ever realized how much power she had over him. Or if she ever left him again.

Her internal muscles tightened on his finger. "You're close, aren't you?" he murmured. "I can feel your sex tightening on my finger."

Her eyes widened, and she bit her lip as the agonizing pleasure swelled.

He leaned closer, his lips near her ear. His warm breath ruffled her hair as he whispered to her. "I love watching you like this, knowing I'm the one making you come."

His words pushed her right over the edge, and she whimpered as her climax swept through her like a wave of molten lava, making her gasp. Shane continued stroking her gently as she came down from the high. He trailed soft kisses along her neck and collarbone, nibbling her soft skin and breathing in her sweet scent. "God, I'm addicted to the smell of your skin," he said.

She melted in his arms, boneless and satiated, so tired she couldn't move.

His expression sobered as he gazed at her. "Don't leave me again, Beth. If there's a problem, give me a chance to fix it. I'm far from perfect, but I'm good at fixing things. And I'll do anything to make this work."

Beth's hand came up and touched his face, brushing his hair. "I shouldn't have walked out on you," she said. "I panicked."

"Promise me," he said. "Next time there's a problem, promise me you'll let me fix it."

Beth nodded. "I promise."

45

The next morning, Shane lay awake watching Beth sleep. Despite the bruises and the cuts on her face, she looked peaceful bathed in the morning light coming through the French doors and high transoms. She lay on her right side facing away from him, with her good hand tucked beneath her cheek.

He'd been awake for a little over an hour, but he just couldn't bring himself to leave their bed. It was a relief to see her so relaxed. After the orgasm he'd given her, she slept through the entire night without incident — no nightmares, no panic attacks.

He really should get up and get to work. He'd missed a lot of work, first dealing with Beth breaking up with him, and then dealing with the aftermath of the attack. He knew without asking that Jake had taken over for him, and between Jake, Liam, and Cooper, everything in the Chicago office was under control. But it was time to pull his own weight. Beth was safe. She was under his roof now, and he had no more excuses for slacking off.

Right now, though, he just wanted to lie here and watch her sleep. It gave him tremendous satisfaction having her here in his home, knowing she was safe, knowing she would be cared for even when he wasn't here. Elly and George would take good care of Beth, as would the rest of the household and the security staff. Especially Elly. He'd seen the look on Elly's face when she'd caught her first glimpse of Beth's battered face. Elly seemed to have taken to Beth like a mama bear taking to an orphan cub.

He checked his phone for the latest updates on Kline. There was nothing urgent on that front — or Cooper or Jake would have alerted him — but he still wanted to know what that fucker was up to.

He was studying the bruises on the side of Beth's face when someone knocked quietly on their door. After pulling on his trousers, he found Elly standing outside their room with a serving cart laden with two covered plates, a pot of coffee, cups and utensils.

"I thought Beth might like to have breakfast in bed this morning," Elly whispered. "How's she doing?"

"She's still asleep," Shane said.

Elly nodded. "Sleep's the best thing for her right now. Do you want me to bring this back later when she wakes? I can keep it warm in the kitchen."

"Shane?" Beth's voice sounded groggy.

"I'm right here, sweetheart," he said, looking back at the bed.

"Good morning, dear," Elly said, pushing the cart into the room. "I hope I didn't wake you."

"You didn't," Beth said. She looked at the bedside clock and groaned. It was almost ten.

Elly parked the cart beside the bed. "I brought you some breakfast, honey."

"Thank you," Beth said, struggling to sit up.

"You're very welcome. What would you like for lunch later? Any special requests?"

"She's going to spoil you rotten," Shane said, helping Beth sit up in bed. He propped several pillows against the headboard for her lean on, and then he handed her a plate with an omelet, bacon, and toast.

Beth took a bite of the omelet and moaned in delight. "This is so good."

"How do you feel?" he said, sitting beside her, digging into his own plate. "Did we overdo it last night?"

"Maybe a bit," Beth said, wincing as she shifted. Every muscle, every movement hurt. Still, she grinned at him. "But it was worth it. You will not hear me complaining. I haven't slept that well in a long time."

"I think I'll have to give you an orgasm every night before bed," he said.

After they finished eating, Beth headed to the bathroom on her own two feet to get cleaned up and dressed.

"After we're dressed, I'll take you on a tour of the house," he said.

"Most of the fun stuff is down here," Shane said, as they stepped off the elevator on the lower level. They were moving slowly, but at least Beth was walking on her own, which she had insisted on doing.

Shane showed her the movie theater that sat twenty people in lush reclining armchairs arranged in stadium seating.

"Nice cup holders," Beth said.

Next, he showed her the pool room, which housed an Olympic-sized swimming pool with diving boards, a two-story twisting tube slide, and a separate hot tub. The exterior wall in the pool room was made up of large arched windows, which let in plenty of sunlight and overlooked a spacious lawn that led down toward a sandy beach.

"I just found my favorite room," she said, taking in the smooth surface of the clear water. Sunlight streamed through the tall, arched windows, lighting up the water. The pool had a zero entry walk-in at one end, and at the far side there were three diving boards, including one high dive.

They were standing in the hallway outside the pool room, observing through a huge picture window, when Beth noticed someone in the water swimming laps with clean, efficient strokes. The Lab puppy, Gus, ran along the side of the pool keeping pace with the swimmer.

Beth watched the swimmer for a moment, admiring his incredible speed and precision. "Who is that?"

"That's my brother Jamie."

"He's really good," she said, admiring the man's powerful strokes. He cut through the water like a torpedo, propelled by his long, muscular arms and legs.

"He should be," Shane said. "He was a SEAL."

Beth looked at Shane. "A SEAL? As in a Navy SEAL?"

Shane nodded. "He was, until about three years ago. He was blinded in an explosion."

Beth watched Jamie reach the end of the pool and execute a perfect turn. "He's blind?"

"Yes."

"Completely?"

"Yes."

"How awful. Is it safe for him to swim alone like this? Shouldn't someone be in there with him?"

Shane laughed. "Jamie's drown-proof. If I jumped in that pool and tried to drown him, I'd be the one who ended up at the bottom of the pool, not Jamie. Trust me, Jamie doesn't need a babysitter."

Further down the corridor, they came to an interior window that overlooked what appeared to be a martial arts studio.

Beth stood at the window and watched Jake pummeling the hell out of a large black punching bag that was suspended from the ceiling by a heavy chain. Jake was barefoot and dressed only in a pair of black boardshorts. His hands were wrapped in white tape, and he was attacking the punching bag as if it were his worst enemy.

"That's gotta hurt," Beth said as Jake hammered the bag mercilessly with his bare hands. He really did look like he was trying to kill the thing. "Shouldn't he be wearing gloves?" she said, wincing when she noticed blood stains on the tape.

Shane shook his head. "Jake doesn't wear gloves."

Beth stared at Jake's muscular torso. It wasn't the incredibly ripped and chiseled abdominal muscles that had caught her attention — it was the large, black tattoo that ran down his left side — a combination of letters and numbers. She stared at him as she tried to make out the word. "Is that a date? March 3, 2005?"

"Yes," Shane said.

"What's the significance of that date?"

"It's a long story," Shane said. "And it's not mine to tell. You'll have to ask him."

In the center of the room, Lia was sparring with her twin on the mat. They went at each other furiously, hitting, kicking, and punching.

"What are they doing?" Beth asked.

"Krav Maga," Shane said.

"They're going to hurt each other," she said, when Liam grabbed Lia and slammed her to the mat, coming down on top of her with a knee to her chest, his hands pinning her wrists to the floor.

Shane chuckled. "If either one of them is stupid enough to get hurt, he — or she — deserves it. They know what they're doing."

Beth watched, entranced, as Lia shot to her feet and came at her brother with a vengeance. Liam was much taller and more muscular than Lia, who was just five-five to Liam's six-feet. But still, she managed to hold her own. She drove him back several feet and got a few impressive hits in before he began pushing her back.

"Is he taking it easy on her?" Beth asked.

"No. Lia's good. People underestimate her because she's a female and because of her size, but she could easily take down a man twice her size. Besides, Liam wouldn't be doing her any favors if he gave her a break. An opponent's certainly not going to take it easy on her if it comes to a real fight."

Beth watched Lia on the mat, envying her power and her stamina. If she could learn to do what Lia did, then no one would be able to hurt her like Andrew did. She'd be able to protect herself.

"Shane?"

"Yeah?"

"I want to learn how to do what they're doing."

"You want to learn Krav Maga?"

"Yes. I want to learn how to protect myself."

Shane put his arm around her shoulders and drew her against him. "No one's going to hurt you again, sweetheart. I promise you."

Beth watched Lia grab Liam's foot as he kicked her. She twisted his foot hard, and he dropped like a stone. She followed him down to the mat and slammed her elbow into the side of his head.

"I want to learn how to do that."

"If you're serious, there are forms of martial arts that would be better suited to you. Like Aikido."

"Could I learn to throw someone to the ground like that? Someone big, like Andrew Morton?" *Or, someone like Howard Kline?*

"Yes, with the right training."

The sound of heavy footsteps drew their attention away from the window overlooking the martial arts studio. Cooper was heading right toward them.

"You're needed upstairs," Cooper said to Shane. "We have company."

"Who?"

"Tyler. He wants to see Beth."

Shane nodded. "I'll come up and talk to him." He looked at Beth. "Wait here. I'll send him down to you."

"Okay," Beth said, barely paying any attention to Shane as her gaze was back on Lia and Liam on the mats.

"Go on inside the studio, sweetheart," Shane said. "There's plenty of seating in there. You don't have to stand out here to watch."

Shane headed upstairs to the command and control office, where he found Tyler Jamison standing at the window overlooking the front drive.

"Hello, Tyler," Shane said.

Cooper followed Shane into the room, taking up a position in the corner. He stood quietly on the sidelines, his arms crossed over his chest.

Tyler stood with his hands on his hips, surveying the sophisticated electronic surveillance center. He was dressed in his typical work garb — a black suit and white shirt. His detective's badge was clipped to his belt, and his gun was visible in its holster beneath his jacket. He was clean shaven, his dark hair short. His eyes narrowed on Shane.

"What can I do for you, Tyler?" Shane said, as if he didn't already know.

"I'm here to see my sister. Alone, if you don't mind."

Shane nodded. "Of course." The truth was, he did mind. He minded like hell. But as Beth's brother, Tyler had a legitimate claim on her. Shane would have to learn to accept that, just as Tyler would have to accept that Shane had a claim on her now, too.

Shane gave Cooper a curt nod.

"She's downstairs, Detective," Cooper said to Tyler, stepping forward. "I'll walk you down."

Beth heard a rapping on the glass behind her and turned to see her brother standing outside the viewing window. He smiled as he beckoned her out into the hall.

"Tyler!" she said, smiling brightly as she walked into his outstretched arms.

"Hey, kiddo." He hugged her carefully. "How're you feeling? You're looking better."

"I'm feeling better," she said. "I'm still sore, but today I can walk on my own."

Tyler kissed the top of her head. "I'm glad to hear it."

"This place is insane," Beth said, laughing. "There's a movie theater and an indoor swimming pool and this martial arts studio. And these are just the parts I've seen so far. This place has twelve bedrooms!"

"Yeah, it's impressive." Tyler peered into the studio and frowned. "But, hey, what do you expect? Shane's loaded. Just don't let his wealth blind you, Beth."

She lost her smile at Tyler's disapproving tone. "I'm not. It's just that I've never seen anything like this in a private residence."

Tyler laid his hands on Beth's shoulders. "Beth, I want you to come home with me. My condo's in a secure building, so you'll be perfectly safe there while we're waiting for Andrew's arraignment and dealing with Kline."

Beth frowned. "Tyler."

"I get it, Beth. Shane's good looking and richer than hell. And the attention he's paying you is very flattering, I'm sure. But he's not good for you. He's a player. He's used to getting whatever he wants, when he wants it, and right now he wants you. But how long is that going to last? How long will it be before he's tired of playing the mighty protector and is ready to move on? And where will that leave you?"

"Tyler," she said, shaking her head. "I — "

"I know you, Beth. You're not a casual fling kind of girl. He'll take what he wants from you, and then, when he's tired of you, he'll kick you to the curb, just like he's done with all the others before you. And believe me, there've been plenty of others. Don't be gullible."

Beth felt the bottom of her stomach fall, and she flushed. "It's not like that, Tyler." *He cares about me.*

"Bullshit it's not!" Tyler began to pace in front of her. "Beth, you're so naive. I've known Shane McIntyre for a long time. He's never with the same woman more than a few months. He's just not a long-term relationship kind of guy. You're not cut out for someone like him. This is only going to end with you getting hurt!"

Tyler took a deep breath and ran a hand through his hair.

"Come back with me. If you want to keep seeing him, fine. I won't stop you. You can date the man, if that's what you want. But don't live here under his roof, letting him use you."

"What the fuck!"

Beth and Tyler both turned to see Lia standing in the open doorway to the studio, her hands gripping her lean hips.

Lia was sweaty and disheveled, and she looked mad as hell as she scowled at Tyler. "Is there a problem here, Detective?"

Beth's face burned when she realized Lia must have heard what Tyler said about Shane. "No, Lia," Beth said, hoping to diffuse Lia's anger. "There's no problem."

"That's not what it sounded like to me," Lia said, glaring at Tyler.

"Mind your own business, Lia," Tyler said, glaring right back at her. "This is between Beth and me."

"Beth is my business," Lia said. "So anything you say to her concerns me as well."

Tyler frowned. "What are you talking about?"

"I'm her primary bodyguard now." Lia crossed her slender, muscled arms over her chest, as if daring Tyler to make a snide comment.

Even hot and sweaty, Lia was a striking figure. In her black sports bra and boy shorts, every lean, curvy inch of her was on display. Her short, spiky blond hair was darkened with sweat, but her blue eyes glittered like diamonds. The lip ring was gone, but the tribal tattoos were still on her face — tattoos that Beth now knew weren't permanent.

"You're the best Shane has?" Tyler said. "Wonderful! Beth might as well protect herself."

"Tyler!" Beth said in reproach. She wondered if Lia could take Tyler down on the mats, despite how much bigger he was. Remembering what she'd seen Lia do to Liam, Beth figured Lia probably could take her brother down. That might be fun to see.

Lia turned her attention to Beth. "You okay, Princess? You want me to get rid of this douche bag?"

Beth chuckled. "I'm fine, Lia. Thanks."

"Is there somewhere we can talk in private?" Tyler said to Beth. "Without an audience?"

Lia shrugged and pointed down the corridor. "I don't think anyone's in the pool room right now." Then she glanced pointedly at Beth. "Scream like hell if you need me. I'll hear you."

Beth laughed. "I'll be fine, Lia."

Beth led Tyler down the hall to the pool room. She glanced through the window and saw that the pool was empty now, the water as still and smooth as glass. Shane's brother must have left.

Tyler opened the door and she stepped inside, the warm, chlorine-scented air hitting her in the face like a heavy, damp curtain. She looked longingly at the water, wishing she could just dive in and escape this conversation altogether.

"Sit," Tyler said, indicating a padded bench.

Beth sat and watched her brother pace. She felt numb, and she resented Tyler for raising these doubts about Shane. And yet, recalling the women from Shane's past that she'd already met, part of her thought that Tyler might be right. There was the ice-cold blond — Deborah — from Clancy's Bookshop that first night they met. And then there was the exotically beautiful and bitchy Luciana, who'd cornered her in the women's restroom at the hospital fundraiser, accusing Beth of putting on some kind of act to snare Shane.

Tyler stopped in front of her and crouched down, his fingers brushing her cheek. "Does your face hurt?" he asked, his expression somber as he surveyed her bruises and cuts.

"A little," she said.

"Your lip's healing nicely."

She nodded.

Tyler sighed heavily. "Beth, I just want you safe and happy." He reached up and brushed her hair back. "But I don't see this thing with Shane ending well. He's used to... well, a different sort of woman. You're too young to handle someone like him. I don't want you to get hurt."

Beth regarded her brother, trying not to feel like her world was unraveling right before her eyes. She couldn't blame Tyler when he was simply voicing the same thoughts she'd had herself. Those women she'd met were in a completely different league. They were older, sophisticated, confident, wealthy... and she was none of those things.

"Please come back with me," Tyler said, coming up to sit beside her on the bench. "You can still see him, if that's what you want. But at least put some space between you."

Beth blinked back the tears forming in her eyes. She knew Tyler was likely right. But she also remembered Shane's words from the night before, as she was falling asleep in his arms. She'd promised him that she wouldn't run again, not without first giving him a chance to fix things.

But if Tyler was right, how could Shane fix this? She couldn't bear for him to grow tired of her and set her aside. It would kill her.

And there was no fixing that.

"How long are you gonna sit up here and do nothing?" Cooper said, pacing the control room. "You know he's trying to talk her into leaving."

Shane leaned forward in his chair, his elbows propped on his knees. "I know." It was killing him to sit here when what he really wanted to do was go down there and show Tyler Jamison the door. But he couldn't do that.

"Then why the hell are you just sitting here?"

Shane glanced up at his friend. "He's her brother. I can't keep her from him. Besides, she has to want to stay."

The fear that Tyler might succeed in talking her into leaving was eating a hole in his gut. How the hell had she become so important to him so quickly? He was in unfamiliar territory here, and it didn't sit well. He was used to being in control — used to being the one who called the shots. But he certainly didn't feel in control now. He wasn't the one calling the shots. Beth was. She could make or break him with a single decision.

Cooper checked his watch. "He's been down there for forty minutes. I think you've waited long enough."

Shane stood and took a deep breath. "Well, there's no point in making it easy for him."

When he reached the lower level and found no sign of Beth in the martial arts studio, where he'd left her, Shane's gut tightened. Through the window, he saw Lia doing pull-ups on a wall-mounted bar. Jake was removing the shredded, bloody tape from his hands, and Liam was doing one-handed pushups. The show-off.

Shane poked his head through the open studio doorway. "Where's Beth?"

"Pool room." Lia released the bar and dropped lightly to her feet. Her expression made it clear what she thought of Tyler Jamison's presence. "That asshat's trying to make her doubt you."

Shane headed to the pool room, pausing for a moment outside the glass doors to observe the pair seated inside. Tyler's arm was around Beth's shoulders, and she was leaning into him. Tyler said something, and Beth nodded, wiping her eyes with the back of her hand. God damn it, he made her cry. Enough.

Shane pushed open one of the doors and strode inside. Beth glanced up at him, her startled expression a mix of surprise and guilt. She hastily wiped her eyes and sat up straight, pulling out from under Tyler's arm.

Tyler rose, stepping in front of Beth, blocking her from Shane's gaze.

"Is there a problem, Tyler?" Shane said, looking expectantly at Tyler, prepared for the worst. If Tyler thought he'd succeeded in talking Beth into leaving with him, then he had another think coming. Shane would damn well fight for her.

"No," Tyler replied through clenched jaws. "I was just leaving."

"Good. I'll walk you out," Shane said. "Beth, why don't you join Lia in the studio?"

Shane followed Tyler out the front door to the black pickup parked in the circular drive.

Tyler opened the driver's door and paused before getting in. "This isn't over, Shane," he said. "Beth needs to be with me. She needs to be with family."

"I disagree," Shane said. "She's not a child, Tyler. She has me now, and I'll take care of her needs."

"Yeah? For how long? Until you get tired of the flavor of the month? Then what? You'll toss her out and leave the rest of us to pick up the pieces?"

"That's not going to happen."

"Shane, I've known you for a long time. I've seen you with one woman after another. You're not a good bet for Beth."

Shane stood fuming because he could hardly contradict Tyler's observations. He did have a lousy track record with women — he had to admit that. He'd just never found what he was looking for before. But with Beth, it was different. And yeah, he knew that sounded lame as hell.

"You're wrong, Tyler," Shane said. "I'm the best bet she has."

Tyler climbed up into his truck. "We'll see about that."

Shane found Beth in their bedroom standing at the balcony railing looking out at the lake. He walked up behind her and placed his hands on the railing, one on each side of her, caging her in with his body.

She leaned back into him, sighing. "Can we walk down to the lake?" she said.

"Sure. But first, we need to talk about this."

"Talk about what?"

"What Tyler said to you."

Beth shrugged. "It was nothing important."

"Bullshit."

Beth flinched at the vehemence in Shane's voice. He was angry. But at whom? At Tyler, or at her?

"I saw you crying," he said, turning her to face him. "Tell me what he said."

Beth shook her head. "I told you, it's not — "

"I know why he came, Beth. He wanted you to leave with him. Now tell me what he said."

Her eyes teared up, and her throat tightened. She'd kept these fears bottled up inside her, and now they came pouring out in a rush. "He said you never stay with one woman for long, and that you'll get tired of me soon. He said you're a player."

"I can't deny what Tyler said, Beth," Shane said, his hands coming up to gently cup her neck. "I'm not proud of my track record, but I never promised those women more than I gave them. They knew damn well what they were doing — I made it very clear to them from the start. It's not my fault if they assumed it would turn into something more."

Beth's stomach clenched tightly, and she felt sick. "Tyler was right. I'm not your type," she said. "I know that's true because I've met two of your former girlfriends, and I'm nothing like them."

Shane closed his eyes and released a heavy breath. When he reopened his eyes, they were filled with pain. "They weren't my girlfriends, Beth."

"Then what were they?"

"They were women I had sex with. That's all it was. You're the only girlfriend I've ever had."

She looked up at him, skeptical and hopeful at the same time. She wanted so badly to believe him. To believe this thing between them was real. But she also didn't want to end up being a gullible fool.

Shane leaned into her, his face just inches from hers. He grabbed her good hand and placed it over his heart, which was hammering hard in his chest. "I love you, Beth. I've never said that to a woman before. I've never felt this way before. I'm in, with everything I've got. I'm offering you everything I am, everything I have."

Searching his gaze, she looked for something, anything, to hold onto. "I — "

"Shh, it's okay. You don't have to say anything right now." He leaned his forehead lightly against hers. "God, I wish I could kiss you," he said. "I wish I could sweep you up in my arms, dump you on the bed, and fuck you until we both pass out." He gave her a lopsided grin as his thumb lightly touched her healing lip.

She laughed. "I'd definitely like a rain check on that."

46

The next morning, Shane propped himself up on one elbow to look at Beth and noticed that the bruises on her face were already starting to change colors. As awful as the bruises looked, Shane knew that the changes were a good sign. She was starting to heal.

Her eyelids fluttered open, and she smiled sleepily at him.

"Good morning," he said, leaning down to gently kiss her forehead. "How do you feel?"

Beth stretched, moaning with pleasure. "Definitely better. The pain's not as bad."

"Good. Do you feel up to a little road trip today? I have a surprise for you."

"A surprise? What is it?"

"If I tell you, it won't be a surprise."

She smiled. "I think I can manage a road trip. How far is it? Where are we going?"

"It's not far, maybe half an hour. And I'm not telling, so stop asking. You'll just have to wait and see. Let's get dressed, and then we'll eat breakfast. Elly said she'd send up a tray."

While Beth finished getting ready in the bathroom, Shane made the bed, and then checked the news headlines on the television. He walked out on the balcony and watched the sailboats, jet skis, and tourist cruises off in the distance. When he walked back into the bedroom, he was surprised she wasn't out of the bathroom yet.

He stood quietly at the bathroom door, listening to make sure she was all right, and heard nothing Not a sound. Surely she should be making at least some noise. The hairs on the back of his neck stood up, and he turned the door knob. As soon as he'd eased the door open, he heard her quiet sobs.

Shane strode into the bathroom, his eyes quickly scanning the room. He spotted her sitting on the edge of the Jacuzzi. Her arms were wrapped around her belly, and she was bent forward, her loose hair falling around her face like a curtain of sunlight. The anguish on her face tore at him.

"Beth!?" He dropped to his knees on the rug in front of her and brushed her hair back from her face. "What's wrong?"

She looked at him, her eyes filled with glittering tears.

"What the hell's wrong?" he said.

She shook her head. "Nothing. I'm sorry, it's nothing," she said, wiping her eyes. "It's stupid. Please, go back to the bedroom."

Shane stood and scooped Beth into his arms. He carried her to the bed and laid her down, and then came down beside her and wrapped her in his arms. "Talk to me."

"I told you, it's stupid," she said, her body heaving as she struggled to catch her breath.

"Do you need your inhaler?"

"No, it's not that."

"Then what is it?"

She sucked in a deep, ragged breath.

"Beth, please," he begged, laying his forehead against hers. "You're killing me here." The sobs started again, quiet and mournful. Shane held her and let her cry until her tears began to subside.

She took a deep breath and steeled herself to speak coherently. "We don't ... need... to take ... a pregnancy test," she said. "I started my period."

Shane was silent for a moment as her words sank in. *A pregnancy test?* And then he remembered their one episode of unprotected sex in his apartment. He'd completely forgotten about it in the aftermath of Andrew's attack.

He kissed her shoulder to comfort her as he tried to figure out what to say. Frankly, he was confused by her reaction. "Did you want to be pregnant?"

"No, of course not," she said. "Well, not really." Once the tears had subsided, her adrenalin levels crashed, and she started shaking. "It's stupid, I know," she said, sniffling. "I don't even know why I'm reacting this way."

"You've had one trauma after another these past few days."

Shane sat up and pulled the bedding out from beneath her, and then he covered her shivering body. When he settled back into bed beside her, he pulled her close, wrapping his arms around her. "Talk to me, sweetheart. Why are you crying?"

She turned her face into the crook of his neck, her voice muffled against his skin. "I didn't want to be pregnant. But the more I thought about it, the more the idea started to appeal to me. It got me thinking... about us having a baby. I started picturing a little boy who looked like you. In my mind, he — I know it's stupid."

Shane kissed the top of her head and laid his arm gently on her belly. "It's not stupid, sweetheart. It's not stupid at all. It's just a little... premature."

She sniffled. "You could say that."

"I love the idea of having a baby with you someday," he said. "When the time's right."

They lay in bed for a while just holding each other. Shane stroked her back as her breathing evened out.

A quiet knock on their bedroom door announced the arrival of breakfast. They ate together at the small table for two out on the balcony.

"The room service is very thoughtful," Beth said, "but

shouldn't we go down to the dining room for breakfast? I don't want Elly going to such trouble."

Shane laughed. "Good luck with that," he said. "Elly's been dying to have a lady of the house for years. I think she intends to spoil you."

Beth smiled as she sipped her hot Lady Grey. "As much as I appreciate it, I'm sure she has enough things to worry about. I don't want her to go to extra trouble for me."

"Tomorrow we'll go down for breakfast and beat her to it."

After they finished eating, they headed downstairs and stepped out the front doors. Cooper and Jake were outside, standing beside the Escalade.

"We're all going?" Beth said, surprised.

"Yes," Shane said, leading her down the steps.

It was a hot summer day, and Beth was dressed in a sundress and sandals. Shane wore jeans and a white button-down shirt, and Beth was amazed how he could make such a simple outfit look sexier than hell.

Cooper and Jake were in jeans, too, but they both had on jackets over their t-shirts. Beth knew why Cooper had a jacket on, in spite of the summer heat — to conceal the gun that he never went anywhere without. But why was Jake wearing a jacket? Was he armed as well? And if so, why did they need two armed guards with them on their little road trip?

Beth leaned close to Shane and whispered. "Is Jake armed?"

"Yes."

"Are you?" There didn't seem to be anywhere to hide a gun on him.

"Yes. I have a small caliber handgun in my ankle holster."

Beth frowned. "Why is everyone armed?"

Shane smiled at her. "It's our job to be prepared for anything. It's nothing for you to worry about."

She frowned. "What could possibly happen? Andrew's locked up, right?"

Shane nodded. "He is. But Kline's not."

At the mention of Kline's name, she blanched.

Lia walked out the front door. "Hey, Princess," she said. "Don't worry about Kline. We've got that covered."

Beth turned to look at Lia and did a double take. Lia's facial tattoos were gone, as were her nose and lip rings. She wore her hair in a cute pixie style — the purple tips were gone, too. She was dressed in a short skirt, a tank top that showed off her tanned and sleekly muscled arms, and sneakers. She looked... normal. She looked pretty, in a girly way. How could this be the same Lia?

"Lia, you look amazing," Beth said.

"What, this?" Lia glanced down at herself. "Oh, it's nothing."

Cooper opened the driver's door and climbed in. "All right, folks. Let's get this show on the road."

Shane opened the rear passenger door and helped Beth step up into the Escalade.

"Where are we going?" she said.

"I told you, it's a surprise," Shane said, climbing in after her.

"Lia's not armed," Beth said, watching her bodyguard skirt around the front of the vehicle. There was absolutely no place she could be hiding a gun.

Shane chuckled. "Lia's always armed. She just doesn't usually carry a gun."

Lia climbed in on Beth's other side.

"Why the makeover?" Beth asked as Lia buckled herself in.

Lia shrugged. "New assignment, new look. It's all part of the job."

"Hey, Rainbow Girl," Jake said, turning back from the shotgun seat to look at Beth. "You're looking good."

"Rainbow Girl?" Beth said, frowning.

"Yeah," Jake said, pointing at her face. "The array of colors on your face is impressive."

"Jake," Shane said, glaring at his brother.

Beth shivered. *That tone.*

"What?" Jake lifted his hands in self-defense. "That's a good thing. It means her bruises are healing."

Once they left the lush, green expanse of the suburb and hit the city limits, traffic picked up. Cooper exited onto N. Michigan Avenue, and they headed west. They weren't far from Shane's office building, and for a moment Beth thought they might be headed there. But in the middle of the shopping district, Cooper pulled to the curb, sliding effortlessly into a reserved parking spot in front of a familiar building.

Beth peered out the window at her favorite spot on Earth. "Are we going to Clancy's?" she asked, grinning at Shane. "Please say 'yes.'"

"You could say that," Lia said, opening her door and hopping out.

Beth followed Lia out of the vehicle, and Shane followed right behind her. Cooper and Jake joined them, and they all stood on the sidewalk in front of the entrance to the bookstore.

The front doors opened and out walked a man who was 90 years old, if he was a day. He was a small man, not even Beth's height, and frail. His posture was stooped, his fingers bent with arthritis. What little hair he had was white and trimmed short, and his face was heavily wrinkled and tanned to a permanent shade of leather. He was definitely a man who'd spent a lot of time outdoors.

The old man walked right up to Shane and offered him a shaky hand. "Mr. McIntyre, it's a pleasure to finally meet you in person," the man said, smiling up at Shane, who towered over him.

Shane smiled back, shaking the man's hand. "Please call me Shane," he said. "And the pleasure is all mine, sir."

Shane put an arm around Beth's shoulders and drew her close. "Sweetheart, I'd like to introduce you to Fred Clancy."

Beth's eyes widened. "Clancy? You're the owner of Clancy's?"

Fred Clancy nodded, smiling at Beth. "For the past 63 years," he said. "And thanks to Mr. McIntyre, I can retire to Florida and fish all year round."

Clancy reached into his trouser pocket with his gnarled fingers and fished out a set of keys on a gold key ring. He held the key ring out to Beth, dangling it from his shaking fingers.

Beth frowned. "I don't understand."

Clancy took Beth's good hand and dropped the key ring into her palm, and then folded her fingers around it.

Beth glanced up at Shane.

"Think of it as... a token of my affection," he said, smiling at her. "If you'll have... it."

Beth stood speechless, her mouth open. For the life of her, she couldn't form a coherent thought.

Lia leaned toward Beth and whispered loudly. "He bought you a bookstore."

That snapped Beth out of her shock. "What?" Beth cried. "I — "

"And I think he just asked you to go steady," Lia added, rolling her eyes. She shook her head. "I didn't think this would be so hard."

Beth turned to Shane, her expression dumfounded. He couldn't possibly be serious! She couldn't even begin to imagine what a business like Clancy's would go for in downtown Chicago. The price tag on the building alone would be exorbitant, not to mention the cost of the business itself. And she knew absolutely nothing about running a business. This was insane!

"It's all yours," Shane said. "Paid for in full. The transfer of ownership paperwork is solely in your name."

Beth didn't know when the tears had started, but she realized her cheeks were wet. She wiped her tears with the back her hand — the one holding the keys — wincing at the tenderness of her face. Good grief, she'd cried more in the past two days than she had in the past decade.

Shane pulled the tail of his shirt out of his jeans and used it to gently dab her tears.

"My dear, would you like to come inside and have the grand tour?" Fred Clancy said, taking Beth's hand.

She looked at Shane, still stunned.

"Go ahead," Shane said. "I'll be right behind you."

Fred Clancy led Beth through the front doors of the shop, Lia close on her heels.

"Come meet your employees," the man said, pointing to a cluster of people standing next to a display of newly-released hardcover books. "They're anxious to meet you."

Beth looked at the display of crisp, new hardcover books and wondered if she should pinch herself. Surely this had to be a dream! She picked up one she'd been looking forward to reading and opened the front cover, loving the pristine feel of the brand new book in her hands. While she adored her e-reader, she'd never lost her love for physical books.

She glanced up and looked around, taking everything in. *So many books.* It was overwhelming. It was like Christmas and her birthday and — she couldn't do it justification — it was like *everything*, all wrapped into one. She couldn't wrap her mind around it.

Beth looked back at Shane, who stood just a few feet behind her, his arms crossed over his chest as he watched her. He smiled at her, and she walked straight into his arms, her good arm going around his waist.

"I know absolutely nothing about running a business," she said.

He shrugged. "That's all right. You love books, and you love this place. That's what matters most. You'll learn what you need to know about running a business — if you want to — and I'll give you all the help you need. Besides, there's a highly competent staff here already who know how to run this place. You're the owner, Beth. You don't have to manage it, if you don't want to. But it's yours now, so enjoy it. Now, go meet some of your staff."

She turned back and looked at the small crowd of employees who were watching her closely. They seemed nervous, fidgeting as they watched her closely.

One woman, a brunette in her mid-thirties, stepped forward. "Welcome, Ms. Jamison. I'm Maureen Ferguson. I'm the store manager."

Beth smiled as she approached the group, reaching out to shake the manager's hand. "Thank you," she said. "It's a pleasure to meet you."

"I'll show you around if you'd like," the woman said.

Shane was poised to follow Beth on her impromptu tour when Jake caught his eye and signaled him to hold back. As Beth and Lia moved on with Fred Clancy, Maureen, and a few of the employees, he and Cooper remained with Jake just inside the bookstore entrance.

Jake finished reading the message that had just come in on his phone, frowning. "It's from the Kline surveillance team. Kline just boarded a bus for Hyde Park."

"Damn," Cooper said.

Shane frowned. "Do they know his exact destination?"

Jake shook his head. "It's too soon to tell. It could be her townhouse or the Kingston campus — they're both on the same route. We'll know if, and when, he gets off the bus."

"I want to know," Shane said.

"He's not going to stop," Jake said. "He keeps getting one step closer to her. He's got a gun, ammo, and now he's casing either her home or her workplace. Eventually, he's going to go after her."

"I know," Shane said, his expression somber.

"What are you gonna do?" Cooper said.

"The only thing I can do," Shane said. "I'm going to take him out. It's the only way to ensure Beth's safety. We'll give him an opportunity to go after her, and we'll be ready for him."

Jake looked skeptical. "You're going to use Beth as bait?"

"Hell no," Shane said. "It won't be Beth — we'll use a decoy. But Kline will think it's Beth, and we'll be waiting for him."

Shane caught up with Beth and Lia on their tour. He put his arm around Beth and drew her close, kissing the top of her head. "I love you, sweetheart."

She hugged him back. "I love you, too."

"Oh, thank God," Lia said, rolling her eyes. "Otherwise, this little outing would have been rather awkward."

~THE END ~

Thank You!

Thank you for reading *Vulnerable*. I hope you enjoyed reading the beginning of Shane and Beth's journey as much as I did writing it. Book 2 in the McIntyre Security series picks up right where this first book left off, as Shane and Beth deal with the impending threat posed by Howard Kline, Beth's plans for her future, and other challenges that come their way.

If you want to be notified when the sequel comes out, sign up for my e-mail newsletter; you'll find the sign-up form on my website: http://www.aprilwilsonwrites.com.

Please Consider Leaving a Review on Amazon.com

I hope you will consider leaving a review on Amazon. Even just a brief comment would be very much appreciated.

Upcoming New Releases

What's coming next? In *Fearless*, the sequel to *Vulnerable*, Kline is coming for Beth, but this time she'll be ready for him. Also, stay tuned for Lia's story, Jamie's story, and a whole lot more in the McIntyre Security series.

To find out about new releases and to receive free and exclusive bonus content featuring Shane, Beth, and other characters from this series, sign up for April's New Release Mailing List at http://www.aprilwilsonwrites.com. This mailing list will be used only to announce new releases and giveaways, and to send out periodic free bonus content. The names on the mailing list will never be shared or sold. And you can unsubscribe at any time.

A Little Bit About Me

I've been writing fiction since the 6th grade, when I wrote and illustrated (in Crayon) a children's book. With the explosion of the indie publishing market earlier this decade, I knew it was time for me to get serious. *Vulnerable* is my first published novel. But stayed tuned, because I have more novels on the drawing board than I can count. I'm working as hard as I can to get new stories out there.

In my professional life, I've enjoyed a long career in education, including teaching college English courses and developing online education for corporations and colleges. Over the years, I've done freelance work for newspapers, publishers, and magazines as a writer, editor, and desktop publisher. I have masters' degrees in literature and in education.

I live in Ohio with my daughter and more than a few dogs and cats. When I'm not writing, I'm reading romance novels and watching movies with happy endings.

I would love for you to get in touch with me and share your feedback on *Vulnerable*. You can reach me here:

Email: aprilwilsonwrites@outlook.com

Website: www.aprilwilsonwrites.com

Twitter: @AprilWroteIt

Facebook Page: search for "Author April Wilson"

It's been my life-long dream to become an author. Getting lost in my characters' lives gives me more pleasure than I can possibly express. Thank you so much for reading my first novel. You've made my dream come true.

~ April Wilson

Made in the USA
Middletown, DE
10 October 2018